# ANNABEL HORTON
# LOST WITCH OF SALEM

Annabel Horton, Lost Witch of Salem
Olivia Hardy Ray

This book is a work of fiction. Names, characters, places and incidents are products of the author's imagination or are used fictitiously. Any resemblance to actual events, locales or persons, living or dead, is entirely coincidental.

ISBN: 978-1-64456-565-0 [paperback]
ISBN: 978-1-64456-566-7 [Mobi]
ISBN: 978-1-64456-567-4 [ePub]

Library of Congress Control Number: 2022948730

INDIES UNITED PUBLISHING HOUSE, LLC
P.O. BOX 3071
QUINCY, IL 62305-3071
indiesunited.net

# Annabel Horton
## Lost Witch of Salem

A Novel
by Vera Jane Cook

INDIES UNITED PUBLISHING HOUSE, LLC

# PART I

# DOMINION

# Chapter 1

Some say I am a stain on your history, a nameless statistic, — a grotesque misfortune that is alluded to in your text- books. I cannot disagree. Allow me to introduce myself as I am. Patience Annabel Horton is my given name, though I refer to myself as Annabel, never much caring to claim a virtue I do not possess. I am in spirit form, for the most part. Though it was not always so.

It was in the year 1692 in the town of Salem, in the state of Massachusetts, that I swung by my neck. Many of us died there, such needless, senseless tragedies.

But I am not here to condemn anyone for my suffering. So, do not be alarmed. As you may or may not know, men who believed they were doing God's work chastised many of Salem's citizens as witches, and brought us to trial. Many, like myself, were hanged. I was eighteen years.

I will tell you what really happened in Salem Village before the century turned. You never learned the truth of it. Your history books do not contain the truth. But I will open the veil of time for you.

It is difficult for me to speak of my physical death but I will share with you all that I can recall of it. Hear me well, new friend. It may ease your pain to learn that death is only a cacophony of singular experiences ... a trick of perception. I did not know that in 1692 as I faced the rope.

1

The texture of the cord lay against my skin with such cruel ambivalence, for it caressed me like the comfort of a lover's hand. I thought it would feel rough and coarse and burn my flesh, but that was not so. The rope was painfully soft, as velutinous as a cat.

What a beautiful spot it was on Gallows Hill, near Town Bridge, just south of Stone's Plain. The morning was ablaze in amber light on the day of my death, and birds fretted in the sky, oblivious to human insanity.

The good Reverend Parris stood before us, his mouth drawn in a somber frown.

"I will pray for your souls, witches," he mumbled. "I will pray to banish the evil from your heart. May ye find God. May ye rest in peace."

So many of the townspeople came to see us die; what an odd curiosity they shared. They stood off in clusters and prayed, "God rest ye almighty souls."

My heart was beating so fast that I might have passed out. My mouth was dry, my eyes nearly blinded by tears. Still, I could see him as he stepped forward, seemingly out of nowhere: A man with an anguished expression. He held my arm with a firm and steady hand. Gently, he led me up the ladder steps.

"Do not be afraid," he whispered as he carefully placed a blindfold over my eyes.

"I am afraid," I told him.

His was the last voice I heard, the last face I saw. I had never seen him before, or so I thought. He was not from my village; I was sure of that. He had features so fiercely handsome that even in my desperate state, I noticed and wondered of the familiarity. His hair kissed his brow in tight black curls that shone in the morning sun. His deep dark eyes gazed with haunting despair into my own. How I hated his pity.

As the rope was slipped around my neck and the knot pulled close against the nape, I felt his whisper once again as it grazed my ear.

"Count to three," he said. "Then turn your head sharply to the right and hold it. Do it girl and be spared!"

But it was quick that a hand pushed me from the ladder step. My fall was brief. My bone broke and snapped in two. My breath left me. I struggled for air but there was none to take in. Death had taken me, death as I had understood it.

I felt my body sway. How odd it was that I could feel anything at all, but I did. I was heavy as a log in water. Suddenly, the heaviness was lifted and I became light as a feather in the wind. Then I lost touch with the earth altogether. My soul rose, vanished into obscurity. I disappeared into semi darkness and I would remain in this shadowy dimension for hundreds of your years, except for occasional life journeys back into living flesh.

Light is no longer the same to me as it is to you. I see your world through shades of gray. All sound in my dimension runs together and I receive only remnants, discordant vibrations from which to decipher language. Movement appears to me as a brief motion wrapped in gauze and released like tiny bursts into reflections of dim light.

When I am not in the form of flesh I live in the confines of shadow. The psychics of your dimension have said that I can be seen floating between the kiss of dusk and the evening moon. Yes, some of you can actually see me, though you are unaware of what I am. You usually ignore me because I vanish so quickly. I simply blend into the surface of your world and disappear — into objects — into trees —into the soft fur of a sleeping squirrel — into anything that will have me.

Before I begin my tale, you must know this: I can also blend into a human body. I can steal your flesh if I choose. But before you judge me, you must understand my loneliness. You have no idea how desperately I desire the physical senses you so cavalierly take for granted. But please, do not fear me. I will not harm the innocent. Hear me out before you cast any stones. There are secrets in my tale worth knowing.

The snap of my neck appears to have granted me immortality as a captured soul, doomed to live over and over again in stolen flesh and blood. Therefore, I take bodies in exchange for my freedom. I want you to understand that if I were to ever choose your flesh, I would mean you no harm. I would simply borrow the luxury of your language and take comfort in the pleasure of your warm beating heart.

Be assured, the process of my abduction is painless. You see, the earth holds time. When I consume a body all I do is absorb time. It is quite simple. My soul moves out of one perception and into another. Let me reassure you that though I can take any one of you, I prefer the flesh of those whom the devil favors and I do not have to go very far to consume the devil's own.

Let us go back to how it all began once I realized my eternal fate. The first body I took belonged to my youngest brother. Oh, I did not take him. That was my first and only mistake. I took his third daughter. She was just ten years but I took her anyway, believing she would be better off, and in due time, she was.

"Father, look at the light," Elizabeth cried as she chased me.

Jeremiah scowled. "Child, do not imagine things that are not there."

The fool did not know that Elizabeth could see me through this opaque shadow that I had become.

"What do I look like, Elizabeth?" I whispered.

I watched in astonishment as she clapped her hands and giggled. "Pretty, pretty," she called. *My God, she can hear me,* I thought.

"Ah, so you see me as I am, as Annabel?"

But I do not think she actually understood my question for she ran and hid from me, chasing me with her eyes as I flitted across the yard.

She was a bright child. My brother's favorite. He favored her a bit too much if you know what I mean.

"Come Elizabeth, sit upon my lap," he called as he patted his legs.

He kept the child on his lap for hours, the bastard. A little game it was. He would wiggle her about and would not put her down until after he had rocked and shaken the poor child to death and had soiled his pants with the sin of his evil.

I took Elizabeth away from that.

"Forgive me," I said softly. "You will soon be with me, Elizabeth. Jeremiah will meet the devil on his own terms ... and let the devil take him."

One night, as she slept, I seeped into her bloodstream like a tic upon a dog, filling her little soul with my own and gently forcing her to leave her flesh.

"You will be safe," I uttered.

I filtered through her blood like a rushing stream until I felt that I had overwhelmed the balance.

"I am afraid," she screamed.

Of course she was afraid; she did not know where she was going. Neither did I. I did not learn what became of her for so many years. I thought that she would be with me. I prayed that she would be with me but instead it was I that wound up sitting on my brother's lap while the fool grunted and groaned in my ear. But Elizabeth was gone. My sweet Elizabeth was gone to a fate that would take me two long centuries to learn.

So, it would seem, I became Elizabeth. I inhabited her flesh and all saw me as Elizabeth. But my own soul was intact and when I caught my

4

reflection in glass it was that of Annabel Horton. You see, I always capture the image of my original soul in the looking glass.

Eventually, my brother Jeremiah fell to his death. I had nothing to do with it. Eventually, in Elizabeth's flesh, I became the wife of a very ambitious man and lived to be almost twenty-nine years old. I thought I would see Elizabeth again when her flesh and blood gave way to a dreadfully congested chest full of mucus that drowned her in her sleep, but as her flesh died, my spirit rose again into the solitude of familiar darkness.

I shall always carry my grief for Elizabeth. My despair has been endless. It was then I swore I would never again consume the innocent. I vowed I would only take evil and alter it through the presence of my soul. It was Jeremiah that should have been forced from his flesh, not sweet Elizabeth. How perfect for me; take only the evil ones, Annabel, and leave goodness alone. Unfortunately, evil does not alter easily.

There was evil in Salem Village in 1692 but it was not in the soul of any of those women they hanged. Poor Goodwife Nurse, now she was the saddest of the lot to be taken to the tree. No more of a witch than poor Bridget Bishop. No one was safe from the devil's fire; certainly I was not, not with my detachment, my disinterest in the other girls of my village and their silly games. You see, I knew I had powers and it kept me apart, but I told no one my secrets. Of course, I only tell you now because it no longer matters.

# Chapter 2

Before my death, one year to be exact, a presence came to me.

"Who goes there?" I called in the dark. His form was like mist. His answer was like wind.

"Leave me, ghost," I whispered coarsely.

The wind became a breeze and caressed my lips. I knew he had kissed me and I shuddered.

"Who are you?" I asked softly.

"Yours," I thought I heard him say.

"You hold me in your arms and yet I cannot see you." I looked around the room. I felt his movement. Once again, he came so close.

The wind was like a dance as it lifted the hair from my brow. I felt him take me in his arms and embrace me, air around my body so light and sensual, touched by a gentleness that caused my heart to pound.

"Show yourself," I commanded.

He circled the room, a tall grey mist. I was sure his hair was black, his eyes as dark as evening.

After that, I waited for him every night, and almost every night he came to me. It was not long before I fell in love with this spirit, as helplessly in love as any restless young woman can be.

These ghostly visits continued right up until my physical death. I always knew when he was near because the air would become faint with the scent of fresh rain and I would feel drugged with the fragrance that lingered in my room.

"You smell like late afternoons in summer, after a rainfall," I told him, but he did not answer. He spoke to me so seldom. It was quite by chance that I heard his whisper.

"Matthew," he said.

"Matthew is your name?" I asked.

I listened so carefully as the shutters moved and some papers on my bureau fluttered like wings.

"Matthew?" I asked again. "Oh, please speak more. Tell me where you come from?"

My illusive shadow was silent.

"Matthew. Matthew," I implored. "Speak to me! Show me your face. Let me see the hand that strokes me."

Suddenly, the wind returned. "I am so far," he uttered.

"A spirit that has found me in his path?" I called. "It must be so."

Miraculously, the papers on my bureau flew around and around, as if chasing each other in a playful game of tag.

I knew he could not reach me, could not fully pass beyond the barriers between us. Yet I felt him like an artist must feel his subject.

"You are tall," I said. "Your shirt has cuffs of white and I have images of your smile. Does time part us, Matthew? Are the centuries between us too vast?"

I saw a shadowy light. It shone before me and revealed a man of great height, but in a split second the light was gone, the image within, too oblique to recall.

Soon after his first visit, I received letters. They appeared out of nowhere. I would find them all over the house, always beginning: *To my wife.*

"What's this?" I stammered as I held the letters in my hand.

*Know that I love you and I'll come to protect you.* He had written.

His notes were always signed with the letter *M*, for his first name.

"Matthew," I whispered. "How is it that you can leave notes about the house and yet not show me your face?"

But my ghost was silent and could not find a way to answer me.

"Why do you sign only with the letter M? I asked. "Is Matthew really your name?"

Silence remained, as still as the night wind beyond my window.

I began to think that I had truly gone insane. Oftentimes, I doubted the presence of my ghost and I questioned Father about the mysterious letters. For surely, I thought, the sun must be too hot and had affected my brain.

"Father, I have received notes of affection. Do you know who sends them?"

Father laughed. "A neighbor's boy must surely be culprit to the bow of Cupid, daughter."

Ha! I knew better. No neighbor's boy in Salem would dare call me his wife. I frightened the boys of my village. They thought me haughty and illusive. Oh, there was a young man from Andover with the courage to court me, and I might have married him if not for my fascination with my ghostly lover, but I never got that chance.

*It must be you who writes me.* I smiled to myself. *Mustn't it be so, Matthew?*

If only I had known then that it would be centuries before I would see the face of my beloved. But in 1692, I could only cherish his words. So I made myself a wooden box and covered his letters with a beautiful purple cloth. I placed all the letters inside. I then covered the box with a square piece of coarse fabric and hid it under the tallest elm tree by Frost Fish Brook. Many afternoons that year I read the letters in the shadow of the branches. The writer's hand was full of lovely twists and loops, and the ink was black.

Had I not of died so soon I might have lived my life with my ghostly lover and never come to know him as a man of flesh. I would have assumed that some lost spirit had written the letters and had found a way to leave them inside the house. But, that innocence was not to be, and it was not fate that made it so. It was Urbain, Urbain Grandier, and the power given him.

# Chapter 3

This is my magic, but is it evil? None of us were evil, and Reverend Parris's slave knew it. Yes, Tituba knew it. The children knew it, too. I begged Father to take me to New York to escape the madness of murders around us but we could not leave the farm, and Father did not believe that any harm would ever come to me. My brothers swore they would protect me, but I knew better. I knew I would be named a witch and taken to the tree. I could not sleep at night or enjoy the sun as it burst upon me in the mornings.

Soon enough, they served me my warrant as I lay in the field praying that God would see fit to help me. Ann Putnam had accused me. She hardly knew me but she had seen me in Andover buying wheat and grain for the farm. My brother James tried to shield my face from hers when she fell on the ground before me and writhed at my feet. She pointed and held her side in pain.

"She torments me!" she screamed.

I fell into my brother's arms and wept.

"Look into her eyes," she called to all who listened. "They are of the devil, green as evil's slime."

I turned from her accusations but she would not desist.

"Begone, witch," she called.

And the townspeople came and stood around me. They looked into my eyes and said, "Yes, it must be so."

"She accuses everyone that comes to mind," I pleaded.

"She is weak and stupid," I heard my brother say.

I took his hand. I knew that I could not prevent my fate surrounded as I was by fools.

I hated the insidious evil that had inflicted the village. "God, cure them," I prayed. "They have surely gone mad."

I knew the truth, and tried to speak it, yet none would hear it. There was only one other that knew as much as I did, the Reverend's slave girl, Tituba. Yes, Tituba knew. She recognized the darkness and made a pact with the devil and the devil saved her from the tree. I made no pact with the devil and so I swayed by my neck in the August sun.

You might as well know the truth now. It was the slave girl that told the children stories of witchcraft. That is true. The stories came with her from the slave ships. They were a part of her heritage. But it was Thomas Putnam that used the Arawat to incite the children.

"Give them your magic," he told her. "I will see you safely removed from Salem when the time is right."

And why should she not survive in a land that sold her kind like meat at the village square?

"What will you have me do?" she wept.

He bent down close and held her face firmly in his hand. "Fill their head with the nonsense that is in yours," he commanded.

So, Tituba planted the seed in the minds of the children because Thomas Putnam bade her to do so. The ignorance and cruelty that surrounded her was amble fuel for the devil's fire. Do not blame the slave girl. She believed she would save her own soul by recognizing evil when she stood in the presence of it.

I will tell you where the evil thrived in Salem. It was in the child, Abigail Williams, and in the deviousness of the town leaders. They should have destroyed the girl right off and recognized the vindictive plan behind Thomas Putnam's perfidious handshake.

What wickedness there was. Surely, both were the devil's prey. Tituba knew this. She also knew that none would accept that evil could dwell in a child's soul. Yes, Tituba knew better, and she saw the devil's presence in the child the day she followed the girl out to Crane River.

It was an afternoon in late spring. I learned of it as I sat in jail awaiting my trial.

Tituba had watched as Abigail Williams held a child's puppy, a sweet thing named Lark, under water, despite the poor dog's struggle for freedom. Tituba had fallen to her knees in fear as Abigail held poor Lark down by his neck and sang a church song as she did. The puppy yelped and whined for air, but Abigail continued to sing, and to giggle, and to hold the poor dog down until it was silent.

Tituba watched quietly as the child dragged the dog's poor limp body from the water and poked it with a stick. The sweet brown hair now matted and wet, and the eyes still open in fear. Then Abigail sat by the dead puppy and sang. Certainly, the child was the devil's own and Tituba knew it. Anyone who was not of the devil would have known it.

Later that evening, Tituba went out to Porter's Hill with fresh chicken blood and called forth the witches of light. She asked for protection against the white man's evil. She called forth the witches but it was the devil who answered her call.

The next morning, when Tituba awoke, she began to tell Abigail tales of witchcraft.

"Drink this potion," she told the child. "And the devil will come to you. You will have the power of Satan's sword."

Quickly, Abigail drank the chicken blood.

*I will do the bastard's bidding,* Tituba thought. *So my neck will not wind up in a noose.*

Soon, under Thomas Putnam's instruction, Abigail, believing herself infused with the power of Satan, convinced the other children to follow her lead and they pointed their fingers at Putnam's enemies.

"There is the presence of the devil in this town," Thomas Putnam told the courts. "We must cleanse our streets."

"Nay, we must cleanse our souls," they cried.

Soon, the entire town fell under Thomas Putnam's control. Under the name of God, Putnam served the devil. Abigail was only possessed with her own meanness. She was a perfect vessel for the devil's insidiousness. The other children were only pawns in Urbain's game to upset the pious and sacred God-fearing village of Salem. Yes, Urbain Grandier, the devil's own disciple, was having his day once again. Urbain had a perfect evil conduit for his plan. But Abigail Williams had no real power. She was no better a witch than Tituba. You must remember, that once the devil's servant was through with Abigail, and Putnam's insatiable hatred, he cast them all aside and left Salem.

I thought that the devil came to Salem, Massachusetts in 1692 because there was too much of God to be found there. I thought he came because Tituba called him and the child Abigail could receive him, but he did not come because of God or Tituba ... or even the demented Abigail. He came, because of me. For many of your centuries I did not know that. But I know it now. The devil rejoiced in Salem, Massachusetts in 1692. But the devil always rejoices. Your world is shrill with the devil's laughter. He continues to make fools of us. Perhaps, he always shall.

# Chapter 4

My youngest brother's first-born son, Judd Patrick Horton, married a woman from Topsfield and he took over her family's farm. There were many offspring. Judd and his wife, Margaret, had five children. Their first-born son, John Jeremiah, moved his family to Boston in 1747. John's daughter, Sarah Ann, married a man called Oliver Stokes in 1766, and they had three children. Several years following the American Revolution, their middle child, Andrew, married Hendrika Van Pelt, from a Dutch family, who had settled in Nieuw Amersfoordt, in the town of Flatlands, known in your day as Brooklyn.

After their marriage, Andrew bought a farm on Hubbard Lane, not far from the Flatlands Town Center. In the year 1806, I took their only daughter. Of course, I walked in the flesh many times prior but I will not take you through so many tedious sojourns. I only tell you of this one because it will have significance later.

You see, they named the child after me. They found me listed in some tired old family record and decided on the name, Patience Annabel, for their new daughter. They did not know, of course, that I was called by my middle name.

"Oh, this is perfect, Andrew: Patience Annabel. And the name shall compliment our child for patience in a woman is surely a virtue."

"Our daughter will be as pure as she is patient, as proper as she is prudent." Andrew playfully kissed his wife. "I wonder what she was like," he said.

"Who, my dear?"

"Why Patience Annabel, my ancestor. Our daughter's namesake."

Hendrika giggled. "Look, Andrew, it says here, right under her name, that they called her the 'beautiful Annabel.'"

"And our daughter shall be the same." Andrew smiled.

Alas, Patience Annabel Stokes was nothing like me. She was an ugly child who lacked humor and grace. Nonetheless, Andrew and Hendrika doted upon her. I kept my distance for many years, for though I detested the child; I remembered poor Elizabeth, and that I had sworn I would never again take the flesh of children.

Patience Stokes developed into an insipid and vacuous young woman. She was vain and cruel. She tormented the servants with senseless and needless demands and she constantly belittled the pretty young maid that Andrew had hired to attend her.

"What is it, you half-wit, I do not wish to be disturbed."

The pretty maid smiled sweetly back at Patience. I admired her reserve.

"Michele Guyon has arrived Mademoiselle."

"Ah." Patience stood up quickly and primped her hair. "Fetch my mirror and be quick about it. I will see him shortly."

"As you wish, Mademoiselle." The pretty maid curtsied and left through the large double doors that closed off the foyer from the sitting room.

I watched as Patience twirled around by herself, nearly knocking a vase from its perch. I followed, unseen, blowing her hair out in wisps until each ringlet fell about her face like spiders around a ball of white yarn. *Whoosh,* I blew and blew again, *whoosh!*

"Mademoiselle Patience!" The pretty maid cried as she came back through the doors holding the silver mirror. It's a wonder she didn't drop it.

"What is it, you fool, why do you gape?"

The poor maid stood aghast, staring at the wild ringlets blown in torrents as if living things had suddenly sprung from Patient's head.

"Be quick, you idiot, I must not keep him waiting."

The poor maid reluctantly handed the mirror to Patience ... who proceed to scream.

"Don't just stand there. Fix me." Patience demanded.

Oh, if they could have only heard my laughter.

"You bungling flea brain, you are hurting me!" Patience cried as I took my exit.

Bored with her vanity, I slid into the parlor and watched as the handsome Michele took a seat.

"My manservant, Philippe," he said to Andrew and Hendrika.

Michele had traveled to the village of Brooklyn with his young male servant, a boy of nineteen or twenty.

"You speak English so well, sir." Hendrika sat, spreading her beautiful orange and gold taffeta dress around her. I only knew of the colors because they were bright enough and penetrated through the fog before my sight.

"My mother was English," he said quietly.

"So, you live over there on Clover Hill?" Andrew asked.

Michele nodded and politely took the tea that was handed to him by one of the servants.

I knew that Michele had had a large house built on Montague Street in Clover Hill, the likes of which I had never seen before. I followed him often to keep myself abreast of it. When the house was completed in the winter of 1806 it looked like a temple and had so many tall, large windows peering through pilasters, that I wondered how anyone could afford such luxury. It stood alone, overlooking the river.

"There's going to be a steamboat launched in Hoboken. This will soon revolutionize the waterway and make my land invaluable," he told them.

"I admire your foresight," Andrew said. "I hope you are correct."

"I would like to extend an invitation to my home on Saturday; will you and your daughter join me?" Michele looked at Hendrika and smiled.

"Of course." Hendrika smiled back and sipped her tea; pleased, I'm sure, that poor Patience had managed to snare such appealing male attention.

"Good. I'll send a carriage."

Though the journey between what is now Brooklyn Heights and The Flatlands was tedious, every Saturday afternoon following his first visit to the Stokes', Michele would send his large, black carriage to Hubbard Lane for Patience and her mother, who thoroughly enjoyed and anticipated the excursion, despite Andrew's protests.

Michele entertained them in royal fashion. Philippe gallantly took their wraps and summoned great platters of food to be brought from the kitchen. I watched with amazement while Michele courted my namesake as if she were a princess. I hovered around her, though of course, she never noticed me. From my shadowy existence, I could make out her short plumb body and her fleshy smile. I shadowed the room from the confines of culinary desire. You see, I longed to nourish my palette with wine and chew the roasted goose that caused Patience and her mother to swoon like idiots.

Michele seemed oblivious to the spectral vision I cast as I moved around the room, but I could swear the young servant, Philippe, could actually see me hovering about — could feel how deeply I yearned for life. I could have gone anywhere, could have stolen the flesh of the Queen of England, if I had chosen. But I was fixated on this strange romance. I was drawn by an intense compulsion to consume my namesake. I was fascinated by Michele's passion for her. She ogled him like a street urchin while he showered her with gifts ... beautiful European treasures.

"I love music boxes," he said. "Here, my dear. I have started a collection for you."

Michele lovingly touched the ornately painted top and opened it gently.

"Can you hear?" he asked as he held the box to her ear. "Listen."

The sweet sounds gathered in the air and Patience pursed her lips and smiled. It was one of Haydn's string quartets, but to Patience's tin ear, it might as well have been the corner cat crying for an evening meal.

Carefully, Michele walked to a cabinet of dark wood. The doors were paned in glass.

"What have you there?" Patience asked.

"French Bull Dogs," he said and held them out. "Look, how beautiful they are. I brought them all the way from Paris. Notice the detail." He handed her two from a collection of Porcelain dogs.

"Exquisite." Patience giggled as she fondled the tiny creatures in her fat little fingers.

"Philippe. Wine for the ladies if you please." Michele turned and the young man servant bowed at the waist.

"Yes, sir." Philippe quickly went to the wine cellar.

Patience grinned at her mother who beguilingly smiled back.

The three sat uncomfortably staring around the room. Patience could think of not a single thing to say to this delightful man, despite inconspicuous nods from Hendrika to speak up.

"You have decorated your home with such fine things, hasn't he, Patience?" Hendrika asked.

"Yes," Patience replied, untying, and retying the bow on her dress.

"Isn't it wonderful to see the river from these windows?" Hendrika smiled, encouraging her daughter to respond.

"Yes." She'd managed to make a mess of the bow and attempted to fix it.

I was relived to notice that Michele's manservant had returned.

"I have a passion for rich, red Bordeaux. Try this," Michele said as he handed Patience a glass."

He tried to teach her to sip the liquid. "Allow the flavor to linger and slowly float to your belly," he said.

But Patience could not master the fine art of wine tasting. She gulped it, and the wine dribbled down her chin and caused her to cough incessantly. Michele seemed amused. He always seemed amused.

He was a magnificent man. He towered over her in height and while his shoulders were broad, his hips were narrow. He was blond. His hair appeared almost white and fell to his shoulders. His face could have been chiseled in stone. His cheeks were high and his skin appeared rough. I could not tell the color of his eyes, though from my ghostly shadow, I imagined an intense blue color that had changed to gray, such as when the sunlight fades and gives way to rain. His lips were full, and his nose was sharply defined by the rugged strength of his profile.

Patience stared at him constantly. He simply sat back in one of his plush regal chairs and grinned back at her.

One day, quite unexpectedly, Michele's carriage pulled up to Andrew and Hendrika's door.

"I wish your daughter's hand in marriage," Michele told Andrew after seating himself on the chaise, a slight blush to his cheeks. Philippe stood by his side and stared at his feet. Hendrika began to weep and Andrew leapt quickly to his feet and extended his hand.

"I would be honored to welcome you into our family," Andrew said proudly.

Poor Patience, she would never have her wedding night with Michele Guyon. As he came to her bed the night of her lavish wedding; I hid in the shadows. The poor thing was lying there smiling like an eager wench when I took her. I slipped into her as she lay there breathing for him. Her breath was heavy as I lingered across her mouth, letting the air around her lips saturate my soul with delirium. How I longed for it. She felt me take her. She felt my soul cling to hers and force it out. She fought me like a captured animal but I pushed my light into her veins. I forced my being into her flesh. My possession was quite brief. Within moments I moved in her bloodstream. She had lost. She screamed just once, and was gone.

My darkness was replaced with a vague sight of your earth. Faintly, I could hear the wood as it creaked under Michele's step. As he entered the room, he wore a black velvet robe and carried a decanter of wine. I lay back on my pillows and stared. He seemed so very different now.

"Michele?" I whispered.

He smiled into the light of the candle. His face seemed to hold thoughts I could not read. He seemed so much older, so much older than the handsome Michele I had seen from my darkness. The lines in his face traversed his skin like *cul de sacs* that led to places I would not trace with my hand, for fear I would never be recovered.

I found myself praying that he would not touch me, would not further reveal his skin to me as it lay against the open velvet like hard white stone.

"Yes?" he answered.

His voice was harsh and seemed to lash out at the night air. He was staring at me as though he sought to hypnotize me. His gaze seemed haunting and sinister. My body stiffened as he moved toward me. Suddenly, I felt myself shudder. The room had become terribly cold. He seemed to be aware of my flesh as it chilled.

"Shall I build a fire?" he asked me.

"Yes," I whispered.

He set the wine near me and walked to the mantle. The nearness of his flesh had repulsed me. *What is happening,* I thought. *How can this be?*

Soon the flames were flickering like fighting cats and the crimson warmth filled my new flesh like food. He turned back to me. I noticed that his eyes looked like fire in the light.

"Annabel," I thought I heard him say.

A chill went down my spine.

18

"What did you call me?"

I took my head from the pillows and sat straight up. I had just become Patience Stokes Guyon. He had never called that horrid woman anything else but Patience.

"Annabel," he said again.

I shuddered as he spoke it. He came to me and took me in his arms. I fought to free myself from his embrace. I would not consummate a marriage with this imposter. I heard the wine fall to the floor. I heard the glass shatter. He held me tighter.

"Who are you?" I screamed.

"Do not fight me, Annabel."

As he held me down, I felt myself in a horrific spin.

"I have you now, my lost avenging angel," he said fiercely.

He took my hair and held my head back with it. I made my hands into fists and beat him wildly upon the arm.

"Look, Annabel," he demanded.

Suddenly a sharp, vivid light blinded my eyes. An awful pain shot through my head.

"I bring you through time, my little one," he whispered.

I felt the earth as it spun around me with such velocity that I had no other choice but to hold on to him and bury my face in his neck. In a matter of seconds, the sharp white light gave way to sky. When I lifted my head, I immediately noticed that my vision was clear and sharp. I had not seen the blue of the sky with such vividness for centuries. I turned quickly around. To my right, was the sea. It was the very same sea that surrounded my village. I was sure of it. My sense of hearing was suddenly as normal as if I were a girl again in Salem. I began to weep as I listened to the sound of water falling over a rock. I had not heard the sound that water makes, as it runs, for so many of your centuries. I felt the dampness of dirt on my back as he held me on the ground and ripped off my gown. The blessed smell of the dirt filled my lungs. My good God! I was surely in the village of Salem again and the devil himself was forcing his dalliance upon me ... wielding his large, hard appendage before me like some proud royal scepter. I tried to free myself but he held me so very tightly. I tried to run back to the home on the other side of the hill where my father must surely be kneeling in evening prayer.

"Let me go, Michele!" I demanded.

He laughed so loud that the tree branches trembled. I screamed out, but he covered me with his face and placed his mouth on mine. I pounded my fists against his chest, but he held me to the damp earth and forced my legs toward heaven with his hands.

"Annabel," he said. "I give you life!"

I fell into darkness. When I awoke, my bed was empty, and the demon was gone.

# Chapter 5

The very next evening, there was a knock at my door.

"Mrs. Guyon?"

Before me stood a police captain. He was accompanied by two officers. I shook my head, barely remembering who I was.

"Yes?" I said.

"I'm sorry to have to be the bearer of bad news." The captain looked uncomfortably beyond me.

"What is it?" I asked, my borrowed heart seemed still.

"A body turned up in the city mortuary last night. He was burned beyond recognition. We believe it to be your husband."

"What?" I held onto the post for support.

"May we come in?" the Captain asked me.

"Of course," I said and stepped aside.

I felt faint and threw myself onto the nearest chair.

"Are you all right, ma'am?" one of the officers asked.

I nodded. "What happened?" I whispered; my question barely audible.

"The man was trapped in a building down there on Fulton Street. It went up in flames from a faulty furnace." The captain stared at me.

I met his eyes. "How do you know it's my husband if the body was burned beyond recognition?"

21

"Well," the captain began, as he looked admiringly around the lavish house. "The building warehoused fine European music boxes and imported porcelain dogs from France. Your husband was from France, am I correct?"

"Yes, but surely you must have more evidence than that. Is this not a city filled with Frenchmen?"

"We found this," he said and held a ring out to me. My heart beat rapidly, for even without the luxury of perfect eyesight I had seen the emerald ring on Michele's finger many times.

"You'll find the initials *MPG* inside the band. Your husband's initials, I presume?" The captain looked apologetic, but I, on the other hand, was not so sure I would miss my husband at all.

So, there I was, the poor widow, left alone to raise the baby I carried from a night I could barely explain.

My son, Matthew Joshua Horton Guyon was born in February of 1807. He carried the name of my ghostly lover from centuries past and my own dear father. I loved the baby with all my soul. For over a century I had given birth to children. Some I had loved. Some were not lovable. But this child was mine. He did not come from borrowed flesh. He came from me. He had my face. My face! Not the face of a woman people saw as his mother, that horrid Patience, but the face of the real Annabel Horton. His hair waved and shone in the light, though it was not golden like mine, but black as night. His jaw line was strong and lean and his eyes seemed to dance in kindness and humor. He was my boy. My Matthew.

How I pampered him. He was, after all, fatherless. But we were rich. Michele had left us more money than I had ever dreamed. Soon, I began to forget that the devil himself might have fathered my child and enjoyed the luxury of living quite well on the devil's money. Of course, I tried to piece together a history for Michele Guyon, but I could find nothing. I questioned Philippe, who had remained with the house, but the boy seemed reluctant to talk to me.

"I can find not a trace of Michele Guyon in Paris, what do you make of that?" I asked Philippe.

The boy merely shrugged his shoulders and looked helplessly away.

"This makes no sense to me, Philippe," I said. "My son's skin is the color of a cashew and his eyes shine black like the evening sky. I am fair and Michele Guyon was fair. What do you make of that?"

Philippe stood there, his face a mask. "Yes, fair," he said.

"Ah," I exclaimed in exasperation. "You are of no help to me, Philippe."

"I don't know what you want me to say, Ma'am."

I realized I was being hard on Philippe and sent him back to his room. I would be better served with my own thoughts. I could not tell Philippe what I was really thinking, he would think me mad— for I suspected that someone like myself — someone able to steal the body of another, had in fact, committed this heinous act of violence against me and had then murdered the real Michele. How could I voice that thought to anyone?

I hoped that Hendrika would quell my suspicions, but unfortunately, she only verified them. I had coerced her into talking about Michele shortly after Matthew's birth.

"I knew poor Michele for such a short time," I began sadly.

"He was such a beautiful man," she reminisced quietly.

"Tell me, Mother. Tell me everything that you can remember about him," I pleaded.

"Well, he was kind and always chiding us, he had wonderful humor."

"And handsome, too. No?" I questioned.

She smiled and took my hand.

"He was so dashing and so dark like his son."

"Dark?"

"Ah, yes. His skin was the color of the sand out by the marshlands and his eyes were like the sky at midnight. I will miss him."

I was shocked.

"Are you sure, Mother?" I laughed. "Do not fool me. He was dark? His eyes like coal?"

"Patience, you frighten me. I never know anymore if you suffer a breakdown. You have not been the same since the morning of his death," she said with concern.

I knew then that I had lain with the devil's own but surely nothing from the devil could have fathered my child. I was certain that this entity had stolen the body of a man called Michele ... and it was this man to whom I identified my son's thick dark hair and deep set almond shaped eyes.

I was overjoyed that Matthew was born of my spirit and had not inherited any resemblance to either the demon, or Patience Stokes, even though I could not explain it. He was clearly mine and he had the delicate features of a priceless doll. Dimples framed his smile and his chin was marked by a cleft. My own chin had such a mark. Of course, I longed to know his father, the real Michele Guyon, but his soul would be lost to me for endless dimensions.

I realized that everyone ... that horrid Patience and her mother, Hendrika ... must have seen the real Michele Guyon while the demon courted and charmed them both in Michele's name, hiding himself behind the eyes of Michele's glance. But I saw only the demon as he pandered in the flesh of the man who had fathered my son. Oh, the demon had a name but I did not know it then. I did not yet remember the face of Urbain Grandier, chosen by the devil to be my nemesis.

But what could it matter to me that a monster had tricked me into believing he was humorous and kind? I had my son and he was innocent, entirely innocent of evil. In all the centuries that I have known men, all sorts of noble men, I have never known a man of such gentility. Not even my own father, whom I adored. No, my son was not of the devil or the devil's lackey. The devil is not so complex as to proliferate kindness. A demon's soul could not be ambiguous. I was sure that there could not be a trace of God in a demon's soul. How wrong this proved to be. But why would the demon bother to force his vile affections upon me? To that, I had no answer.

So be it. I certainly would not call the devil forth for explanations. I wanted no part of him. I could not explain what had happened to me and I refused to become obsessed with it. I only knew that the man who called himself Michele Guyon had been a fake and a murderer. Why should the real Michele be prey for the devil, I pondered? But I had not a clue and I prayed never to know.

My son grew so tall that I was always after him not to stoop and from the moment he could walk he became my gallant and protective knight, always checking to see how I felt and whether or not I needed tea from the kitchen, or a shawl to put about my shoulders. I never entertained the notion that he might have powers that could move time aside or reach out past tomorrow and return from the journey. No, I simply assumed he was as normal as any other child and did not even look for hints of the craft. Then, in his thirteenth year, my innocence was shattered and I was faced with the unimaginable.

We could not find Matthew for five days. We searched everywhere but there was no trace of him. I was frantic. Andrew and Hendrika did all they could to console me but I felt as if I would die of grief. At just that moment, when I feared I might never see my son again, he appeared at my bedroom door as if by magic. Philippe stood by his side.

"The boy has returned," Philippe announced reassuringly.

"Good God!" I cried.

"Mother!" he said excitedly. "I've been to a strange place."

I fell to my knees and held him in my arms. I wept from happiness. I was so overcome with relief to have him back that I did not even ask him where he had been. But then, he began to tell me.

"I have been to a strange place, Mother. There are lots of children there and they speak funny. They run into walls and call me the devil." He laughed.

The color ran from my flesh. I held him firmly and looked into his eyes.

"How did you get there?" I asked him.

"I'm not sure, Mother."

I stared at Philippe who was listening intently.

"Tell me more, Matthew," I asked quietly.

"Well, the children," he continued, "they run around pointing at me. 'There he is! Can you not see him? There! There!'" They point and scream at me. They say I torment them and tell them to do things."

"What kind of things?"

"To roll on the floor. To beat their heads with their fists."

"Have you ever seen these children before?" I asked him while my heart pounded in my chest.

"No, Mother. Never."

I knelt before him.

"Matthew, I do not ever want you to see these children again. The children are evil and they may not let you go. Do you understand? This is very important."

I looked up at Philippe who stood very still, his dark skin nearly white.

"Leave us, please, Philippe," I said and wondered what on earth the poor boy could be thinking.

"If you'll forgive me, Miss Guyon," he began, "but perhaps it is time."

"Time, time for what?" I quipped.

"The truth," he said simply.

Something in his expression frightened me. I dismissed him. *How dare he intervene*? I thought to myself. "No information you might have

25

is of any interest to me. "Please leave us," I commanded and returned my attention back to my son.

"Yes, ma'am, if you insist" he said with a long sigh.

I waited for the door to close behind Philippe before I spoke.

"You must promise never to go there again. Please, Matthew. I beg of you."

He made me a promise and I believed he would honor it. I now knew that my son's powers were far greater than my own, for at that time I could not re-enter another dimension without killing off the body I was in. I followed a linear path because I was consumed by human consciousness and the human mind believes in chronological order. But my son's experience of time was far more advanced. He could absorb the walls of gravity and travel through. In 1820, I wanted only to believe he simply spoke to ghosts. Now I know better. Now I know that he pushed beyond the barriers of perception.

I kept a watchful eye on Matthew after that and I believed he never experimented with his powers again. I ignored Philippe's attempt to speak with me about the incident, though I knew how much he wanted to. I was grateful that my son had gifts, that he had the sight to see his mother as the real Annabel Horton, but I would not discuss our powers. My ancestry, at that time, was as much a mystery to me as I would insist it would remain to Matthew. I was deathly afraid to accept this special ability we both possessed and I shunned any belief in the supernatural. I raised my son as a good Christian. And despite that one incident, he seemed to have a perfectly uneventful adolescence.

Eventually, I remarried. The demon had been correct about the invention of the steamboat and now, with its close proximity to Manhattan, Clover Hill was becoming a sought after spot on the Hudson River. I met many of the families who began to build houses around the area, and eventually, I was introduced to a wealthy businessman who had never married.

"Why, Patience Stokes Guyon, I am so honored to make your acquaintance." And with that Seth kissed my hand, his eyes traveling up to mine.

He was plain and short and not put off by the ghastly appearance of Patience Stokes.

"How lovely you are, like a lone dove perched upon a spring branch in full bloom."

26

"You flatter me so, sir," I said with a smile. "A cherry tree, I hope. I do love them."

"Pink and delicious." He smiled with a blush to his cheek.

I was amused by Seth and became increasingly fond of him. His laughter was infectious and he loved my son, and would have, no doubt, done anything for either of us. He courted me with sincerity and dined me on exquisite food.

"Fit for a Queen," he would say, handing me a *Foie Gras.*

I pretended to adore the fine cuisine, but unfortunately, all that I could actually experience was my unquenchable desire to taste that which I could not.

"My dear Patience," he would say. "I would almost swear that you do not experience your food. Let it sit upon the tongue before you swallow. Taste! Taste is everything." He'd close his eyes and softly chew.

"And always cleanse the palette with wine when you move from meat to vegetable," he'd say as he sipped on the liquid and ran his thumb and finger across his mustache, softly smiling in my direction.

Poor Seth did not realize that my palette was an empty vessel that hungered to feel the sweetbreads upon my tongue and even the water that washed them down. The useless body I had stolen only gave me a reflection and a voice. If he only knew that I could barely feel his embrace.

My son approved of my relationship with this boisterous and endearing man and went into business with him when he was nineteen years old. Seth manufactured ink. At first, Matthew thought it was a common trade, but Seth soon gained his respect.

"A man must earn his living," he told Matthew. "A man builds his character by providing his community with an honest days work."

My son had always cared about art and music but little else, and though I appreciated our mutual interests, I asked Seth to instill a sense of economics. I did not want Matthew to become complacent and limited. I often feared he might. He was a delicate man whose only friend, thus far, had been the servant, Philippe. So I welcomed the developing relationship between Seth and my son. For the time being, we had more money than we needed, but if it were the devil that gave me this child, then what would prevent the devil from claiming his fortune? Then, what would become of my son?

Seth was happy to teach Matthew the printing ink business and I believe that he caught on quickly, and even grew to enjoy the work. I had spoiled him terribly all his life so I knew that I must insure that he could survive the devil's blow, should the devil decide to strike.

"It's time for you to take a wife, Matthew."

I was concerned, women did not hold his interest for very long. Though he was terribly amusing and attracted many a young woman to grace our parlor and peer at him from behind their fans, he seemed bored by the attention.

"In due time, Mother," he said. "I'll know her the minute I lay eyes on her, I'm quite sure of it."

"You will be grey by the time that happens."

"Oh, Mother." He laughed. "Then she will be as grey as I."

Well, he was, after all, my son, of my spirit. Hadn't I found my desires nurtured in a ghostly prince, my beloved Matthew, a man that had appeared as a shadow in my arms more than two centuries ago? I knew that my son also possessed my talent to absorb life from some other time. How could I expect this boy of my flesh to satisfy himself with girls of his day if girls of his day could not capture him?

As for me, I had not even allowed Seth to kiss me during our courtship. However, Seth's intentions were earnest. The night he proposed, I heard his step on the front walk and noticed that his eyes, even from my shadowy sight, appeared to sparkle. He had Philippe take his cloak and he entered my parlor with a sheepish grin.

"My dear Patience," he began, as he fell to his knees before me, and took my hands.

"You know how I feel about you and I hope you feel the same. Close your eyes, dearest."

I felt him slip the diamond on my finger, and as I opened my eyes, he threw his face in my lap. "Will you marry me?" he whispered.

I agreed to marry him. You must understand, my son needed a mentor and I was lonely. Men saw me as that horrid Patience, not as the beautiful Annabel. They treated me with politeness and indifference, as though I were actually a homely woman, or one past thirty. But, Seth loved me and said that I had inner beauty. *Ah, Seth, my darling Seth, if you but knew whom you take in your arms. I was called beautiful, the beautiful Annabel,* they would whisper behind me. Ah, well. Yes, I agreed to marry him but our marriage lasted only one year. Urbain saw to that. Read on. I will tell you more.

# Chapter 6

You do not understand evil. I can see that. It is too prevalent in your world for you to comprehend the subtleties. It has infiltrated your earth so entirely that your consciousness accepts it and your vision misinterprets it. Evil is everywhere. Oh, how the devil makes a fool of you. But let me continue.

My son came to me one evening as I sat beneath the oak tree that graced our rear yard. I sat there often, for the branches offered me shade from the sun. *God's music,* Father used to say of trees. "Yes, dear Father, God's music." I thought. "And one thing the Devil can not alter."

"Mother," he said as he came toward me, my beautiful son. He walked with his chest out and his head held high.

*What is this?* I thought as I noticed his usual smile replaced by furrows that formed lines above his nose. He sat and took my hands.

"We must talk," he said.

I sat up sharply. I saw it immediately, a form, dark like a shadow, and it passed quickly behind him.

"Shall we go inside?" I asked, with some amount of concern.

My son seemed not to hear me.

"Mother, I'm in love!" he said.

Again, I saw the ghostly form. It did not pass so quickly this time but paused for a moment, hovering behind my son. I stared directly at it and wondered if I could shoo it away.

"Mother, did you hear me? I'm in love," Matthew said earnestly and squeezed my hands.

"I want to hear all about it. Everything," I said as I tried to ignore the presence that now shifted its position and moved about the yard, resembling what some of you might call a spirit.

"Let's go inside, my dear. I've caught a chill."

I moved swiftly toward the house. Matthew ran ahead to open the door. I noticed his furrows were gone and his face now glowed.

"Mother, she is beautiful. She is the most beautiful girl I have ever seen," he said as he led me into the parlor and sat me down.

It was then I heard it. Laughter. It was low at first. I shuddered. Then, suddenly, it faded.

"Mother, have you heard a word I've said?"

My son got on his knees before me.

"Yes dear," I answered. "You are in love and I want you to tell me all about it. Tell me all about *her.*"

He paused and the furrows returned.

"What is it dear?" I asked as I reached out and touched his hair.

"Do you love me, Mother?" he asked, with eyes that searched mine so seriously, and hands that held my own so tightly, that he might have cracked my bones.

"What kind of a question is that?" I asked. "You are my life. I worship you," I answered.

He put his face so near to mine; I could detect the faint sweet scent of his breath.

"Do you know me to be sane?" he asked me.

"Are you afraid to tell me about her, Matthew?" I smiled. "Is this girl of yours a two headed monster?"

He laughed then. "Oh, Mother," he said, "quite the contrary. She is beautiful."

"Oh, Matthew," I whispered. "Is she is an actress?"

He put his hands to his eyes and he laughed so hard that tears formed and fell down his cheeks.

I stood up quickly. I heard another laugh other than my son's. Someone was laughing with him. I felt afraid and agitated.

"Matthew, I demand to know more about this girl!"

I walked to the mantle and stood before the fire. I felt the darkness follow me.

Matthew came to me and took my hands again. I was bewildered that he seemed not to be aware of this menacing presence.

"Mother," he said. "Forgive me. I've upset you. I didn't mean to. Come, sit back down and I will tell you all about her."

As he led me back to the sofa, I heard the laughter behind me, loud and insane. It came from the mirror above the mantle.

My son sat beside me.

"Mother, do you remember when I was a child and I went to that place where I had no right to be, but I felt the air in my lungs and the sun in my eyes all the same?"

My blood turned cold and I stood up sharply.

"Matthew, you promised never, never to go there again." I took his face in both my hands and looked deeply into his eyes. "Have you betrayed me?"

He brought my hands down from his face and held them to his lips.

"Yes," he sighed.

There was a long pause between us. I heard the laughter rise so loudly that it hurt my ears. I stood up and ran to the mirror. Briefly, so briefly, I saw the form of a man. Yes, there it was. The blond, broad demon now stared back at me, with eyes that glowed red, from the glass.

"The devil!" I screamed. "It is the devil's doing."

"Mother!" My son ran to me and took me in his arms. "I never returned until last year. I swear it. But they called me ... those children kept calling me back and when I returned they went wild, and screamed, 'there, he makes me do this and that ... look there, look there, look there ... he is the devil ... do you not see him?' I know this sounds crazy, but there is a girl, Annabel, and she is in danger. Mother, I must help her ... those children will surely have her killed."

"Annabel?" The blood in my borrowed veins ran cold. "No!" I screamed and turned back to the shadow.

"Mother, you must not worry for me. I love this girl with all my heart. She is my Annabel. My beautiful, beautiful Annabel."

"Your Annabel?" I said to him. "You cannot love her."

The memory of the ghostly presence from centuries past turned my flesh crimson red and I burned as if I were on fire.

"Yes, Mother. I must find a way to be with her. I have a power ... a power that allows me to enter time. It is not a dream. You know it is not a dream."

"Oh, my God," I whispered. "Dear Lord, no!" I cried. "You cannot love this girl."

Matthew ran to my side.

31

"I must save her, Mother. I must try. Please understand."

I fell to my knees. "You cannot save her, Matthew. You are centuries too late. Her soul has rotted in time like the flesh she lost."

I turned toward the mantle where I knew the demon lingered in the shadows like slime on the water's surface.

"You bastard!" I screamed.

The laughter filled my eardrums and reverberated against the walls. My son's horrified sadness gripped my heart and tore it open.

"You bastard!" I screamed again.

But the demon only laughed.

"What do you want of me?" I said as I fell to my knees and beat my fists against the floor.

But the devil does not answer you. The Devil leads you. The devil uses you.

My son's despair, and my own horrified confusion, tortured my days and turned my nights into sorrowful weeping and endless pacing. I assumed that my son had been there in 1692, as I lay in my bed and fell in love with him. We were surely witches ... the two of us, pawns for the devil's deviance, but surely it was God that granted us power and not Satan. Why won't God speak to us as clearly as this demonic spirit? Why had God allowed this evil? But, both God and the devil were silent now, and I had only my son's sorrow to haunt me, not seeing the girl again was torturing him. The son whom I had always doted upon, and to whom I was the anchor and the angel of his childhood, would now give him nothing but pain.

I refused to let him speak of this "phantom from his imagination" again and I insisted that he take a wife. He pleaded with Seth to talk sense to me, to allow him at least his bachelorhood, but my dear Seth regretted not marrying earlier, and therefore, invested a great deal of his time in helping me find an appropriate bride for my son.

Andrew Stokes, the man who had fathered Patience, in whose flesh I lingered, had a distant cousin by the name of Oscar Everett Stokes. Oscar had married and moved to Chatham, New York, before the century turned. He and his wife, Katrina, had three daughters. The two oldest, Alice and Sarah Ann, had married, but their youngest daughter, Maebelle, was just twenty. It was Maebelle to whom I married off my son. I did not like her. She was a bit odd. Her features were very irregular and her voice was thin. However, she adored my Matthew. He grimaced at the sight of her, and my heart ached for him, but I had to act quickly.

"I will never have a wedding night with her," he told me.

"Please, Matthew," I begged. "This is for your own good. You cannot follow around a ghost for the rest of your days."

"I will go to my Annabel again. I will find her waiting." His fist hit the side of the table and his handsome face was distorted in distress. "Please, Mother. Do not make me marry Maebelle. I cannot stand her."

"I am sorry, Matthew. But I insist that you start a family."

"For God's sake, Mother. Is there no one else in the city of Brooklyn for me?"

He was angry ... terribly angry. I wanted the earth to swallow me. If it were possible to shoot the devil in the heart I would have shot him. But alas, the devil dies not by gunshot.

"I am sorry, Matthew. I insist on this. Please, trust me."

He turned from me and left the room. His fists were tight and his eyes were teary. I felt this heart I had stolen beating as if it would burst open. From somewhere in the shadows I heard the devil's laughter. The air around me was cold and stunk of must. I spit in the direction of the darkness but the devil's laughter did not cease.

# Chapter 7

Maebelle Stokes and Matthew Joshua Horton Guyon were married at St. Evangeline Christian Church on July 26th, 1829. I bought them a new house on King Street in Manhattan, close to Seth's manufacturing plant on Varick Street. Seth moved into the house on Montague Street after we were married in October of that same year. But my son was not happy and Maebelle complained of his long evenings at the theater and his endless conversations on literature and art with Philippe, from which she was excluded.

"He recites Lord Byron's poetry into the air, as if to a lover," she told me.

"I am sure he is reciting to you, dear," I said reassuringly.

"He is not," she insisted. "He shares his passion with another."

I could not intervene. I mourned the loss of my son, for his anger had created a distance between us, but I could not change the circumstances and permit any exercise of his power.

Soon, Maebelle became pregnant. I was thrilled that their marriage had been consummated. I prayed that her love for my son would eventually penetrate the barriers of his resistance, and ultimately, I hoped her determination would win her a place in his heart. I was convinced that a child would awaken him to the responsibilities of the dimension he was in. I did not want him to even think of "his Annabel"

34

again.

Seth and Matthew renamed their company, Quality Printing Ink, and set up lucrative contracts with major publishers. The bank was willing to advance them on a loan so they could expand to a new location on West Street and hire more employees. We might have all eventually been happy. I was beginning to see a tolerance develop in my son for Maebelle's awkward, but endearing affection for him. And Seth was filled with energy and plans for the future. We were all excited over the birth of the child, and I felt that Matthew's anger had subsided. I began to fantasize that I had imagined my identity as Annabel Horton, and had never seen the devil's face. If it were not for my beautiful image in the glass, I might have all together forgotten that I was a transient in their world.

They found Seth's body in March of 1830. I knew it was the demon that had caused me this grief, but I could not prove it. And even if I could, who would believe me? They said that Seth had drowned at the Fulton Street Pier while waiting for a ferry into Manhattan, and that my son, Matthew, had probably drowned with him.

"Matthew Guyon's body is probably adrift in the river," the police told Maebelle and I. "It should surface."

"Was there a witness?" I asked tearfully, and the policeman shook his head as Maebelle sobbed in my arms.

I sought out the devil and demanded he justify this cruelty, this vindictive act of violence. But the demon cowered behind his evil and would not show his face again for many years.

They never found my son's body but they were able to return a gold pocket watch that I had given him on his eighteenth year. Strangely enough, the watch was found in Seth's pocket, but it was clearly engraved *to Matthew from his loving Mother.*

My son's child was not yet born, and though I pitied poor Maebelle, I could not bring myself to comfort her. My despair had crippled my desire for life. For thirty days I stayed in doors and would not look upon the light of day. I thought about killing this horrible flesh that I had borrowed and freeing myself from the pain that I felt. But this much I know, when the flesh dies, spiritual pain continues. I prayed that my son might still be alive, but I prayed in vain. I prayed until my anger at God overwhelmed me. Finally, I sought solace from my son's child.

Matthew's daughter was born at the house on King Street, on June

6th, 1830. I was there at the moment of Meredith Mae's arrival on earth.

"Oh, God, she is so beautiful," I cried as Maebelle held her out to me and I rocked her in my arms.

The child so eased my grief. Maebelle was quick to allow me to care for her. Perhaps, she was still too despondent over Matthew's death to nurture the child. Eventually, Meredith Mae stayed with me entirely. I did not care or need to know why Maebelle did not want her. The bond between my grandchild and I was apparent. She was the prettiest child I had ever seen and she had her father's beautiful almond eyes. There seemed to be not a trace of Maebelle in her.

My son was eventually declared dead, and though Maebelle grieved, she remarried shortly after Meredith Mae's birth. She and her new husband, Malcolm Jacob Northrup, had three other children in quick succession. Maebelle then ignored Meredith Mae all together and the child was content to pretend that I was her mother. Of course, I had to open the house to visits twice a month. Maebelle and her husband would bring the other children, and Meredith Mae and I would have to pretend we enjoyed their company. It was an abysmal bore to be tied to these peculiar people, but we did our best to make them feel welcome.

Malcolm assumed the position of lord and master and insisted that I do this and that with my money. I told him my attorney managed my fortune and I was quite content.

But Malcolm believed he had some inalienable right to my estate. I am sure he calculated that my death could not be far off and surely he would become the executor of all that I would leave to Meredith Mae.

"You have no right to assume that I am frivolous with money, Malcolm," I calmly reiterated over and over again.

"Well, women, dear Patience, are better suited to other things than managing money. What do you know of it, you make none?"

His arrogance was a sore spot of constant tension. He treated my servants poorly, as well, and I was always apologizing for his behavior. He believed himself to be better than people of a different skin tone. He felt that his white, fine masculine features were the mark of beauty, and he and his kind were fashioned in the likeness of God. Poor fool, I thought. He thinks this false proximity to God gives him the right to control the earth.

Maebelle doted on Malcolm Jacob Northrup in much the same way she had doted upon my son. Their children resembled them in both their features and mental limitations. Their oldest daughter, Catherine, was a cruel child. She was a bossy little brat and she was consistently in a foul temper. Poor Catherine had a rather hooked nose and a portly body. Unfortunately, she resembled Malcolm's father, the stoic Ebenizer Ryan Northrup. Their other daughter, Beth Anne, resembled a broomstick. She was skinny, like Maebelle, and her hair stood straight and rough.

How jealous they were of Meredith Mae! Meredith Mae was the beautiful child to whom strangers stared adoringly. Her sweetness brought her gifts from little boys and her kindness brought her prayers from those she had touched with her generosity. But, my Meredith Mae's qualities went ignored by her immediate family. Her sisters slapped her when they thought that no one was looking, attempted to trip her down the stairs and stole her favorite toys. Her mother, Maebelle, considered only her usefulness, and Malcolm ... that horrid man ... leered at her as if she were prize cattle.

Thank goodness their last child was a boy. They named him Jed. He was a bright child with an honest affection for his sisters. Malcolm adored his son and treated his girls as an afterthought. Maebelle used her daughters to run her errands and keep her house tidy while she spent Malcolm's money on china and the latest fashions. She took great care of her son, however; perhaps, she believed that he was superior to her daughters.

Meredith Mae and I dreaded their visits, but we accommodated them so that I might remain sole guardian of my granddaughter. She was my son's child and did not belong to Maebelle. And she certainly did not belong to Malcolm. It was not until the child was ten years old that I learned how intrinsically connected we really were.

# Chapter 8

It was the winter of 1840. I had Philippe light a fire in the library. The snow fell like music from the sky and covered the streets in a white enchanting dance. My darling, Meredith Mae, sat at the window and traced her name in breath on the glass.

"Would the misses like cocoa?" Philippe asked as he stoked the wood. The red and yellow embers leapt up the chimney to die a cold death in the February air while the fire cackled and cracked at us, as though it could will us to burn.

"Oh, yes," cried Meredith Mae. Philippe smiled as the child ran into my arms. "Philippe always makes the fire speak," she said gleefully.

"You have to tickle the wood and feed the flame." He smiled.

He clearly loved Meredith Mae and the child loved him in return. I was grateful for Philippe. After Matthew's disappearance, I so needed the strength of his demeanor and the sad and compassionate smile he gave me when I beckoned him. I sought solace from conversations by the fire and the murmur of his voice. Philippe had been such a strong and refined presence in my life all these years. He had always been an educated man, and I never questioned that. It was terribly unusual to find a servant reading, and I was surprised by the hours he devoted to teaching my granddaughter European history, and amusing her with tales of literature. He and my son had been more like brothers and both

38

shared an avid love of poetry and music. Since the moment he had insisted upon remaining with the house, I had become very fond of Philippe. I sensed a bond between us that I did not fully understand. He was my only friend and he seemed to have a profound understanding of my despair. We spoke often about the complexities of the human spirit. I did not enjoy the developing alienation that I felt as I perceived the years to pass, but Philippe would laugh at me, and often succeed at getting me to laugh at myself.

"It is not the changing years that create alienation. It is your soul's response to change," he would say.

"This nineteenth century world of manners and beauty makes me feel so unbearably isolated," I would tell him. "And it only gets worse as the years go by."

"Well, yes." He would laugh. "It's certainly a century of attitudes, isn't it?"

But, in all the years that Philippe and I spoke of so many things, I consistently avoided questioning him about his association with Michele Guyon. When he attempted to broach the subject, I dismissed him. Eventually, he acquiesced to my wishes and muttered some stories that I sensed were only half-truths, told only in some fashion to placate me.

"I was bought in Virginia," he told me. "Mr. Guyon said he was traveling east, said he was going to build a house in Brooklyn and import objects of art from his native home in France."

"Interesting," I said. "And do you have any family?" I asked.

"Yes, ma'am, my sister, Emie."

I imagined she had been left behind when he joined the man called Michele Guyon.

"And this man eventually freed you?" I asked him.

He nodded and looked off. I knew there was more to Philippe's story but I did not want to know it. I fought desperately to maintain my own illusion of privacy, while I respected his, as well.

"And Michele? How do you remember him?" I would ask casually, avoiding any intensity to my question.

"Not fair," he said. "But dark."

I doubted that Philippe was telling me the whole truth, but he had learned not to offer information unless I specifically asked for it. From the first moment I saw him, I felt he could see beyond the veil. I was convinced that he and I had seen the same Michele Guyon ... the same blond demon with the cold and penetrating stare. But, for all these years, I had not been ready to discuss my nature with anyone. Not

Philippe. Not my own son. It was, after all, my witch's power that had cost my soul this darkness. But then again, perhaps my fear of this power had cost me my child.

After Philippe went off to make the cocoa, Meredith Mae insisted on a game of hide and seek. We had played it often. I let her hide and then I would run about the house attempting to find her. She usually hid in the same places, under the bed, in the attic or behind my bedroom door. This particular afternoon, however, I could not find her. I looked for at least twenty minutes before I finally summoned Philippe.

"I cannot find Meredith Mae. Do you think she went outside?" I asked him.

He shook his head. "She would not go outside," he finally answered.

"Do you know where she is?" I asked.

He put his hands across his chest and stood firm, silently staring at me.

"Philippe, I am becoming concerned," I said with some agitation.

He began to mumble something that I could not make out, when I heard a sound on the stairs. A moment later, Meredith Mae was standing in the doorway of our front parlor.

"Where on earth have you been?" I cried as I ran to her.

"I went to the tree," she said.

"What tree?"

"The one I always go to."

"And just what tree is that?" I questioned.

"The one by Frost Fish Brook," she answered.

I laughed because I did not know what else to do.

"Frost Fish?"

"Frost Fish," she replied.

The Frost Fish Brook runs right by Leach's Hill in Salem, Massachusetts. Meredith Mae had never been in Massachusetts. She had not been out side of the state of New York. *What an imagination she has*, I thought. I had often told her stories about a little treasure chest that I had buried under the tall elm tree near the Frost Fish brook. I told her that the chest contained love letters from my future husband, and that the letters were wrapped in purple cloth and placed inside the chest. I told her that some day I would return for the letters, and perhaps, she would come with me. The child loved the story and made me repeat it often.

"Well, you have had a long trip. I hope you will not go quite so far away next time," I said.

"I only came back for the cocoa."

I laughed, despite myself, and then I noticed a small bundle in her hand. "What do you have there, Meredith Mae?"

"Letters," she answered proudly and held them out to me.

My hand shook as I reached out for the small and dirty parcel she held. The cloth was familiar, though it looked so old. I blew away the dirt and the vivid purple cloth shone through. As I opened the cloth, old torn letters fell to the floor. Some of the papers were ripped into several pieces. I reached down and held them in my hands. The all too familiar writing caused my heart to beat like a cannon just fired.

*To my wife*, one read, *I will protect you. To my wife, my beautiful, beautiful Annabel,* said another.

"My God," I wept. "These are mine."

Philippe came immediately to my side. Meredith Mae stood over me and stroked my hair. I turned to my granddaughter and held out the delicate pieces of torn paper. "Where did you get these?"

"I went to the tree, Grandmamma. The tallest elm ... and I found your letters. I thought you would be pleased."

Meredith Mae, I am not pleased. Tell me, child. Did you see anyone?"

"Only Papa."

"Papa?" I asked softly.

"Yes, Grandmamma. I saw him. He put his arms around me and told me to tell you that he is safe. He tells me that all the time."

I pulled the little girl to me and held on to her arms.

"Papa?" I asked again.

It was then that Philippe knelt by the child.

"Your cocoa is in the kitchen, Meredith Mae. Go on and have it before it gets cold," he told her, as he tenderly rubbed some dirt from her hands.

She looked at me for a moment and I smiled briefly.

"Yes, Meredith Mae, go have your cocoa. I will join you in a bit."

I watched as she went and closed the door behind her. After a moment, Philippe came to me.

I turned to him sharply.

"How do I look to you Philippe?" I demanded as I walked up close to him and stared at his face.

"Miss Cummings?" he muttered.

"What do you know of this?" I demanded more furiously.

He held both of his own hands up to me in what looked like a plea of admonition.

"I have suspected something for quite some time."

"Yes, Ma'am?"

"How do I look to you?"

"You look fine, just fine, Ma'am," he answered, and seemed to want to put his arms about me for comfort, but dared not.

"No, Philippe. Be specific! What color are my eyes?"

He hesitated and turned his head.

"What color, Philippe?" I looked him squarely in the face. I knew that he would not remember the color of Patience's eyes. Men barely paid attention to her. He stared back at me.

"Green, Ma'am," he said finally.

"Green, you say? Green? Ah ha!"

Philippe gave me a soft and reassuring smile.

"The real Patience Guyon had brown eyes," I told him.

He avoided a confrontation, yet he did not cease smiling.

"Only one with power can see me as I am. It is Annabel Horton who has the green eyes ... not poor Patience.

Philippe remained quiet.

"We are two of God's witches, you and I, Philippe. Do not pretend that I am a crazed female and you are a humble servant. Speak to me now!" I demanded.

"I have wanted to for such a long time," he finally said. "It is you who has forbidden it."

"Why have you not told me that Meredith Mae has the power?" I questioned.

"You know yourself that you would not listen to me. You sent me on some errand every time I attempted to tell you who I am, and what I know."

"Who are you, Philippe?" I asked him. "And what do you know?"

"There will be time enough for that, but for now, we have a more important situation to discuss."

I felt the pressure of his fingers on my wrist and noticed, perhaps for the first time, that his one hand was so large it might have covered both of my own.

"And just what situation is that?" I asked.

"He wants you back," he said simply. "That must be it."

"Who wants me back?"

"Urbain."

"Urbain? Who is Urbain?" I felt terribly confused, for I had not known the blond demon's name. I had not any awareness of my connections to Urbain in that moment.

"The blond demon that possessed Michele's body, Urbain Grandier, from the caverns of hell. He wants you back in Salem. His curse has been upon you from the moment you were born."

"What curse?" I asked sharply.

"You only recall yourself as Annabel Horton, the witch from Salem, but your spirit was born in Loudun."

"Loudun? France? But I am English," I answered in disbelief.

"Perhaps so. But your soul was born in Loudun. I believe your great aunt served God in Loudun."

"As a witch?"

"As a nun," he answered me solemnly.

"I am a Puritan," I said proudly. "We are not French Catholics."

"Look, your great aunt was a French Catholic nun," he insisted. "Grandier seduced her. He seduced all the Ursuline nuns. He made a mockery of God. He caused them all hysterical fits. A church full of nuns crawling the walls like animals in heat ... screaming for Urbain ... as blasphemous as the hysterical children of Salem. It was this great aunt of yours that finally turned him in to Cardinal Richelieu. The priests had named him a witch and said he put a spell on all the nuns of the Huguenot St. Pierre-du-March Church."

"What became of him?" I asked, feeling the stolen flesh on my arm run cold.

"They crushed his legs and then burnt him alive," he answered me. Then he added. "He was the local curate. Did your mother ever speak of him?"

"No. I know nothing of what you tell me," I told him.

"He put a curse on all the descendants of those that sent him to the stake." He sighed. "But Madeline was his prize, the beautiful Madeline de Brou. Still, he cursed her soul for eternity and swore vengeance on her descendents."

"What does history say became of this nun?" I suddenly felt a strange connection to the tale he told me.

"No one knows. Some say God let her go for turning away the devil — freed her soul from remembering the shame."

"I am not the niece of a nun."

"I tell you, Madeline de Brou's little grand niece stands before me," he insisted.

"Nonsense," I proclaimed loudly. My mother was Caylus Moreau Horton, and we are English, and my mother never spoke of this nun."

He laughed. "In Puritan Salem? Well, I would think not."

"Nuns are celibate. They do not know men." I walked up close to him and searched his eyes. "Urbain could not have violated a nun."

"Perhaps you will return to this church and find your ancestry in the stones of that madness. Seek out this Claudette. She can tell you the truth."

"What is your real identity?" I demanded of him as if he were still my servant.

"I am Michele Guyon's son."

I was confused and agitated and began to weep again. "I do not understand," I cried. "I could get no information on Michele Guyon. He does not exist. And you cannot be the son of a white man."

"He exists," he insisted. "He is born in 1946. And I am his son. I could not reveal that to you for so long. I wanted to, but I could not. You were not willing to hear it and might have sent me away."

I rested my head back on the chair and let out a long sigh. Then I began to laugh. I stood up and pointed toward the door that Meredith Mae had closed behind her. "If he is not born until 1946, then how could *she* be here? Her father was born in 1807; her father is Michele's son."

He looked at me and smiled. "Come now ... what does the future mean to us? And what of time? There is no time, only one chaotic second upon which humanity has imposed order."

"Who fathered my son? Someone put a seed in me. And it was not that bastard, Urbain," I yelled at Philippe, still laughing as if I would lose my mind.

"Yes. You are correct. One of the nuns gave birth to his only child, centuries ago. A girl. He was still a man then. Now he can only use the bodies of living men to impregnate women. He used Michele's body to have a wedding night with you, but it was not Urbain's seed that fathered your son. He cannot father children anymore, he is merely mist. We are all quite sure of that."

"Where is my son?" I asked quietly.

"He exists now in the linear year 1692, in Salem, Massachusetts."

My heart pounded against my chest and the thought of holding my son in my arms again almost lifted my feet from the floor. I turned back to Philippe.

"My son is alive and safe? Why did you not tell me sooner?" I put my head in my hands and began to weep so loudly I feared my granddaughter would hear me. "If you knew all this time ... Why did you not tell me?" I cried.

"For all these years I have wanted to speak to you, but I felt your soul was buried in fear. I knew that when we finally did speak, that time would not be an issue. I did not mean to hurt you, but time has no value to me in this dimension. When I return to my own possession of space, I will have lost only moments."

"My son? Swear to me that he is safe."

"For now, he is safe. But Meredith Mae has told me that the children are becoming worse. The trials are almost over."

"The trials have been over for centuries. This does not make sense to me." I screamed. "My son saw the children. Now my granddaughter sees the children. You tell me the trials are still happening? How can this be?"

"There is only *now*," he said. "And *now* is all there is and all is contained therein."

I looked at him as if he were mad.

"You must return," he spoke quickly.

"I am lost in linear space. I can only go forward," I told him in despair.

"Time does not have motion. You are gifted beyond your awareness," he said to me in a whisper. "You can go anywhere. Return, and take new flesh."

"And where is Urbain?" I questioned. Can he crush my spirit before I steal a new body?"

"Philip cleared his throat and answered me. "No. Urbain will not crush your spirit. He has already doomed it to darkness, but your power is as great as his. You must accept that."

I stared at him. His face was the map of gentility, and yet, I had one more disturbing question.

"Why were you serving the devil's slave, Philippe? Once Urbain possessed this Michele Guyon, why not leave the devil to his own deeds?"

"I stayed to protect you. One day you will understand. The demon could not prevent it. He seemed to find it amusing that I insisted on remaining at your side, but unfortunately, I could not control his evil. I came with Michele Guyon in search of you. Urbain knew that we would. He possessed the body of Michele Guyon and left it when he had no further use for it. I had to remain then, for your sake."

"Why would Michele allow himself to be possessed by the devil?"

"Michele is not yet a strong witch. He has mastered what any human being can master with practice, but he does not have the power to overtake the devil at this point."

"Why would Michele Guyon be in search of me?" I questioned. "And whose body did they find charred to the bone in the warehouse?" I asked him.

"A homeless man that fit Michele's description. Urbain exchanged his clothes with those of his own. He put Michele's ring on his finger and murdered him there in the warehouse. Then set fire to the building." He looked at me sadly. "Michele was then dispossessed and returned to his dimension in tact."

"And that is where he is now?" I asked. "In his own dimension?"

"For now."

"Why did Urbain not kill Michele?"

"He cannot kill a witch. He can only possess one."

"And where is Urbain?"

"He could be anywhere."

"What if I do not return to Salem?" I asked sharply.

"Your son will hang on Gallows Hill. His spirit will linger in darkness and he will be as lost as you are," he answered softly.

"My God!"

"He lives as a new widower. He has told them that he has a young daughter. He is happy, but in danger."

"Have you seen him? Have you been there?"

"No. Meredith Mae has told me. She visits him while you nap."

I felt an overwhelming desire to put a stake through the devil's heart. I got up and went to the tall wooden doors. I opened them onto the front hall and looked up the stairs toward my granddaughter's room.

"I will attempt the journey, but I will take the child with me," I told Philippe. "I want us all to remain together. I assume you are also coming? I will need you."

"Of course. It will not be easy for you to re-enter another dimension. Your conscience mind has accepted the order of time, and that concept must be destroyed and replaced with a true vision. Meredith Mae and I will help you. Your granddaughter can dissolve the barriers of time and walk through in her own flesh and blood. But you must kill off this Patience Guyon. Your borrowed flesh cannot yet cross. You must steal a new form as soon as you are revealed in that dimension."

"And whose flesh should I steal, Philippe?"

"Why not the flesh of the girl, Ann Putnam?"

"Yes," I said softly. "But, yes, of course. How sweet is justice. Yes, it makes sense to me. But one last thing, Philippe."

"What?" He looked at me with eyes so sad I wanted to weep.

"Who is Michele Guyon?" I asked him.

"I told you. He is my father," he said simply.

# Chapter 9

The following day I called my attorney, William Davenport, and told him to draw up an estate trust for my granddaughter, Meredith Mae, to be paid to her in her twenty-first year, just in case I never returned. I made provisions for the money to be reinvested and all dividends to be paid back to the estate until that time. I retained the rest of my money in my name, and in the event of my death, I named Meredith Mae as my sole heir. But, I also included a provision for my son. I told William that my son was to share the estate, should he ever be found alive, and that fifty percent of whatever the estate was worth be given him.

That evening, I informed Maebelle and Malcolm that I would be taking the child abroad to finish her education and we would be gone several years. They were relieved to be rid of us and asked that we send cards and gifts. Maebelle gave us a shopping list a mile long and Malcolm insisted he be given power of attorney over my estate during my absence.

"Absolutely not," I said with a hearty laugh.

"But Patience," he began. "Be reasonable. If something were to happen to you,

William Davenport would gain a large percentage of your fortune and we would all have to rely on his judgment until Meredith Mae comes of age. Does that make any sense?" he asked as he stared at me with a scowl on his face, as if I were a total fool.

"William Davenport is my trusted advisor and attorney. I pay him well to insure the security of my granddaughter. The only vested interest you have in my estate, dear Malcolm, is your own greed."

Malcolm let out a long and tedious sigh. Then he gathered up his family and we all said rather cold goodbyes. That foolish Maebelle asked me to reconsider her husband's interest in our well being.

"He is a good man," she told me as we shared the perfunctory hug.

I looked at this pathetic creature that I had once thrust upon my son in a moment of desperation.

"No, Maebelle. Malcolm is not a 'good' man. He is an evil man. And he would see your daughter starving on the streets of Brooklyn if he had just an ounce of control over her money."

Maebelle stared at me in disbelief. Her eyes filled with tears.

"May God forgive you," she hissed at me before following Malcolm, and those horrid children of theirs, down the stairs of my home. I would not miss that family, yet the end to which poor Maebelle came would one day cause me sadness. You will know of it soon, as well.

With my financial affairs in order, we then sent for Emie, Philippe's sister. Of course, she was not a slave in Virginia, but from Philippe's dimension of the twentieth century. When she appeared in our parlor one rainy afternoon, I was startled by the familiarity I felt between us, but I quickly dismissed it, for there was so much on my mind. She was a lovely girl, but she seemed so different, so strong and self assured for a woman. She was not as dark as Philippe, but she was clearly of mixed blood. Her features were delicate, and she hid her very large eyes behind the oddest little wire-rimmed glasses. I noticed that her eyes were not black, but green, like my own. The first time she saw me she put her arms around me and held me so tightly that I thought she would squeeze the air out of me. Philippe said that she was a powerful witch and that they could communicate through meditative writing and thought. Emie would run the house in Brooklyn for all the years we would be gone. Of course, Patience Guyon would never return to Montague Street in the nineteenth century, and her body could never be found. If it were, a murder investigation would certainly hinder our plans.

To dispose of poor Patience we chose a quick and simple wound to the back of the head. After her death, Philippe would bury the weapon

and throw the body to the river, way out, where it would drift to the sea and never be found. The spirit of Annabel Horton would return again to darkness. But remember what I have told you. This darkness is not death. For this witch, it is the opportunity for life. And life is not what you think of as *time*. You think that space is out, and that time is long. But I tell you that time is a curve in the universe – a dimension that does not reach backwards or forward. Time curves out into a different perception. My consciousness was also confined by the belief that the past is behind me. Before my physical death, I had to destroy that belief. It was not easy. Philippe made me a labyrinth. For hours I walked it. At some point, in the process of my meditation, I finally began to experience the shattering of space.

"Human consciousness creates order," Philippe told me softly as I walked. "Let the order dissolve and feel the power of your soul to push order aside."

"Are you really the son of Michele Guyon?" I begged him to tell me.

"In the chronological year 3082, God is redefined and consciousness is altered," he continued.

"Then religion must be changed by this new discovery of God?" I questioned.

"Of course."

"How do you know that, Philippe? Do you gaze into a crystal ball?" My eyes were closed as I walked. Surprisingly, my voice came out more like Annabel, the human being I had been in 1692, instead of the higher pitched Patience. "You do not answer my question, Philippe."

"Which one?" he teased.

"Who are you?" I asked again.

"I am Michele Guyon's son. I am born many, many years from now."

"Your mother?" I asked. "Who is your mother?"

"Annabel Horton," he answered.

I laughed so hard my sides hurt me and I lost my balance in the labyrinth.

"You'll make me fall."

"Listen to me. And concentrate!" he commanded. "All humanity is born knowing and forgetting the nature of the universe. You will also forget. You will also remember."

"What will I forget and remember, master?" I giggled like a young schoolgirl.

"Beginnings," he went on, oblivious to my jesting. "Humanity is constant. Humanity craved life and found itself on earth. Humanity created earth, which is beautiful, but restrictive, and the process of evolution is tedious."

"How can there be evolution if all is now? How can anything be tedious?" I questioned more seriously.

"Humanity imposed order on the gift of life. We feel tedium. We watch time pass and we record history, but all life is contained in the same moment. In the linear year 3082, the human soul will be redefined by a greater evolution." Philippe walked behind me and spoke in my ear. "It has already happened. All time is contained in space. You must push through the walls of human reality and see with your soul."

"What of God?" I begged him. "Tell me where to find God."

Philippe laughed. "God? How can you find what isn't missing?"

"What of the devil? Is he destroyed by this discovery of God in 3082?" I asked.

Philippe smiled. "God and the devil ... the unanswered conundrum. How can God exist if I cannot see the face of God, or the devil for that matter?

"I have seen the devil," I told him.

"You have seen the devil but not God? Would you recognize darkness if you had never seen light?"

"Philippe, like most prophets, you speak in riddles."

"Prophecy connotes a future. Well then, back to the unanswered conundrum. If the future is created out of the present ... then where is the past? If God is the infinite language of humanity, than what language is humanity to God?" He returned my smile and continued. "Are you ready to die?" he whispered.

# Chapter 10

I went to my granddaughter's room. *What a beautiful child*, I thought. Her lips were in a soft pout as she slept. Her thick rich hair embraced the pillow and looked like it could have been a fine piece of silk. I softly stroked her brow. Her beautiful dark eyes opened and beheld me like a treasured friend.

"It is time," I told her. "You know that I will not feel pain. You know that my spirit will follow yours?"

The child smiled softly and reached out her arms to hug me.

"I will go first and lead the way. You must not lose spiritual sight of me, Grandmamma," she whispered firmly.

Philippe had promised me that she would not witness my murder. He told me that the child's body would pass out of this dimension before my physical body was destroyed. I was frightened, of course, but also excited to see my beloved home − to walk beside my father and wade my toes in the river again − to sit in the hard wooden pew of the Lindal Hill Chapel and sing the old church hymns.

We left the house on Montague Street at midnight and went for a carriage ride down the River. Somewhere, near a short bridge, we stopped. It was raining badly, and there was mud everywhere, but we had waited for the rain. Now that it was here, we were excited to get it all over with. Philippe hid the carriage under large imposing trees.

Meredith Mae and I walked up close to the bridge, but kept ourselves hidden from the road. It was a fierce, black night. Under a large tree I stared into my granddaughter's eyes as we held hands.

"Are you ready?" I asked her.

She looked at me sweetly and nodded. Soon, she started to sway and hum. I knew Philippe stood behind me with a pistol pointed at the back of my head. I do not know how long it was that we stood together like that, but at some point, I could no longer see the black night, or hear the heavy rain. Meredith Mae was all that I saw. I heard nothing either, not even the sound of her singing. Then, in one fantastic second, the body of my granddaughter was replaced with emptiness, and in almost that same instant, a quick sharp fire in my brain threw back my head, and with some mighty force; I flew out in circles so fast that I lost sight of everything, except my own speed.

Suddenly, I stopped moving, and it was then that I knew I had returned to darkness. Through this opaque mist, I could see Patient's body on the ground. The fear subsided and the anxiety of weightlessness set in. I watched Philippe tie stones around her wrists. The body of Patience Guyon Cummings had fallen in an almost seated position, the white dress now filthy, the hair, a bloodied knot, and the shocked still open mouth, that seemed to catch the rain like drops of wine, was still.

# Chapter 11

I saw nothing before me. Yet, I was in motion. I screamed out for Meredith Mae, but she did not answer me. I realized then that I hadn't a voice to be heard. I felt that I was weeping, though I could not shed tears. I demanded that Philippe come to me. But he did not come. I was alone and adrift in a black shadow, which slowly and gradually revealed a white light. The light was three-dimensional, and in it I could decipher movement. I realized that I was looking at a vision of people that appeared to me like streaks of lightning. They had form, and seemed to be made up of white fire. No, I was not in heaven and I did not have a ghostly vision. I was looking at life as it is in 1692.

I no longer had a body of flesh and blood but I felt myself as a human form. I began to walk, and to feel that I could almost touch the earth, but I felt nothing under my feet. I seemed to be floating, but I noticed that I was able to control the direction in which I wanted to go. I was on a street. I could make out a familiar building. People passed me by in familiar dress, and though I could barely see anything but white forms, I detected the familiarity. Everything I heard was distant and terribly low. I tried to touch the ground beneath me, but I could not reach it, or feel it. I struggled so to grasp it, to hold something in my hand but all of substance evaded my touch. Everything I reached for seemed to disappear, though I knew I beheld a material earth.

I continued to walk. It was not long before I knew exactly where I was. My shadowy vision revealed the lanes of my childhood. I struggled to find Salem Common and the direction of the North River. From there I would find Salem Village. I followed the river toward Northfields and Orchard Farm. I passed people on horseback. The smell of dirt began to tease my senses. I passed by Ipswich Road and the old lane that led to Thomas Putnam's land. I continued east toward Birch Plain. The Mile Brook of my childhood beckoned me but I kept along the path that would take me to the cut off that led to my father's farm. Soon, I turned north. I struggled to catch sight of the trees that swooped before me like miraculous arms, that fell to the earth. I could almost see the color green, in the dazzling white light of images.

Before long, I stood at the front door of my father's house. He drifted before me like captured lightning in human form. I screamed out his name but he did not hear me. My voice came from some far away chamber that seemed to break up and fall away as I spoke. I entered my home and reached to touch objects that I could not feel. I struggled to lift the plate from the table but I struggled in vain. From a great distance, I heard prayer. I followed the voice up the stairs and into the room that had once been mine, more than two centuries ago.

I could not believe what I beheld! I gasped and screamed, but my voice fell around me like shattered glass. There was my son, Matthew. He was kneeling at the bedside and he held a woman's hand. He prayed earnestly. I reached for him but he only stirred and went back to his prayer.

"Philippe!" I screamed. "Come, help me! Matthew is here!" But my words were lost in this shadow that encased me like a coffin of darkness.

I struggled to see the woman on the bed — my bed — Annabel Horton's bed. "Who sleeps there, I wonder?"

I found the opposite side and reached out to touch the girl's shoulder. As I did, she stirred, and my son's body stiffened. He watched as the girl's eyelids moved and slowly opened.

"Who goes there?" the girl whispered.

Matthew shot up quickly and ran to the door.

"Mr. Horton!" he called. "Come upstairs! She has finally spoken!"

Mathew rushed back to take her hand. I reached to stroke his cheek but I could not feel his soft skin on my palm and I wept bitterly. My weeping was uncontrollable. My despair was so deep that I did not pay attention to the girl whose eyes had now fully opened. I kept reaching for Matthew's cheek and screaming that I could not feel it.

"There is no greater pain than this," I called to God.

Suddenly, I knew she had reached out for me, as if in comfort. I struggled to see her face. It looked familiar, but I did not know it. Large tears fell from my son's eyes. They glistened in the white light and I could see his happiness. I could feel that a great weight had been lifted from his heart. My father ran into the room and passed through the shadow that housed me. He did not know how I longed to throw myself in his arms.

"Annabel," he wept. "Good God. Our prayers have been heard. She has spoken?

Annabel, my child"

"Annabel?" I screamed from my darkness. "Annabel? I am Annabel. Who is this impostor?"

I raged across the room. I sought attention but I was ignored. Yes, Matthew and my father ignored me, but not the girl. No, the girl followed me with her eyes. This I knew.

"I am Annabel. Do you not see me, Father? Matthew? I am here. Look here."

They paid no attention as they doted on the girl in my bed. The girl stared right at me. She reached for me again, and suddenly, I sobbed in disbelief. All at once, I remembered the familiar face.

"Dear God," I whispered as I struggled to see her more clearly. In a moment I knew. Yes, I knew whose body was covered in the blanket I once felt against my own skin. It was the child who had seen me in my darkness. The little girl I tried to save from my brother, but who was lost to me, and whose loss I carried with great despair.

"Elizabeth," I wept.

I walked closer. She was now a young woman. My soul was so overjoyed that I fell into her arms and held her as best as I could in my transient state. She sensed my presence and began to cry.

We rejoiced together, though neither my father nor Mathew could see me in the girl's arms. My father wept openly and Matthew held the girl's hands tightly. She was weak, as if she had been asleep for a long time.

I prayed that Philippe and Meredith Mae would find me, but surely, I would rob the flesh of the girl, Ann Putnam, without them. I was eager to have a voice, to have weight upon the earth. It must have only been moments before a loud knock came at the door. I followed my father down the stairs. I felt Philippe's presence before he entered.

"I am Matthew Guyon's servant," he said to my father. "I bring him his daughter."

I struggled to hold Meredith Mae in my arms but she did not see me. She did not know that tears of joy ran down my face. That embrace between my son and his daughter is one I will always cherish, for it was clear that death had never robbed my granddaughter of her father's love. Even in my shadow of darkness, I felt the despair of absence filled with his tenderness. I wanted to join in their happiness, but instead, I could only look on from a great distance.

My father's house was filled with excitement that evening as they sat around the girl they believed to be Annabel Horton and told her that Governor Phipps had disbanded the hangings, and the trials were over. She looked at them sadly and spoke in a hoarse whisper.

"These hangings you speak of appear to me in a dream. They seem to be memories that offend me but I do not recall them clearly."

"That is just as well, my child," my father said to her as he stroked her hair.

I knew I had to find Thomas Putnam's house and steal the flesh of that wretched girl or I would be lost to this darkness, where not even Meredith Mae, or Philippe, could find me.

I left the house, with its warm fire in the kitchen and the long wooden table filled with eggs and bread. It was difficult to find the road, for my white world had grown dim and I assumed that the earth's darkness had thrown a shadow over the white fire. *It must be a dark night,* I thought.

I had never really known Ann Putnam, or her father, Thomas, or even the girl that lived in their house, Mercy Lewis. We were friends of the Porters' and did not attend Reverend Parris' church. In those days, the town was divided by ones loyalty to a particular minister. The loyalties were so intense that spying and paranoia infiltrated the village like a virus. It was difficult to know the Putnam's because they only mingled with their own and seemed suspicious of everyone else. I knew Ann on sight and everyone knew the Putnam house. They were the most powerful people in Salem and many said they were vengeful and cruel, though never aloud. I would feel no regret as I stole into Ann's room and watched her sleep. After all, she had been my accuser. It had been she that had condemned me to my shadowy infinity.

She looked the same as I remembered her ... blond and thin. I noticed that her lips were full and her lashes were dark and long. I would not mind this flesh. She was a pretty girl. She had thrown her blankets to the floor and the fire in her room shone on her and revealed the sweat on her young firm arms. I looked closely. Her breasts were lifted up and her lean legs grappled with sheets that barely covered her. Soft blond hair caressed her calves like the fuzz of a peach. I wanted her to know that I would take her and I would not be gentle in the consumption of her body. She had doomed me to this. She had said I afflicted her ... that I came in the night and tormented her. "Well, now I am really here, dear Ann, and you will not live to condemn me further."

I covered her with my form. From my shadow coffin I lay myself over her and I willed her to wake. She felt me and smiled. "Smiled?" I sneered. "You dare to smile at me?"

She did not hear me. She moved under me slowly, as if I were a lover in the night that had sought her skin beneath me. I pushed harder until I felt myself lock with her bloodstream. I felt myself like warm water filling her bones with my soul. Oh, I was delirious in my taking of her. She screamed. They all scream when I take them but this pleasure of Ann Putnam's screams, my accuser, drugged me with such power that I was able to stare in her face and watch the blue eyes behold me in fear. It was then that I kissed her, and she struggled under me and fought my mouth with her own. I covered her face with the enormous shadow of my soul and I pushed myself into her living flesh. In the moment of her flight, she cursed me to hell. I had held her like an eagle with her prey. I had forced her soul out, and I had gone in like a child to the womb.

I knew from some darkness she watched as I stretched my lovely young body against the white sheets and sighed like a fresh new bride. I could only imagine her despair at the loss of life, as she knew it. Then I laughed as she vanished into some darkness of her own, with a destiny I was never to learn.

Philippe found me in the fields of my father's farm. I had gone out before dawn to walk barefoot in the wet grass. I could actually see the sun rise for the first time in centuries. The cool morning air sent shivers through my brand new flesh and the birds thrilled me with their song. I was delirious as I danced in the soft meadow and pulled the bark from trees to hold against my lips. I lay on the damp earth and tickled my face with the brown red leaves of autumn. I listened as the breeze caused the leaves to dance and hungry rabbits and deer scurried over the hillside. The air was sweet with the scent of fires and the pretty, light color of blue peeked through a blaze of orange and sent puffs of white clouds across God's canvas.

Philippe called to me. "Don't let your father find you on his land. Not with the face of Ann Putnam."

My delirium ended when I realized I would never communicate with my father again. The girl lying in the bed, that had once been mine, was his daughter now and I was the enemy, the girl who had condemned his child to the Gallows.

"What year is it?" I asked Philippe.

"It is October 3, 1693."

"My neck was broken on August 19, 1692. How could my body be lying upstairs in that bed?" I demanded of him.

"Do you remember one who put the rope around you and told you to turn your head to the right at the count of three?"

"I do," I answered.

"Well, you listened, and you did not die. Your spirit left your body and you should not have had a heartbeat, but when they returned for you they found that you were warm and had a pulse."

"The girl has been asleep for fourteen months?" I asked Philippe in amazement.

"More or less," he said. She has not been fully conscious for fourteen months. Your father and Matthew bathed and fed her. She awoke periodically but never spoke a word. She would look around the room as if everything she saw was strange and then she would return to sleep. The morning of your arrival she fully awoke and began to talk. Just like that."

"Yes. I was there in the room, though no one could see me. Except the girl, Elizabeth, she saw me."

"Elizabeth? Matthew calls her 'Annabel,'" he told me.

"I am Annabel. The girl is Elizabeth ... my brother's child ... not yet born. I thought you knew everything."

He smiled at me.

"Patience Annabel Horton, your soul is free of incestuous thoughts. Your long ago lover did not come to the girl. Matthew has never loved anyone but Elizabeth ... no-matter what name he knows her by. It is Elizabeth's face he sees when he looks at her, not yours."

"Her soul aged in my old flesh?"

"Precisely."

"Philippe? Who returned for my body?"

"Your father, and your son, Matthew."

"Who saved me? Who turned my neck so it would not break?" I asked.

"Michele Guyon."

I walked toward the old pond I had loved as a child. Philippe followed. The face of the man with the dark curls had often come to me in dreams with so much more clarity than I actually remembered in my waking life. If I could hold on to my dreams I might have been able to sketch his face in the dirt.

"I do not understand what poor Elizabeth is doing in my skin. If I did not die then why am I not in my own flesh? I am Annabel Horton and I want possession of my own body." I said with a fury I did not know I felt. His answer was stern.

"You cannot take the flesh without killing the child in it. Your son, Matthew, loves the girl, Elizabeth. He does not see his mother in the girl's face. He never has. Now, he will recognize his mother in Ann Putnam's face. If you take back your flesh, you will have to explain to your son what you've done with his bride. Remember, it was you who took the child to begin with."

"And now I know to what fate my darling Elizabeth came."

The loss of my own flesh tortured me, but at least, my niece Elizabeth was not lost in darkness. This gave me some solace. I had loved Elizabeth like my own daughter and began to feel a great relief that it was she who had captured my son's heart.

"I want to see my son," I said.

"We will wait until your father goes out to the fields and then we will enter the house."

He sat on the grass beside me and leaned his head back against a tree. I sat on the ground before him and threw stones into the pond. Philippe spoke to me in whispers.

"It is not yet known in Salem that the girl, Annabel Horton, did not die. If they knew, they would surely know you were a witch and most likely come to burn the flesh off what is now Elizabeth's body. It would be most suspicious and strange to these people. They still believe that they have acted in a sane and fair manner. As Ann Putnam, your friendship with Annabel Horton will protect Elizabeth and Matthew. They will respect your wishes and leave the girl alone. The accuser embracing the accused will allay any attempt to cast misfortune on the Horton family. I must tell you, that Matthew is not liked in this town. He is seen as an odd stranger. They refer to him as 'that dark, effete boy with the waves in his hair.'"

I thought of my beautiful son with his fine manners, and I smiled. My son walked with a gentleman's posture, so befitting a nineteenth century man of wealth, with his legs always neatly crossed and his hands folded; he spoke in low tones with a slightly affected lisp. I laughed to myself and thought how out of place he must appear in a town surrounded by Indians and inhabited by Puritans.

"Now that we are all together," I told Philippe. "Let us leave this time and go back to Brooklyn."

Philippe sat up and looked at me sadly. "You don't understand?" he said.

I returned a pensive frown and shook my head from side to side. He continued.

"Your son, Matthew, will never leave Elizabeth's side. If you want to remain with your son, then you must remain in Salem. Elizabeth has sight, but not power. She cannot move her soul, as we can, in this dimension."

I realized in that moment, in a state of horror, that I was to be held prisoner in Ann Putnam's flesh until my new daughter-in- law's natural death.

"And what does the devil gain from this, I wonder."

"Your son was about to be accused. The day you appeared in Salem, Governor Phips declared that none would be tried on spectral evidence and he disbanded the witch hangings."

"Then why does Urbain call me back? What possible plan could the devil have for me now that the children have lost their power to destroy anyone else?

"He has lured you back to Salem. He knows that you will not leave your son."

"But why? What foul trick does he play with me?" I questioned Philippe.

Philippe remained silent and looked back toward the house. I tried to read his thoughts, but I could not.

Satan loves to tease our sense of responsibility. This I knew. You must see that in your own world with all the lies you live with. You do know that you are one of his greatest triumphs, do you not? He rejoices in your century. If you look for the devil with the right intention you will find his thumbprint on your heart every time you turn in the wrong direction. But his objectives are often senseless. I pondered the devil's plan for me in the chronological year 1693, and I was to search long before I learned of it.

"Unfortunately," Philippe sighed as he turned in my direction, "we must follow the Devil's lead if we are to alter it."

# Chapter 12

My son was overjoyed to see me. Meredith Mae held on to my dress and would not let go. Poor Elizabeth smiled at me tentatively, but without recognition, as I sat by her bedside and stroked her hair.

"Do you blame me now, Mother? Now that you see how sweet my bride is?"

My son knelt by Elizabeth's side and brought both her hands to his lips.

I recognized that there was some physical similarity between the girl and myself. With great relief, I also realized that my son had always looked upon the face of dear Elizabeth, and not my own. His ghostly form in my life must have been nothing more than a genetic memory that had haunted my waking dreams. Somehow, when I took the poor child from the clutches of my oldest brother, Jeremiah, I had exchanged my experiences with hers. In return, I had become a figment in time, and my identity as a human being was lost. I was nothing more than spirit condemned to shadow. My image in the glass was a painful reminder. The great love I felt for my father was a bond I could never again enfold.

I left my family before my father returned from the fields. I walked slowly back to the Putnam farm. The tears in my eyes obscured my vision and I found myself wandering on the old Meeting House Road. I took the shortcut back. It was a trail I had taken many times, as a child, but it did not seem to lead me to the hill that bordered on the Putnam's land. I grew tired and lay under a large tree with towering branches that shielded me from the afternoon sun. On the ground under me the grass was covered in leaves, luteous and dry, that broke and cracked in my hand.

I felt an ache that I could not soothe. It was as if I had never been born. Yet, I remembered myself as a girl chased by my brothers, and scolded by my father for petting the pigs and bringing baby chickens into the house. The memory of my mother returned to me in perspicuous images. She had died so young. They say I look just like her. My father could not speak of her without weeping. On our land there is a marker, and she is buried there in the ground under it. Once, as a child, I lay my face on the earth over her grave and her whisper touched my ears and startled me. I was so frightened that I never went back. She had whispered to me what sounded like the name, *Annasha*. If only I had listened. I might have raised my hand to the devil sooner. But my mother was pious and never spoke to me of witchcraft. Perhaps, if she had lived to see me mature, she might have.

I must have fallen asleep recalling the way my mother would tilt her head to one side and scold me with a teasing smile. My longing for her lay heavy on my soul as it had the day Papa told me her spirit was with God. The air was sweet with a cool, crisp breeze and I nestled back on the ground and let sleep take me. I had not slept so deeply since I inhabited my own flesh. It seemed that my senses were as alive to me in this borrowed form as they had been when I walked the earth as the real Annabel Horton, days when my step was light with youth and my face could be captured in eidetic reflections that rippled in the waters of our brook.

I must have slept for hours because it was almost dark when I awoke to the sound of loud maniacal laughter. I put my hands over my ears and looked above me. Black clouds were moving quickly over a gray and unwelcoming sky. From the light of the stars, I thought I saw the form of a man and a woman. I stood and called out. The moon rose and covered the couple in a shower of light. I froze in fear. Surely, it was the girl, Abigail Williams! Yes, surely it was she that stood naked and scowling before me like a rabid beast of the field. She threw back her wild hair and screamed.

"Witch! You afflict me! You torment me!" She then fell to the ground and laughed in hysterical fits. "Begone bitch!" She pointed at me with one hand and threw dirt at my dress with the other.

Then the demon laughed loudly. There he stood, naked beside the girl, the malevolent and fallacious Urbain Grandier. His chiseled face turned to me. His smooth massive body stood tall and imposing. I could see the scepter in his hand pointed toward the girl's open mouth. It appeared like a large thick whip that he brandished proudly. I shielded my eyes and fell back. The demon smiled.

"Annabel, come to me."

I instinctively held my right hand up before me, and instantly the great Urbain flew back several feet, as if he had been thrown.

"Never, bastard!" I shouted.

I stood, and believing I now held some power from God in my fingers, I put my hand up before me once more, and lo and behold, the devil jolted so far back that I could not see him. I saw only the demented Abigail on the ground.

"Begone demon!" I screamed and held out both my hands.

But his laughter invaded my hearing with such force that I fell to my knees. In an instant, I felt his grip on my hair. He pulled me up until my feet were several inches from the ground. Then he dangled me like a dead pheasant. His laughter was so loud it caused a sharp pain in my head.

The naked Abigail sat on the ground quietly smiling. I saw her eyes as I remembered them, the one turned in toward the other. Urbain dragged me now by my hair and forced my body upon the naked girl. I screamed and spit in her face.

"Bitch!" she hissed at me.

The demon laughed and turned me around. I fell off the girl and he lay above me.He brought my lips close to his. His large tongue invaded my mouth and I almost gagged.He pressed me close to his chest and I could feel his large phallus against me. His fingers bore into my flesh. I felt my skin burn under his touch. Then the demented girl pushed him off me and buried her head between his thighs. I held my hands straight out before me and stared into his eyes.

"Return to your darkness, devil!" I commanded.

He was thrown from the girl and landed sharply against the trunk of a tree. My heart raced frantically but I ran to escape. In my panic, I tripped and fell on the ground. As I turned to find my way, I watched the demon recover and pull the naked girl up his body. His laughter reverberated into the night sky like the echo of thunder. The girl's legs were around his waist and her horrid face hung upside down. The phallus was buried inside her. Her hair fell to the dirt. Her cross-eye found me.

"Witch?" she screamed. "Watch the devil fill me with his seed."

I found the strength to stand.

"Take your whore back to hell," I screamed.

He put out his hand and pointed his fingers at my heart. My skin was seared and my flesh opened. I felt the burn so deeply I could barely stand it. But I kept my hands straight out before me. My eyes never left his. This time, he flew back against a tree with such force that the girl, too, was thrown. The moon's light had faded and the night was now dark. I looked to find Urbain, but all I saw was the naked girl, who also searched for him. Then, in an instant, he reached out of the darkness and fiercely grabbed me by the neck.

"*Au revoir*, God's little avenger," he whispered.

In one split second, he had disappeared in a violent strike of light. I picked myself up and turned on my heels. I forced myself to run back down the dark dirt path. I screamed until my throat closed up and I could scream no more. I ran back to my father's house with out looking behind me. They all heard my screams and had come out to the field to comfort me, all but my father, who stood silently on the porch steps of our home and did not move.

"Help!" I yelled with my sore and raspy throat. "Dear God, Help!"

I fell into Philippe's arms. He held me and moved the hair from my eyes.

"Grandmamma has seen the devil." I heard my Meredith Mae whisper.

"Yes," said Philippe. "She must have seen Urbain."

"Welcome back to the seventeenth century, Mother." My son Matthew said tenderly.

My father ordered me off his land. Philippe offered to take me to the Putnam farm by carriage. I was distraught and frightened.

"What does the demon want of me?" I whispered.

"I believe he has left Salem. At least, for awhile." Philippe reassured me.

The horses trotted quickly forward in the rain. I breathed in the dampness and wondered how my soul could feel so tortured when the rain fell on my lips and the cold night air penetrated my lungs. "How will I ever live in the Putnam house, Philippe? How will I bear it?"

He kept his eyes in front of him. His face was stern and sad. "It will not be forever," he told me.

But it was forever. For years I lived with Thomas Putnam and his family. I learned of the family's treachery and cruelty during the trials. I discovered that Tituba had been promised salvation for her part in the incitement. I was let in on family secrets that included the rape of Mercy Lewis and the planned and manipulated accusations against John Proctor and the others. I discovered the feebleness of Reverend Parris and the molestation of several of the children by the examiners. I learned that the only sin of the accused was either arrogance or innocence. For years, I turned over and over in my bed at night consumed by hatred and rage. I yearned to bring the dead from their sphere of time and banish the demons from a forgiving heaven, to a purgatory ruled by a vengeful God. "Let there be no forgiveness in hell for the unmerciful," I wept.

Thomas Putnam forbade me to read — except for the bible. If it were not memorized to his specifications, I would be made to kneel for hours and recite the psalms I had forgotten. I could not hold opinions that were different from his. Once, when I told him that the theocratic foundations of our society might one day be questioned, he beat me with a leather strap.

It was difficult for me to escape to my father's farm in the mornings because I had to account for every moment of my time. There were days when I could only spy on my family from the shadows of Cherry Hill. I would sit crying in the open air and watch

Meredith Mae and Elizabeth carry milk from the North field. I could see Philippe washing down the horses or mending the roof. Far off in the distance, I knew that my son was on the old plow with my father. What a terrible farmer he was and how he hated it. I smiled to myself knowing how hard he would try to please, but how desperately sick he was of the dirt under his nails and the physical exhaustion he felt at the end of the day. He could not bear owning just one simple pair of pants and he found the winters on the Massachusetts hillside pernicious and interminable.

I ached to join my family, but we could only steal moments when Father was away in Andover, or when he was distracted by his daily chores. Sometimes, he would visit long enough with my brothers and I could spend whole hours sitting in the sparse pine kitchen conversing with my family. I would tell Thomas Putnam that I was praying, and memorizing the Bible, but it was not very often that I could steal these moments. I would risk a beating if I stayed away too long.

Though we dared not admit it, we longed for the grand luxury of our home on Montague Street. Not even Meredith Mae or Philippe could get used to the austerity of the small quiet rooms, reflecting a precious simplicity so contradictory to our understanding of comfort. Matthew's tales about the city we called Brooklyn, in another dimension of time, fascinated Elizabeth. She listened intently when we spoke of women walking under pastel parasols and brightening their faces with rouge. She listened to our stories of spontaneous dimensions with pensive and complaisant acceptance, but I knew she doubted us. She had recuperated well from her transformation out of darkness to land fortuitously in the body of Annabel Horton. Her spiritual image ingrained in my lost features like symmetry captured in clay. Of course, her only recollection of the trials were contained in the shadows of genetic omniscience. It was assumed that the tragedies were too frightening to carry in memory. My son was clearly happy, so I hid my misery as best I could. But, one morning, my brother James caught me on the farm and went for his pistol. Matthew jumped him and James ran from the house in a rage. He was furious that we would allow Ann Putman into our home. I could not control my sorrow that day. My own brother whom I loved ... the brother that had taught me to climb trees and had always shielded me from harm ... did not know me. I wept bitterly after he left and told them all how unbearable it was to live without them ... to pretend that I was a Putnam when the very thought of the Putnam's caused me such disgust.

On my next visit, Matthew suggested I return to Brooklyn and live in peace.

"To return to what — an empty house — Malcolm Northrup and his horrid family? No, Matthew. I will never leave you."

I brought his hand to my lips and kissed it.

"So be it, Mother," he whispered. "But I wish you would reconsider."

"I will never leave you," I repeated firmly. "Not ever."

# Chapter 13

My father's land was adjacent to the Cloyce farm. Peter Cloyce lived in a tiny house at the foot of The Mile Brook. His wife had died after the birth of her last child and he was left alone with his seven children. He was a friendly man that spoke often to everyone, and yet, was a friend to none. The Cloyce's had always attended Reverend Parris' church, and not the Chapel on Lindal Hill, where my family always gathered on Sunday mornings. Yet, my father was there when they laid his wife Ruth to rest, and as a child I played in the fields with his youngest sons, Daniel and Isaac. After dark, Peter Cloyce could always be found at the Ingersoll tavern, a popular meeting place for the people of Salem Village. Since the death of his wife, he only seemed interested in farming and drinking. He left the care of his youngest children with his two oldest daughters, Sarah and Susanna. Almost every evening he would stop at the door of our house and yell for Father, "Joshua Horton, come join me for beer and leave a hard days work behind you."

Father would laugh and rise to the window, "I shall keep my wits about me, Brother, but the Lord bless you."

Peter Cloyce would then continue on down the road to join his eldest sons at the Ingersol Tavern, and there they would drink beer and liquor, and share family tales with their neighbors, straining the ear for gossip as the crowds gathered. Father had few close friends and preferred the company of his sons and their family.

He considered Peter Cloyce to be an ass with the face of a man but it was after the witch trials that my father's tolerance for him evolved from a casual politeness into a fierce resentment. Father would never forget that during the trials Peter had been quick to judge the accused and yet complacent and indifferent toward the accusers. Father said he revealed a weakness of character in a time of great need and community suffering.

Upon my return to the dimension of the late 1600's, I was acutely aware that the town had remained torn apart by the trials and senseless hangings. The people still argued over the guilt or innocence of those who rotted in the town jail, or swung by their necks on Gallows Hill. But life went on. The afflicted girls matured into women and some of them even joined hands with the sons of those they had injured. Three of Peter Cloyce's children married into families whose sisters and wives had been accused of witchcraft. His fourth son, Samuel Cloyce, married Mary Harding who had accused half the town of Andover of the devil's sorcery. And though the village tried to heal itself by random acts of benevolence, the suffering of those who had been victimized haunted the happiness of those responsible. But everyone made the best of their lives and sought to live in God's righteousness. The ministers preached forgiveness and the people of Salem searched their hearts for the courage to honor God. They prayed for the souls of those murdered but they avoided apology. That would not come for several years.

Peter Cloyce had a brother by the name of Ezra. Ezra returned to Salem Village in the year 1698, with a wife and three small daughters. Unlike his brother, who was more simplistic than malevolent, Ezra Cloyce wore evil in his smile. His eyes were a curious cinereous color with lids that were lined in blood. His teeth were large and his body bent like a long lean twig so that his head walked out in front of him. His back stooped as if it might swallow his neck. He was a huge hulk of a man with hands so large he only needed one to lift his youngest daughter into the wagon.

He and his brother built a house on the Cloyce land for Ezra and his family. Ezra's house also bordered the Mile Brook, but it was shielded by two large apple trees and faced away from the road. When it was finished, it seemed to dwarf Peter's small and unassuming farmhouse, so the brothers decided they would move Peter's farmhouse to face the mountains. When the work was completed, Peter's house had been set back from the road, as well, and several rooms had been added. My father's rear yard now faced the front door of Peter Cloyce's new home.

Father told the brothers that he owned fifteen feet of the land taken up by Peter Cloyce's new house. Peter and Ezra disagreed with the deed map my father produced and refused to pay my father for the use of the land. Now, my father is a gentle man and would have easily turned his head and ignored an issue not worth more than fifteen feet of land, but my father's beloved view of the brook had been completely obstructed by a house that he considered a reckless and grotesque investment. To add further salt to the wound, Ezra Cloyce refused my father access to the brook that ran past the fifteen feet of land under Peter Cloyce's house. Peter's diplomacy was lost on Ezra's meanness, and eventually, both men opposed my father and agreed that he not access the brook on land he actually owned.

The feud between the three men went on for several months. My brothers finally insisted that Father turn to the courts to settle the matter and either order the Cloyce brothers to pay my family a rent for the land they were using, or have the house torn down and rebuilt.

The courts eventually sided with my father and the Cloyce brothers were forced to buy the fifteen feet of land they were trespassing on. My father was also granted an easement, which provided him access to the brook. Ezra Cloyce exposed his vengeance for my father by shooting at his dogs and tearing down the small bridge he had built with my brothers over near the old Planters Farms. My brothers, James and Jeremiah, often returned bruised and bloody from confrontations in the field with Ezra.

But out of all the men in our family, it was my son, Matthew, whom Ezra Cloyce truly hated. I was distressed to learn that he appeared on our land one afternoon when Father was in Andover. He walked on the land and began throwing pebbles at my son.

When my son yelled at him to stop, Ezra paused for a moment, and then turned away, as if he might leave. But then, he gave a little laugh and began to throw the pebbles again. Philippe went to intervene and Ezra Cloyce drew a pistol.

"I only throw pebbles. Can the boy not take it?" he asked. Then he made odd sounds in the back of his throat and began to taunt Matthew with cruel and hideous remarks.

"Daffy man. Come darn my socks. Here daffy, daffy. Me wants a wife like you."

"Get off our land, Mister. I'll shoot you if I have to."

I was told Matthew walked right up to him and stood firm. Ezra Cloyce held his side and made loud wheezing sounds from the back of his throat.

"Is that right, Daffy? What are you going to shoot me with? That pretty daffy finger of yours?"

He then made obnoxious chuckling sounds, like a hungry pig, and started shooting his pistol on the ground around my son's feet. Matthew stood very still, but Philippe later told me he could hear Matthew's heart pounding in his chest. Elizabeth must have heard the shots because she ran from the house screaming and throwing large objects at Ezra Cloyce. She had brought two pots from the kitchen, and after one hit his knee, and the other ran into his arm, she began to grab dirt and rocks from the ground that she angrily threw at his face. He had been startled by Elizabeth's unexpected charge so Philippe was able to jump on him and wrestle him to the ground. Ezra Cloyce gave Philippe two heavy punches to the chin and almost knocked him out with those huge brawny hands of his, before he turned and ran back toward the Cloyce farm. All the way back they could hear his laughter as he leapt over the brook and called behind him. "Daffyyyyyyy. Daffyyyyyy. Daffyyyyyyy."

My son said he was not afraid of Ezra Cloyce. But I was afraid. I began to feel as I had on the day of my sentencing. My chest was explosive and my body shook. "Please, Matthew," I begged. "Let us return to Brooklyn."

My son laughed. "Mother, Annabel...."

I corrected him quickly. "*Elizabeth,* Matthew. I am Annabel. The girl is Elizabeth ... a spirit not yet born."

"Forgive me, Mother. I will try and remember. *Elizabeth* is not touched by God as we are. She cannot move the walls of time. And I will not walk through with-out her."

"Let us teach her our power then," I told him. "She is of our blood," I insisted.

He looked at me for a long time and then reached out to hold me.

"All right, Mother. See that you are careful not to frighten her, though."

He kissed me on my forehead and I promised that I would do nothing to harm her. I begged him to protect himself against Ezra Cloyce, and he assured me that Ezra Cloyce was a harmless brute who would eventually tire of tormenting our family, but if it would give me some relief, he would arm himself against anymore surprise visits by keeping his pistol on him when he was in the south field near the house, or near the brook that bordered the two farms.

While Matthew worked the fields with my father I spent hours with Elizabeth. I did not talk of potions and of spells, as Tituba had once spoken of with the children. No. I spoke of the mind and the power within to shatter the vision of flesh and blood and see with the soul. The girl listened pensively. Philippe made a large labyrinth way out in Birch Plain and she walked it for hours. We waited for the presence of infinity. We hoped to see a second in which Elizabeth would vanish, when the line of gravity would be delicately revealed in the ripple of the wind. But, poor Elizabeth could only weep and fall to the ground, "Annie, I haven't power. I try, but I only feel quiet and relaxed. Nothing more."

She called me Annie, as everyone else did in Salem, though I told her once that I was Matthew's mother.

"Shish, Annie. What will I do with you? The witches have all returned to Satan. If you go around telling people that, they shall press you to death, or surely hang you from the tree. You're but a girl's age, Annie."

I wondered how much Elizabeth really believed and what magic she actually possessed. Certainly, I could see that she did not have the power of Meredith Mae or Matthew, but she could feel cold spots on the earth. She was sensitive to the pull of time, and the gentle shift of the environment that occurs when one passes a dimension of violence, or passion.

When the labyrinth failed to guide Elizabeth to the inner sanctum, when it failed to expose her to that confrontation with perception that sends the soul beyond the flesh; we lay her in the fields and hummed. We held hands and closed our eyes. The sound that Philippe and I made came from the memory of our ancestors. From the echo of those who had given us a power we could not account for. We followed the voice of those kindred souls and were led into a low and sonorous breath that we pushed out from deep within. After several minutes, Philippe and I could move beyond our bodies and feel the vertiginous surface of gravity release us. We could turn and see the physical world. We could see ourselves lying in a bed of daffodils and hear the call of our breath in the wind. But Elizabeth sat solid and impenetrable, her mind a mirage of images and preconceived realities, which we could not threaten with this greater knowledge of pure and infinite life. We would return to the harbor of flesh and stare sadly at Elizabeth's artless attempts to master transmigration.

It was during this period that Philippe informed me that he was receiving distress signals from his sister, Emie. We had passed ten of your chronological years in Salem, and Meredith Mae was just about to approach her twenty-first birthday. It was decided that she would return to Brooklyn and I would remain behind with Philippe until we could train Elizabeth to follow us through time. It might take the passing of several more years, but I could not leave my son to rot among the provincial tyrants of Salem. I was also distressed and concerned by my daughter-in-law's disturbing dreams, and Ezra Cloyce's continuing trespasses on our land. Matthew was forced to carry his pistol everywhere now but it did not stop Ezra from running along the brook and calling out crude and unwelcoming names, throwing rocks and dirt at my son, who still chose to ignore the asinine antics of such an ignoramus as Ezra Cloyce.

During her third month of training, Elizabeth grabbed me fiercely in the field after two long hours of meditation and forced me to the ground beside her. She then wept bitterly in my arms.

"What is it, child?" I asked.

"Oh, Annie. I feel such darkness that I have not been able to sleep. My dreams disturb me. I am afraid but I do not know why I am afraid."

I shunned the possibility of a premonition, and yet, I knew that Elizabeth was not without sight. Though I resisted, I was unsuccessful, and I consumed her fear that day, as if her dreams had been my own dark premonition all along. I was no longer able to walk in the light of the sun without a great darkness shadowing my soul. The sight of Ezra Cloyce caused my heart to race, and chills penetrated my borrowed flesh like injections of ice. I wondered what part in the foreboding dreams the nasty fool would play but I had no crystal ball to enlighten me, just a darkness that taunted me.

The demon, Urbain Grandier, had not returned to Salem since that twilight I came upon him in the field. Yet I knew he lingered near my stolen breath like the sour taste of spoiled food. I did not know then why he had beckoned me to Salem, but each rising day, I looked behind me as I walked the roads of my village, as if stalked by a madman.

Soon after my return to the seventeenth century, I learned from my son that he had actually abandoned his desire for "his Annabel" during that period in Brooklyn when we had all been so happy. He told me that he had become content to think of his experiences as a romantic misguidance, and he planned to devote himself completely as a father and husband to Maebelle. He assured me that he had been welcoming the birth of his daughter with more joy than he had ever dreamed possible. He admitted even falling in love with Maebelle.

"I swear, Mother," he whispered. "If it were not for the man at the Fulton Street ferry that day we would all be sipping brandy before the fire in our grand parlor, or listening to Mozart at that little square by the river. God, how I miss it." He sighed.

"What man?" I questioned.

It was then he told me that he had been approached at the landing that day by a man of great height, with hair of gold and eyes that turned like a gray angry sea. The man told him that Annabel Horton had sent him. Would he please come? She was in great danger.

Matthew said he was distressed by the man's message but he did not make up his mind immediately. He thought for quite some time while the man with the steely eyes begged him profusely.

"Who is Annabel to you?" Matthew had asked him.

"My daughter," said the man. "Please. I know who you are. Go to her. She needs you."

"And what of my family here?" My son had asked, his heart torn and his hands shaking.

"No prison of earth can hold us. I know your power. Return in time and claim what you will. My Annabel will die. Return then."

Matthew said he stared in the man's eyes and saw large tears fall upon the strong cheekbones. "I beg you. Annabel will die. Her last wish is to see you."

"All right. I will move my soul to see if I can save her," my son had said.

"Bless you," said the imposing stranger.

Matthew reached in his breast pocket and handed his watch to Urbain.

"Give this to my stepfather. He stands there at the water's edge and waits for me. Have him bring it to my mother and tell her that I will return before the small hand passes the stroke of midnight twelve times."

Urbain looked toward Seth and smiled.

"Will you do that, sir? Please."

"Of course," assured the demonic Urbain.

Matthew then told me he went into a small clearing across from the pier. He did not say goodbye to Seth but he could see Urbain approach him. He sat in the warm light of the sun, and in a matter of moments, he moved through eternity like a whisper of wind.

"Why did you not return when the small hand of the watch turned around twelve times?" I asked him sadly.

"When I arrived in Salem I was told that my Annabel was in prison. She was to be hanged in nine days. None would let me see her." He took my hand and continued after a long and sorrowful sigh. "I went to Joshua's house and told him of my feelings for his daughter. Of course, by this time, I knew the stranger on the pier had lied to me and he was not Annabel's father, but too much was happening around me to concern myself with this lie. I told her real father that I was a widower from Boston and that Annabel and I had met at the meetinghouse before the town went mad. I said that we fell in love and had spoken of marriage. 'Are you the one that leaves her those notes?' he asked me. I knew nothing of notes, but I said it was I who had left them. He was surprised that his daughter never mentioned my name but he felt my sincerity and together we shared our grief."

My son looked at me sadly and continued.

"It was terrible for us, for there was nothing we could do to prevent the hanging. On the ninth day, we remained in the chapel until we knew the time of her death had passed and her body had been thrown in the shallow grave they dug for the witches' corpse. We planned to go in the evening and steal the body so that we could bury her properly. My eyes were blind with tears as I reached down to enfold this woman I loved. But then, I leapt back quickly and grabbed Joshua's hand. 'Dear God, she is not dead!'" I told him.

"Joshua sank to his knees and wept so loudly that I had to cover his mouth. I reached in the crude dark hole to lift the body. Her flesh was warm to my touch. I placed my ear on her bosom and heard the beat of her heart. We rushed her back to the house and told no one, not even James and Jeremiah. We did not know whether or not she would live much longer but I begged for her hand in marriage. Mother, forgive me, but I could not leave my Annabel then. Not while she clung to life.

Not while my prayers might save her."

"You married her before she gained full consciousness?" I asked and wondered what minister would perform such a ceremony. "You married her though Maebelle was pregnant with your child?"

"Yes. I married her before God and the Reverend Porter's blessing. He did Joshua the favor. The Reverend is a man of great compassion. He prayed with us often. For fourteen months we fed Annabel and walked her around her room. We showed her the moonlight and raised the curtains to let in the morning sun. She did not seem to see or care for me at all, but I would not give up. She had not spoken a word and seemed completely dazed. Then, a miracle occurred, in the fourteenth month she opened her eyes and spoke. 'Who goes there' she said. It was enough. God heard us. This woman was the wife given to me by God. Be her name Elizabeth, or Annabel ... She is my love, not Maebelle. When the Lord answered my prayers, I knew it clearly. So you see, Mother. I could not leave. My life is here. It will always be wherever she is."

I smiled and kissed his slender, delicate hand now marred by cuts and dirty nails. "I understand," I whispered. Then I told Matthew that Seth's body had been washed up in the waters off Fulton Street that day, and he had been lured by the devil's lackey, the bastard, Urbain Grandier. His jaw tightened and his eyes filled with tears.

"Why?" he implored. "Why would he kill Seth?"

I did not have an answer for my son. But I will tell you this about the act of murder. It is an act of evil so heinous that all humanity is crushed under the weight of it. Oh yes, I am certain that Urbain killed Seth Cummings for the sport of it. Only those that serve the devil are capable of plunging a sword into the heart of another, for a millisecond of mastery achieved at the cost of salvation.

How the act of murder offends me and yet how perilously close I came to fusing my soul with the devil's heart.

"My sister's thoughts concern me," Philippe told us. "She is in distress and I fear that something is wrong." He had begun to say this often and we each felt a growing concern.

"It is time for Meredith Mae to return home and take over the house, claim her fortune. It will put all our minds at rest," I said; I had known for a while it was inevitable.

My son took Elizabeth's hand. "Yes," he began with a smile. "We will all join her once my wife has learned to master her soul's journey through time. Do you think you can master it, darling?" he asked.

"Oh, yes, Mathew, I will work hard. I know I will travel soon."

Of course, I had my doubts that Elizabeth would ever rise an inch in spirit to leave her flesh and I did not like to send my Meredith Mae through the dimensions alone, but I was not yet ready to leave. I knew that I could not yet feel secure in successfully training Elizabeth without Philippe's great power to guide us, so I could not spare him just yet either.

"Emie will help Meredith Mae resolve any financial problems that may have arisen in our absence," Philippe assured me.

So we said a sad farewell near the great willow trees on Birch Plain. I marveled at my beautiful granddaughter who had become a woman so gracious that even my own lost image paled beside her. Her face was a sweet soft blossom that caused one to smile. Her lips were full and mischievous and her almond eyes were enchantingly shy and heavy lidded. I knew, despite such feminine beauty, that she was strong enough to face any misfortune.

We embraced together on the Plain that day. We held Meredith Mae in a circle and Matthew wept like a small boy.

"God, go with you, daughter."

"And with you, Father."

It was the last thing we heard her say before the late spring breeze released her. No sound existed for just a second, and then, the three of us prayed into the quiet stillness, into the glorious miracle of this great earth. Oh, if only we could hold this thing called *time* and rattle the order we have given it, then we all could have followed behind her, but we could not leave Elizabeth. We simply could not. We had to remain and live in the illusion of years, and months, and seconds, and confront grief like any mortal soul. And it was grief that awaited us back at my father's farm. A grief so dark and dangerous that the shadow of the devil came out of the darkness and whipped across the earth in a thundering barrage of lightning that fell across our path like swords.

# Chapter 14

The rain fell heavy on our backs and the night was black and empty of stars. Thunder shot out of the sky like large cannons aimed above us. Razor sharp streaks of light cut through the darkness and lit up our faces as we ran toward my father's land. We heard loud shouting as we approached the brook; agitated shouting that tainted the warmth of the tiny house and caused this hybrid flesh of mine to chill.

"No!" I whispered and grabbed my son's hand. "Do not go there. Something is wrong."

"What is it, Mother?"

"Shish! Stay very quiet," I told them.

We paused beside the barn and strained to listen. Elizabeth's screams cut through the night and Matthew began to run toward the house. I swiftly followed and pulled him back.

"Do not move," I demanded as my body shook and the beat of my borrowed heart raced forward. Philippe's eyes were wide with fear. Again we heard the screaming and the shouts of men that called out in the night. They seemed to be calling for Matthew. I turned to Philippe frantically. "'Brother Guyon,' they seem to say. Do you hear the same?"

Philippe reached out for Matthew's arm. "You must hide. I feel we're in danger."

Shivers overtook me and I could barely stand. Suddenly, I heard

Ezra Cloyce's great bellowing voice. It was filled with rage. "Murderer! Murderer!" he shouted. "You will hang by your neck! Murderer! Come out of the night, coward!"

"Good God." I whispered. "What shall we do?"

But there was not time for an answer. A great bolt of lightning fell on the roof of the barn and the large planks of wood that we thought shielded us could not conceal us from the brilliant shawl of light that revealed our huddled shadows to the men who hunted us.

"There! There he is!" one called in the night.

"Let us get him!" yelled back the other.

Elizabeth's screams could be heard coming toward us as she ran. We stood still and quiet. We could see them all stampeding toward us, a great charge of people running like angry bulls while we stood perplexed and frightened. The night was so thick with the storm that we had to strain our eyes to see. Suddenly, out of the darkness of this unyielding torrent of rain, the huge hands of Ezra Cloyce reached out for my son's neck and threw him to the ground.

"Murderer!" he kept shouting as he hit my son's face. My screams echoed Elizabeth's as I pleaded with him to stop. But Ezra Cloyce kept punching my son. I could hear the bruise upon the bone as it was struck. Someone grabbed me and threw a coat over me and carried me back to the house. I screamed for one of them to help Matthew. I watched as Elizabeth ran inside the barn and returned with a large shovel. I could see her beating Ezra Cloyce on the back with it until one of the men picked her up and carried her away. She was brought kicking and screaming into the kitchen where they had taken me. They sat me by the fire. My father sat with his head in his hands. He lifted his face to me sadly as I spoke.

"What is going on here?" I demanded.

"What are you doing with these people, Annie Putnam?" Asked Brother Osburn, one of the neighbors to the Putnam farm.

Before I could answer, my father interjected.

"You are not welcomed here, Sister," he said.

"Please." I searched his eyes earnestly. "I am a friend. Have I not apologized and have I not done it publicly? Please sir. I beg your forgiveness." My father sighed and put his head back in his hands. I turned back to Brother Osburn. "What is happening here, Brother?"

At just that moment my son was brought into the house. Brother Jacobs and Brother Small were holding him. Elizabeth ran to him and began to weep uncontrollably. Matthew's face was covered in blood and his lip and his eye appeared cut. I gasped loudly and began to moisten a cloth.

"Please," I implored. "I want to wash his cut."

"Why are you here, Sister? Does Brother Putnam know of this?" Brother Small asked. I proceeded to ignore him and washed my son's face. But my answer was not pressed because Ezra Cloyce had entered like a great gust of wind. The door was thrown back loudly and something fell from a shelf. John Darling and Daniel Rea, two more neighbors of the Putnam land, were restraining him.

"You are to be arrested for the murder of Peter Cloyce, Brother Guyon," said Brother Rea.

Elizabeth began to shout. "No! No! That cannot be so. He would never do such a thing."

"Peter Cloyce is dead?" I turned to John Darling. He nodded his head and stared at my son.

Matthew turned to them and asked slowly, and yet, indignantly. "What proof have you of such a crime? I had no argument with the man. Why would I kill him?"

"Your pistol was found on the floor by his body." We have reason to believe he owed you money and when he did not pay you became enraged and shot him," said John Darling.

Matthew began to laugh quietly, and as best as he could with his lip so full and sore. He glared at Ezra Cloyce. "So that's it, Brother Cloyce? You force me to carry my pistol so that you can steal it when my back is turned?"

Ezra Cloyce stood so quickly that the chair he had been sitting on flew against the wall and fell on its side. I screamed as the man leapt once more toward my son. But both Joshua Rea and Alexander Osburn restrained him and ordered him to desist from further outbreaks.

"The truth will be uncovered in the court, Brother Cloyce," said Daniel Rea.

"He killed my brother for the money. Look here and then at us. He is desperate because he cannot farm. The other one is old. This daffy one can do nothing."

"I said the truth will be known in the court, Brother." Daniel Rea then turned to Matthew and said they would be taking him to the town, to Brother Corwin, the High Sheriff, and the rest is up to God.

I looked at the faces of the men who had left my own fate up to God, and who believed that God's will was done in the ignorance of the punishment they bestowed on the witches of Salem. "Fools," I uttered.

"Bastardly sanctimonious fools," I whispered under my breath.

"Sister Putnam?" Brother Darling turned to me. "I will take you home."

# Chapter 15

My son was taken to the county jail in Salem Town on May 15th, 1704. The following day, I sent Philippe to toss a note that I had written, and tied with a stone, into his cell. Father and Elizabeth were able to visit Matthew, but the prominent Ann Putnam, who had condemned his wife to the Gallows, could not. It had been eleven of your years since the town learned that Patience Annabel Horton had survived the rope. Ever since then, poor Elizabeth had become a curiosity, and even children came to the edge of our land to stare at the house, hoping to glimpse the great witch of Salem. My father and brothers were still treated with respect, but Matthew was considered an odd man who did not fit in and his daughter, Meredith Mae, was often compared to Martha Corey, for she often let her hair fall about her shoulders, and some had even spied her swimming in the great pond near our house. Poor Martha Corey and her husband had always been two of the town's most unusual people, but capriciousness was not a valued commodity among the people of my village in the late 1600's. The couple had been undauntedly arrogant in their intelligence and audacious with their wit. Martha had a great flair for color and Giles had an uncanny ability with carpentry. He made things of extraordinary beauty for the time. You must understand the Puritans of my day. They were not gentle people and they mistrusted creativity. Martha and Giles Corey were doomed by the will of mistrust and confusion that dominated their society. They were handsome people who were blessed by God with a passion for joy. But handsome people unnerve the plain and dull of spirit. Joyous people are often called fools and their intentions questioned by those who are not as blessed.

I learned that Martha Corey had been hanged only a month following my own misfortune. Poor Giles had been pressed to death. I was told that it took him three days to die. His strength of will did not surprise me. Though the town was now ready to offer apology to the families of those who had been victimized by the accusations and wrongful deaths, the mentality of the witch trials was still intact. My son was looked upon by the town as a man very much like the arrogant Giles Corey, who had cursed them all to hell as he lay under a multitude of rocks that were crushing his bones. Here was another man who would not humble himself, who would die before he would plead for mercy. I knew that this town would never accept my son's innocence even if it could be proven. There was only one way for my son to save himself. I prayed he would listen to me that day Philippe brought him my note. I had written simply:

> *Darling boy, please beckon the powers of your soul and fly from heaven onward. We will meet at Montague Street. Make haste! I fear the worse. Please! Do not linger. Elizabeth would want your safety.*
> *Your loving mother.*

I waited for my son's answer but it did not come to me. I begged Philippe to go by the prison and demand that Matthew move his soul to safety, but Philippe came back distraught and angry. It seems that he could not see him or get close enough to catch his eye. I walked up and down Essex Street trying to sneak into the jail, but the doors were closed to me, and those passing by stared at me as if I were mad. I feared they would report my behavior to Thomas Putnam so I was forced to wait at home for word.

My son's trial began two weeks following his arrest. Women could not enter the court as spectators but my brothers told Elizabeth everything. She met me on Birch Plain near the labyrinth each day to inform me of the progress. She wept bitterly because the evidence seemed insurmountable. The most damaging of all was that they had found his pistol next to Peter's body.

"Oh, Annie," she cried. "Matthew told us that he had misplaced the gun. This was only a few weeks ago. Father said it was probably in the barn. He told Matthew not to worry, that it would show up soon enough. Father told this to the courts but they do not believe him. Oh, what are we to do, Annie? What are we to do?"

"What other evidence have they?" I asked her.

She wiped her eyes and continued. "The money that the court had ordered Peter Cloyce to pay Father was never paid. They know that Father had two letters sent requesting the sum. Father told the court that the letters were not answered and his next intention would have been to have a jail sentence imposed if arrangements were not made to pay the money owed. Then Ezra Cloyce told the court that Matthew trespassed on the land and threatened his brother if cash were not received in a fortnight. Ezra said that Matthew had intimated that his family was in dire need of the money and he would kill for it if he had to."

She then took my hand and held on to it tightly before she continued.

"On the afternoon of his brother's death, Ezra testified that he saw Matthew leaving Peter Cloyce's house and asked him what business he had there, to which he said Matthew had replied, 'You know what business, Brother.' Oh, Annie. I fear for him."

She put her head on my shoulder and wept profusely.

"What else is there?" I asked, once I was able to soothe her.

"Ezra then said he thought nothing more about it until his wife told him that she had heard a shot several minutes before Ezra arrived home. It was then he thought it best to check on his brother. When he entered the house, and called out to him, he received no reply. He called again. Still, there was no reply. He then climbed the stairs to his brother's room. Again, he called out but only silence was returned to him. He opened the door of the bedroom and found his brother lying in a pool of blood."

"Good God!"

"What are we to do now, Annie? What are we to do?" she asked tearfully.

I took her hand and brushed the hair from her face.

"Can you master the soul's flight?" I asked her.

She shook her head sadly and wiped her eyes. "My soul remains fixed. I beg God to release it. But my soul does not rise. I am sorry."

"Do not stop trying," I whispered and kissed her brow.

My son was found guilty of the murder of Peter Cloyce based on the evidence against him. No one questioned why he would have been in Peter Cloyces' bedroom or why he would have left his pistol behind. I prayed all during the trial for Matthew's freedom, his soul's freedom. I waited desperately to hear from him, but his answer did not come until after the verdict was received. I had prayed he would use his power to escape. Surely, that was the only protection God offered him. But that was not to be.

Elizabeth found me in the Chapel the day following his sentence. She held out a small piece of parchment. I immediately recognized my son's hand.

> *Mother, I cannot leave Elizabeth to bear the ramifications for my actions. How will it look to the town if I vanish from my cell? How will she hold up her head under the hocus pocus of my disappearance? Or worse yet, will she and her brothers be blamed for my escape and brought to a trial of their own? No. I cannot subject them to any more misfortune. Oh, that Elizabeth could move her soul so that I could find her in the safety of our Brooklyn home, but that is not to be. Let her then live out her life in peace and let my soul find solace in the kingdom of God. Bless you, dear mother. May God protect those I have loved.*
>
> *Forever, your son, Matthew.*

His hanging was scheduled for the 29th of June. I now had only ten days to change my son's mind and give him the will to live on. I had to remove any more excuses to choose this absurdity over life. I had to cause a despair so compelling that it would drive my son to flee this arrogant pompous world of blind inhumanity, and I had to act quickly.

# Chapter 16

I knew that Ezra Cloyce had killed his brother. I also knew why, but it would never matter to the town of Salem and I was not out to prove my son's innocence. I was out to keep him from Gallows Hill. If he would only believe me, I would tell him that Elizabeth had found her freedom, had mastered the soul's flight, and waited for him in the safety of the nineteenth century. Then, surely he would follow. But how was I to convince him that she had vanished from this dimension and found her way in the great vast eternal space of time? I knew that he would never believe a lie. Matthew only humored our efforts in training Elizabeth to move her soul.

"Mother," he had said to Philippe and I. "I shall love Elizabeth in this time, in this century. I shall grow old beside her. But her only real power is this spell of eternal affection that she has cast upon me."

Philippe and I disagreed adamantly. We insisted that she was a dormant witch that feared a release of her power because her Puritan mind was filled with the nonsense that the witch is not of God — that the witch is of the devil. But Matthew only laughed at that and told us that she had been levitating her body three times a day to please us, but only a miracle from God would levitate her soul.

So what was I to do? I had to save my son. His tender decency broke my heart but decency would not save his life. I knew what was best, as a

87

mother always knows, always, even when the child matures. I knew that I had to take control of Matthew's destiny. I was driven by love's madness to do so for certainly he would not save himself.

Ezra Cloyce was responsible for my grief. That much I knew. I had watched that wench of a wife of his with Brother Peter Cloyce. I had seen her eyes follow the man as he loaded his cart with grain. I had watched the blush of her skin when he stood near. I knew desire when I saw it. I watched her breasts rise and her mouth dry up and the need of her tongue to wet her lips when Peter Cloyce was passing. It was she that stayed on the farm while Ezra worked as a blacksmith in Salem Town. She and Peter were alone on the farm, except for the youngest children, and they were often up in the fields with their older brothers. There was time that could have been found together. Maybe Brother Cloyce was only murdered for his thoughts. But I think it could have been proven that they were warming the bed together when Ezra confronted them. But there was not one to prove the truth in Salem Village. Truth was a long tale of shallow conclusions in Salem.

Any fool at all could have observed the changes in Ruth Cloyce since Peter's death. I heard she testified without a tear shed. But there was a rage in her eyes where there was once only tenderness. The pretty sweet features of her face had been replaced with a stern and frightened mask. I can assure you, Ruth Cloyce wanted Ezra's neck in a rope on Gallow's Hill as much as I did, but in the long run, his death would not matter to me, would not force my son to flee his flesh. In only a matter of days, my Matthew would be killed. His soul would be contained by time. No, not lost to shadow like mine but discovered in ubiquity with his gracious decency still gleaming in his eyes. Perhaps lost to me forever. Eternally lost to me. This is what I believed. I had no other knowledge that would prove otherwise.

Poor Father would have to sell land to pay off Matthew's jailer fees. How sorry I felt for Father, but I could not help him. And I knew that more sorrow would follow. I knew that Elizabeth would die by the age of twenty-nine. This is what I believed. I thought it was her fate to die at that age. Hadn't I lived out her life for twenty-nine years? But, I was proven wrong, and it would be centuries before I would discover just how long my precious Elizabeth would inhabit flesh. The spirit, when not contaminated by circumstances, always controls fate, and Elizabeth's spirit sought life ... a long and fruitful one. In 1704 my knowledge was still limited. I knew that my oldest brother, Jeremiah, and his wife, would have their third child the following year. I knew it would be a girl they would name Elizabeth. I also knew her soul would inhabit flesh until the age of ten years and then her flesh would become the first victim of Annabel Horton, witch of Salem. What I did not know, was that it was I that gave her spirit flight and shattered her destiny, through the magic of my darkness. But, I did not have that knowledge in 1704. In 1704, I believed that Elizabeth was fated to die before the year was out. If I were to tell my son that Elizabeth would be dead in less than a year he would think that I was trying to trick him. He would not move in time unless he knew for certain of Elizabeth's death.

How cruel life is. We were now in the eleventh year of our return to Salem.

Elizabeth was twenty-eight. In just four months she would be twenty-nine. She would never see that day, or so I thought. I was convinced that the fate of her flesh would not permit it. Oh, if only I could convince Matthew of that. We would all simply grieve and then bury her. Philippe and I would return to our lost dimension in Brooklyn, saddened but yet blessed by having had her presence, however briefly. My son, Matthew, would feel the same and gladly flee his fate to join us.

Why is it that life is far crueler than it is kind? I knew that my son would shun this notion. So, I knew what I had to do to save my child, though God forgive me for it.

I begged Elizabeth to meet me at the labyrinth each morning and together we spent as much time as we could steal in meditation and walking. My father needed Philippe to help in the fields so we were often alone, Elizabeth and I, humming and praying. By the fifth day, just four days before Matthew's sentence was to be carried out, I had her lie in the field and concentrate only on the twenty-third psalm.

*"Yeah, though I walk through the valley of the shadow of death, I shall fear no evil, for thou art with me; thy rod and thy staff, they comfort me. The Lord is my Shepherd, I shall not want. In verdant pastures he gives me repose...."*

I could see that she had finally mastered a very deep meditation. She was lying on her back and her hands lay loosely at her sides. Her eyes were closed. It seemed as if she were hardly breathing. I carefully brought my hands over her body and levitated her from the earth. I then gently turned her around three times before I returned her to the ground. She never stopped humming and praying.

On the day before my son was to be hanged; I released my hands from her levitated body and clapped them over her. She did not stir. I knew that it was time to carry out my plan. When the deed was done, nothing would prevent my Matthew from returning to his life in Brooklyn. It was only Elizabeth that kept him here and it was only she that could release him from this fate, this horrible fate that awaited him.

I slowly removed Thomas Putnam's pistol from my apron and took aim. It took both my hands to hold it steady. I pointed the gun at her heart. Beads of sweat fell down my brow. Tears of grief nearly blinded my sight. My fingers held fast to the trigger. I cocked it back and heard the click. I took steady aim. Elizabeth remained in deep meditation, barely breathing.

Could I really do this? Could I kill this girl I loved to save my son? Could I live with the lie I would tell him? My heart raced and I dropped the gun to my side. *She was so distraught. She has taken her life,* I would tell Philippe and Matthew. But would they believe me? My breath was heavy and my mouth dry. I would make them believe me. *This murder must be swift,* I thought. *There must be purpose to it. Blind purpose.*

I took aim again. I could not look at the sweetly sleeping face. I pointed the pistol at her heart once more, and was about to fire, when I heard the call.

"Mother! Mother! No!"

I looked around frantically searching for the voice. I saw Philippe as he came running across the field, his eyes wide with terror. He slid to his knees before me. His chest heaved with sobs. "Find God now, Mother," he cried. "This is where you find God. Choose God, Mother!"

I froze, and stared at Philippe. My hands still aimed the gun at Elizabeth's heart. My fingers burned against the metal. A great shadow loomed across the field and darkened the sky over us. In the distance I heard laughter, Urbain Grandier's laughter.

I turned toward the great darkness and screamed as I have never screamed before.

"Bastard! This is why you lure me to Salem, to make of me a murderer? What sickness there is in your soul, you demon bastard," I cried.

"Drop the gun, Mother!" Philippe ordered. "Let there be God, not Satan."

"No," I wept. "No."

"Please, Mother. Do not do this."

I let the gun fall to the ground. Philippe reached out and held me in his arms. The darkness deepened like a sudden summer storm, descending down upon us, and the wind ripped through the trees with a fierce cry. I closed my eyes and wondered. *Will I ever be forgiven for what I might have done?*

Then, as fiercely as it came, the darkness vanished. The great roar of laughter faded in the lost wind. We only turned to the west for a moment, as the brilliant sun began to set.

When we turned back, Elizabeth was gone.

"My God, she has mastered it." I turned to Philippe. "Quick. Make haste."

He dropped to his knees and made the sign of the cross.

"I pray she is safe," he said.

"Do you think she is really gone?"

I looked about me.

"Yes. She is gone. But God only knows where."

"We have very little time. Take the cart and go to Matthew. Tell him of Elizabeth's journey. Demand that he take action quickly. Then return to me and tell me what he says."

Philippe ran to go and I stopped him. I reached out and held him close to me for a moment and then I searched his eyes. "Make him believe you, Philippe."

"I'll try."

Philippe ran swiftly down the hill. I fell to my knees and prayed. I prayed until the darkness became alive with stars and all the distant houses were warmed with the unity of evening.

I was still lost in prayer when the dawn found me. I knew the Putnam family would be frantically searching for me, but I did not care. If God saw fit to answer my prayers I would never look upon the face of Thomas Putnam again.

Finally, I could hear the old cart as it wobbled along the path. I watched anxiously as Philippe left it on the side of the road and ran to me as I sat huddled under a large, towering Sycamore tree. His eyes were wet with tears. My heart stopped its beat and I held my breath.

"I have told him. He seemed startled by the news. But they don't leave him alone for an instant. We could not talk," Philippe told me as he breathed heavily and quickly.

"Did he believe you?" I asked him.

"Yes. I think he did."

"Then he will find a way."

"Let's ride to the hill. We must go quickly. The cart that takes the prisoners will pass the town bridge. We can see from the Northfields if he is in it. Pray that he is not."

Philippe and I made great haste toward Orchard Farm and over the great Northfields. The people we passed stared at me curiously, for I must have worn a wretched expression as I clung to Philippe's arm. Once we were just on the other side of the river we saw that a crowd had gathered on Gallows Hill. We did not wait more than ten minutes before the prisoner's cart approached the bridge. We could see that there were several men in the wagon. I strained to see if Matthew was among them but it was Philippe that saw him first and let out a cry.

"Oh, God," I gasped. "What is it?"

"Matthew is with them," Philippe said sadly. "Oh, God. He is in the cart."

"Quick," I said. "Let us take the bridge."

Philippe rode the horses swiftly until we were not far behind the prisoners. I could see that their wagon was not moving as fast as ours. I had Philippe stop our wagon so that I could reach it on foot. I ran toward the road. I could see Matthew sitting on the right hand side of the cart. I was able to run beside him. I heard one man call out that Ann Putnam was running beside the prisoners. They yelled at me to get back. But I did not listen. I saw Matthew. He tried to reach for my hand. People yelled at me from the road and I was ordered to stand back. I was grabbed away from the cart and pushed into a crowd of people. Dirt covered my face and my body was soaked in perspiration.

"Sister Putnam," said a woman I knew from the Parris congregation. "Do stay back from the cart. You could get hurt."

Standing next to the woman stood a man with a very white shirt on. His hair was black and fell in curls. He was a man of great stature. He held my eyes with his and I felt as if I had been shot with lightning. But I could not concentrate on the familiarity I felt. I called out for my son. "Matthew!" I yelled. "Matthew!"

The man with great statue ran to where I now stood. He bent down and whispered. "Go back girl. All will be well. My God, it's good to see you!"

"What?"

Then Philippe caught up to me and ran to my other side.

"That man," I said as I turned to Philippe. But the crowd had thickened and I could no longer see the man.

"What man?" asked Philippe.

"He is gone. It does not matter now."

We turned our attention back to Gallows Hill. The men were being taken from the cart and led to the tree. I watched my son take the steps to the rope. I fell, limp and trembling, into Philippe's arms.

"Please, let us go. I cannot watch my son hang by his neck," I cried.

We left the Northfields without looking back and rode sadly to the chapel on Lindal Hill. It was there I prayed until dusk. I prayed for the safe flight of my son's soul to God. I prayed that he had not suffered. I told Philippe to go with Father and collect the body for burial.

I was alone for many hours. I knew Thomas Putnam would have half the town up looking for me, but I cared not a bit. My son had been hanged for a crime he was innocent of and were they to throw me in a fire that evening; I would have offered no resistance.

It must have been dusk when I finally heard Philippe return. He walked slowly toward me. His large dark beautiful eyes were filled with grief.

"We have taken the body back to the Farm. He is to be buried shortly. They are all searching for Elizabeth. They think his death has driven her away, perhaps even to take her own life."

"He is really dead?" I whispered.

Philippe did not answer me. The tears that fell to his cheeks were my answer. I pressed my hands into the wooden seat and my head jolted back like a wounded animal. My cry was unrecognizable ... like the moan of a dying dog.

Philippe came quickly to my side and together we knelt before the altar. We cried like children, without shame or pretense. We cried from a place so deep in our soul that all else but our grief had ceased.

We might never have noticed the great shadow that fell over us and covered the chapel in darkness, but the darkness turned so black that we could not help but lift our heads.

The only light we could see came from the simple cross at the center of the altar.

It glowed the purest white I have ever seen. The darkness deepened and chilled the air around us, but the glow from the cross expanded and seemed to swallow the darkness, swallowed it so completely that the little chapel was now completely consumed in white light.

"Did you see that?" I said, wiping the tears from my face.

"Listen," Philippe whispered.

From a great distance, so great a distance, we heard a gentle hum, as if there were voices from very far off that offered us comfort.

"Do you hear that?" he asked me.

"Yes," I said softly.

Then, we watched in amazement as a brief form appeared before us and quickly vanished. It had looked like a man but we could not be sure. The brief image had left us with an overpowering sense of peace.

"Do you feel that?" I asked Philippe.

He was just about to answer me when my brother James suddenly came running through the chapel door.

"Philippe!" he cried. The body is gone! Matthew's body has disappeared! Good God. We cannot account for it. God help us."

"What do you say?" asked Philippe in amazement.

"The body! It is gone! We laid it out in Father's bedroom. When we returned, it was not there," my brother said frantically.

"Praise God!" yelled Philippe, and threw his arms around me.

"Praise God!" I wept and kissed Philippe on the cheek.

My brother James looked on in horror.

"Your family knocks on all the doors of the village looking for you." James finally said, suspiciously, once Philippe had released his arms from around my shoulders.

"Yes, Brother Horton. I will return now," I assured him.

I caught Philippe's eyes as my brother hurried him out. They were filled with an anxious acknowledgment. If only I had known then how much of your chronology would pass before I beheld his blessed face again. But my only thoughts at that moment were about returning to the warmth of our Brooklyn home and finding my family in safety.

I knew it would be difficult to die, difficult to kill off borrowed flesh. The control of the soul's flight is not easily mastered and I had no intention of extinguishing the body of Ann Putnam, and exposing myself to the darkness, without Philippe at my side. I planned to hide and wait for him to come to me in my father's barn, for he always knew that is where I hid when I wanted to speak to him, and together we would return to the dimension of 1851.

I found the night so black that I could not see the hand I held before me. The moon was a sliver of light in the sky that was covered by a shadowy mist. I decided to walk back toward my father's farm and wait until I could find Philippe alone. I would shield myself in the barn. Lightning bugs flitted before me as I felt my way east. My steps made crackling sounds in the dirt and the night air smelled like damp warped wood. I had just started to turn and walk along side of the Mile Brook when I heard a rustle in the trees above me. I turned slowly.

A large animal was perched in the tree. His ears were pointed straight back and his face was fierce. He was surely a catamount. The thick coat was tawny and the eyes of the beast were as vibrant as a sunset, steadfastly holding me in his gaze. The colors of the cat's eyes leapt out of the dark night with a shock of brilliance. In the stillness, I could hear its' breath. I did not move. The evening bugs flew before my eyes and I prayed for God to save me. But God existed in my eyes, as much as in the eyes of the beast. Our value to God was one and the same.

I stared at the creature. He revealed a terrifying confidence. I begged myself not to stir. I held my breath and watched as he began to move his body slowly toward me. His gaze continued to hold mine. I heard a low ferocious sound stirring in the back of his throat. The lips curled back and his sharp long teeth stretched across the black night like needles.

I stood very still while my heart pounded and petrified tears formed at the corner of my eyes. I reached in the pocket of my apron for the pistol I had concealed to use against Elizabeth. In my horror, I realized it still lay in the field. Then, suddenly, I felt it, the presence of a man. He was standing on my right, about three feet from my arm. From my peripheral vision I could see the white, blond hair that fell to his shoulders. His hand was extended toward me.

"Urbain?" I whispered.

The beast in the tree did not turn but continued to stare at me. Its' breathing became more intense.

"Come to me, Annabel," said Urbain, as he held his hand close to mine and almost touched my fingers. "Come to me."

It took only a moment for me to respond. My eyes never left the cat.

"Go to hell," I whispered.

The animal drew back his lips I heard a low growl that slowly increased in power.

"Come to me, girl."

"Did you not hear me, demon?" I said, "go to hell."

"Foolish wench." He laughed.

Then, like the sound of a whip in the night, Urbain vanished into darkness. I heard the echo of his laughter as it lingered in the humid inertia of the summer air. The catamount moved swiftly. Before I could take my next breath, the animal had leapt out of the tree like a beautifully agile dancer, and bore his prodigious jaw into my flesh.

I did not die quickly. The mighty head that knocked me to the ground had ripped my flesh open with its teeth as it continued to tear at my limbs with its claws. Like great knife wounds gouging my flesh the powerful animal tore at me and tossed me about like a piece of meat.

I could not scream or defend myself. I could not find death fast enough to escape the profundity of my wounds. I could feel the great weight of the beast on my chest, the vicious ambiguity of the fur against my skin, as it was ripped from my body like paper from a box.

In a matter of seconds, I lay in a pool of blood and watched in horror as the great cat feasted upon my bones.

# Chapter 17

Disconcerted to find myself so violently torn from life, I wandered in bleak darkness, confused, and much too frightened to stir from my shelter of oblivion. I grieved for Ann Putnam. How could I not, for even she did not deserve the fate that my soul's flight had bestowed upon her flesh. Whatever memory I carried as Annabel Horton, lost witch of Salem, was shattered by my violent death and lay dormant. I sought God. I wanted to wander peacefully in a place like heaven. I wanted to sit with angels and have God comfort the atrocity of my passing. To my great despair, I was unmercifully alone.

But do not think that Annabel was entirely forsaken. From my shadow of darkness, I felt my witches' power like a mighty eagle soaring skyward. Though my loneliness lay as an infinite wound upon my soul, my power to return to life was the elixir that redeemed the fate into which I fell, like an embryo, coiled around its innocence, coiled but not incognizant to the power within.

My despair was a solitary confrontation with the mystery of my journey. In due time, I was healed by a desire to return to earth's reality and reunite with the chronological order imposed upon it. I had lost approximately two of your years in infinity, so it had been twelve years since I had seen my beloved home. I was ready to return. I willed myself to conjure up the house in Brooklyn. I sketched it into my mind's eye.

97

Soon enough, I could see the street and the tall, white columns teasing me like an ambiguous apparition. I held the image before me until I could hear faint sounds and see the white light of living humanity move through a gauze of shadow, like lost ghosts. I forced my soul out of darkness and into the dimension I beheld. In what you would refer to as milliseconds, I floated before the house on Montague Street.

There had been changes. I could feel the differences the last twelve of your years had brought. Many more mansions had been built on the water, and on the side streets off Montague Street there were houses made from brick. I could make out taller structures, with lavish windows and steps that led up to front doors that held not two, but three, even four floors. There were many more stores and places of business on the streets of Brooklyn Heights, and far less farmland. Still, I was able to find my home. From my shadowy darkness, I could still see the great, lavish driveway and the tall, gracious windows that stared out over the river as if the house were a breathing thing. The open windows seemed to me like welcoming arms and beckoned me close.

As I entered the house, I could see that nothing was as I had left it, though I was quite pleased with Meredith Mae's improvements. I assumed, of course, that it had been she who had decorated my house so splendidly. The drapes around the windows were magnificent. Through my fog of vision, I could make out a green and gold pattern that swooped to the floor and fell from valances. I tried to speak. The furnishings were far more variegated than I had remembered them. I tried to say aloud that my home looked like something out of a painting or a museum, so fine a vista of taste, even more refined than I myself had arranged it. I longed for life just to be able to sit in my parlor again and run my fingers over the silken threads and deep, plush cushions that seduced me into chairs and left me yearning for the pleasure of the body in repose.

I could barely wait for legs to get me up the stairs and arms to throw around my granddaughter and my son. I had missed them so. The sooner I could find myself a body to inhabit, the quicker I could show my affection. I had given not a thought to whose flesh I would take this time around, whose being I would harbor, or whose blood I would consume. *Ah well*, I thought, there will be time enough to find the devil's own.

I longed to see Matthew and Meredith Mae as they came through the open door and sensed my presence. I assumed that Philippe had followed my flight and was waiting, perhaps even nestled in the soft pillows of a settee, just waiting to startle me and ask me where on earth I've been. I wondered of his reaction when the poor torn remains of Ann Putnam were found near the Mile Brook.

Well, I thought, there would be plenty of time for catch up. Meanwhile, I would have some fun and I would make them sense me. I would do funny ghostly things, if I could master it. I would will a plate to fall from a table, or a door to slam. I might even survey the neighborhood and haunt the living earth in a misty light, confuse the human interpretation of the supernatural. I would appear like a faded daguerreotype in a pane of glass and tease reality from my prism of infinite existence.

I was enjoying my mischievous plans when I could vaguely see two forms appear before the house. I was so excited by the idea of seeing Matthew and Meredith Mae that I found myself spinning around like a top. I was spinning so rapidly that I was almost out of control. Finally, I was able to stop myself and position my shadowy form right at the bottom of the stairs. If I had breath, I would have certainly held it as I waited for the open door.

To my horror, it was not Meredith Mae, or my son, Matthew, that entered the house. It was that awful Malcolm Jacob Northrup. I recognized him as best as I could from my opacity. I struggled to see who had entered with him. I forced myself close; so close that Malcolm looked up and swatted me away like a fly. The girl that entered with him was familiar. She stared in my direction, as if she could see me. I came closer, so close that I felt an electric currency that pulled me to the girl. It was like being caught in a storm. I felt myself held fast, unable to disentangle. She seemed to hold my presence for a matter of seconds, and then, she held her arms straight up and I was released.

I found myself on the opposite side of the room. Something about my connection to her had strengthened my memory and I was able to clearly recognize Emie, Philippe's sister, and her strange wire glasses. She was still staring at me as if she knew exactly where I hovered in the room. Malcolm removed his coat and I watched in horror as Emie took it and placed it in the closet. *My God, he seems to live in this house*, I thought.

Then, I heard Emie's voice whisper "Yes," as she continued to look directly at me.

Malcolm turned sharply. "What did you say?" he asked her.

"Yes. You are right," the girl answered.

Malcolm furrowed his brows. "Right to what? I've said nothing."

"Oh?" she responded innocently. "I thought I heard you say what a fine day it is."

Malcolm looked at her as if he might strike her. "I am going to nap. Wake me in an hour."

I watched as Malcolm climbed the stairs and headed toward my old bedroom. I was enraged, so much so that I could barely contain my movements. How dare this bastard move about my house as if he owned it? I felt myself transforming into a red glare of light. Red seems to be the color I become when I feel myself in a tailspin of rage. I flew behind Malcolm. I had become so red a glare by now that I knew I was giving off a light he might be able to see, should he turn in his tracks. Emie reached behind me and was somehow able to hinder my movements. I resisted her. I was furious, but her command was powerful. I turned reluctantly and followed her back into the parlor.

"I can see you," she whispered. "Listen to me."

I hovered near, though not near enough to be swallowed by her energy again. I could hear her well enough without the intensity of being held in the energy force of another soul.

"Malcolm has taken over the house. Meredith Mae is on Tilden Street. There is a Catholic Church there, St. Joseph's. A Priest has given her a room in the convent."

I wanted to speak, to question her, but my voice fell and shattered in the air. Yet, the girl seemed to understand the answers I sought. She leaned forward and spoke directly to me.

"Your attorney, William Davenport, was killed in 1851. I will tell you more about that after you have found a body to inhabit. His practice was taken over by a man called Louis Boussidan. Malcolm was able to convince him that Patience and Meredith Mae had perished abroad, for we could produce no letters, no proof of their existence. He then had himself and his daughter, Catherine, declared the heirs to your fortune. We stood by helpless as Malcolm took possession of the house and everything in it. When Meredith Mae went to Boussidan, to plead her case, he told her that he had no proof that she was Meredith Mae Guyon for all of her papers had been destroyed, and no-one could identify her, or would identify her."

My despair could be felt, for Emie began to weep from her chair.

"Please forgive me, Mommy. I tried but there was nothing I could do."

I had no time to comfort her. I flew up the stairs so fast that I actually caused a small wind.

I found the scoundrel disrobing. He was half naked. His right foot trapped in his breeches and one hand on the bed for support.

"Vermin!" I cried from my shadowy circle of light as I spun around him with such force that he lost his balance and looked up. I slammed my soul into his neck with such vehemence that he began to choke and fall backwards until he lay on the bed with one knee up and the other prone. I reached deep into his heart and clung to the beating organ like a vampire thirsting on blood.

Soon, I felt myself in his arms as I stretched my soul through his flesh. His face was now grimaced as I glared my image into his eyes. I began to feel the oddity of his genitals, the massive thickness of his chest and the uncomfortable fat on his belly.

"I damn you to hell," I hissed.

He captured me for just a second in his eyes. He screamed and found himself imprisoned, unable to move. I smiled as I took him. I felt his spirit leave with such speed that it rattled me. Someday, you will know the speed of the soul when it leaves. It is like a shot from a pistol.

But alas, the bastard was now gone and there I was in his fat and unappealing flesh. I sat on the edge of the bed. I had been made dizzy by my own emotions, emotions that lingered and caused an odd vertigo when I stood. Also, you must understand, it does take a moment of adjustment to harbor the male body when my soul is of the feminine. Though you live in the flesh many times as male and female, your original soul is one or the other. You see, all opposites live in what we have come to call "God," who is opposite of nothing, and neither male nor female. If that were so, the devil would be an opposite of God, such as in good and evil, but the devil is only the opposite of angelic, the wicked Lucifer cast from heaven's purity, the fallen angel. Interesting tale.

I stood and went to the mirror. Malcolm had not aged well in the last twelve or so years. His hair had thinned and he was almost bald. He had gained at least seventy-five pounds and he seemed to be short of breath, as well. I ran my fingers through his hideous beard and vowed I would cut it off immediately.

Once I had his breeches back on I went to the top of the stairs. Emie was standing there grinning up at me. We ran to each other like parted lovers, meeting somewhere at the center of the staircase.

"Oh, Mommy, Mommy. How I have missed you," she wept, and held me so tightly my breath became short.

It seems that both Emie and Philippe insist that I am their mother. I decided to ignore the implication. I had more important things to do, such as get in touch with this fool of a lawyer.

"Where are Matthew and Philippe?" she asked me.

I stood back from her embrace and felt the brows above my eyes form into arches. I looked at her with an increasing anxiety that caused poor Malcolm's heart to pound. Beads of sweat formed below the hairline and fell like drops of rain down the massive cheeks and into the facial hair. This flesh was causing me great discomfort for the beard began to itch me horribly.

"Why, they are here with you. Are they not?" I asked her, scratching at myself with Malcolm's perfectly squared off nails.

She took my hands. "I have not seen them," she said, as she led me down the stairs and into the parlor.

I had now become so short of breath that I sat myself on the large couch that I spotted across the room. Malcolm's body seemed too amplitudinous for most of the dainty and pretty chairs strategically placed before paintings and next to tables, as though awaiting tea and conversation with well appointed gentry.

"But they surely left before I did. They followed Elizabeth. Where is Elizabeth?" I asked her.

She followed me to the couch and sat beside me. "I have not seen anyone but you and Meredith Mae. I have been trying to communicate with Philippe but I am getting nowhere. There's some hindrance that I experience, and I cannot get through to my brother. I need your power to help me."

My anxiety deepened and I felt this horrible flesh I now inhabited sweating profusely under the arms and about the legs. The borrowed brain felt sluggish and I must have looked at Emie helplessly.

"He smokes cigars," she told me. "And I think he takes opium. Quite a bit of it."

I leaned back into the cushion and felt the fat on his body shift.

"We must go immediately to Meredith Mae," I told her. "I will handle that fool of a lawyer. Summon us a carriage, but first get a razor from the upstairs bedroom and shave this horrid hair off my face."

Even with smooth and freshly shaven skin Malcolm was not a handsome man but he was certainly rich enough to camouflage his misfortune behind well-fashioned suits. I made him appear as dapper as possible, and I must have succeeded for I noticed that woman fluttered their eyes as I passed them on the way to our carriage. They smiled demurely as I walked by them. How amusing it was. I found myself throwing out my chest and fondling my pocket watch every time the attention was given me.

I became uncomfortably aware that I did not have as much control over this flesh as I usually have over bodies I have taken, though I assumed that it would only be a matter of time before the impulses left to linger in Malcolm would dissolve. But, much to my shame, I even felt sexual desire when that horrid Beth Anne showed up with her young daughter. Just as we watched the Barouche pull up, Malcolm's flaccid organ began to grow in the presence of his own grandchild.

"Wretched beast," I whispered to Emie. "What is she doing here?"

To my great relief the organ withdrew and lay flat and inconsequential.

"Father, where are you off to? You promised to watch little Rachel while I shop."

I noticed the child hid behind her mother and stared at me with hateful eyes.

"I'm off. An emergency. I'll explain later."

I jumped into the waiting carriage as quickly as possible and Emie followed my lead. As I turned to look behind me, poor Beth Anne was pouting, and her face had turned so red that I almost laughed out loud. But the child she had called Rachel stood staring back at me with a look so disturbingly haunting that it sobered me.

"She seems unnaturally wise for her years," I whispered. "Very unhappy for one so young."

Emie obviously did not want the driver to overhear our conversation and told me quietly that she was suspicious of something and would explain later.

It was just at that point that we stopped in front of the Church on Tilden Street. It was a Saturday afternoon in late summer and the Church grounds were alive with flowers. The church had just recently been built, for I did not remember it. It was a magnificent structure with towering steeples and high, beautifully stained windows. The roof was peaked and the doors were arched and made of wood, with large metal crosses hammered into them. We stood for a moment, just outside, and watched as the bell rang from its tower. We admired the gracious, red, and gray structure before placing our hands on the metal crosses and pushing the doors in.

Inside the church it was dark, and the only light seemed to come from a multitude of candles that shone and flickered near the altar. We stood just inside a little anteroom, for we did not know exactly where the convent was or how to get there.

As soon as I stepped into the church I was aware of a cold chill that started slowly at the base of my spine and filled my borrowed flesh like a lightning jolt. For several seconds, I shook from the effect of it.

"Are you cold?" Emie asked me.

"Something is wrong," I told her.

We stepped further inside the church. Emie dipped her fingers into the holy water and made the sign of the cross.

"You are a Catholic?" I asked.

I was surprised to see her make such a sign even though I remembered that Philippe had done the same in the fields when we realized Elizabeth had passed through time.

She looked at me in a strange way. "Yes," she whispered. "And you? You are not?"

"I am a Puritan," I said proudly. "And in another life, a Christian."

"Oh."

That was all she said as she took my hand and we neared the altar. The darkness was somehow a comfort and the coldness had dissipated, leaving behind warm air and the pungent scent of incense. The stained glass images seemed to transport me and I found that great tears uncontrollably ran from my eyes. I felt consumed with despair and a state of confusion overtook me. I walked to the cross, to a statue of Jesus, limp, and bleeding from his wrists, and I fell to my knees.

Emie ran to my side. "What is it, Mommy?" she cried.

"I am not sure. The soul of Jesus," I whispered, "commands me."

Emie knelt beside me and bowed her head before Jesus, as well.

"Yes," she said to me simply.

I was about to pray, when suddenly; I felt the same cold chill again that I had felt earlier and I turned quickly behind me. To my great horror, a Priest stood in the shadows, his face hidden by a dark hood. He slowly moved toward me. I froze so completely that I don't remember breathing.

"It is the devil," I whispered to Emie. "Urbain."

I quickly stood up and threw my arms out ahead of me. The demon was thrown to the back of the church wall. I spoke before he could reach me again.

"Begone Demon!" I screamed and kept my arms rigidly pointed at his heart. Emie ran quickly beside me, and she too, put both her hands straight up before her to keep the demon at a safe distance.

"Begone!" we both shouted at once.

The Priest fell to his knees and we watched in horror as his body shook in great spasms, and finally fell into a heap. Emie and I stood silent and stared at it. To our horrified embarrassment, a sweet young man removed his hood and crawled along the floor, trembling before us.

"Who are you?" he wept. "Who are you?"

"I'm so sorry," Emie apologized quickly and ran to the Priest to help him to his feet. "We are looking for the gentleman's stepdaughter, Meredith Mae Guyon. We are told she is here at the convent," she said.

"Oh? Yes," the young Priest responded nervously. "Yes. She is here. Father Jacques has given her a room at the top of the stairs".

We waited for him to lead us to her but he stood and stared, still trembling, and said nothing.

Finally, I spoke. "May we see her?" I asked.

He looked for a moment from Emie to me. He held on to the pew as if he needed to collect his balance.

"How did you do that?" he asked.

"Pardon?" I said, though I knew to what he referred.

"Lift me off my feet like that?"

"I am sorry, Father," I said quickly. "I did nothing."

"Oh? Well, perhaps I tripped then." He laughed. "I have been known to fall over my own feet."

"Please, Father. May I see my stepdaughter?" I asked.

"Oh, yes, of course. I will take you to her. Come this way."

The young Priest walked swiftly and ushered us up a tall flight of stairs. From each landing one could look down and see the Nave below. I turned at the second landing to search for the demon; for I knew he still lurked in the shadows and had walked in the flesh of the innocent young Priest to trick us.

Over in a dark corner of the altar I noticed a dark hovering form. I stopped and stared at it. In only a matter of seconds, a blond devil, its eyes shining with a red, yellow glare, walked out of the darkness. I could hear his laughter. I could feel my skin begin to burn as the demon looked up and stared back at me. He wore a Priest's collar.

"Annabel," he called. "Look here."

I noticed that the statue of Jesus had fallen to the floor and lay in pieces. The demon's laughter was a long, low growl that bellowed out through a web of darkness, slowly rising in intensity until I clutched my ears with the palms of my hands.

"Jesusssssssssssssssss." The devil hissed from his darkness. Jesusssssssssssssssssss."

"Devil be damned!" I commanded. "Return to your hell!"

"What's that?" The young Priest turned to me on the stairs as I stood staring down on the altar at the deranged devil.

"Lucifer be damned," I said simply.

"Oh, yes," he said earnestly as he made the sign of the cross over his heart and tenderly kissed the rosary that graced his neck with a Saint's benevolence.

"Oh, yes. The devil be damned," he whispered.

# Chapter 18

It was a cold dark room he led us in to. I could feel the dampness on my borrowed flesh and see the sunlight fighting its way in through a narrow slab of window. Meredith Mae was sitting on a small cot in the far corner of the room. She was not alone. My body stiffened at the sight of the woman beside her, though I did not know why. I could feel Emie's hand tighten in my own.

Meredith Mae ran into my arms. The young Priest blinked his eyes and clutched at his rosary.

"I will leave you alone," he uttered and left the room quickly.

Meredith Mae hugged me so tightly that Malcolm's horrid flesh began to sweat again, even though the room was cold and the women had shawls about their shoulders.

"What perfect flesh you have stolen this time, Grandmamma," she whispered in my ear. "What a perfect choice!"

I forgot about the devil in the Nave below. I was too overjoyed to see my granddaughter after so much chronological time. The smile across my face was broad and Malcolm's heart was pounding so rapidly that I had to sit. I looked around the room for a chair.

"It is so good to see you. So good." She laughed as she hugged me. "But where is Papa? Philippe? Where are they?"

"We do not know," I told her sadly.

"Elizabeth?" she whispered again.

I shook my head.

"You don't know where they are?"

I felt her grasp on my arm.

"No," I repeated. I told her that I had been quite sure they had arrived safely at Montague Street and was very distressed to find out they were missing.

Meredith Mae sighed deeply and spoke softly.

"Emie told me there was some tragic barrier in her communication with Philippe but we had so much difficulty here that we could not concentrate on it. Still, we thought they surely would have crossed with you. We must try and find them!"

It was then I turned to the stranger who had remained on the cot. She looked up at me with a glance so familiar that I rattled my soul to remember, but I could not recall her. She was eyeing me with a raised brow.

I bowed my head to her and when I looked up I could not help but notice how deeply she searched my eyes.

"Ursula Boussidan," she said, and stood to offer me her hand. I detected the dialect of her native France.

Boussidan?" I asked as I stooped and kissed the hand she'd held out to me. It had been an impulse that was so instinctive that I could not prevent myself from doing it.

"Ursula is Louis Boussidan's sister," Meredith Mae's sweet voice rang out. "She is trying to persuade her brother to re-open my case."

"Isn't it your brother who is responsible for Meredith Mae's grief?" I asked her.

"No, Mr. Northrup. You are responsible for her grief, and therefore I find your heartwarming embraces quite contrary."

I was not sure how I would explain my change of heart. I noticed that her mere presence caused an odd anxiety in Malcolm's chest. I could not honestly tell if it was my own emotion or whether it belonged to him.

"And just why would you help my granddaughter?" I asked as I led my massive flesh toward the cot and sat on the edge of it.

"Granddaughter?" she exclaimed and turned to raise her brow at me.

I realized quickly that I must now be cognizant of referring to Meredith Mae as my *stepdaughter*.

"That is certainly amusing considering you deny any family blood at all between you," Ursula quipped.

Emie took the only chair in the room and told the woman that I had suffered a fall and it had affected me terribly. "He's just recently come to his senses," she explained. "He's willing to give Meredith Mae back her share of the estate."

"Oh?" Ursula said and sat beside me on the cot. "You now wish to give Meredith Mae back the very estate you took from her?" she asked incredulously.

I noticed with great difficulty, since my sight was very foggy, that she was quite beautiful. I could see that her hair was dark and worn up under a large violet colored hat. Her eyes were a piercing blue and her bones were noticeably strong. They were high above the cheek and left an attractive shallowness below. Her lips were lovely, and even without a smile a dimple appeared in her cheek. Yet her handsomeness unnerved me and I did not know why.

"That is exactly what I am saying, Miss Boussidan." I smiled.

"I see," she said and continued to stare at me with an unnerving intensity.

I looked at Meredith Mae as surreptitiously as possible for I wanted to conceal a hint that she get rid of this woman, perhaps with a slight nod of my head, or a wink. To my surprise, my Meredith Mae sat beside Ursula on the other side of the cot and took her hand.

"I have the greatest sympathy for Meredith's Mae's financial loss and I give you my word, Mr. Northrup, I will see to it that Louis looks into this more carefully. I will insist he hear me out. You see, I have considerable influence over my brother and he is not above admitting that you have deceived him. I believe that this young woman is indeed your stepdaughter and is entitled to her full estate."

"As you wish." I winked at Meredith Mae. "She can have it all. I want no part of it. As a matter of fact, I am on my way to tell your brother to give her what she is due," I said as I stood from the cot and hoped she would take her leave.

Ursula Boussidan seemed shocked that I would say that, and even a bit disappointed to have a fight taken off her hands. Her lips fell open and she stared up at me contemptuously.

"You admit then that you took the estate spuriously and with malicious intent?"

She peered into my eyes with a penetrating inquisitiveness. I felt a shiver run through my soul.

"I have had a change of heart, Miss Boussidan. I have come here this afternoon to offer my stepdaughter the house and the entire estate. Now, if you will let us get on about our business?"

Ursula got off the cot and stood before me. I noticed she was quite tall and very thin. She had hardly any breasts, and yet, her diminished figure did not obscure her beauty.

Though it was not a beauty I would have nestled poor Malcolm's body against were I so inclined, for it seemed so self contained and unapproachable.

"You had better be telling me the truth, Mr. Northrup, for I have become very fond of your stepdaughter." She turned to my Meredith Mae at that very moment and cupped her face in her slender hands. "Take care, my precious," she whispered and bent to kiss her upon the mouth, briefly, but with a lingering emotion that horrified me.

She then returned the shawl to the bed "I will take my leave," she said.

This time, she stared into my eyes so long that I coughed and turned my face away. She looked briefly to Emie before turning on her heels and leaving the room. We could hear her footsteps on the stairs. Meredith Mae sat and stared past the door, as if transfixed and unable to move. From a far distance, I heard laughter, menacing and evil laughter. I turned sharply.

"Did you hear that?" I asked them.

The laughter was an old familiar reverberation that seemed to emanate from the Nave, several floors below us, and yet, it felt as close to the ear as the summer wind that flowed through the window. Certainly, it was Urbain. It was low, masculine laughter that rose in intensity, as if it would deafen us. Suddenly, it died as quickly as it had begun. In its wake a horrid smell permeated the small room. It was a familiar smell, like that of the body's odor when it goes unwashed.

"Let us get out of here," I said to Meredith Mae. "Let us return to Montague Street."

"But Father Jacques. I must tell him good-by."

"No. There is not time," I insisted.

Emie ran to Meredith Mae and forced her to her feet. "Meredith Mae, there is evil here. We must leave quickly."

"This is a church, a Catholic Church. The devil cannot enter here." She almost laughed at us.

"Come quickly," I said sharply and pulled her out the door.

I had the carriage stop at Boussidan's office since it was on our way. I wanted to amend the terrible circumstances and restore the estate to its rightful beneficiary. I told Emie and Meredith Mae to wait for me while I confronted the scoundrel who had gone against my wishes. I also wanted to learn what exactly had happened to William Davenport. I could not imagine my dear friend turning his accounts over to mere strangers when his own son had been ready to enter a partnership with him. I had trusted his sworn promise to never allow any part of the estate into Malcolm's hands. I feared he had met with foul play, though I prayed that my instincts deceived me and this Boussidan was simply an honest man who had been taken in by the bastard, Malcolm, in whose flesh I lingered, like the soul of a pigeon trapped in the body of a hippopotamus.

I was concerned about this Father Jacques, as well, and kept seeing Urbain in the Priest's collar, could he be camouflaged within the flesh of Father Jacques? Yet, Meredith Mae insisted that Father Jacques was a kind and gentle man who knelt with her every evening in prayer and had come to her rescue like a saint, or an angel.

"Why? Why did he come to your rescue? Who is he? Is he really a Priest?" I asked, hoping that my worst fears were not going to be realized.

"Grandmamma. You are being unfair. Father Jacques is a man of God. Trust me."

But, I did not trust that my Meredith Mae would recognize the devil if he stood before her carrying a scepter and breathing fire. I had seen how she swooned over that horrible Ursula. I looked at Emie, who seemed to be reading my thoughts. As the carriage approached Boussidan's office, Emie whispered that she would keep a close eye on Meredith Mae. We both must have feared she might walk back to the church, since we were not far, to thank the dubious Father Jacques. And I preferred that none of us ever set foot in that church again.

I climbed the two flights of stairs to get to the law offices and had to rest at the top before I entered. I remembered how swift my step had been as Ann Putnam, and even in the flesh of that horrid Patience. I felt the weight that Malcolm carried and was particularly distressed by the way I had to maneuver my thighs to keep them from rubbing. I swore that I would starve this flesh until these pounds were dropped, and yet, I found myself craving something to put in this stomach of his. Despite my insufficient sense of smell I could pick up a very faint odor of cheese, and wondered where it was coming from.

The old secretary that William had employed was gone and to my great shock, there at the desk sat Malcolm's oldest daughter, Catherine.

"Father! What are you doing here? What happened to your beard?" she asked me.

"I wish to speak to Boussidan. Please tell him I am here."

"Why?" She narrowed those small eyes of hers and peered at me.

"Do as I say daughter," I commanded.

"He has just arrived back and I'm not sure he will see you. He seemed quite out of breath."

"If you do not tell the man I am here, I will walk in there myself and announce my own presence."

She laughed.

*How absolutely disrespectful*, I thought.

"Sure, sure. Whatever you say, dear Father, but I told you that he has just returned and may be busy," she hissed at me sarcastically.

I was somewhat taken aback and eyed her curiously. It was clear that she and Malcolm were not as close as he appeared to be with Beth-Ann. I watched impatiently as she moved some things around her desk before she went in to Boussidan's office, as if stalling.

Finally, I heard her tell Boussidan that I wished to see him. After a moment, she came out and motioned for me to enter. I could feel her eyes peering into my back as I passed her by, as though she would sooner toss me into a fire, were one burning.

Louis Boussidan was sitting behind a large desk with his head bowed. He was engrossed in some papers. He did not pick up his head as I entered. I noticed that his hair was dark and fell to his shoulders and he appeared slight for a man.

I began to speak immediately as I sat my body in the chair opposite him. I told him I wished to turn the entire estate back to my stepdaughter, that I had come to my senses and it had all been some terrible mistake that I now wished to rectify. I mentioned something about a fall and how it had affected me. I was speaking so rapidly that I took no notice that he had lifted his head. Finally, my winded monologue came to an end and I asked him to draw up the necessary papers. It was then I brought my attention to his face. He looked at me and smiled, his eyes a brilliant blue and the bones above his cheek so strong they caused a hollow below. His lips were full, and without a smile, he showed a dimple.

112

"Astonishing," I whispered.

"Pardon?" he asked in his native tongue. He leaned forward in his chair. His hair was in a man's cut and his shirt was that of a man's, as well; above his lip, he touted a fine mustache.

"You are twins?" I asked quietly.

He nodded his head and smiled. "Yes."

"The resemblance is remarkable," I said. "I did not think the opposite sexes could be identical."

He ignored me. "My sister has persuaded you?" he asked, looking past me, as if straining his neck to see Catherine.

"Well, actually, no. I have only just met your sister," I said, as I stared at him intently. He also caused me to trace back through my memory, to wonder why I felt I had known him in some distant future, or woebegone past.

"Really?" he said with an odd scowl. "Well, then, you know my sister is insisting that Meredith Mae is the real beneficiary. As I'm sure you are aware?"

I said nothing and he continued.

"Now, you say she is, in fact, your stepdaughter?" Louis stared at me with incredulity, as if I stood before him naked.

"That is precisely what I am saying."

Louis got up and sat on the edge of his desk. I noticed that his legs were long but as thin as Ursula's had seemed. He lit himself a cigar and stared at me. There was a strange tilt to his brow as he searched my face.

"Cigar?" He smiled.

I shook my head. Smoking was a foul habit I detested.

Louis laughed. "How very odd." He smirked.

"What's that?" I questioned.

He ignored me and continued. "All right, Malcolm, I'll play your little game. How much of the estate do you wish to relinquish?"

"All of it," I answered quickly.

"That leaves you penniless." He sucked deeply on his cigar and blew the smoke at me.

"Penniless?"

I leaned back in my chair. I realized that Malcolm Northrup would have to retain a portion of the estate. It would look foolish to cut himself off without a dime and I did not wish to draw attention to my actions. I simply wanted the money back where it belonged.

"I will retain twenty-five percent of the estate," I told him.

Louie got off the desk and went back to his chair. "And my share, I assume, will be left intact? That would leave fifty percent to Meredith Mae, not seventy-five."

"William Davenport did not own a share of my estate. He was paid a monthly fee. What is this nonsense?"

Louis shot up quickly and pointed his dastardly cigar at me like a weapon. "We agreed to this two years ago. Are you mad?"

I was breathing heavily. I noticed that Louis had a bottle of red Bordeaux on the shelf behind him and a plate of Brie. He saw me staring at it.

"My lunch," he said. "I would offer you to share it with me but Catherine and I always take lunch together, and there's not enough."

"Look, Louis," I stood and rested my hands on the desk. "I will expect compendiousness in this matter. The estate is to be returned to Meredith Mae Guyon with the exception of twenty-five percent, which will remain in my name. Keep your share, for now."

"And Catherine?"

"Catherine?" I quipped. "What about her?"

Louie looked toward the door that had been left partially opened. I watched as he crossed the room to close it.

"The walls are still thin," he whispered.

"Give her two percent of my share," I said to him.

He looked at me as if I had just said something ridiculous, but he said nothing.

"By the way, what happened to William Davenport?" I asked casually.

Louis eyed me oddly. "Just how badly has that fall affected you, Malcolm?"

A chill went down my spine, and yet, I pressed him for answers. "Humor me, Louis. What happened to William?"

Louis spread the Brie on his finger and sucked it into his mouth. Before he answered me he poured himself a glass of the wine.

"William Davenport was murdered in this very office on August 10th, 1851. I bought out the practice from his son, Silas."

"Silas is a lawyer as well. Why should he turn the practice over to you?" I asked.

Louis met my eyes as he sucked on yet more of the Brie.

"Silas was arrested for the murder of his father within six weeks of the crime. Have you no memory of that?"

"On what grounds?" I almost rose from my chair in disbelief. I remembered Silas as a sweet and considerate young man.

114

"Well, for one thing, they argued constantly and brutally, and for another, a witness came forward and said that she had seen Silas enter the building only minutes before the shot was heard."

"What witness?" I asked. It was incredulous to think that Silas could hurt anyone.

Louis smiled and leaned in close to me. "Why, your own dear daughter, Catherine."

I sat there silently taking it in. Something was terribly disconcerting and I felt sick from the smell of the Brie, and even sicker staring at the cheese that had stuck to Louis' lip and lay there like misbegotten scraps.

"Call me when the papers are ready." I stood up to go. Louis rose, as well, and crossed to me. He stood only inches from my face. The lashes over his eyes were thick and dark. His shoulders so small I might have cracked them with my bare hands. I watched as he licked the cheese off his lips, like a blood wound, and stared into my eyes so deeply I felt a flush to my skin. To my horror, I felt the flaccid organ between Malcolm's legs grow until I could feel it touch the material of his trousers. *How very odd*, I thought. *How very odd, indeed.*

# Chapter 19

Once back at Montague Street I told Emie that our priority was to contact Philippe and discover why he and my son were not with us. Emie told me she would try and reach her brother but for the last two years of chronology communication had become very difficult. "It is the first time in our lives that Philippe is unable to transmute his thoughts, or to move through the barriers of space," she said.

"Grandmamma's presence will help us," Meredith Mae said as she went through the house lowering the lamps. She insisted that Emie lay back in a large chair that she had placed on the bare wood in the parlor.

"Why did you remove the rug?" I asked her.

"A circle is needed," she told me, and took a piece of chalk from the cupboard and drew a circle around the chair. "Lay back," she told Emie as she placed her in the chair and put her palms up facing the sky. Emie then laid her head back on a soft pillow.

"She looks too comfortable," I whispered. I feared that sleep would take her before Philippe could find her.

"This is not difficult," Meredith Mae said confidently. "The will that unites us is greater than the flesh that keeps us parted."

My granddaughter sat me down before Emie and turned to take my hands. "Hum, Grandmamma. As we did on the night of the rainstorm, out near the marshlands, and do not be pulled back by the mind."

We sat together for what must have been hours. The oil in the lamps burned off. Emie remained in the chair as Meredith Mae and I sat at her feet, holding hands, and pushing out long sonorous sounds with our breath. The candles burned one-quarter inch from their holders and still we hummed. Emie appeared in a deep sleep. I could hear her breathing, soft and steady, lulling me into a mindless darkness that held nothing but random thoughts, and images that made no sense at all. I let them come and go, as if they appeared on a slate that was quickly erased and then filled anew with faces and impressions, appearing as negative images, real, but yet, not real. Nothing was familiar. In my distress, I searched for my son.

"Matthew," I called. "Where are you?"

"Do not try so hard, Grandmamma," Meredith Mae whispered. "Only hum and call upon the soul."

"I am sorry," I said sadly. I had not opened my eyes. I could still hear Emie's breath and my own voice, so unappealingly masculine, trailing behind Meredith Mae's gentle sounds with some low vibration I found in the pit of Malcolm's stomach.

Hours surely passed. The candles burned to almost nothing. I felt drunk and mildly delirious. My mind wandered aimlessly. The shapes that appeared before me were those I had never seen before, barely human — forms with out sense, or meaning. Ominous — humorous — they came and went while the inner lobe of my ear held nothing more, or less, than pure sound. Emie's breathing had long since quieted. I could no longer hear Meredith Mae's voice. My only reality was a vast endless and resounding monotone that I continued to send out in my breath like some wayward chant.

I do not know how long we sat before the images changed — a blur at first, and then, as sharp as life. To my amazement, I finally saw my son so clearly that I might have touched him. He was putting wood into a fire. I sensed that the barriers around the dimensions had faded, and yet, I still had not entirely entered my son's reality. I could only stare and walk through, like a ghost, if you will. Yes, precisely like a ghost.

I could see that there were men around him. I did not know them. I wanted to call out but I could not use my voice, and my son did not know that I watched him.

"I have found Matthew," I whispered from this vacuum between my son's perception and my own.

"Where is he?" I heard Meredith Mae ask sharply.

"In a room. A room in a house."

"Look around the room," she whispered. "What do you see?"

I moved my eyes as if in a trance. "Matthew is talking. He is talking to men.

Most of them are dark, as dark as Philippe," I answered.

"What are they talking about?" she asked me.

"A tunnel."

"A tunnel?"

"Yes," I assured her as I looked around. "They are very intense. Their brows are lined and they appear angry. They are very passionate about moving something through the tunnel."

"Where is Philippe?" she said to me.

"I do not know," I whispered as I continued to search. I was surprised that they could not see me as I walked amongst them. I noticed a door at the end of the room. I struggled to open it but I could not. Then I heard something. Someone calling. The voice was close, so very close to me.

"Who is there?" I asked.

"Philippe," The voice answered, but it did not come from my vision. It came from Emie.

"Philippe?" I said and turned toward Emie.

"Where are you?" I heard Meredith Mae ask.

"Petersburg," she whispered in a voice so strange that I could not tell whose it was.

My heart began to pound and I felt as if I would pass out. I looked about the room in my vision and noticed it was very sparse, very similar to my father's house in Salem.

"What year are you?" I uttered.

"I am Philippe. They think I am a runaway. I am injured," Emie whispered.

"Good God!" I exclaimed.

"Help us find you," Meredith Mae pleaded. "What year? What year in Petersburg?"

I watched as my son spoke to some man he referred to as "Pastor" about moving the bondsmen.

"They are speaking about moving some men to Vermont," I told them.

I kept trying to touch my son but I could not. I could hear Emie moaning and trying to speak. Some man started to talk about the route into Canada that was most difficult to detect when suddenly a great banging could be heard. At first, I thought it came from the vision, but it did not come from my son's world. It came from mine. Some hideous pounding on the door that shattered my hold on Matthew's existence and exorcised him like some frenzied Priest with holy water on a mission against the devil.

"Damn!" I shouted. "What is that wretched sound?"

Meredith Mae ran to the window to look out. I noticed it was morning and we must have been in our trance for over twelve hours. Emie was shaken.

"Are you all right?" I asked her.

"There is a great pain in my leg," she whispered, and reached to touch the spot. "Philippe has been shot. He lies wounded and that must have been why we were unable to connect. The Civil War, have you heard of it? A future war some twelve years from now."

I was about to ask her more about it when Meredith Mae turned to us.

"Catherine is at the door and she seems quite agitated."

"And what has she to be agitated about, horrid beast that she is," I said, standing with great difficulty, for the blood in my legs seemed to be boiling over and I could barely feel them to make them work. "Well, I suppose we must let her in."

Catherine seemed aghast as she walked into our parlor and found Emie comfortably ensconced in the most plush and lavish chair and her stepsister opening the door and offering her a morning coffee as if nothing were unusual.

"Father, what is the meaning of this?" she demanded as she walked straight to me and locked her eyes with mine like some enraged lover.

"Whatever is the matter, daughter?" I asked as I lowered my self into the closest available chair in order to stretch and massage my poor legs. To my horror, Catherine turned from me and grabbed Emie by the throat.

"Get up, you insidious wretch and mind your place." She then tossed the girl out of the chair and onto the floor at my feet. "Are you out of your mind, Father?" She screamed. "To allow a slave girl such privilege?"

Meredith Mae ran to Emie and helped her up. "Emie is not a slave. This is Brooklyn, Catherine. There have not been slaves in Brooklyn since 1824."

"Are you all mad? She sits openly in your parlor? And what is this, a mark on the floor? How curiously Satanic." Catherine knelt by the chalk mark and looked strangely at the way the chair was placed in the center.

"I thought it was mother that could trace her ancestry to the witches of Salem?"

"What is your purpose here?" I asked her.

"You know full well what it is." She glared at me.

"Speak your mind."

I leaned back in my chair and raised my arm straight out with my palm extended at an acute angle. I realized it had been a natural masculine gesture, as if I were a king bestowing a gift upon my subject. I had seen many men make such a gesture and it now came quite naturally to me.

She glared hatefully at Meredith Mae.

"Get them out of here," she ordered me.

"I certainly shall not. Say what you will before them," I said.

She seemed to shake with rage, her face so violently red in color that it appeared in my haze as a humorous contrast to the milky white color around her eyes. I found that I laughed aloud, though I had not intended to do so. I realized I appeared as arrogant as the original inhabitant of this ungainly flesh.

Catherine walked close to my chair. I thought for an instant she might strike me. Instead, she leaned in as if she might kiss my very mouth and grinned with such loathsome maliciousness it caused my heart to pound loudly.

"This intimacy with your slave does not surprise me, eh, Father?" She leered at me.

"But Meredith Mae? I will not speak before her. Send her from the room."

I rose from my chair and commanded her to treat her father with more respect. "I take no orders from you, Catherine," I told her.

"Oh, yes you do." She came and stood so close to me that I could barely breathe.

"I will call the authorities in a heartbeat," she whispered. "The child will tell all. The child will confess your perversion."

Something in her threat alarmed me and I looked over to where Meredith Mae and Emie sat together, straining to hear what she had said to me. I could tell that they had not heard a word.

I stared at Catherine and thought quickly. Of course, I had no idea what she was talking about and needed to find out as much as I could. Her words had left me with an uneasy feeling of disgust. I looked over the top of her head and met Meredith Mae's eyes. "Leave us," I said to both of them.

Once Catherine and I were alone in the room I expected her to explain the entire meaning of her threat, but she did no such thing. We were simply standing there staring at each other, waiting for the other one to speak, when suddenly her left hand went to her hip and the finger of her right hand shot up into my face like a weapon.

"Not one dime leaves the estate. Do you hear me, Father? Not one dime does Meredith Mae get or your little perversion becomes public knowledge. Do you hear me?"

I wanted to ask her what perversion she was referring to but I was thoroughly confused. I did not know what to say. I stood there looking at her monstrous scowl until I had to sit. I had to think. She followed me to the couch and stood before me.

"Why would you do this? Why return the money to that woman when you worked so hard to win it? We have won. It was a brilliant, brilliant plan. Not to mention, a dangerous one. What in God's name are you doing, Father? Have you gone as mad as Mother?"

I continued to stare at her in disbelief. "Maebelle?" I whispered. I could not think fast enough. I had been so preoccupied with everything that I had not even wondered of Maebelle. "What has become of her?" I asked.

Catherine stared at me quite similarly to the way in which Louis had looked at me.

Then she laughed. She laughed with such jocundity that she fell into a chair.

"What is so funny?" I inquired.

Catherine appeared to be crying as she wiped her eyes, but of course, there were no tears.

"The opium has dulled your senses, Father."

"Yes, yes. I do not remember things," I chided quickly. "Where is Maebelle? I can't recall. The drug affects me so."

But I was not to learn of poor Maebelle's fate so quickly. Catherine had now composed herself and continued to stare at me.

"Listen you old fool," she whispered hatefully. "If you do not return to Louie's office this morning and reverse your requests, I will destroy you. Do you understand, Father?"

We sat for a minute, sitting across the room from one another, our eyes meeting in confrontation, each waiting for the other to speak once more.

"Well?" she finally commanded of me.

"I will consider your request," I said quietly. I knew of nothing else I could say until I learned more about Malcolm's indiscretions. I had to know if she could, in fact, blackmail me.

Catherine slowly lifted herself from the chair, for she had become even more portly than I remembered her.

"I trust you will make the right decision," she said as she turned at the door to face me. "The money will remain in the estate of Malcolm Northrup, as it was originally set up between us — you and I, and Louis. Do you remember, Father?"

"Remind me, daughter." I said, as gently as I could muster, for I wanted terribly to strike her down.

"The money belongs to us, to me and to you. An even split, and of course, Louie's share. See how generous I am? But nothing is to go to Meredith Mae. Absolutely nothing."

"And what of Jed?" I laughed, for I remembered Malcolm's son and how he doted upon him. "And what of Beth-Ann?

"Jed?" she exclaimed incredulously. "Jed? Oh, Father you really have gone mad. What does a Priest want with money but to give it to the poor?"

"Oh, yes, yes of course," I said quickly as she turned to go.

"Beth-Ann is to have none of it?" I wondered how Catherine had ever gained so much control over her father.

"She is too much of an idiot to share this fortune. And besides, you have favored her always, haven't you? You owe me at least this."

She looked at me with such hate that I felt inclined to put my arms around her and comfort whatever grief the bastard, Malcolm, had bestowed upon her. Instead, I kissed her cheek.

"An odd gesture Father," she whispered in my ear. "And much too late."

I followed her outside and watched as she lifted herself into the waiting Hanson and beckoned the driver to leave. I looked after the carriage. I had a very strange sensation within the body I now inhabited. I was craving something that caused me shame. Images flashed across my brain, so quickly at first that I could not distinguish what they were, and then, they slowed until they moved before my eyes, as if I were a voyeur peering from behind a wall. I looked on in horror as I saw the child Rachel appearing in the vision. The child, Rachel, disrobed and weeping, and there I was, locked in Malcolm's body with some awful compulsion to force the girl to her knees and brace myself behind her naked flesh.

"No!" I screamed from the depths of my soul and shook my arms before me as if I might wipe the awful image from my mind. "No!" I screamed again. Emie and Meredith Mae ran outside and held me. I shook in their arms. The devil's laughter resounded against my brain and I saw the sky as it turned black and deep, and dark clouds passed swiftly overhead. He was there. I was sure he was there searing into my brain. I fell to my knees.

"Oh, God." I screamed. "Where are you?"

"Here," spoke the devil. "Here is your God."

"The devil's slime, Urbain. You are the devil's slime."

I rose to my feet and shook my hands in the direction of the devil's malignant presence. Emie and Meredith Mae looked frantically about for they clearly did not hear him as I did.

"Come and be still, Mommy." I heard Emie whisper as she led me back inside the house and into the parlor. I followed like a helpless lamb.

"Be calm, Grandmamma," Meredith Mae said tenderly as she sat me on the couch and rested my feet on a small footstool.

"The bastard is a deviant," I wept.

"What do you mean?" they asked in unison.

"He has violated the child. He has tainted the earth. I saw the image of it in his wretched mind. Catherine has threatened to expose this perversion."

"The child, Rachel?" Emie asked me. "I have long suspected it."

"Why did you not prevent it?" I cried, enraged, as I stood and hit my fist against the flat of my hand.

Malcolm's father, Ebenizer, they go off together." Emie took my arms and turned me to face her. "I could not be sure. I could not follow them and I could never be alone with the child to ask."

"Ebenizer is still living?" I was aghast. "The old man must be nearing one hundred years."

Emie nodded. "He is quite old. But spry enough."

I sat back in the couch and put my head in my hands. I knew I had to find a way to bring my son and Philippe home. I needed them. I longed to rid myself of Malcolm's body, his disgusting desires. I thought of Ursula and how fine it would be to inhabit one so beautiful. However, the very thought gave me a chill.

"What should we do, Grandmamma?" Meredith Mae asked intently.

"The only thing we can do, and let Malcolm go to the devil. We shall keep the money. It is ours. I will take care of the vermin, Ebenizer."

"You will be jailed if Catherine exposes Malcolm and the child validates the story. You may be jailed forever and unable to die, to pass to another dimension."

Emie sat on my other side and took my hands in hers.

"Unfortunately, we do not have the time to further meditate and find Matthew and Philippe. I am going to Catherine's and I will tell her that I refuse to give her any part of the estate, except for the two percent promised, and she can do what she chooses. We must assure that the money is returned to us and then we will act quickly to recover Philippe and Matthew. We will all leave this century behind us."

"You can't take it with you, Grandmamma," Meredith Mae smiled.

I returned her smile, "oh yes, we can. We will find a way to move the money until it shows up in the right dimension. In the meanwhile, let Catherine expose the bastard, Malcolm. We will kill him off before he is ever jailed and I shall choose another victim, a lovely victim. How unfortunate that Malcolm will escape the public humiliation he so rightfully deserves."

"But how will you die?" Meredith Mae asked me quietly.

"I shall fall before a bullet; lose my breath in a river. Ha, perhaps find myself at the end of a sword. After my confrontation with the cat, I fear nothing."

I started toward the door and touched the hair that had appeared on my skin overnight. I could actually feel the bristle against my thumb and forefinger as I brought them down my cheeks to rest against my chin.

"Catherine owes me some answers. An innocent man has been jailed and we must help him if we can. I owe William that." I turned to Emie. "Why didn't you tell me about the murder?"

"I started to, but then thought it best to wait until after you had taken a body. There was so much for us to catch up on. Besides, William was dead and unable to help us. I thought it inconsequential how he died."

"Inconsequential? You did not think it suspicious?" I questioned.

"What could we do once the trial was over? My only intention was to wait for you and the others to return. I never knew Silas and thought perhaps it was possible he had killed his father," Emie said.

"Silas has a reputation for a short temper," Meredith Mae added. "He seems nice enough but he was once involved in an argument over a carriage accident and hit the man who accused him of recklessness."

"Well, that does not make him capable of murdering his own father. What disagreement could have driven him to such means?"

I wondered if I would ever be able to prove that it was likely Malcolm, or even Boussidan that had murdered William.

"Did you know it was Catherine that swore she witnessed Silas at William's office the afternoon he was shot?" I said as I turned to them.

"Yes, and I also know she is in love with Louis and would do anything he tells her,"

Emie told me.

"I think they were all involved in a monstrous, deadly plan to steal the estate." I thought aloud as I ran my hands again over the short stubble.

"Perhaps that is why none of them would identify me," my granddaughter said sadly.

"What of Jed? He did not remember you as well?" I asked her.

"Jed is abroad. He is a priest in France at a small country church. I don't remember the town but it is not far from Paris. He has been there since he took his vows."

"Why, France?" I asked curiously.

Meredith Mae shook her head and seemed not to know. I found it an odd coincidence and wondered if his path had crossed the Boussidan's in this quaint country church. I could feel my body begging for sleep but I knew I had to find my answers before Malcolm was found in a ditch and the estate wound up entirely in the hands of Louis Boussidan. I instinctively knew that Catherine was utterly dispensable in this deadly plan, and I sensed that I did not have much time.

"Shave me quickly," I said to Emie. "And then show me the way to Catherine's."

# Chapter 20

Catherine was happy to see me at first. She was confident that I had already been to Louis's office and had told him not to bother with the transfers. She was almost radiant as she twirled around the room and smiled at me from pasty thin lips.

"Meredith Mae will make a lovely nun. I'm sure that crazy Father Jacques will help the wretched and penniless creature as she struggles with the torments of poverty." She laughed.

"I have no intention of forcing Meredith Mae from her house. It is I that should be begging Father Jacque for his generosity," I said seriously.

She sat me in a lavender chaise that stretched before a Persian rug with the most unusual colors I had ever seen. The rug looked as if it had been drained of its life and nothing remained behind but whatever was left of the faint hue of bile.

"Why Father, your kindness is a new weakness. The opium has mellowed you so completely that I would swear you are a counterfeit, certainly not the father I know."

She peered at me so intently that her eyes disappeared behind her flesh and all that I could focus on was the puffiness of her cheeks.

"Well, so be it. Let the wretched girl have the house as long as I have my share of the money; you can both go to hell." She sat opposite me on some strange looking chair that had neither legs nor arms.

"Do you have a cat?" I asked her.

I had heard a soft cry, as if a cat was calling for milk.

She threw back her head and laughed with such gaiety that a strand of hair fell from her head and dangled on her forehead like a long thumb.

"Oh, but you are amusing, Father."

It was at that point that I heard the knocks, several knocks followed by the cries. I listened intently while Catherine rang for the servant.

"It is precisely the hour I have my morning coffee. Will you join me?" She seemed to twirl and spin around as if someone had wound her.

"I am sure that Louis was quite pleased that you came to your senses. I wish to hear all about it. I will not see him until noon."

I stared at her and said nothing. It was clear to me that she had already spent a great deal of my granddaughter's money on the most distasteful objects I had ever seen. Over the mantle was a huge mirror with two enormous serpents carved into the frame. On the floor, near the door to the library, she had placed a statue of indiscriminate interpretation and various paintings adorned the wall, appearing to me as visions in a nightmare.

"I see you did not inherit my taste." I smiled.

"Oh, I picked none of this," she told me. "You know that it was Louis who refurbished my home. They are perhaps too sophisticated for you, Father?"

I could see in her eyes as she spoke his name that she was completely seduced by Louis Boussidan. I suspected by now that she and Malcolm had hired Boussidan to swindle Meredith Mae by offering him a share of the money, but I did not know who had actually killed poor William. I was not yet sure how Ursula was involved either.

"Do you know Ursula?" I asked her.

I noticed that a blush came to her cheeks.

"Yes. In a way," she said softly.

I stared at her as the servant girl came and set the tray upon the table. I listened as the knocking continued and the cries became louder. I stood and went to the foot of the stairs. I could hear walking above, restless walking and crying, as if someone were in great pain.

"Who is up there?" I shouted.

Catherine stared at me as if I were stark raving mad.

"Who is up there?" I shouted to the servant. The girl shook as I took her arm. She began to cry.

"You're hurting me, sir," she said.

"Who is up there?" I demanded.

The girl looked at Catherine, who continued to stare at me in disbelief. Finally, she went to the girl and took her from my grasp.

"It's all right Eliza; let him go see for himself. His memory fails him."

I ran up the stairs until I stood on the landing. For several seconds I heard nothing. I looked in the rooms, behind the open doors, and I saw nothing. Suddenly, there was a scream, followed by the cries and the knocking on the floor. I found the stair that led directly to the attic and stood behind a latched door. The cries within were haunting. I pulled on the latch and could not open it.

"Who is there?" I called. "Who is there?"

I heard only crying, and it seemed as if someone had fallen before the door and was scratching on the other side.

I ran to the landing and called down. "Get me the key." I ordered Catherine who looked up at me with the most peculiar grin. "I order you to get me the key," I repeated and waited until she sent the servant girl for it.

I went back to the door and knelt down to listen. I could tell the cries were a woman's. She had begun to cough. She had stopped crying but continued to cough badly while I waited for the key. I did not know what I would find on the other side of the door, but the girl, Eliza, was clearly afraid and ran back down the stairs the minute I put the key in the lock.

She was so thin I barely recognized her. She had on a torn robe and her hair was straight and stringy and fell to her shoulders. She was perspiring badly, for the small attic room was hot and the air was fetid and so massive that it was difficult to move about. My head was stooped for I could not stand upright. I loosened my shirt immediately and stared at the huddled creature in the corner. She did not even lift her eyes as I entered.

"Maebelle?" I said sadly. "Good God, Maebelle. Is it you?"

She swayed gently from side to side. I went to her, reaching out to touch her arm. Suddenly, she leapt out at me as the catamount had done when I walked as Ann Putnam.

"Bastard!" she screamed as she kicked my legs and ripped her nails down my face. "Bastard!" she wept and flung her arms at me furiously.

Her eyes were wild as she struck me. I fought for her hands so that I could hold them down at her side. I jumped back as best as I could to avoid her rapid kicks as she attempted to hit me with the flat part of her foot.

I was able to hold her arms down and push my leg behind hers. I forced her to the floor. I sat over her and held her hands above her head. We were both breathing rapidly and I could feel poor Malcolm's heart about to explode. Maebelle wiggled beneath me as though trying to escape my grasp but she was clearly weak. After a moment, she desisted all movement and lay there staring up at me. I wasn't sure if it would be wise of me to let her go. I could feel the burn on my skin where she had scratched me and I felt the blood on my lips.

"Listen to me, Maebelle. I mean you no harm," I whispered.

"Give me some!" she yelled at me. "Give it to me, now!" She ran her tongue over her mouth and her eyes seemed to disappear in the top of her head.

"Give you what?" I questioned. "What?" I leaned in close to her face and searched it.

"My medicine!" she screamed. "Let me drink it," she said more softly. She began to writhe under me, screaming out again from the top of her voice.

I looked behind me to see if Catherine had followed me up the stairs but the door behind me had closed. "Catherine!" I yelled. I called her name several times before she finally appeared in the doorway. "Good God, help me!" I told her.

Catherine walked slowly to where I sat straddled over Maebelle's body. She held a small pouch in her hand and what appeared to be a glass of brandy in her other. She knelt before me and held the pouch up and brushed my nose with it. Maebelle began to breathe heavily.

"Do something," I said to Catherine.

Catherine opened the pouch and poured the tincture into the brandy. She turned the brandy glass around three times until the laudanum was made, and lifted Maebelle's head to sip it.

"I know you prefer it in the pipe," she said to me.

Maebelle finished everything in the glass and returned her head to the floor. I felt her body go limp and I knew she would no longer fight me. I released my hands and got off her. I was breathing so deeply I thought I would faint. I sat Malcolm's large body on the other side of the room and stared at Maebelle. She was smiling at me and had begun to hum softly. Catherine looked on as though she were thoroughly amused.

"How long has she been like this?" I asked her.

"For years, Father. Please. Don't pretend you do not know that it was you who started her. It drove her quite mad. She will probably die because of it. Does that make you a murderer?"

I ignored her remark and turned my attention back to Maebelle. She appeared almost normal, now. She stood up and walked to a small table. She reached for a brush and began to move it through her hair until it became full and flowed from her face. We watched as she put it up in a chignon with small pins. When she was through she smiled at herself in the mirror. I looked on sadly. I remembered how she had once loved my son. She was the mother of my granddaughter. She was of my blood. She did not deserve to end here in an attic, locked away like an animal, loved by no one, living only for a drug that would eventually kill her.

I slowly came and stood behind her. I put my hands on her shoulders and looked at her image in the glass. "Very pretty," I said quietly. "You look like a queen."

Her face had altered so completely that I meant every word. I touched her hair softly and felt the tears fall to my cheeks. I reached up to brush the tears away and it was then I noticed that Maebelle had almost ceased to breathe and was staring back at me through the glass, as if I were a ghost.

"What is it, poor dear?" I asked her softly.

She bent her finger at me and beckoned my ear to her lips. As I bent down, I could feel Catherine stiffen behind me.

"Yes?" I asked.

"Who are you?" she whispered.

"It is Malcolm, your husband," I said softly.

Maebelle laughed as she stood and took my hands. "Husband? Husband?" she said as she giggled and turned me around in a circle. "Why you're a woman, and a very beautiful one, I might add."

Maebelle had never had the sight. Whatever it was about the drug that had given it to her, I did not know, or care, but I knew she could see the real Annabel Horton as clearly as Emie and Meredith Mae.

"Leave us," I said sharply to Catherine.

"Gladly," said Catherine. "If you wish to spend your time with a mad woman it is your affair. I shall finish my coffee in the parlor. You may join me when you've had enough of her ridiculous hallucinations."

Once I heard Catherine's steps on the stairs, I turned back to Maebelle. She had moved herself to a corner of the attic room and stared at me as though I were an apparition.

"I will not hurt you," I said softly and reached for her hand. Slowly, she let me lead her back to the vanity table. She stood on the tip of her toes and looked at my face.

"Were you always a woman?" she whispered and gently stroked my cheek.

"I am not really … Malcolm," I told her.

She took a small pencil sketch that was encased in a leather frame from the table and showed it to me. "My son, Jed. She said proudly. "He's a priest."

I looked at Jed and saw the same sweet face he had had as a boy. "Where is he a priest?"

She returned the picture to the table as she answered me. "France. Loudun, France," she said.

"Loudun?" I whispered. I realized my suspicions might have some validity. "Has he friends there?" I pressed her.

"Just another young priest," she said.

"Who? What priest?" I asked her quickly. I realized I had frightened her for she retreated a bit toward the wall. I walked to her slowly and smiled. "Do not be afraid.

I will not harm you."

"Who are you?" she asked me again.

"Annabel Horton," I said. "Lost witch of Salem."

She smiled then, and told me she could trace her family back to Salem.

"What priest did Jed know in France?" I asked her. "Was it Father Jacques?"

"Who is that?"

"Do you know Meredith Mae?" I asked her.

"Of course. My daughter. She died abroad."

I wondered just how much Maebelle could really help me for I assumed she had been locked away in this attic for years. I also feared the drug had deteriorated her mind to the point where reality was a fine line. Still, I needed answers. I walked to her and sat her near me on the small cot. I took her hand and held it in my own.

"I'm going to tell you a story, Maebelle. Would you like to hear it?"

She nodded like a small girl and nestled her head against my shoulder. I leaned my head against hers, as she tentatively took my hand.

I told her everything, because I thought she was insane enough to hear it — my childhood in Salem where I played by the open sea and ran in the fields between the farms to tease my brothers while they tilled the land — the accusations against me, trials by men made mad by their own deceptive virtues — and my death on Gallows Hill — I told her that I became a lost spirit and wandered for years claiming the flesh of those the devil favors. But it was not until I mentioned Matthew that she began to tell me *her* tale. She began in a whisper, but soon, she spoke clearly and with full voice. She wept as she relayed how Matthew had drowned in the Hudson River. She told me how much she had loved him and how desperately she had fought to win his heart. The memories she relayed were as clear to me as the face that I now beheld, though my vision was still murky and opaque, I could see her eyes, and watch, as her expressions changed.

"Our baby...." she began.

"You never loved her, " I said softly, but without accusation.

"Yes." She contradicted me, "I did. I saved Meredith Mae," she whispered.

I remembered how easily she had given the child up to Patience, but I said nothing. She sat straight up and leaned her back against the wall. I could not see her face as she spoke; yet, I heard her pain and did not let go of her hand.

# Chapter 21

"I was foolish, but not so stupid or shallow that I did not know grief." Maebelle turned sharply to me and stared at me so intently that I did not know whom she saw.

"Please go on," I said as gently as I could.

"Matthew was my Orpheus. Matthew was my heart."

She spoke more softly now.

"But it was not I he sought from Hades. It was never I he sought. Our marriage was arranged. He would not love me, except for one brief shinning moment when he clutched me in the dark. He came to me in all his sweetness, with gentle strokes and such murmurs of affection."

She turned her face to the wall and began to recite a poem. I knew it well. Matthew had loved it.

*The dew of the morning sunk chill on my brow.*
*It felt like a warning of what I feel now.*

"Lord Byron. Do you know it?"she asked me. "Matthew bored me incessantly with

Lord Byron."

I smiled and squeezed her hand. Matthew had recited the poem often, with his head back and his long legs stretched before the fire as he whispered the verse, his hands over his heart, tears welling up in his eyes, as if love were some destructive weapon and not our only glory.

"Ghosts are too far distant," I had told him. "Lost to perpetuity, Matthew."

I knew Maebelle was also remembering how he ached in his melancholy for nothing he could name.

"But he came to love me," she said. "And in one of those sweet, ecstatic evenings he gave me my daughter, my Meredith Mae. He lost his sadness to this joy, the birth that we awaited. Matthew and I had created a life! I was no longer the dull and ignorant girl who worshipped him. I was a woman worthy of his heart. He loved me then. He honored me.Matthew Joshua Guyon loved and honored me."

I knew the tears fell to her cheeks as they did to mine. I knew she brought her hand up and wiped the tears away. I let mine fall. She deserved to see them.

"Go on," I said gently.

"But he must have found his muse buried in the river's deep because he did not return to hold this gift of life to his heart."

I sighed, as she said that, and brought her fingers to my lips.

"Is there a place in heaven where one can see the earth, I wonder? See the earth and share the sorrows of vulnerable love and the simple joys of mindless frivolity? Is it one and the same to the dead, or have they no tolerance for our defenseless hearts?"

She paused, as if she wanted me to answer her. When I didn't speak up fast enough, she continued, though I would have told her that we are always defenseless, always vulnerable to love, which in the end is always more a thing of joy than of grief.

"My baby was born without a father. I gave her to the grandmother, Patience Guyon, Matthew's mother. It ached me to hold her and to love her. I was a coward. I couldn't bear the grief. I couldn't stand the pain. 'Here,' I said to that horrid Patience. 'Take her.' The woman hated me and was so pleased to receive the child. She loved her. She loved her as I loved her."

My flesh burned as I remembered my distaste for Maebelle, my elitist opinions; the coldness of my own heart to accept so readily that she had not embraced Meredith Mae as I did, with my entire soul. I carefully squeezed her hand.

"I married quickly," she said. "I married to escape what I could not control. Unquenchable sadness. A delirium of depression so deep I sought distraction. Malcolm came to me like a magnet, one so drawn to my need, so drawn to my despair. 'Take this,' he crooned in my ear and fed me the laudanum as if it were honey on my lips."

She laughed so strangely then that it frightened me and I turned to look at her. She had closed her eyes and a strange smile appeared on her face. I touched her, as if to draw her back. I could not lose her now that she yearned to tell me so much.

"Maebelle," I whispered. "Then what?"

"Who are you?" she screamed at me and released her hand.

"Annabel Horton. Lost Witch, as lost as you. I am not Malcolm. Please, go on. Go on," I pleaded passionately as I reached back for her hand.

I watched as her eyes glazed over but she began to speak again. I noticed that she now spoke much more rapidly and her voice had taken on a raspy quality.

"Oh, how soothed I became in my delirium, in my obsession, and how Malcolm fed upon my grief until I could face the morning sun and smile on my neighbors, as if my heart were unimpaired. I would have taken the child back then, though Patience had lost so much, as well, two husbands, a son. And I was unsure of my own strength. I married Malcolm, not out of love. It was for need. I sought his presence at my side so that I might hold my head up in society and feel approved. Married and approved. And, of course, there was the laudanum, my embrace with heaven. How else could I maintain such total delirium if not for the laudanum that Malcolm fed me as if I were a child on medication? I welcomed it."

She seemed to fade away from me again and I spoke up quickly. "And after? What happened after you married, Maebelle?"

She opened her eyes and looked at me inquisitively. "Annabel?" she whispered.

"Yes, yes." I cried. "A friend, finally now, a friend."

She put her head back on my shoulders as she continued.

"It was a few years later that Malcolm began to insist we take back Meredith Mae. All of a sudden. Just like that. Ah ha! I couldn't imagine why Malcolm Northrup would want this child of my prior marriage when it was only at the age of three, or four years, that he showed any interest in her at all. However, I refused to take her from Patience at this point and we argued often. I told him that if we left the child with Patience, Meredith Mae would inherit her fortune. Then he said, 'fine, then let's take her week-ends.' He didn't love the child. I had given him three of his own. His interest confused and unsettled me."

I took my other hand and brought it over my chest so that it rested upon her arm. "Did you ever discover why he wanted Meredith Mae to return to your home?" I asked.

"Oh, yes," she sighed. "Yes, I did. I sensed it from the beginning, though I dared not think it."

I let out a long breath. I loved her so completely for protecting my Meredith Mae from Malcolm that I began to weep openly.

I felt the small pressure of her fingers on mine as if offering me the comfort I owed her.

"There were sacrifices," she told me then. "You see, I had no more love to give after I gave my child to Patience. Three children I had with Malcolm. I sacrificed each of them."

"What do you mean?"

"My son to God, Catherine to the devil and Beth-Ann to sin, to sin and contrition."

"Contrition?" I asked with a smile.

She began to cry. She freed herself from me and stood from the bed. "Yes, contrition!" She screamed at me. "Contrition!"

I held out my hand to her. "Please. Sit by my side. Let me comfort you."

She was weeping uncontrollably and fell to her knees. I slid from the bed to the floor beside her. I put my arms around her until the crying ceased. Gently, I led her back to the cot, but we sat on the edge this time and she put her head on my arm.

"Beth-Ann was only a child. A child. He never wanted Catherine, of course. 'She is ugly.' He would laugh. 'She will need a fat dowry to win a husband,' he would tell me over dinner. Only Beth-Ann was worthy. Not beautiful, like Meredith Mae, but worthy enough. Beth-Ann who adored him."

She spoke so quickly, as if she wanted to tell me everything and in the telling erase the tale. Her voice retained that scratchy quality, as if it pained her to talk. I listened, though my heart was sick to hear it.

"The old man, Ebenizer, would come and they would follow each other while I sat at the table. 'Say Malcolm is a good man one hundred times,' he would tell me.' And I would sit there and say it while the child bathed. The child bathed, and the old man Ebenizer went upstairs, into the bath, while Malcolm fed me my laudanum. The old man would stay in there for a long time, a very long time. Then, out he would come, back into the kitchen with his mouth set tight and tell Malcolm to dry Beth Anne, and Malcolm would go upstairs and dry the child while I sat in my delirium. The old man slept in the chair after smoking his pipe. I knew what they did to my daughter and I could not fight against this monstrosity. Take my soul, Annabel, witch that you are. Lay it at Satan's door. Take my soul for God will never have me."

With this admission, she wailed out so deeply that Catherine heard the cries. I could hear her footsteps coming quickly up the stairs. But Maebelle would not be stilled.

"And the child would come from the bath with such haunting in her eyes. I took more of the laudanum. I turned my face away from my daughter's eyes. Good God. They put her on her knees in the corner and told her to pray. To pray as if it were *she* that had sinned, to ask God to forgive her for what? For being innocent? Oh, how I hated him. How I hated him. He saw the hate, saw it on my face and he would lean in close. 'Malcolm is a good man. Say it one hundred times while the little whore prays, one hundred times. Malcolm is a good man. Malcolm is a good man.'"

Catherine stood in the doorway and stared, as Maebelle lost herself in some wild delirious screams.

"Get out of here. You've upset her," Catherine called to me, as she screamed for Eliza to bring more of the brandy.

I rose slowly and took to the stairs. I wanted to rip this vile flesh from my bones, to rip this vile flesh from my soul. Instead, I stopped at the foot of the stairs and went back in to the room.

"I will be taking her out of your attic, as soon as possible. I will bring her where she can get some help. First, I have business to attend to."

"She's insane. You can't take her from here," Catherine yelled over Maebelle's screaming.

"I am taking her. And I am not relinquishing the money. I will give you a portion of my twenty five percent to live on, and nothing more."

Eliza came running into the room but Catherine did not take the brandy from her. She walked directly to me as Maebelle continued to scream.

"What did you say?" she asked me.

"You heard me. Seventy-five percent of the estate will be returned to Meredith Mae. It belongs to her. You were never entitled to it and certainly Louie is not entitled to no more than a fee."

I expected her to hit me but she did not. She laughed. She laughed as loudly as the hysterical Maebelle was screaming.

"Then I will go to the authorities immediately and tell them what you have done to the child, if you don't die first, Father," she said with such hatred that my heart skipped a beat and my blood ran cold."

"What? Who would kill me?" I asked as I grabbed her arm and held it tightly.

She shook herself free and ran to Maebelle to administer the laudanum, but not before I heard her say, "who else, you fool."

# Chapter 22

I had to see Silas. I had to question him about his father's murder, if I were to help prove his innocence. I also had to insure that the estate was returned to the rightful beneficiary before Malcolm wound up in a ditch. I knew that I did not have much time now that I had insisted upon a transfer of funds. I suspected that Louis Boussidan was the scoundrel behind this deviousness and I began to form a plan as I sat in the carriage that took me to the county jail on Jay Street.

As I suspected, Silas refused to see me. I insisted that a message be brought to him and told the officer that I would wait for his reply. I remembered that when I inhabited the flesh of Patience Guyon and had agreed to attempt my passage through time, I had given William a code word so that he would always recognize my wishes and be able to honor them. I knew that I was leaving the body of poor Patience to the fish in the Hudson and I had wanted to insure that I could always communicate with William, if I needed to. I never planned to remain in Salem, Massachusetts, in a century of such Puritan piety for as long as I did, but I protected myself from the possibility that I might.

I carefully wrote the code word on a piece of paper and told the guard to insure that Silas read it.

"If anyone should ever come to you and say the word, 'Annasha', you must acknowledge whoever it is, for whoever utters the word 'Annasha,' carries my instructions," I had told William on a wet afternoon in 1840.

"Annasha?" he had asked me quizzically. "How odd, Patience. How very odd."

Still, he honored my wishes, as I knew he would, for honor was valued then, so ambiguous a concept in your twenty-first century world but not so foreign in nineteenth century chronology.

"What does it mean?" he whispered.

I remember smiling. How could I resist the truth knowing he would never believe it?

"Annasha is the name my mother calls to me from the grave."

How he laughed at me. "Patience," he had said. "Your imagination is most endearing. I will honor the call of 'Annasha.'" With that, he had taken my hand and held it as he smiled and elongated the name once again. I prayed now he had passed the code word to his son.

"He will see you," the guard told me as he came back around to where I was sitting. "Follow me."

I walked behind him as he led me through a locked door and down past several cells. Men sat staring at me as I passed, their eyes held a challenge I did not understand, but it left me feeling as if Urbain lingered in their desperation like the smoke that precedes fire.

Silas was brought to me as I stood behind the iron bars that separated us.

"Whom have you tortured to learn of that code, you bastard?" he spat at me.

"You must trust me," I whispered. "I am here to help you."

He threw back his head and laughed. He laughed so hard that tears fell on his cheeks. I watched him, and waited, before I began again.

"Listen Silas, you have no choice but to trust me. I want to get you out of here and clear your name. I know you did not kill your father."

"Why help me, Malcolm? I am taking your place in hell."

I took a deep breath. I had suspected that Malcolm was responsible for involving Boussidan, but I was still unsure which one of them had actually pulled the trigger on poor William. I needed to know everything that Silas knew in order to assure his freedom. So I relayed to him the most preposterous story. I knew he would think me mad if I told him that I had robbed Malcolm of his body and he was nothing more than a flicker of meaningless evil, adrift in an infinite paradox, but perhaps he would accept that I had found God, and in that miraculous transformation I was spared any memory of evil wrongdoing. Silas looked on, transfixed, while I shed such easy tears and told him that I sought absolution in his forgiveness. I thought I had certainly moved him for he reached to touch me.

"You remember nothing? God spared you your memory?"

"Yes," I answered. "I remember nothing, so you must tell me what happened so that I can clear you. I owe your father. I owe it to myself to take responsibility for my actions."

"But if God spared you, why should I return you to your sins?"

I did not want to waste my time with Silas in philosophical meandering. I thought quickly.

"The priest has willed it. In confession he advised me to know my soul."

Silas searched my eyes. Finally he spoke. "I find it difficult to believe you, Northrup," he spat at me once again.

"Who else is there to help you, Silas?"

He continued to stare at me. His mouth was set tightly and his jaw was firm. "All right, what difference will it make to me anyway?" He sighed.

"You must relay it to me as if I were a stranger," I told him.

"Are you playing with me, Malcolm? Because if you are......" He leaned forward and clutched the bars before him, and even through my opaque sight I could see his knuckles turn white.

"You have got to trust me," I cut him off.

He leaned back and stared at me for several moments. "I guess I do. Don't I?"

I relaxed my body and shifted Malcolm's massive weight. I listened intently to Silas as he revealed this most disturbing tale.

"We had not seen Patience and her granddaughter for many years, yet we continued to carry out Patience's instructions just as she had advised us," he began.

"Yes, yes." I said, "and what about me?"

"We did not see or hear from you for several years, as well, but then, one day in 1847, you burst into Father's office and insisted that Patience and Meredith Mae had perished abroad, yet you could produce no proof of their death. Still, you declared yourself beneficiary and demanded the estate. For God sakes, man, don't you remember all this?"

I ignored him. "Is this around the same time that Louie Boussidan came here from France?"

"No, he did not arrive until later."

"Then what, Silas?"

"My father refused you. You see, Patience had told us to expect this behavior from you if she did not return soon enough. And so we ignored you, which only made you more furious. You retained a lawyer, in order to force proof that Patience and Meredith

Mae, were indeed, dead. But Father and I produced a will that declared that the estate never be turned over to Malcolm Northrup, not even in the event of her death."

I smiled at how diligently William had followed my requests. I had written in that will that if Meredith Mae and Patience were to be proven dead, the money was to go to several Christian Charities for the care and well being of orphaned children.

"Then how did I finally get my hands on it?" I asked him as I leaned into the bars.

"Boussidan," he whispered.

"Go on," I said.

"It was shortly after this that Jed went to France. Don't you remember that?"

I shook my head. "No, why France?" I asked him.

"He said he was drawn to the country, and of course, Father Jacques..."

"Father Jacques?" I interrupted.

"Yes, he was a great influence on the boy and was able to find a parish in the country, I don't remember the town, but it's not far from Paris."

"Loudun?"

"I don't really retain French. I'm sorry. Anyway, he went abroad and the following year he wrote to his sister Catherine and asked if she might put up his French tutor. It appears his tutor was moving to America to study law. Just until he found a place of his own."

"This tutor?" I asked him. "Was it Louis?"

"Yes. Louis came in 1848 and stayed with Catherine. He even refurbished her home. Have you memory of that?"

"Unfortunately, yes," I said.

"He stayed for quite some time. A year or so, I believe. He became a citizen in 49' and set up a law office on State Street in 1850. He was hired, at some point, by Malcolm and Catherine to help them contest the will."

Silas stopped and stared at me.

"Go on, go on," I said quickly.

"They lost. You lost. No proof of death. The original will was upheld. For God sake, don't you remember anything?"

I shook my head sadly and he continued.

"Clearly, Catherine was madly in love with Louis by this time, and together they must have concocted some hideous plan to steal poor Patience's estate, once they realized that conventional legal channels were lost to them."

"Catherine and Louis?" I said aghast. "What about me? What about Malcolm? Wasn't I involved?"

"I'm sure you were all involved. After Father's murder and my arrest the estate changed hands. The will was destroyed. There was that mysterious fire that burned all the old wills? Anyway, a new one was forged but I could not prove that."

"But Meredith Mae had already returned in 1850."

"Everyone denied that she was really Meredith Mae. She left Brooklyn at the age of ten. And besides, Louis was now in charge of our accounts."

"Why did you sell your practice to him?"

"I never did. Louis has proof of a contract that I never signed."

I stepped back, as if I needed more air. Silas leaned in closer.

"I think they used you, only because they needed your name, but they would have gotten rid of you sooner or later. There's rumor ... There's rumor about you, Malcolm. They would have blackmailed you right out of your share of the estate. They're evil, those two. I'm sorry. I know she's your own daughter but...."

"Rumor?" I said softly

"God bless your transformation," he whispered.

"Thank you," I uttered. I quickly brought him back to the matter at hand. "Who is responsible for your father's murder? If not you, then who?"

"I was nowhere near that office on the afternoon of August 10 th, but I couldn't prove it. Wednesdays are always my gardening days. Anyone would have known that."

I noticed how he clenched his fist and put his forehead to the bar. I felt his despair.

"Where was Boussidan?" I asked quickly.

"He was seen by several people at a Pub on Alistair Street. He dined there every Wednesday. Besides, he was never a suspect."

I was shocked. Clearly, it was Malcolm then who had murdered William. "Good God," I cried. "It was I?"

"No. You dined with your associate at Barron's. You were seen by many people for you argued with the waiter over a discrepancy in your tab. You were loud and caused quite a stir."

It was all he could get out before the guard came and began to escort him back to his cell.

"Wait!" I yelled. "Then who killed William?"

"Good God, man. Isn't it obvious?" And with that he disappeared behind a door.

I took a long breath. Somewhere, the answer was clear but I could not yet accept it, or allow myself to know it.

# Chapter 23

Evening was starting to fall as I walked back to the house on Montague Street. I had sat for hours at the small square by the county jail to ponder how poor William's murder had come about, but my hours in deep meditation had not brought me any closer to the truth. I finally arrived at the conclusion that a triggerman must have been hired to carry out the crime and all I needed to do was prove the conspiracy and who was behind it.

The air felt cool and pleasant against my borrowed flesh as I walked. The sun appeared as an enormous orange ball that began a dramatic decent behind the perfect crescent of the earth. Women in beautiful pastel dresses passed me by with smiles and gentle, nodding heads. Men walked gaily at their sides with their arms extended in a proud manly showing of chivalry. They too, nodded as I passed — a gentleman's acknowledgment between us. I smiled to myself at how privileged I felt in the flesh of a wealthy man. Children called me "sir" and circled me with laughter as they ran in playful pursuit of each other. How glorious to feel utterly winsome, to be completely alive and contained in this conformity of pure and passive innocence. I blessed the beauty of this glorious experience — a moment in which only love of life existed, without the tedium of order, and the despair of death.

There was no one home at the house on Montague Street when I entered. I was curious and wondered where they were, my Meredith Mae and Emie. I had so much to tell them. I hoped they could shed some light on who might have killed William and how I could prove it to the authorities.

The house was welcoming. We had left the front windows opened and the evening air blew in with the scent of hyacinth and roses. I realized, that since my return, I had not had the time to truly revisit this house that I so loved. Now, I needed that solace and I walked through the rooms touching the frames around the doors and stroking the backs of chairs. The rooms welcomed me with a sweet tranquility as I gazed with approval at the tasteful revisions. I remembered how large the house had seemed when I first saw it from my hazy opacity as Patience Stokes. It had been a considerable structure for its time and had looked to me like a great white temple. The house had curves and there was a swirl to the staircase that I had not seen in other houses of the century. The rooms were regal and yet not overbearing. I was glad that Malcolm, at least, had the taste to honor its character.

I went into the library on the second floor, a room I had not been in since my return. I lit the oil in the lamp and sat in a comfortable chair with beautifully clawed arms. I noticed the books on the shelves were all leather-bound and did not look familiar. I stood and began to read the titles. I found there Hobbes, Descarte, Spinoza, Aristotle. "How odd," I mused, and wondered if this were Emie's taste in reading for I myself had nothing but literature, and of course, the Bible. Though I searched the shelves, I found no Bible and the only literature the shelves held were some obscure texts that I had no familiarity with. I took one book from the shelf and sat back down with it. It was a large dusty book and I could not read the language, for it was written in German, but some words were familiar to me and I was able to interpret brutal references to the measures taken against German witches by Pope Innocent VII in 1484.

I was a bit aghast to find such a book in my library. I lay my head back against the soft contours of the chair to contemplate who might have changed the collection of literature that I had cherished. I knew that Malcolm had never had an interest in books of any kind, with the exception of Almanacs. Yet, I saw not one Almanac on the shelf. As my eyes searched the room I noticed the table upon which I had kept the music boxes, the ones that were given to Patience before her marriage. I walked to one that did not look familiar to me and opened the lid. It played a beautiful waltz by Johann Strauss, *The Redetzky March.* "How very lovely," I crooned. I noticed that the entire room was filled with a beautiful collection of music boxes, some as tiny as a pin chest.

"I cannot believe that Malcolm would care for such sweet and delicate beauty," I said aloud.

The laughter was low at first, as if it were only over my shoulder. I shuddered, for the room had suddenly turned quite cold. The oil in the lamp lowered though I had not touched it.

"Who goes there?" I whispered.

It was then I sensed a presence in an old wooden chair that was turned away from me. I stood transfixed, unable to move. I saw that the wind had turned quite fierce and had picked up the drapes with a sweep as they blew towards me.

"Welcome home, Annabel," the devil spoke.

The air was now cold upon my flesh and I felt chilled.

"Who goes there?" I commanded, though I knew who sat there as surely as I knew that he would turn in his chair to face me and that I would be held in his sight like a tack on a magnet's rim.

"Annabel," he spoke again.

The dim light from the lamp cast shadows in his eyes as they flickered in collusive dominance and he appeared from behind a natural darkness like the vision of the moon on a black sky. I noticed, with horrified fascination, that he sat staring at me in the garb of a Catholic Priest. The hair that fell to his shoulders glistened so golden from out of this illusive illumination that it appeared as a halo, as if he were an angel of God.

I spat out sarcastically, "Father Jacques, I presume?"

On his lap he held a Bible. I recognized it as my own. The cover so frayed, and yet, the title remarkably untouched and clear.

"You were looking for this?" He held it up but I said nothing. When I did not reach to take it. He tossed it on the floor.

"Nonsense," he said. "Utter nonsense. I never quite believed it."

"Leave my house at once!" I ordered. "You are not welcomed here."

"Your house?" he bellowed and laughed so loudly that the very foundation seemed to shake from it. "Why, this is my house, Annabel. This is my favorite century so I have adopted it as my own. Now, I return for my wealth and my wife, and I find you in the most ungainly flesh. Tsk, tsk."

"I am not the wife of Urbain Grandier. I am the wife of a man whose flesh you stole."

I looked in his eyes as squarely as I could, for the fire from them seared my flesh. It was a frightening experience to confront this demon, this disciple of the devil, as beautiful as any God.

"You ambiguous bastard," I wanted to cry out. He might have easily been called Adonis or Zeus. I trembled before him though I did my best not to.

He stood and came toward me. He towered over Malcolm, who was not a short man.

I noticed the squared off lines of his jaw and the great broad shoulders under the priest's robe. As he held the cross in his fingers, I noticed the smoke that fizzled from his flesh. He smiled at me as his skin continued to burn.

"If you were a prettier man, dear Annabel. I would have my way with you. Perhaps, I should anyway." He walked close to me and spun me around. "Perhaps, you are not so bad." He laughed loudly, as I released myself from his hold and ran to the bible. I held it up before me like a shield.

"Begone, demon!" I screamed.

He was laughing so hysterically now that he had to sit. I noticed that he rubbed his eyes with his hands.

"The bible means nothing to me, little Annabel. No power there. It's useless information. Don't tell me you believe the rubbish of those old fanatics."

I held the bible close to my chest and bent my lips to kiss the edges.

"Jesus," I whispered. "Send him back to hell."

"Ha!" He spat at me. "You fool! Why not worship Goethe or Spinoza? Jesus was a bully to inflict such dribble on humanity for three millenniums."

I looked up quickly. "Three millenniums?" I remembered what Philippe had told me, the discovery of God in 3082. "What happens then?" I asked him.

He came and knelt before me and took my hands in his.

"The dark decent. The age of despair. The shattering of hope." He rose to kiss me then, he was hard upon my lips. I felt his arms force back my own, until I could not move.

"You bastard!" I screamed as I turned my head to spit out the saliva he had left on my lips. "God lives," I wept, and managed to free myself from his embrace. "Jesus will not die. Not ever."

He slapped me then, so hard that I fell back and felt my neck as it snapped. He had stunned me, but he had not killed me.

"You share your aunt's blindness, Annabel. Jesus hides in parables. I am alive in man. I foretell the future, like Nostrodomus. Jesus is lost to antiquity and to the feeble prayers of those who praise him. I host humanity. The world is my kingdom. Jesus lies beneath the stones and weeps. I walk among the clouds and laugh." He came to me and took both my hands again. "Am I of God?" he asked me. "Or is God of me? Did I need the challenge of God's eternal goodness to amuse me for eternity, or was I created to amuse God?"

With that, he took my head and pressed it against his testicles so that I felt them forced against my mouth. He pressed me hard against him until I ached from it. I heard him laugh as he continued to press, and the organ grew from behind the priests robe as he continued to force my face between his legs.

"Behold, Annabel," he whispered. "God's creation or mine?"

In a flash, he was gone. I sat, unable to move for several minutes, and then, just as I was able to lift myself from the floor; I heard the front door slam from below. Meredith Mae called out my name.

"Grandmamma!" I could hear the distress in it.

"What is it? What's wrong?" I asked her as she flew into the room.

"I've been looking for you everywhere. I even went to Catherine's. She said you left there by eleven."

"I spoke to Silas, and then I sat by the old square near the jail," I told her. "You've been crying. What is it?"

"Emie is gone. She went to Philippe and Papa. I tried to pass through with her, but she forbade it and insisted I stay here with you."

My heart sunk. I had hoped we would all be able to pass into the dimension that held my son and Philippe, but I also knew how concerned she was about her brother's wound.

"Do not worry," I whispered. "She will return them to us safely. I am glad she was finally able to move through."

I kept my arm around Meredith Mae. The devil's presence seemed to linger about us, like must after a long rainy season.

"I have had a visitor from hell," I told her.

"Urbain?"

I nodded.

"Well," she looked up at me sadly. "You are about to witness yet another demon. It is Thursday evening. Malcolm always visits his father on Thursday evenings. You probably should keep up the tradition or the old man will just come here looking for you."

"Perhaps he can shed some light on William's murder," I told her. "I'll leave promptly."

As I stood to gather my things I heard the devil's laughter reverberate in the angry thrusts of the wind as it threatened a late summer storm. But it was not low and manly laughter as it had been in the library. What I heard was a maniacal, staccato giddiness that followed me through the streets of Brooklyn like an evil child in pursuit of a weaker soul to torment. I pulled my hat down over my eyes as the sky opened. I barely made it to Ebenezer's door before the rain raged in a thunderous outburst, and fell about me like a sword from the ancient god, Zeus, demanding reverence.

# Chapter 24

No one answered my knock as I stood huddled under a partition before Ebenizer's house on Willow Street. The rain continued to saturate my suit as I rapped upon the door. I feared the lightning would certainly strike me from behind as it shattered the night with an uncanny repetition. I was just about to investigate whether or not there was a rear door to try when Beth-Ann suddenly peered her head out and called to me. I was startled to see her, for it was Ebenezer I had expected.

"Father, what happened to your key?"

I hurried inside and immediately took off my hat, which had been thoroughly drenched. She took it from me and shook it furiously. I watched as the rainwater fell to the floor and lay on the wet wood, causing tiny puddles around her feet.

"I will get you some hot tea. Meanwhile, give me your coat. We'll hang it in the back to dry."

I got out of my coat and looked for the old man.

"Leave your shoes here and I'll bring you a pair of Papa's slippers," she said as she left the room. I noticed she spoke very quickly and her eyes darted all over, never resting anywhere.

"Thank-you, daughter," I called to her and walked into a large parlor after removing my shoes. I assumed Ebenezer was somewhere in

151

the house for certainly he would not be out in this horrid storm.

The parlor was dark and the drapes were drawn against the city street. I had an uncomfortable feeling as I stood looking at the room, as though I were seeing something cast aside, something once precious to someone but no-longer valuable. The lamps were lit low but I was still able to notice how terribly untidy the room was. There were papers thrown all over the floor and used pipes were left on tables that had not been cleaned. The ashtrays still held tobacco and some of the chairs had torn threads in the faded fabric.

I walked to the fireplace and stared at a large oil painting of two small girls. The children in the painting appeared wickedly and sadly mature. It unnerved me to look at them. There was something salacious about the entire environment that thoroughly disgusted me.

I was still staring at the painting when Beth-Ann appeared with my tea and the slippers. She handed me the cup and then sat before me to put the slippers on my feet. I noticed she caressed my legs a moment before sliding on the soft leather shoes that had to be worked a bit to fit Malcolm's extra large foot. She sat across from me and continued to move her eyes quickly, as though she were searching for something.

Finally, I spoke."How are you this evening, daughter?"

"Proper, Father. Very proper."

She spoke so quickly that I barely understood her.

"And Rachel?" I inquired. "How is Rachel?"

" Also proper, Father. Rachel is a proper girl."

I noticed that I myself was picking up her speed as I asked her where the child was.

It was then she giggled. "She's a good girl, you know. A very good girl."

"Yes, yes." I said. I realized she did not answer my question directly so I asked her where "Papa" was.

She giggled again. "A very proper man," she said, "papa is."

*Oh dear,* I thought to myself. *The girl is quite deranged.*

I sighed deeply and sat back in my chair. I noticed the dust that flew about me as I positioned my body against the cushions.

"You look different, Father," she said to me.

"Oh, yes. My beard. I have shaved it."

"Oh."

"Tell me, Beth-Ann, " I began. I wanted to see if I could, at least, get some information out of her. "Were you ever asked to identify Meredith Mae for that attorney Catherine hired?"

152

"Of course," she whispered as she leaned down and began to pick up tiny debris from the rug. I could not exactly tell what it was she had found to extricate.

"And you could not identify her?" I continued.

"Of course not," she said as she continued to pick at the debris. She had positioned herself so far over the rug that I could not see her face.

"Tell me dear, where is your husband?"

By this time I was quite concerned that a woman who appeared this incompetent was bringing up a child and I prayed, at the very least, that the father was cognizant. She raised her head to look at me, but said nothing.

"Your husband, dear girl. Where is he?"

Her eyes kept darting all over the room and never met my own. It is difficult to explain but I knew she was staring directly at me, from her perspective, even though her eyes never ceased their movement. I remained silent for several moments, awaiting her answer, but she only continued to sit and move her eyes about.

I stood quickly. I burned with a fever that I was sure had scorched my flesh but I did not know what had caused it. *What in God's name is the matter with me?* I wondered. I felt so dizzy I thought I might fall. From a great distance I heard the devil's laughter, like the annoying hum of a ubiquitous fly, and in a flash, Ebenizer stood before me as if he had been flown in from some unknown destination.

"Malcolm, my boy. What has kept you?"

I stared at the old man though I wanted to knock him down. He was as thin as a twig, and his scalp was pink and covered with large brown marks and wisps of thin white hair. His chin hung like a chicken's gullet and his teeth were as brown as the used tobacco in the unwashed ashtrays.

"Father," I said. "I was held up with some business at hand. My apologies."

He laughed as he winked at me and walked slowly to a chair. "Ah, well, you are here now," he said, as he used his cane to help drop his body into the torn and once regal button back chair. Once he was seated he turned to smile at me. "What business at hand has you so busy, boy?"

"I am trying to clear Silas' name. I do not believe he killed his father," I told him as I stared into his eyes. He was breathing very heavily and he kept placing his tongue under his lip and moving it as though he were utilizing it as a toothpick.

"What do you care whether or not Silas killed his father?" he asked, as he stared now at Beth Ann, who still continued to pick tiny pieces of debris from the rug. I noticed she put the debris into the palm of her other hand, though I saw not one speck of anything there.

"An innocent man is in prison. Haven't I some responsibility for that?"

He laughed and I could swear I heard his bones rattle. "No, I don't believe you do," he said.

"What do you know of the murder, Father?"

I leaned forward now in the dusty old chair and held my hands together in front of-me. The old man raised his eyes to the ceiling a bit and then closed them as he spoke.

"Crazy family you married into, boy. That wife of yours can trace her line right back to them Salem witches."

"What has Maebelle's family to do with any of this?" I asked.

He opened his eyes and looked at me, eyes shadowed by mountains of skin and haunted like the blood eyes of a slaughtered calf.

"Well, I always thought it was funny when that girl of Maebelle's came home, after all them years, and proclaimed herself as Patience's granddaughter. Well, we knew she was telling the truth, but be damned if we'd let on to that, hey boy?" He laughed and slapped his leg. "She was still the same little pretty thing she was when she left."

"So you wouldn't identify her?" I asked, sitting up further in my chair until I was almost at the edge.

"Hell, no. What's the matter with you, boy?" He leaned his head back and closed those awful eyes. "Yes, pretty thing she was. Ah, pretty, pretty little thing. We tried to get our hands on that one, hey son?"

When I didn't answer he turned to me and smiled.

"Well, got ya that house and all that money, didn't it, son?"

I lowered my eyes and stared at the tip of the old man's shoe.

"Nice house up there by the river, hey, boy? Strange though, the way that Priest came in and redid it right before you got it, lucky thing for you. Damn place looks like a museum. Must be worth a fortune."

I swallowed so hard I almost choked. "What?" I exclaimed. "Father Jacques? Why would he redo my house?"

"What are you all excited for now? You got it, didn't you? What do you care?"

I wondered why neither Emie nor Meredith Mae had mentioned that it was Father Jacques who had decorated the house in my absence.

"When did Father Jacque refurbish the house?" I asked the old man as he looked at me quizzically.

"What's the matter with your memory, boy, and where the hells that beard of yours?"

"Look, Father. This is important. When did the Priest restore my house?"

"Right after Meredith Mae came back. Before that, there was some servant girl living there and she wouldn't let the Priest touch it. Then, when Patient's granddaughter returned, Father Jacques talked her into restoring it. Told her it had once belonged to his grandfather, or some bull crap like that. Anyway, the girl thought the place was tired and agreed to it. Damn Priest has money. They say he don't honor his vows, you know," Ebenizer laughed. "Those priests must want it bad, uh?"

I sank back into the chair and held my face in my hands.

"Child is waiting for you, boy." I heard him say.

"Who do you think killed William Davenport, Father?"

"Ask that slick little French boy. The one that's got Catherine lifting her skirts." He leaned forward on his cane and smiled so broadly that I could see every rotten tooth in his mouth.

"Or better yet, ask Catherine." He laughed loudly and used his cane to position himself comfortably. "Go on to the girl, Malcolm, before she falls asleep."

I walked to Beth-Ann so that I stood between her and the old man.

"Where is the child?" I asked her.

She didn't answer me but I followed her eyes up the stairs and surmised that Rachel was in one of the upstairs rooms.

Suddenly, I understood what Maebelle had meant by contrition. I leaned in close to her face and whispered, "God forgive you."

I climbed up the stairs and called out Rachel's name. I walked down the hall and looked in the tiny bedrooms but it wasn't until I got to the far room that I found her.

She lay in a large bed with crumpled, dirty sheets that smelled like the old man's breath. The girl was not crying but she held her fists tight on the sheets and looked past me.

"Rachel?" I whispered.

She did not answer me. I came and sat at the edge of the bed. I felt her body stiffen, but still, she did not look at me.

I reached to take her hand and it lay listless in mine. I brought my hand to her face and tenderly brushed her long dark hair aside and stroked the tiny cheeks. I felt the tears form in my eyes. The child glared at me.

I took her in my arms and felt her body go limp at my touch, as if she would not have cared if I had strangled the very life from her. I wept, as if my tears could choke this wretched Malcolm to death and cleanse the earth of this evil violation of human dignity, of this violence against goodness, and this malevolent attack against innocence.

"You're safe now, little girl," I told her. "There will be no more harm to you."

I picked the child up in my arms, but not before I wrapped her in a blanket I found in an open chest that reeked of nidorous fumes, as if charred by fire. I then took her downstairs. The old man and Beth Ann stood to their feet when they saw me.

"Father, where are you taking her?" Beth Ann ran toward me.

"Malcolm, what are you doing?" Ebenezer asked as he tottered at the end of his cane.

I walked to Beth Ann. It was not pity I felt, and yet I knew that pity would have been entirely appropriate.

"You bring your own daughter here to be raped by this vermin?" I said to her as I turned to Ebenezer.

"Watch your mouth, boy." Ebenezer raised his cane and I realized he still had the strength of a much younger man.

Beth Ann looked at me in that odd way of not looking at me. "Papa is a fine man. A fine and proper man," she said as her eyes darted. She began to pace back and forth. "Papa is a very fine man, a very fine man!" she screamed at me.

I walked to the old man. "If you send the authorities for this child I will break every bone in your body. I will snap off your limps as if you were tonight's dinner."

The old man came toward me as if he might strike me, but I must have frightened him because he thought better of it, and retreated.

"What the hell is the matter? You want the little whore? Go on, take her."

Ebenezer shrugged his shoulders and walked back into the parlor. I looked at Beth Ann, who was still pacing. "You will obey me, daughter," I said, "You are not to come for this child, or send anyone for her. Is that understood?"

I noticed that she nodded and only ceased her pacing when she picked up Malcolm's shoes and shoved them in my hand. She slammed the door behind me and began to scream out what a good man Ebenezer was. I could hear her screaming it over and over again, even after I was halfway down the block with the child. I walked quickly, until all I heard was the wind spinning around, causing bracelets of leaves to jingle in a sweet beckoning dance above me, and Beth Ann's screaming was finally lost to distance.

The storm had retreated back to heaven, as if leaving atonement for the violence. There was now a gentle calm upon the earth. The night was cool and alive with the sparkle of stars. I took the night air deep into my lungs.

The child lay limp in my arms and looked at me with terrifying mistrust.

"Don't worry, precious girl. I am taking you as far out of hell as I can," I told her, and tenderly kissed her forehead.

"What have we here?" Meredith Mae asked as she took the child from my arms.

"Put her to sleep. I have taken her, though I haven't a clue as to what I will do with her now."

I leaned my hands on the banister for support. I was exhausted and realized I hadn't slept in days. I wanted to question Meredith Mae about Father Jacques and why on earth she had ever allowed him to refurbish our home, but I could barely stand. I followed my granddaughter upstairs with the child and stopped briefly at the door while she tucked Rachel under the covers.

"I wish to question you about Father Jacques but I cannot stay awake another minute. We must talk, though."

"Of course, Grandmamma. Sleep now. I'll be here when you awaken."

I kissed her goodnight and retired to my room. I barely remember getting out of my clothes, but I must have managed, for when I awoke the next morning I was in my nightdress and had slept quite comfortably for over twelve hours. I did not remember my visit with Emie right away. It was not until I opened my eyes and lay there staring at the ceiling for several moments before I recalled it. I suddenly remembered that I had been awakened by a gentle shaking at least an hour before dawn. When I opened my eyes, I could barely make her out in the darkness, but then, she leaned down close to my ear and spoke to me.

"Mommy. It is I. Emie. Don't be frightened."

"Emie?" I sat straight up in bed and hugged her tightly. "Where are the others?" I whispered.

"They are not with me. I'm afraid I will be going back. I just wanted you to know that we are fine. As fine as we can be under the circumstances."

"What do you mean?" I asked as I took her hands.

'Oh, Mommy, it is unbearably hot where we are and the oppressive stench of blood is everywhere. It is so crowded that I must sleep on the floor," she said sadly.

"That war?" I asked her. "The one you mentioned?"

"Yes, it is the War Between the States. I wear the old clothes of a soldier who died just as I arrived, for my dress became soiled after I assisted in the amputation of a man's arm, despite violent protests from the soldiers who would not trust a Negro with such a task, much less a woman. How strange to travel the barriers of space and not find paradise at the end of my journey. How brutal to know the outcome of history and have no power to prevent its misfortunes."

I looked at her sadly. "A war on our land?" I asked incredulously.

Again she nodded. "I'm afraid so. It is 1865 and the War Between the States has been killing our soldiers for over four years now. I studied this war in history class, Mommy.It was a noble war to abolish slavery, and yet, no war is ever really noble. How can it be? It was a war fought for a human cause yet these dead men will never know their victory."

"Philippe?" I asked.

"Philippe is in great pain. There are several wounded men here. We are trying to heal them so that they can be sent back to the battlefields, though I regret to see them regain their strength, knowing their fate. They are bitter and frightened, and many of them will die before the war's end. Philippe has a bad head wound. The soldiers assume he is a runaway and he is kept downstairs beyond that door you saw during your meditation."

"And Matthew?" I asked. "My son?"

"He has learned to be a doctor. At least, that's what the men believe he is, and he is doing a fine job assisting the others," she told me.

"Why is he there?"

"I don't think even he knows the answer to that. He wound up in a Pastor's house in Virginia, in the year 1860, when he passed through time and space to follow Elizabeth, but she is not here, and if she is, we cannot find her."

"Then why not come back?" I asked her.

"Matthew will not leave Philippe's side and his wound prevents him from moving his soul."

I sighed deeply, as Emie snuggled beside me in the bed and took my hands. I noticed that she carried the foul odor of death and blood on her clothes.

"The men are kept upstairs in the bedrooms and the Pastor's living room is used for operations," she told me. "Philippe appeared in 1861. He was mistaken for a runaway slave and shot in the leg. After the war started, he remained with Matthew to help the Pastor with the wounded soldiers and whatever doctors could be brought from Richmond."

"How many years have they been in that place?" I cried out.

"Papa has been there almost five years. Philippe was shot a second time, an irate soldier claimed that he was responsible for the death of his friend and tried to kill him. Philippe's wound was to the head and much more severe than his first wound. He is lucky to be alive, but he is very weak and certainly does not have the strength to move his body through space. But neither he nor Matthew would leave this place if they could, not until the war has ended and the last soldier has been tended to."

"And when will that be?" I turned to her quickly.

"Philippe and I know that the war will end soon at Appomattox and we have told them to expect the Union victory."

I ran my hands through my hair. "What of Elizabeth?" I whispered.

"Matthew says he has no idea where she is for her soul does not respond to his call. He tells me he was drawn to this time and place in chronology, but he doesn't know why, since Elizabeth seems so absent. He is distraught and has thrown his grief into saving these men. He openly protests slavery. Before the battles began, he and the Pastor set up a route to help the runaways. Many people are sensitive to the cause and have offered shelter to the bondsmen. The Pastor's house is now used as a hospital for it is not far from Petersburg, where a gruesome battle is being fought. Though slavery is rapidly losing its appeal, the Confederates still feel they will be redeemed for this war because they believe that God sanctions slavery. How can I tell them, Mommy, that God is not the white mans dominion? So many of them will die like slaughtered beasts believing that it is somehow noble to go to war and kill so that dignity can remain only with the white and the wealthy. What maniac created it so? The only nobility I see is in their blindness."

I took her hand, for I felt her pain, as if it were my own.

"And what of my ancestors, Mommy?" She smiled sadly. "Did they rejoice in this war? The context of slavery has made it inevitable that we fight this atrocity, but what fatal act of cruelty ever acknowledged slavery as the right of property for these fine southern families to begin with?" She clenched her fists and I knew that whatever she had seen had left its scar across her vision so that no future chronology could ever be known without this knowledge.I put my arms around her and tried to comfort her, but I knew my white flesh had incorporated the delusion of superiority, taught, and administered by fools, but none-the-less, instilled for centuries in the collective consciousness of Caucasian descents.

Almost, as if she read my mind, she continued.

"White people often show some genteel kindness to people of other colors, but sometimes, I think that it is only a sense of superiority that allows this kindness. I am consumed with anger, but it is not greater than my despair. If we can lay this all at Satan's feet, I will feel more inclined to forgive my white brothers and sisters for this shameful violation of human dignity. If only I was protected from history, by the illusion of death, but I am not. The misery of this war has scared our souls before God even though the most precious sacrifice lay at our feet. Man's inhumanity and the karmic retribution of that inhumanity, never ceases. If we do not honor life, we will die in the fires of war. I have seen the future, Mommy, and there is nothing to protect it from the past. God will not seek vengeance but certainly must cry out in shame at our atrocities."

With that, she held me tightly and vanished before I could hold her. Before I could tell her that we are all foolish souls, adrift in our own delusions, before I could tell her how very much I loved her.

# Chapter 25

The next morning, I relayed Emie's visit to Meredith Mae and we sat together in silence and held each other's hands. I knew that we were both saying a prayer for their safety.

"Emie said the end was near. The final battle at Appomattox, I believe she said, was approaching," I turned to Meredith Mae hopefully.

"How horrifying. A war on our own soil, how absolutely horrifying," she said.

In the meanwhile, I insisted we meditate that evening and search infinity, if need be, for Elizabeth's whereabouts. I could feel my son's grief, and I knew that if he could call out to me it would be in a plea for Elizabeth's safety. He would want me to use this great power that he believes I have to find his beloved. I sent a promise, from the depths of my existence, that I would attempt to call upon this illusive power to command her presence. I hoped, somehow, that he heard my words.

Rachel sat in the very same chair that Emie had used during our meditation and listened, somewhat distractedly, to our conversation. I noticed that Meredith Mae had come up with some new clothes for her during my slumber and the child looked quite beautiful perched upon the pillows, clutching a new doll that seemed almost a replica, with large round eyes that stared at nothing in particular but seemed aware of everything.

"How are you this morning, Rachel?" I asked her.

"Fine," she answered to the doll that she held before her and danced on her lap.

I had no idea how on earth I would be able to protect her and wondered if she had any magic of her own.

"Rachel..." I began, as I walked to the chair, and as gracefully as possible, considering the flesh I inhabited; I knelt before her. "How do I look to you?"

She continued to dance the doll on her lap and did not respond.

"Am I pretty, Rachel?"

The child nodded but I could not be sure if she were answering to the doll or to me.

Gently, I took the doll away from her. She looked into my eyes with a horrible scowl on her face and pressed her lips so tightly together that I feared she would crack a tooth. Still, I pursued. I had to know if this power from God had been passed in the bloodline. It took only a sip of opium before Maebelle saw the face of Annabel Horton. I had to know if her grandchild had at least as much power. I knew that I would never be able to leave her behind should we ever have to move our souls through to another dimension.

"Rachel, describe my face. I want you to do that."

She held out the doll to me and stuck out her tongue. I sighed and returned to my chair.

"It is obvious she sees me as Malcolm," I said to Meredith Mae, "She clearly hates me."

"She is only a child and she has been through a lot." Meredith Mae gently touched my shoulder as she got up and took the girl to the kitchen where I presumed she would make her some toast and cereal. I sat and waited for them to return to the parlor. I felt restless and I noticed that I craved the cigar that sat nonchalantly on the table upon which I rested my arm. "How unusual," I mused. I picked up the cigar and put the end of it to my lips. I noticed how enjoyable it felt to hold the thing in my mouth and taste the sweet tobacco. I found myself reaching for a match. I was in the process of lighting the cigar when Meredith Mae walked back into the room.

"Grandmother!" she screamed at me. "What on earth are you doing?"

"Smoking." I laughed as I tossed the match in the glass tray and puffed the smoke out before me. Meredith Mae sat aghast and stared at me without closing her mouth.

"Aaah," I sighed. "Very pleasurable."

"Grandmamma, you'll develop a habit."

"Nonsense," I quipped, and continued to puff and run my tongue over the wet paper as I held it between my lips. "Now, tell me about Father Jacques. Why did you permit him the luxury of decorating our home?"

"This house belonged to his family. Did you know that, Grandmamma?"

I took the cigar from my mouth, though I already missed it. "Meredith Mae, this house was built in 1806 by Michele Guyon, or at least someone posing to be your grandfather. The bastard left the house to me. The deed says 'Guyon', not Grandier or Father Jacques."

"But he seemed so adamant. He insisted that the house had been in his family for years and his brother was the last to live in it. He practically broke out in tears when he relayed how his brother was killed abroad, just before his plans to refurbish it. He asked me if he could please honor his brother's memory and restore it to the specifications left in several drawings that he produced for me. They were very beautiful. How could I refuse? He begged me, Grandmamma. And he is a Priest."

"Why didn't Father Jacques inherit the house?"

"Perhaps, it felt too grand for a Priest and he sold it to Grandfather."

"What was his brother's name?" I asked her.

"He never said."

"Who paid for the restorations?"

"He insisted on using his own money, though I offered to share the cost. He said the church would never allow him to spend his money in so frivolous a fashion and he asked if it could be our secret."

"How very generous of him. And you agreed?"

"I agreed and promised to let him come and spend time here. He's a kind man, Grandmamma."

"You do not recognize evil, do you, child?" I asked her.

She looked at me quizzically.

"I do not believe that Father Jacques is evil," she said sternly. "When Malcolm produced that new will and took the house over, it was Father Jacques that offered me shelter."

"Father Jacques' real name is Urbain Grandier, and he is the devil's disciple, not God's," I said softly.

"I love you, Grandmamma. You know that, but I do not accept everything you say as the gospel."

"Urbain Grandier is probably responsible for all of our grief. He is only using your naiveté to take back his due, for I assume we lie in the lap of luxury because he has willed it. But the devil has a price, Meredith Mae."

She stared at me as if she did not understand where I could get such thoughts.

"I see no similarity between Urbain and Father Jacques," she said to me.

"Have you ever seen Urbain?" I asked her.

"No, I have not, but you have never seen Father Jacques."

"That is not entirely true," I said, just as the doorbell chimed. We looked at each other for a brief moment. I could see the pain in her eyes, for she hated disagreeing with me, but I knew she was unrelenting in her trust of this Priest. She kissed me briefly before answering the door.

Louis Boussidan entered our foyer with a large folder tucked under his arm.

"Mademoiselle Guyon, your stepfather? He is here?"

"Oh, yes. Right this way," she said and led him into the parlor.

Louie entered the room quickly. I noticed there was an unusual effeminacy about his walk and wondered if it were a French characteristic. He took Meredith Mae's hand and brought it to his lips after he acknowledged my presence. He then made a grand and eloquent bow.

"I am honored to see you again, Miss Guyon," he said in his most charming French dialect.

He turned to me and extended his hand. He immediately noticed the cigar burning in the ashtray and looked around.

"Have you company?" he asked me.

"Oh, no," I told him quickly. "Have a seat, Louie."

He sat opposite Meredith Mae and I noticed the way his eyes traveled over her face, as if startled by the grace of the sun's shadow on a mountain. Finally, he smiled.

"Pardon me, Mademoiselle Guyon, for staring, but your beauty often takes me by surprise."

"Thank-you, sir," she said demurely.

"It is a fine summer day, is it not, Mademoiselle Guyon?" he said with a smile.

"Please, sir, call me, Meredith Mae."

He smiled at her once more, and sat more comfortably back in his chair. "And you will call me, Louie?"

I brought the cigar to my lips once again and felt quite drugged by the aroma of the smoke as it hit my nostrils. The two of them appeared to be flirting, as their eyes were engaged in a chase of long legato glances. I puffed until I was blowing a good deal of smoke into the room, and at one point, I coughed badly. Louis eyed me oddly.

"Is something wrong, Louie?" I asked him.

"No, no nothing, Monsieur Northrup. It is nothing. I have brought the papers."

He opened his folder quickly and got out some documents.

"I have set up the estate as it was intended for Meredith Mae and....."

"The value?" I interrupted.

"Well, that is hard to say."

He held the documents in his hand and looked at me.

"Try," I quipped.

"Well, several million... but we cannot know an exact figure, the estate holds various assets."

"And my twenty-five percent, then. How much does that equal?"

"Approximately ten million dollars, minus of course, Catherine's two percent."

"And you, Louie?"

He looked uncomfortably at Meredith Mae.

"These figures are approximate values, but I would guess, several million as well."

"I see." I put my cigar down and stared at him. "I intend to employ my own lawyer to renegotiate your 'fee' as you call it."

He looked at me as if he might strike me.

"Tell me, Louie, what is your opinion?" I asked him.

"Opinion? On what?"

"On who killed William Davenport?" I said simply.

He looked uncomfortably at Meredith Mae and then turned to me.

"I believe that Silas killed his father. There was a witness."

"Yes, yes, Catherine, my dear daughter. How convenient."

"Do you doubt the word of your own daughter?" he asked me, with a familiar raise to his brow.

"Let us just say that I do not believe that Silas murdered his father."

"Then what do you believe?" he asked me with an odd smirk on his face."

"Leave the documents for me to go over. I will sign the necessary papers and bring them to you in the morning." I said and dismissed him.

"You have not answered my question, Malcolm."

He sought my eyes.

"In due time, we will know the truth."

I let my eyes lock with his and felt an unsettling arousal.

He ignored the implication and continued, "I have drawn up a will for Catherine," he told me. "You are her beneficiary. That is, until she marries. I have brought you a copy."

"How amusing." I smiled as I took the contract from his hand and looked it over.

"And if you should die, Malcolm. Your assets go to Catherine. Is that correct?"

"Draw me up a new will, Louie. My assets go to Matthew Guyon."

"Matthew Guyon? Who is he?" Louie asked incredulously.

"My father, sir," Meredith Mae told him. "He has been missing, but we believe he is not dead."

"And if he should never return, Meredith Mae receives his share. She will be the executrix of my estate."

"And to Catherine, or the rest of your children?"

"Nothing."

He looked at me as if I were somewhat insane as he stood and reached out for my hand.

"As you wish, Malcolm," he said into my eyes.

Meredith Mae also stood and offered Louie her hand. He held it for a moment and smiled sweetly as he brought it to his lips.

"Mademoiselle Guyon," he said softly. "Can you ever forgive me for any grief I might have caused you?"

"I hold no animosity toward you, Louie," she answered softly.

"Would you honor me then with a carriage ride this Sunday? We can ride through Cadman Plaza. It is lovely there."

To my great dismay, my precious granddaughter blushed like a schoolgirl and agreed to see him. I almost protested, when all of a sudden, Rachel came running from the kitchen and began to giggle and throw her arms around Louie. I was shocked to see the child so animated.

"What have we here? Little Rachel?" he asked.

"You know the child?" I caught Meredith Mae's eye. She looked on as puzzled as I was. Rachel seemed to be squealing in delight.

"We are old friends." He laughed as he twirled her around. "Old friends."

"We have never seen her like this. Why, she is a different child," I mused.

"Really? How interesting." He turned to Meredith Mae. "Sunday at noon?" He grinned as the child continued to giggle. Meredith Mae nodded and took Rachel's hand as Louie closed the door behind him.

"Well, what to make of that?" she turned to me with a curious expression.

"Rachel," I leaned in toward the child, "how well do you know Louie?"

"Very well. We take the ferry across the river and play make believe almost every weekend."

# Chapter 26

My granddaughter saw a good deal of Louie Boussidan over the next several weeks, despite my disapproval. They often took Rachel with them when they went for long walks near the waterfront. I was perplexed by the relationship between Louie and the girl, who seemed as utterly charmed by the scoundrel as Meredith Mae, but I could only sigh and nod my head when they chatted on and on about this or that amusing ditty that Louie came up with during the course of a day.

I asked Meredith Mae whatever had become of Ursula and I was told she appeared to of vanished into thin air.

"Blown off on her broomstick, I presume?"I laughed gaily.

Meredith Mae shot me an unappealing frown and I decided I would let the matter drop. I was relieved and hoped I'd seen the very last of her anyway.

Catherine was infuriated to learn that she was not the beneficiary in my will and had Louie revise her own will to reflect her philandering spirit. I learned that a percentage of her estate was to be left to the Institute for Medicinal Herbs and Remedies and another ten percent went to some Historical Society for the Preservation of Landmark Buildings. I told her that I was quite pleased with her choices, to which she scowled and told me they were Louie's choices and she cared not a bit where her money went after she was six feet under, as long as I received none of it. She then told me that Louie was to be the executor and primary beneficiary of her estate.

I said nothing. Of course, I thought she was an idiot to trust him, but I was not concerned with Catherine's interest in Louie. It was Meredith Mae's developing infatuation that concerned me and I watched helplessly as she and Rachel spent more and more time with this compelling, yet odious individual.

I thought it best, at the time, to ignore the relationship between them and trust that my darling grandchild would eventually see through his ambiguous veneer; so I concentrated my energy on locating Elizabeth's soul. Since I did not have a clue as to how I would go about proving Silas' innocence I thought my efforts would be better spent discovering Elizabeth's whereabouts, at least for the time being. But I received no contact from her, no sense of her presence, despite my many hours of meditation. Meredith Mae was of little help to me during this time because she was so distracted by Louie's pursuit of her.So, I took my meditations alone and walked the labyrinth that I had painstakingly reconstructed from memory, in the rear yard of our house, under the apple tree that Matthew had loved to climb in his youth.

I did not blame Meredith Mae for her youthful lack of interest. She was clearly falling in love with Louie, even though I intimated that I thought he was nothing more than a handsome French philanderer. She told me not to worry, and insisted that they were only good friends. My attempt to talk seriously about the obvious flaws in Louie's character seemed to fall on deaf ears. I searched all of Brooklyn for an appropriate substitute who could seduce her from Louie's mendacious charm, yet she found fault with every young man I brought to her attention.

"Don't you think Louie has a dark side?" I asked her.

She tossed back that lovely head of hers and laughed gleefully. "He is only pensive, Grandmamma. Not dark. And only sometimes."

"I feel he is mendacious," I said cautiously.

"Oh, poo." She laughed and tossed her curls.

"Even a bit effeminate," I added.

"Oh, Grandmamma." She blushed and avoided further comment.

I sighed and stared at the floor. In my heart of hearts, I was scheming to steal her away to some future dimension as soon as Emie and Matthew returned with Philippe. Yet I feared she would not follow, and that I would be stuck with this insidious little man as my grandson-in-law. I also feared that Meredith Mae would choose to die a natural death, if she were to marry Louie, and that natural death could obliterate the luxury of infinity for her.

Finally, I believed that my prayers had been answered. It was the night I returned home from taking Maebelle to the sanitarium that I had found for her on Long Island. It had been a long trip and I was terribly tired when I arrived back in Brooklyn four days later. I was quite relieved, for I now felt that Maebelle would be well cared for, and maybe even eventually restored to some modicum of sanity in due time. The doctors had given me hope and I had made financial provisions that protected Maebelle for the rest of her life, whether she was restored to sanity or not.

I was happily relaying this to Meredith Mae as we sat in our parlor, when the doorbell chimed, and much to our surprise Catherine stood grinning at us.

"Daughter," I began. "Your mother is going to be fine. I have..."

She cut me off and walked right up to Meredith Mae. "I don't give a damn if the woman falls in a hole and can't find her way up for air."

"You're terribly unkind, Catherine." Meredith Mae put her hands across her chest and glared at her half sister.

Catherine held out her hand. "Haven't you ever noticed my ring?"she said loudly.

Meredith Mae took the hand that Catherine suspended in the air like a puppy's paw and stared at the glistening diamond.

"No, I have not. It's beautiful," she told her.

"Well, you should have noticed it. It's from Louie."

"Louie?" Both Meredith Mae and I spoke at once. I went straight over to Catherine and stared at her finger. The damn ring sparkled back at me like a cluster of stars.

"Why should Louie give you a diamond?" I asked.

"Oh Father, Please. You knew of this. I am to be his wife. We have been engaged for months."

I noticed the quick tears that came into my granddaughter's eyes.

"I must have forgotten," I said.

Catherine turned and glared at me.

"You knew of it, Father, and gave us your blessing. Now you pretend you've had a fall and remember nothing. Just what game are you playing?"

"Well, yes," I stumbled, "I remember nothing of your plans. I am sorry."

I looked despondently at Meredith Mae who had the most heartfelt look.

"Well, let me just remind you that I am engaged to Louie Boussidan." She looked at Meredith Mae with a hideous grin. "He and I have so much in common, secrets that would astound you, secrets you would not want to know."

She bent so close to Meredith Mae that I almost stepped between to separate them.

"Do not flatter yourself into believing that my Louie loves you," she said to her. "He is amusing himself with you. Perhaps he seeks to understand my father's sudden infatuation."

Catherine laughed loudly and abruptly left our home. We could hear her laughter all the way down the street. I went to the window and watched her as she practically skipped away.

When I turned back to Meredith Mae, to comfort her, I realized she had run from the room. I remained where I stood, in an odd state of grace, at once delirious to be rid of that scoundrel, and yet, infuriated beyond reason that he had pierced such a trusting heart.

# Chapter 27

I searched endlessly for Louie but I could not find him. He did not return to his office and he was not dining in any of the restaurants that I was told he frequented. I thought a good thrashing would be most appropriate for dishonoring both women, and then I would finally wash my hands of him for good. But it was Friday evening in late summer and many people with even a modicum of money went to the ocean at Coney Island. I had recently heard him speak of a small house he rented there in the summer months. I assumed I had missed him and would most likely be unable to confront him until his return.

I was absolutely convinced that Louie and Catherine were behind the plot to kill William and frame Silas for the murder. I was just as convinced that Louie would break off his engagement with Catherine now that Meredith Mae stood to inherit fifty percent of her initial fortune. It was clear that Catherine was dispensable and was too much of an egotist to admit it. But I also knew that my granddaughter would eventually be in the utmost danger if she ever agreed to marry Louie, and I knew that is precisely what his objective now was. I decided that I must find something on the bastard that would reveal his true intentions to Meredith Mae, for her innocence gave her no insight into the nature of men. I had to prove his part in this crime as quickly as possible and show the bastard up, otherwise, I feared that this wiry, slippery little scoundrel would double talk his way right back into her heart.

Meredith Mae had mentioned that Louis lived in one of the bachelor row apartments on Clark Street. She had also mentioned that the house was at the end of the street, very near the water, and that it was recognizable by a large brass lion knocker on the front door.

I could see the lights of lower Manhattan as I stood staring across the river. Fortunately, it was a cool evening, well after nine, and I noticed that most people were happily bedded down for the night. There was hardly a soul to notice as I found the building and made my way up the steps. It was just at the moment I entered inside that I almost bumped into a pleasant young man as he passed me at the door.

"Excuse me," I uttered.

"Evening, Mr. Northrup," he said. "Beautiful night, isn't it?"

I was startled that he knew Malcolm by name and realized that Malcolm was no stranger to Boussidan's dwelling. I thought it best to see if I could take advantage of the young man's friendly nature.

"Yes, it is." I returned his smile. "Boussidan? It seems I've forgotten his apartment number. Do you know it?"

Just as I suspected, the young man was most helpful and continued to hold the door open for me. "All the way up, sir," he pointed. "First door at the top of the stairs."

I was breathing heavily by the time I got to the top of the landing. I had to put my hands against the door and rest for several minutes before I had the energy to toy with the lock. I took the clip from my tie and was able to slide it between the door until I could push the lock back. I was then able to turn the doorknob and enter.

The moon was full that evening and afforded me ample light to look around the small apartment. However, I decided to light a lamp so that I would be able to read any incriminating documents. As I walked into the parlor I saw a long desk that appeared to be made of cherry wood. It was accented with some wonderful gold inlay. A large, upholstered chair, framed with a band of acanthus leaves, stood in front of the desk. As I admired the furnishings I assumed that this must be where Louie worked, for I saw books and piles of papers. I sat myself in the chair, lit the lamp, and began to browse through his desk. I observed that most of the papers were letters. I picked up several that began *Dear Papa*, but continued in French, so I could not read them. However, one letter began *My darling Jeanne* and continued in English: *how long must we abide this wretched charade before I can come to you and steal you away from that beast you married? I hope that Count Elemont will vacation long enough for us to be alone. How you would laugh to see me fool the world with my gallantry, my chivalry! I long for your lips, ma Cherie, the corners of your blessed smile to find with my own; and that whisper near the lobe of my ear that produces a delirium to rival the richest opium. Is this bizarre plan worth our separation, my darling? I question that every time I lay with that fool who squashes my flesh. Ah well, soon we will be rich, and it will not matter, and you and I, mon chere, will be as far away as the wings of your magic will take us.*

"Ah, ha!" I whispered, "Why, the little bastard!"

He had not finished the letter and it did not appear to make much sense to me, but it did prove that he was, at least, involved in some plot or other, and there was now even another woman aside from Catherine. I would be able to prove foul play to Meredith Mae. I quickly looked through the neatly stacked books until I found a small spiral that appeared to contain names and addresses. In it I found a listing for a Jeanne Elemont on Charles Street, in Manhattan. I scribbled down the address and wondered how often he visited this woman, since it would not take more than an hour to reach her.

I leaned back in the chair and let my eyes travel over the room. It was beautiful andso light that I barely detected color. There were many small tables around, and at least three settees, upholstered in a powder blue fabric and trimmed in a wooden garland of fruit and flowers. I noticed what appeared to be a woman's cape draped over one of the chairs. I stood to touch it, and found that it was delightfully soft to the touch and lined in purple velvet. I assumed it belonged to this Jeanne Elemont, for it certainly was too sophisticated for Catherine, and Meredith Mae preferred more simple clothes.

The door beyond the parlor led into Louie's bedroom. The bed was large and draped in what appeared to be a brilliant marquetry of floral paneling. There were many pillows piled on the bed. In front of a window that looked out on Clark Street, there was a table, and on it were many colored bottles and paper boxes. It appeared to be a woman's vanity table. "How strange," I muttered as I sat myself down. I found at least a dozen perfume bottles of the sweetest and most alluring scents. "This is most unusual." I chuckled as I continued to snoop. Curiously, I discovered several bottles of glue in a drawer and a collection of the loveliest mahogany boxes, inlayed with gold designs. I stared blankly at the one I held in my hand. It looked curiously familiar. When I raised the lid the tiny box began to play the most beautiful melody. It was unlike anything I had ever heard and I was perplexed that I could not place the tune. I carefully turned it over and found that it was inscribed *To U, from your eternal admirer.*

It was then I surmised that Ursula must share this apartment with her brother because it was much too ridiculously feminine for a man, and the box, of course, appeared to be inscribed to Ursula. I also opened the armoires and found some women's clothes among the many fashionable men's suits. I did not make any important connection, at that time, to the music box. I cringe to think that I could have been so stupid. I was sure that the scoundrel would now be exposed for the libertine that he was and we could dismiss him once and for all. I folded the letter and tucked it neatly away in my vest pocket. I breathed a sigh of relief as I hurried down the stairs and into the summer air.

All the way home I pondered how I would break the news to Meredith Mae about the woman named "Jeanne Elemont," and some obvious intrigue that Louie was involved in. I was anxious about telling her, and relieved to find I would not have to confront the issue until morning, for when I arrived home I found a note on our foyer table from Meredith Mae. She had apparently decided to spend the evening at St. Joseph's and she had taken Rachel with her. She wrote that she would have one of the nuns care for the child while she spent some time alone, to think things through, and to quietly meditate on her own. She told me that I shouldn't worry, that both she and Rachel would return by eight the following morning.

So, now I would be able to give considerable thought as to the most delicate way to present Louie's obvious indiscretions, but unfortunately, I was exhausted that evening and could barely remain awake. The walk from Clark Street was at least a half a mile and it had tired me, and though I was grateful for the extra time alone, Malcolm's poor body reacted in extreme fatigue and I took to my bed almost immediately.

I do not know how long I was asleep before I felt it. I did not open my eyes right away for I had no idea what was happening to me. I only knew it was pleasurable, so pleasurable that opening my eyes was terribly difficult. It actually took several seconds for me to realize that someone was kneeling over Malcolm's body and was riding his stiff, wretched organ as if they were on a horse. I found myself moaning like a dying animal and through this delirium I could hear another voice moaning with my own, as though we were singing a bizarre duet. I forced my eyes opened and looked up. The moonlight was softly silhouetting the body of a woman, though I could not see her clearly. Her dark hair fell before her and covered her face. Her legs were long and fit around Malcolm's bulk with ease. I seemed to be holding the woman up with my hands as she squeezed my palms and began to scream and to laugh at once. I could see the attractive crevice of her breasts and realized they were small and firm. I felt some wild spasms in my body that I could not control, and before I knew it, I felt myself losing touch with everything except this delightful explosion that prevented me from tossing this woman off poor Malcolm's organ.

I finally lay back and opened my eyes once again. Malcolm's wretched heart was beating rapidly and I felt his hair, wet with perspiration, against his brow. The woman slowly lifted her head and stared at me with a smile so iniquitous that I shuddered.

"At last, my darling," she uttered. "We are finally alone."

I blinked several times and continued to stare at her.

She pointed her finger in my face and began to chatter.

"I am so angry at you, bad boy. You move Meredith Mae into the house so we cannot speak. You barge into Louie's office where Catherine overhears everything." Then she leaned in close, so close I felt my heart skip. "Have you lost your mind, *mon chere*?"

"Good God!" I gasped, as the moonlight revealed her features and her face hovered over me like an incorporeal hallucination. "Ursula!"

"Were you never going to come to me on your own, my bad boy?"

"Well I..." I stuttered. I was still in a state of shock and could barely speak.

I watched as she threw a robe around her and lit the lamp. The low flame flickered in the room and her beauty seemed opaque and almost tangible in the soft obscurity.

"What is this nonsense about your memory, my precious? You spoil our plans very badly. You tell me to befriend Meredith Mae, to keep her preoccupied, and then you move her into your house!"

I stared at her blankly. I quickly realized that if I played along, perhaps I would have my answer concerning William's murder.

"I suffered a fall, clumsy oaf that I am. I had a memory loss." I laughed and sat up in the bed to look at her.

She stared long and hard into my eyes. Then I felt her hands on my face. "Foolish man," she whispered and kissed me. I found myself drawn in again to pleasurable feelings I fought to control. Fortunately, she laughed and sat back.

"Why have you restored the estate to Meredith Mae?" she asked me. "We plan the perfect murder. We devise a brilliant scheme and you show up at the convent like a mad man and insist that we return the money to her. Are you under a spell, dear Malcolm? Have you been vexed?"

"Well ... you see ... I had a change of heart. I could not toss the poor girl in the street."

"I see," she said. "Now Louie is to marry *her* and not Catherine? I wish you would have told me what you are up to."

I was so startled that I hoped my shock had not shown on my face. I composed myself as quickly as possible. "Why not?" I said quickly.

Ursula laughed and shrugged her shoulders. "You are a cold man, Malcolm."

"Is that my allure?" I smiled.

She turned and looked at me harshly then. "Your allure?" She laughed loudly. "Oh, please. You take a fortune and toss it out the window and you expect me to find that alluring? It is I who am taking the risks here."

"What risks, Ursula?" I asked, trying to appear nonchalant.

I watched as she went to the top of my burrow and helped herself to a cigar. I looked on in horror as she lit it and sat at the edge of the bed.

"I don't understand your logic," she began. "Catherine will expose you. You're a pedophile, darling. I don't care what she says about me. No one will believe her, but you? You will be ruined."

"Well...." I began slowly. "Perhaps, we should devise her death, as we did William's."

She smiled again and blew the smoke near me. I had such a desire to light my own cigar at this time that I rose from the bed and did so. I was aware that she continued to smile and to watch me as I puffed. I sat down in the chair opposite her and the two of us sat there smoking and talking about murder as if it were the most natural thing in the world.

"And who on earth will we get to kill her?"

She glared at me and I tried not to let my confusion show. So, apparently a stranger had not murdered William. I could not let Ursula notice my apparent ignorance.

"Just a thought." I smiled.

She sighed and leaned back. With her hair down in the moonlight and her long legs arched upon the bed, the cigar between her lips, she almost looked like a very pretty boy.

I was still staring at her; still mesmerized by this alluring androgyny when she spoke the words I shall never forget.

"Then you must get Meredith Mae to accept *my* proposal. She must marry *me*."

I stared back at her, unable to speak, unable to understand what she had just said to me. I'm sure my mouth dropped and I might have even gasped when she said it, but she appeared not to notice, and continued.

"You must deal with Catherine, since it is you who has turned our plans upside down. I suggest you send her abroad or see to it that she has a carriage accident, you understand?"

I nodded slowly.

"You have robbed her of the only romance she has ever had or is likely to ever have again. She will destroy you for that if you don't destroy her first."

"And you and I?" I whispered softly. "Where are your loyalties, Ursula?"

She laughed loudly and put the cigar out in the tray.

"I am a woman, Malcolm. What will Meredith Mae ultimately want with me? We shall do away with her immediately after the marriage. You will join me in France after the money is transferred to a Swiss bank and we will live happily ever after, my darling." She kissed me and looked into my eyes. "I must return home. I have waited hours for you once I saw Meredith Mae leave with the girl. Where were you, my sweet?"

"Well, I had business ... Had to dine out...." I began carefully.

"We will not be alone for a while now. I will take Meredith Mae abroad once I have won back her heart." She looked at me and winked. "That will not be so difficult. I have already insisted she renew her passport."

I said nothing and she continued.

"The poor girl will have an accident there."

She laughed and went over to the other side of the room. I watched in utter fascination as she raised the light in the lamp and began to slip her long legs into trousers.

"No? What do you think?" She turned around to look at me. "Or perhaps we will let Catherine murder her in a jealous fit. Um? Catherine is good with murder."

I stared at her dumbfounded. It slowly began to make sense.

"Yes," I said softly. "She certainly killed William without a hitch."

I watched Ursula carefully. She did not answer me but I knew, finally knew who had pulled the trigger on my dear friend, William. I sat up further in the bed and rubbed my brow.

*Poor Catherine*, I almost said aloud. I wondered if she had done it for love, or for money, but I would come to realize that she did it for neither. It was hate that drove Catherine. Unfortunately, for her, it was always hate.

I looked over at Ursula as she continued dressing. What evil they were, she and Malcolm, driven not by greed but by emptiness. It is always there, in the emptiness that the devil charms his prey.

I watched as she took the spirit gum and touched it over her lip. I looked on with astonishment as she pressed on a small mustache and tightened a large bandage across her chest before reaching for her shirt, vest, and jacket. When she had finished dressing, I saw only a hint of the woman who had fondled my face with all the grace of my own mother.

"It is a shame women cannot walk alone at night. This costume is most annoying."

*Dear Lord*, I thought silently, *how will I ever spare Meredith Mae the embarrassment of this disclosure?*

So, now I had my answers, answers that I was not sure what to do with, for I could not prove that Catherine had murdered William any more than I could prove the real sex of Louie Boussidan. And if I revealed this charade to Meredith Mae, would it only further humiliate her?

I now knew that Ursula and Malcolm had devised a plan to rob Meredith Mae of her fortune, a base and deceptive plan that involved the seduction of Catherine by the spurious Louie, in order to use her to murder William Davenport. They must have known that Silas would be an easy target. His solitary gardening on Wednesday afternoons would provide no witness to his whereabouts and, of course, Catherine's word would be utterly believable.

*How perfect*, I thought. Clearly, Ursula had charmed everyone. She would probably have gotten away with the marriage to Catherine, inherited the rest of the estate, and then disposed of her. Poor Malcolm thought he and Ursula would live happily ever after in France with a fortune in their bank account, except the idiot, Malcolm, did not realize he was being used. He would surely wind up in the bottom of the Seine while the executor of the estate met up with her true love, Jeanne Elemont.

I sat for hours in my room trying to decide what I could do to spare my granddaughter any further pain. I decided not to reveal Louie's true sex but only to expose this indiscretion with the other woman. I decided I would follow Ursula's every move until I discovered when they rendezvoused. I would learn all that I could about the nebulous Louie/Ursula and present my granddaughter with enough evidence to expose his character, without exposing *his* true gender.

# Chapter 28

I was not at all surprised to see *Louie* the following afternoon. Meredith Mae and Rachel were reading together in the library when the front door chimed and I saw his unmistakable shadow beyond the lace.

We smiled wickedly at one another and then *he* peered beyond me.

"May I speak to Meredith Mae?" he asked like a child pleading for candy.

"I'm not sure she will see you, *Monsieur*," I told him.

"Perhaps, if you will inquire...?" he urged.

I stepped away from the door and he entered behind me. I was about to call for Meredith Mae when I heard her footsteps approach. She stopped abruptly when she saw that it was Louie.

*"Mademoiselle..."* he began.

"Sir?" she said with a blush to her face.

"It is Saturday."

"Yes, it is," she said.

I looked from one to the other.

"What is so special about Saturday?" I inquired.

"Well, I always take Rachel for a .... how do you say it ... an outing."

"You do?" I was surprised, for I never realized he took the child by himself. "Is that so?"

I looked at Meredith Mae.

"Yes, Louie always takes Rachel on Saturday afternoons. I shop, and we meet up later. The child would be bored with my shopping. It takes me hours."

"I see. And where do you take Rachel, *Louie*?" I asked, trying to be as calm as possible. But it was Meredith Mae that answered me.

"We go into Manhattan," she said. "It seems Louie has often taken Rachel into the city to play. The child likes the ferry ride."

At the mention of Manhattan, I turned sharply to Louie. I certainly had my proof of his liaisons with this Elemont woman. He must take the child with him when he visits her. Perhaps, I could follow them and validate my suspicions and on the following Saturday, I would convince Meredith Mae to accompany me to the woman's house and I would be able to prove his infidelity.

"Of course, *Louie*. I will get the child ready."

I left the room but did not go immediately upstairs. I stood behind the door to listen. I heard the scoundrel tell Meredith Mae that he had broken off his engagement to Catherine. She remained silent and nothing was said between them for quite some time. I was just about to leave when I heard Louis' voice.

"Will you meet me this evening on Greenwich Avenue for dinner?"

She must have turned away.

"Please, Meredith Mae, please listen to me. I had no idea I would feel the way I do about you. I was confused, so terribly confused."

"I am very angry at you, Louie. You should have told me."

I heard the tears in my granddaughter's voice.

"Catherine has wanted to announce our engagement publicly, for weeks, but I told her I wasn't sure of my feelings anymore. She must have known that I was falling in love with you. That's why she came here."

"And are you in love with me, Louie?" I heard my granddaughter ask.

Then I heard nothing. I wondered what my Meredith Mae must be thinking. I turned my head to peek in, for I could not help it, and I knew I would not be seen. To my horror, she had walked over to the scoundrel and was kissing him. There she was, with her arms around him, lost in some mindless, endless kiss.

I burst into the room and pretended that I had not seen what I had very clearly seen before me. "Rachel will be ready shortly," I blurted out.

They stepped apart and Meredith Mae turned her back to me, most likely in embarrassment.

"You will meet *him* later?" I asked her, with an emphasis on the scoundrel's gender.

Meredith Mae turned uncomfortably and stuttered a bit.

"Yes, yes. We will meet for dinner. Louie will accompany us home. We will be fine," she said. I noticed that the blush to her face was more pronounced.

*Poor dear,* I said to myself. *I had better act fast*

I waited until they left the house and followed not far behind. I watched as Ursula, perfectly disguised as Louie, helped Meredith Mae into the waiting carriage. I noticed that he kissed her hand before lifting Rachel up in front with the driver. I could hear the child giggling, and though I was delighted to see her so happy, I was distressed that this fake had so much influence over both of them. The child still had not warmed to me, and though I understood her reasoning, I resented her fondness for *Louie.* As I watched them, I could not help but think to myself that they appeared like the picture of convention, as engaging and affectionate as any other American family about to embark on a Saturday afternoon adventure.

Fortunately, I was able to wave a Hansom on Flatbush Avenue. I told the driver to take me directly to the piers. I knew there would be only the one o'clock ferry into Manhattan and I wanted to be on it before they arrived, for I feared being noticed if I had to board after them. My driver was talkative, but the horse was brisk and I managed to scurry up the plank just as Louie's fancy black carriage pulled up to the dock.

I stayed inside the cabin where I was able to observe the playfulness between them on the outer deck. My granddaughter wore a beautiful wide brimmed hat that she had to hold with her hand, for the wind on the Hudson was quite lively that afternoon. The scoundrel kept stealing kisses and instead of pushing him off, she laughed and coyly turned her face to the left, and then back again to smile at him.

*How terribly in love they appear*, I thought to myself. "How shameful it all is." I sighed and thanked God that I would soon be able to show this insidious character up for at least partial deceit.

Once the ferry docked I let them depart before me and watched as *Louie* found a Hansom for Meredith Mae and blew her a kiss as she rode off. I noticed, with some trepidation, that there were not many carriages about and I wondered what I would do if Louie got into one with the child and rode off. Just as I was completing this thought, that is precisely what he did. I watched in panic, as their carriage went north on Whitehall Street, at quite a fair clip. I looked about frantically and saw not one empty carriage. Fortunately, I had Jeanne Elemont's address in my vest pocket and could only hope that that was their destination.

It took at least twenty minutes before I spotted an empty Hansom as it turned the corner on State Street and headed right by South Street where I stood in Malcolm's poor flesh, a sea of perspiration as the August sun unmercifully baked me. I was able to dry myself off a bit once inside the cab and there was a modicum of a breeze when the horse was able to master a full trot, but nothing like the lively air I had just witnessed on the open river.

"51 Charles Street, Sir," I finally heard the driver call out. "This is it."

I stuck my head out the window and looked around. The house was next to an old church. It was wooden in structure and sat on about a quarter acre of land. Up the block there were newer houses that were red or brown in color. The church was made of stone and was very small. A statue of the Virgin Mary stood on the front lawn. She held the baby Jesus in her arms but she did not look at him. She appeared to be looking inward.

I paid my driver and stood outside the church. I hadn't a clue as to what I would do next, for I wasn't sure where Louie and Rachel really were. I had no other alternative but to wait and see if I could prove his presence at Jeanne Elemont's residence. I waited a terribly long time and realized that Ursula might not emerge until closer to the dinner hour, which I knew would be four o'clock. I decided that since I had an hour or more to wait, that I would explore this quaint Catholic Church that appeared as run down as any I had ever seen.

The door creaked as I pushed it open and once inside it was so dark that it took a moment for my eyes to adjust. I could hear voices raised in song but the sound was very strange to my ear. The doors into the chapel were to my right and they were partially opened. I wondered what Mass could possibly be in service on a Saturday afternoon. I looked around me and saw that the holy water vessel was empty and the cross that bore Jesus' crucified body was hanging upside down.

*How curious*, I said to myself as I walked closer to the partially open doors.

The singing grew louder as I neared. I could not recognize the song, for it was in a language that was unfamiliar. It did not sound like a hymn, it seemed to resemble a chant. I saw fire flickering against the walls as I peeked through the dark opening of the door. To my horror, I saw people dressed in black capes, their faces hidden by hoods. They were kneeling before a leader, or high Priestess of some kind. She stood before them with her hands raised over her head. I could see that she held a sharp, long knife in the air. I stood back quickly. I knew what I was witnessing. This was far more diabolical than Tituba's voodoo rituals. This was the devil's Mass. Fear consumed me and I ran for the way out, but just as I was about to push myself into the waiting sunlight, I heard loud overbearing laughter and I could not move. It was Urbain. I knew it by the chill I felt in my bones; I knew it by the stench of his evil.

"GOD OF THE LIGHT. GOD OF THE DARK. COME FORTH IN THE SPIRIT OF AIR AND LIFT ME TO YOUR KINGDOM. COME FORTH IN THE SPIRIT OF WATER AND LET ME DRINK THE BLOOD OF SACRIFICE. PRINCE OF DARKNESS. ALMIGHTY LUCIFER, GOD OF EARTH. GOD OF FIRE. IN THE NAME OF SATAN WE HAIL THEE, GOD OF ALL BEINGS. GOD OF THE DARK WISDOM. WE SACRIFICE THIS CHILD IN YOUR NAME, IN YOUR BLOOD. GOD OF ALL THINGS. HAIL SATAN. HAIL SATAN. HAIL SATAN," he bellowed.

I turned sharply. He stood in the corner, hooded and dark, his eyes like fire, his breath like smoke.

"Down!" he commanded. "On your knees before me!"

"No!" I screamed and turned from him.

He flew to me and spun me around. I spit in his face. He slapped me hard and lifted me as though I weighed no more than a feather.

He carried me into the chapel and wrapped me in the hooded cloak. I found my self on my knees, surrounded by men and women who huddled over me and chanted in whispers. Finally, I lifted my head. The high Priestess still held the knife in her hand; its long steel blade pointed over the table before her, and on the table a child lay on her back covered by a white sheet. The child's eyes were closed as if in a trance. It took only a moment more before I realized that it was Rachel. I looked around frantically. Urbain was holding me by the shoulders. His fingers pressed into my flesh and I writhed in pain. I looked back at the high Priestess. Her hood fell behind her. Her blond hair curled almost to her waist. Her lips were full and her eyes so blue they appeared transparent.

"The child!" I screamed.

The chanting drowned out my calls and the people moved around a circle that was drawn in the middle of the floor. There was a five-pointed star at the top with both points pointed up toward the Priestess.

"Ursula! Where are you?" I screamed. "The child is in danger!"

I looked about frantically, searching for Ursula, but I did not see her until she stepped from the crowd and took the child in her arms.

"Ursula!" I screamed again but she never turned. She took the child and held her up toward the Priestess who lowered her knife only inches from the child's heart.

It was in that moment that I found my strength. Some miracle awakened my power, my power that is mightier than a coven of fools who practice nothing but evil and bring shame upon the souls of those whom God has honored as true witches.

I reached behind me and grabbed Urbain's hands. I squeezed them so hard that my teeth began to grind and I knew my eyes were flames in their sockets that burned with a fire so deadly it could have brought down the church. I rose to my feet and tore off the black cape of darkness, and I held my hands out straight before me.

"Get back from the child!" I hissed. "Get back or I will kill you all."

Like moles or frightened rats they scattered. The woman who had held the knife now cowered. The hooded demons now ran and Ursula stood naked under her cape and glared.

I faced the mighty Urbain. "Fall before God!" I commanded as I held my hands before me and pointed my fingers into his fiery eyes.

"God the Father," he hissed. "God the Father ... Jesus the son ... Jesus the son ... Mary, Mary, quite contrary. God the Father." He laughed and put his hands to my heart. "Idiot!" he shouted, and then, he was gone. His priest's robe and collar had fallen to the floor and a small puff of smoke, where he had stood, rose in a spiral and stunk as badly as an old carcass.

My chest ached where he had touched me but I ran for Rachel, who had remained in a deep trance. I took her up in my arms and flew as quickly as I could, in Malcolm's wretched form, to the doors. But something made me turn just before pushing them open.

When I looked back at the Priestess, I saw that the knife she held was aimed at my back.

"Is this your Jeanne Elemont?" I said to Ursula as she stood looking at me like some demonic monster that had risen from the dead.

She went to the woman and embraced her from behind.

"Yes, it is, Annabel." She smiled.

I felt a power that I did not realize I had. It came from some capacious level of consciousness. Somehow I knew that all I had to do was think of what I wanted and I could manifest it. So I turned, and with just the power of my thoughts, threw both women fifteen feet back until they landed against the altar with a hard thud. It did not take long before the knife Jeanne Elemont was holding flew quickly and landed in the door, just as I closed it behind me.

My fear was gone. I felt oddly vindicated. I smiled as I picked up the crucifix and gently replaced it right side up. My Meredith Mae would surely reject the demon now.

# Chapter 29

How inauspicious it was to recognize this extraordinary power to will my mind and exert my soul to self preservation in the face of danger, to even conquer the devil and send him back to the fires of his infinite limbo. *Why the bastard feared me*, I thought to myself. To fear is to recognize the existence of God. *Then could the devil have a soul as well?* I wondered.

I was not to have my answer so easily. No, I was not to know Urbain Grandier's relationship to God for several centuries, but I did know that I had the power to send him scurrying back to his infernal damnation. I had the power to protect myself against his insidious little plots to hurt me and those I cared for. But, I was soon to lose the ability to exercise my power. You see, I was about to fall prey, once more, to this angel of malicious intent, this devil whom my great aunt revealed to God as the Priest of the unholy. I, Annabel Horton, lost witch of Salem, would soon forget my identity and I would walk on the earth as if I had never walked in infinity, as if I had never known the devil's touch or received God's wisdom. Read on and I will tell you what came to be.

I quickly put the child to bed once we were back at the house on Montague Street. She had slowly come out of her trance and I was able to question her about her suspicious excursions into Manhattan with Louie.

"We go there often," she told me sleepily.

"Do you always go to the church?" I asked her.

"Oh yes, and we play games." She giggled.

"What games?" I softly pinched her cheek as I inquired.

"Games to the devil." She laughed, wide-eyed and quite innocently.

"Uh, uh," I whispered. "Games to the devil? And what might that mean?"

She yawned and closed her eyes as she continued.

"I pretend to call forth the devil and he comes and lights candles all around me."

"Does the devil ever hurt you?" I asked.

"It is making believe," she answered, but I pressed her further.

"Does he ever hurt you?"

"No, not ever."

She glared at me and I assumed that she remembered that it was Malcolm that had hurt her, and not any make believe demon. I kissed her goodnight and quietly left the room. How could I convince her that Louie was bad and meant to harm her when in fact, he had only made her laugh? How could I make her understand that Malcolm was now the good man, when in fact it was Malcolm that had violated her innocence?

I sat downstairs in our parlor and waited several hours for Meredith Mae to return home. I was relieved when she finally walked in around ten o'clock that evening. I wondered what lies the vicious woman had relayed to my granddaughter in order to protect herself from the truth, a truth that I would now reveal.

Meredith Mae came through the door breathless, and I could tell by her smile that Ursula had no doubt convinced her that nothing unusual had happened that evening.

"Grandmamma," she said when she saw me. "Were you spying on us? Louie told me that you followed him and insisted on taking Rachel home. Is she upstairs?"

"Meredith Mae, you must listen to me. I have something unpleasant to reveal to you. Please sit down."

I watched as her smile faded and she sat down, rather self-consciously, on the couch. I noticed a blush to her face and she did not look at me but stared at the hands that were folded together in her lap.

"My dear," I began. "I regret to inform you that I discovered your Louie in a devil's mass. He practices the dark magic and may even be

Master of It."

She looked at me strangely for a moment before she answered.

"He is a student of the occult," she said softly and raised her eyes to me. "He is interested in all metaphysics. It's a hobby."

"I see," I said carefully. "He had the child in the mass. He was sacrificing Rachel to the devil," I told her slowly.

She laughed, as if I had told her something amusing, and small tears came to the corners of her eyes. I watched as she brushed them away.

I waited before I began again. I sat forward on the edge of my chair.

"I believe that Louie is a disciple of our own Urbain," I told her.

She brought her hands to her face as I waited for the information to take hold. I wished I could read her thoughts, but I could not. Finally, she spoke.

"How do you know that he sits more on the side of Urbain than he does of God?" she asked me. "Perhaps he is a good witch, like us."

"He lies to you," I whispered.

"What lies?" she asked quickly.

"There is a woman, a Jeanne Elemont. I have a letter."

I nervously reached in my vest pocket and handed her the folded piece of paper.

She read it quickly and then crumbled it up and threw it on the floor.

"It is I, Louie loves." She turned to face me. "The letter is dated months before we met. Did you notice that?"

"No," I stammered a bit and knew that I had no choice; I had to reveal this creature's real identity. "Ursula and Louie ... you see, they...."

She cut me off and put her fingers to my lips.

"No more," she whispered. "He has asked me to marry him."

"You cannot!" I screamed. "*He* is not a man!"

"He is all the man for me," she answered indignantly.

"Wait!" I reached out for her arm as she started for the stairs. "You don't understand."

"Forgive me, Grandmamma, but I will hear no more against him," she said to me with tears in her eyes.

"You are in danger," I screamed out.

She put her arms around me and held me to her.

"All who love are in danger," she said.

I cried openly then, for I knew I could not penetrate her innocence. Soon enough, she would learn of the deception.

"All right," I said and stood back to stare at her. "I see that I cannot convince you otherwise about Louie."

She shook her head and looked at me sadly.

"Do you trust me, Meredith Mae?" I asked.

She nodded a simple "yes."

"Then know this. Louie Boussidan is a sham. Louie Boussidan would kill you for a dime. You must always be one step ahead of him. Do you hear me?" I asked her and again she nodded.

"Do not turn your back on him. Protect yourself. Protect Rachel. Will you promise me that?"

"Yes, Grandmamma," she whispered.

"Your soul will see the light, as well as your eyes. Of that I am certain."

I went up the stairs to my room and turned just once to watch as she opened the door to her bedroom and entered. If I had only known, at that moment, as she looked back to smile at me reassuringly, that it would be centuries before I would ever see her blessed face again. Had I of known, I would have never closed my eyes to sleep that night. I would never have left her side to fall exhaustingly, and effortlessly, to dreams.

My granddaughter and Louie Boussidan eloped the following evening. My despair was overwhelming but I had not the power to prevent the events from happening as they occurred. However, I planned to follow them to France when a distraught Catherine revealed their destination.

"Where else do you think they would go?" she hissed at me tearfully.

Several days following this news I was returning home from a visit with Silas when I found the authorities at my home. They had been waiting for my return and looked rather somber and austere as I approached. One man, in particular, put an arm around me and brought me aside.

"We must speak with you, Mr. Northrup," he said softly.

I opened the door and stepped inside. I motioned for them to enter.

"What is it gentlemen?" I asked as they gathered in my parlor.

The man who had placed his arm around me stood back and looked sadly into my eyes before glancing at the floor.

"Your daughter, sir ... Catherine Northrup."

I somehow knew what he was going to say though it still gave me a shock to hear it.

"She has taken the very gun that killed William Davenport and placed it to her temple. I'm sorry," he said.

I fell into a chair and wiped my brow. She was obviously so distraught from Louie's elopement that she saw no reason to go on with life.

"She's left a note, sir," I heard him say.

"May I see it?" I asked as the officer reached in his breast pocket and held it over to me.

I read the note quickly. Of course, Catherine took her revenge. She indicated that it was Louie Boussidan that had masterminded the plot to kill William Davenport. She went on to say that it was she who pulled the trigger and she only wished she had aimed it at Louie, as well. I handed the note back to the officer and smiled sadly to myself.

A few weeks later, Silas was released from prison and vindicated for the crime. I was overjoyed to see him regain his freedom and resume his practice, but I shed few tears for Catherine Northrup.

I knew that *Louie* would not return to Brooklyn for many years. I feared for Meredith Mae's safety, particularly now that she must certainly be aware of his real gender. I was planning to move Rachel and myself abroad as quickly as possible so that I might reunite with Meredith Mae. I had received several letters from her that were postmarked from a village not far from the Spanish border and I was hoping to find them there. Curiously enough, she wrote that she was quite happy and mentioned nothing of what I would have presumed would have caused her a good deal of shock and disappointment. I was perplexed and wondered if the diabolical Ursula was forcing her to write such happy, frivolous letters.

I had just booked passage on The Queen Victoria and had arrangements to close the house and take up residence in France, when the police showed up at Montague Street to question Malcolm on allegations of child abuse, a charge that was revealed in another letter that Catherine had mailed to the authorities on the day before she took her life. These allegations were mailed, I assume, because she wanted her confession to be a separate issue, or perhaps, she decided to kill herself after she mailed the letter. But the police were not taking the matter at all seriously because Catherine's sanity was now under consideration. It seems that she had also declared that Louie and Ursula Boussidan were one and the same person. This revelation struck the police as bizarre and ridiculous, so they dismissed the charges against me on the basis of malicious rumor uttered by a distraught and unstable female. Unfortunately, there were those who took the matter to heart.

On the evening of Silas' release we celebrated at a steak house not far from his residence on Hick Street. I was on my way home, mellowed from several glasses of lager, that though I could not taste still gave me a delightful buzz. I was just crossing Joralemon Street and making my way east toward Remsen when I was jumped from behind. There were several men who grabbed me and forced me into an alleyway.

"Child raping bastard!" one yelled as I caught his fist on my jaw.

"Rotten scum," yelled the other as he hit me in the stomach and caused me to fall back. I was knocked in the head from behind by another and kicked to the ground. But it was not this violence that killed poor Malcolm. It was his ticker that gave way. I felt the awful burn in his chest and the tight spasms cutting off his air as they continued to thrash him. I fought for breath but it was if a giant foot was standing on my chest.

The men continued to punch Malcolm long after his heart had stopped and he lay with his eyes wide opened, quite obviously dead. Of course, I fought to regain life to this body but my plea was rejected and off I went, like a burst of a sudden wind, into a darkness of indiscriminate thought. I prayed for Rachel and my granddaughter, just as death injected itself and I screamed out Matthew's name as the breast of infinity clasped me.

Beyond the death of flesh and blood, far beyond the layers of time and space, I felt my Mathew near me. From some revealing distance, I felt him force his breath into my lungs. Unfortunately, my memory began to fade, even though his dear face was once again so close.

I struggled frantically, but I soon lost this image of my son. I fell into some timeless space for what seemed like forever. I became aware of nothing but my soul's detachment from any human flesh. Somewhere in infinity, I began to lose all awareness of myself as Annabel Horton and I was pulled by something beyond my control. All I can remember of it now is that I heard someone breathing. I followed the breathing for a long time until I realized it was coming from a body that I was now in, though I had not a clue as to how I got into it.

I felt enormously confused. Voices from far away seemed to be telling me that I was regaining consciousness. They appeared to be doctors, but my sight was so unclear. Still, I was able to see that they were dressed in white robes.

"A near drowning" I heard them say, as if from a great distance. They were strangers. I had never seen them before. That I knew. They spoke in an unusual way and appeared to me even more absurd than the language they spoke, a very strange English, sloppy and ungainly.

I could see that I was in a light green room. The room was small and had two windows. From the windows I could see what appeared to be buildings, though their great height startled me. I rubbed my eyes, for everything appeared so vague. I knew I was very high from the ground. The great height caused an uneasy anxiety and the more I let my eyes travel to the windows, the more a vertiginous nausea overcame me and I could not help but grip the sides of my bed. One of the men in white had taken my hand and squeezed it. His hair looked like an enormous mop and almost made me laugh out loud.

"Welcome back, young lady." He smiled. "You've had quite a brush with death."

I stared at him blankly.

Dr. James Welty," he said as he held out his hand.

"Doctor?"

"You were pronounced clinically dead," he said solemnly.

"I can not see clearly," I told him.

He pulled a light from his pocket and searched my eyes with it.

"There appears to be nothing wrong with your eyes," he said as he peered at me.

"Where am I?" I asked.

"New York Presbyterian Hospital," he answered. "You fell off a boat into the Hudson River. Do you remember that?"

I searched my mind so much my head began to ache. "No," I said.

"Your parents have been notified. They're taking a flight out of Boston."

"Oh." I smiled meekly.

"You made the evening news." He grinned.

I smiled back and asked for a copy of The Gazette. It made him laugh.

"You have a friend outside that's been waiting to see you." He returned my hand to my stomach. "Are you up for it?"

In my confusion, I nodded. Before I could ask him my name he left the room.

Moments later, he returned with a man I thought I had never seen before. The man ran quickly to my side.

"Annie," he cried. "We thought we'd lost you."

"Good God, who are you?"

"You don't know me?"

I shook my head.

He turned sharply to the doctor who came and leaned over my face.

"Do you know who *you* are?" the Doctor asked me.

I shook my head from side to side.

"How about the president of the United States?"

"William Henry Harrison?" I answered.

The Doctor laughed loudly.

"Um." He held up his hands. "How many fingers?"

"Ten," I said quickly.

"Do you know your name?"

"No," I said.

"Ann Peckham. It's a temporary memory loss." He sounded as if he were trying to soothe me. "Not unusual. Let's give it a few days."

He gave the man with the dark curls a reassuring touch on the shoulder and left the room. I noticed that the man with the dark hair seemed to be very tan from the sun and he wore a funny pair of pants. They were blue and had large wide cuffs. Above his waist he appeared to be wearing underwear for his arms and neck were quite exposed. I tried rubbing my eyes to see him more clearly but my vision remained opaque.

"Are we related?" I asked him.

"Not exactly. I'm your neighbor. I live down the hall from you. I saw on the news how you nearly drowned in the Hudson. I got here as quickly as I could."

I studied his face, the sweet dark curls that fell on his brow and the eyes that searched mine with a concern that clearly revealed his affection.

"I have no idea who you are but you are very tall," I said softly.

It was then he took my hand and shook it.

"Michele," he said, illuminating a gentleness that caused me to stare. "Michele Philippe Guyon."

# PART II

# REPRISAL

# Chapter 1

Michele took me home from the hospital in a very strange but appealing Hanson. There was no horse attached to it! The speed of the cab unnerved me, at first, but then I found myself getting used to it, even enjoying how little time it had taken to get from one place to another. However, once we arrived, the pretty little street Michele told me I lived on did not look at all familiar. Even as I climbed the stairs of the building I had no memory of ever having done it before.

As it would turn out, Ann Peckham lived in a very small space on the island of Manhattan. There were five flights of stairs inside her house and four doors on each floor. I asked Michele if, in fact, it were a rooming house. He must have found that amusing because he laughed.

I stood at the top of the stairs and noticed that I was in an ugly hall. I felt enormously disappointed. How awful it appeared to me. I could see through my opaque vision that the walls were a dingy yellow and the doors were a rather putrid brown. I stood before the door askance. I tried desperately to recall myself there but I could not. I was petrified of the noise coming from behind the doors and I kept putting my hands up over my ears. The noise seemed just as piercing as it had been from the Hanson. This world was too loud, much too loud. I did not know it then but your modern dimension of space was quite an affront on my soul.

Michele eyed me strangely as he unlocked the door to apartment 2C, and I cowered like a threatened animal before it. He handed me back my purse.

"You live here, Annie."

"No," I said and shook my head

"Come on."

He held out his hand and reached for the fist I had shoved defiantly into a pocket. But something in his eyes made me trust him. I unloosened my grip and allowed him to lead me inside.

"What is it?" he said to me as I looked at the gruesome furnishings. I must have scowled.

"This is all of it?" I asked, with a bewildered look as I noticed that the walls did not lead into other rooms.

"Yes," he told me. "Just another New York breadbox, I'm afraid."

"It is so like a prison," I said. "All it needs are the bars."

"You talk funny," he said suddenly.

"What?"

"The apostrophes, you don't shorten your words. You pronounce everything. It's unusual. You say, 'It *is* unusual'. See the difference? It's like some old English. People don't usually talk like that."

I found nothing unusual about my speech patterns and avoided comment.

"It is so distasteful here," I said instead.

He smiled mischievously. "Yes, it's the food. Chinese — Indian — Italian. It's dinnertime. People are eating all sorts of things. That's what you smell."

Actually, I had hardly any sense of smell but I must have had a funny expression on my face and he assumed I detected cooking odors.

"Chinese? Indian?" I laughed. I couldn't help myself. It seemed so peculiar to think of people eating such strange food.

He grinned back at me.

"Do you remember anything at all about your surroundings, Annie?" he asked as I stared at the peculiar furnishings.

I shook my head. As I continued to observe the horrid room, I noticed some pictures over a mantle that should have harbored a working fireplace, but instead, was completely covered with part of the wall. I could see you couldn't burn any wood in it. It was utterly useless.

"How strange," I uttered as I walked to the mantle.

I was startled by the color in the little pictures. I thought at first that they were fine little watercolors, but then I noticed how shiny and realistic they appeared.

"Who are these people?" I asked him as I stared at them curiously.

"Well, let's see," he said as he came to me and looked at the little pictures in their clear frames.

"That one there is a photograph of you, Annie, with your mother and father. And this one here is your brother, Bill."

I searched the pictures intensely. I was staring at strangers, particularly my own face. The girl Michele called "Annie" had a familiar expression but I knew instinctively it was not my own.

"My hair is not so dark," I told him.

He gave me a strange look and held up another small-framed photograph.

"Here you are with that boyfriend of yours."

"Boyfriend?"

"You don't remember?"

"Let me see his picture," I said.

He handed it to me. It was different than the others, larger, and framed in glass, with a fancy wooden border. It was not in those shiny colors like the others either. As I took it I was immediately startled by what I saw yet I was not sure I understood my own reaction.

"What is it?" Michele asked.

Perhaps I had turned pale. Without thinking, I let the picture fall to the floor. I could hear, as if from a great distance, the glass shatter.

"I do not like him," I said fiercely.

Michele went quickly for a broom to sweep up the glass.

"Are you all right, Annie?" he asked as he swept the pieces up.

Before I could stop myself, I ripped the photograph from the frame and tore the picture into pieces and threw the pieces near his feet.

"Why did you do that?" he asked me. I could see that he was quite startled.

Without thinking, I answered, "I know the devil when I see him."

Michele sat back down and stared at me. I had the feeling I was acting differently than girls he might be used to so I went and sat opposite him. I thought it best to change the subject and not say whatever came into my mind.

"I hate this room. It is ugly," I said nonchalantly.

"Well, let me throw some light in here."

He got up and went to the window and drew up a shade. Outside, I saw a tree.

"That is pretty," I said.

"Come, sit near me." He grinned and motioned with his hand to a place beside him on the bright, orange sofa.

"Where am I?" I whispered as I sat.

"Greenwich Village," he told me. "Charles Street."

I sighed deeply. I remembered nothing, not even my name, and yet, I was feeling a comforting familiarity with the young man at my side, even though I suspected that he thought me quite insane.

"You are familiar," I said. "But not in the way you think you are familiar."

He looked into my eyes for a long time before he spoke.

"You're different, Annie. I don't know what it is, but you are very different then the Ann Peckham I knew before the accident."

"Tell me about the accident," I questioned. I had some fading recollection of feeling deliriously happy but I could not connect it to anything. But, then again, perhaps my happiness had only to do with nearly drowning in the river and being miraculously saved from doing so.

"He took you boating."

"Who took me boating?" I questioned. Michele nodded to the empty frame on the floor.

"What happened?" I asked, though I suddenly had a vertiginous loss of balance and knew Michele had reached for me.

"The boat tipped over," he told me. "And from out of nowhere a man jumped into the river from a passing ferry and swam to you. He managed to pull you aboard another boat that came to your aid, and I believe he kept breathing into your lungs until you came to."

"Where is this man?" I questioned.

"In all the commotion he vanished and we were unable to thank him. It was almost as if he had disappeared into thin air. I think he came to the hospital and inquired after you but no one really knew for sure."

"Do you know his name?"

Michele shook his head. "Perhaps he simply wanted to avoid the publicity and took off before all those pesky newspapermen could bombard him."

"Was there anyone else on board the boat I fell from?" I asked.

"Only that boyfriend of yours, who seemed to have mysteriously escaped without a scratch," he said sarcastically. "He told the authorities that he was knocked unconscious for a moment and when he regained consciousness he found himself under the boat and didn't see you."

"You don't like this man either," I said. Michele looked away. "Were you jealous?" I asked without censoring myself at all. I knew it was a rather brazen thing to say but the words tumbled out of me.

"No," he said emphatically.

"Why not?" I questioned. "You are very drawn to me, I think."

"Yes, I am drawn to you, but it's weird that I am. Oh, I don't mean anything offensive by that. I mean, you're quite beautiful, but before the accident you were just a neighbor, nothing more. Yet now I feel that there could be more between us. But that's ridiculous," he said as he turned away quickly and looked out the window.

I remained quiet. After a moment, he turned back to me. "We've been living across the hall from each other for three years and we have been nothing more than friends. You have a very jealous boyfriend and my attentions are elsewhere."

"And who are your attentions on?" I teased, feeling a surprising disappointment.

"An apparition," he said sadly. "I'm sorry, Annie. I'm a bit obsessed with the occult. It's a hobby and all my energy goes into it. You used to tease me about it and call me an idiot, but I'm afraid I'm in love with a ghost."

Something in his sadness made me tear up and I began to cry. I put my head in my hands and I sobbed as if my entire soul had just been caressed by his words.

"I'm sorry, Annie," he said. "I didn't mean to upset you. Was it something I said?"

"No," I answered through my tears. "You do not understand. I am crying because I feel good."

"About what?" he asked me.

"About your saying that you love a woman long gone, a ghost, as you call her."

He took my hands in his and looked deeply into my eyes, as if the color he found there fascinated him.

"Who are you?" he whispered as he searched my face. "You're different. Very different."

"Take me to a looking glass," I commanded as I rose to my feet.

Michele took my hand and led me to a door. When he pulled the door back, I saw a looking glass there.

"Aha!" I whispered. "Look!"

My image in the glass smiled back at me, not the face I had seen in the photograph, but one so familiar and appealing.

"I suspected that I would not look like your Ann Peckham," I said.

"Jesus," I heard Michele whisper as he walked up close to the glass and touched the image.

"And there I am." I smiled. "That is so much better."

Michele continued to stare at my reflection. "You are not Ann Peckham," he whispered. "My God, you resemble a friend of mine, younger but so similar."

"I am not the woman in the photograph," I said quietly. "I am not Ann Peckham."

Michele seemed stunned and could not even open his mouth to speak to me.

"I am not Ann Peckham," I repeated. "Though she does appear to look like someone I know."

"Who are you?" he finally asked as he looked back to me. "How can the glass reflect a different image from what I see in the flesh? Good God, who are you?"

I shrugged my shoulders. I had no answer to give him.

"I have a friend," he began. "She is the one you resemble in the glass but she is several years older than you. She might be able to help solve this mystery."

"Who is this Ann Peckham and why is she familiar to me?"

"Her full name is Ann Arlin Peckham," he told me as he reached out and touched the reflection of my hair in the glass. "Does that mean anything to you?"

"No. That name is not familiar."

"Her family is from Massachusetts. Do you remember her mother? Her father?"

I shook my head. Michele was still a bit shocked and kept staring at me with wide-open eyes.

"They visit her regularly. She's always terribly upset after their visits. They want her to transfer back home, to a local college, and marry some boy called Todd Sheehan, especially her mother." He laughed. "They hate this new boyfriend of hers and I can't say I blame them."

"And why does she not marry Todd Sheehan?" I asked him. "Is he not a good man?"

"She is in love with this ex-priest, this Jacque somebody or other."

"What do you think of this Jacques?" I whispered.

"He's a schmuck." Michele laughed.

"A what?" I had never heard the expression.

"A blowhard," he said seriously.

"Is she rich?" I asked.

"Her family is. They're an old American family and her father became very wealthy in investment banking. Ann Peckham lives very simply, though. She's a student at New York University, an art history major. I'm sure her father helps her with her rent. This is New York, after all, but she waitresses part time."

"Are you rich?" I smiled.

"Hardly," he laughed. "I'm a professor."

"You are a professor?" I smiled back. I liked this man more than I wanted to. I let myself trust it, for instinct is all one has when memory is missing.

"I teach History," he told me. "I've written a few books. I have a continuing education class for adults and I teach several undergraduate courses in American History at New York University."

"History?" I smiled. "What do I remember of history, I wonder?"

"I don't know," he said. "You tell me."

"I do not have memories, yet I feel that I know something important. The knowledge is not in my memory at all, but in my soul," I said. "Does that make sense to you?"

"Annie, tell me everything you know, everything you can remember. It might help."

I looked at his face. I wanted to weep again. He was so handsome and sweet. Have you ever seen a face that made you want to weep, simply for the compassion and strength of character found there? That was Michele, for me. He was clearly a sensitive and tender man, and his face revealed that. But he was also strong, oh so terribly firm around his jaw. I loved the way his hair curled tightly near his brow and the color of his eyes was such a pretty shade of brown, and shaped like an almond nut. The familiarity comforted me. I knew him. I knew him entirely.

"What is it, Annie?"

"Do not mourn history," I told him suddenly. "It is just an illusion. That girl of yours is not gone. She is not a ghost."

"What do you mean?" he questioned.

"Life does not pass."

"Doesn't move on?" he asked with a grin, as if I jested him.

"No," I said.

"Then how do you define progress?"

"What progress?"

"The television? The telephone? Space travel? How about electric lights, look?" He got up and seemed to perform magic.

"My God," I said. "How did you do that?" I rose to my feet and began to turn the electric lights on and off. It seemed to be the most fascinating thing I had ever seen and I laughed as I played with the switch.

"If there were no history, Annie, there would be nothing to discover."

He seemed so sure of himself but I had no earthly idea what he was referring to: telephones — space travel? How bizarre.

"All is contained in now. We find what is already there, like God," I told him. "The soul does not know progress. The soul simply is and discovers what already is."

"Then why do we suffer death, Annie, what merciful God would allow it?"

"God did not choose despair or grief for us; we chose it for ourselves by agreeing to become flesh and blood. Life contains opposites. Grief is the opposite of joy and that too, is ours. All of life is opposite to something. But the soul has no opposite. Like God, it contains both life and death simultaneously. But being a soul is not the opposite of life and being alive. Death is the opposite of life. The soul simply is, like God. In order for the soul to know God, it must agree to be born to that one eternal moment where nothing passes prior to something else. We believe it does but our belief only gives order to the universe, nothing more. The end is the beginning. Do you see?"

"I can't say that I agree with you, Annie. Take the Civil War and something like the ignorance of the Salem Witch trials? They have passed into history," he said sternly. "Thank God history contains that."

"The Salem Witch Trials?" I suddenly felt cold and began to shake.

He moved close to me and put his hands on my shoulders.

"Annie, what is it?" he asked and I felt his touch on my flesh. How good it felt.

"I do not know," I told him.

"I'm teaching a course now on The Salem Witch Trials. Last semester, I taught a special class on The Civil War. At the moment, I am learning about American Indians and the tribes that lived here in the Northeast. That would make for a great course. I'm considering the subject for my next book. It's rather fascinating." He laughed and turned to smile at me. "I didn't mean to upset you. That's just what came to mind." He took my hand and squeezed it. "I'm a bit obsessed with the eruptions of history."

"I have been to Salem," I said.

"You have?" He was surprised.

"Yes, I think so, but I do not really remember."

"Well, you are from Massachusetts," he told me. " I mean, Ann Peckham is from Massachusetts."

"My soul was born in Loudun," I said quickly.

"Loudun? Where's that?"

"France."

"You're French?"

"No, English. But perhaps my mother was French." I put my head back into my hands and began to cry again. "Oh, I do not know who I am or where I have come from."

"Annie, that friend I mentioned, she really may be able to offer you some explanation. She's a psychic. Perhaps she can help you get your memory back. Perhaps she can explain why the image in the glass is not this," he said as he held up the picture of Ann Peckham.

I looked up at him and felt comforted.

"A psychic?"

"Yes, I see her often. She was one of my students last year. We became quite friendly. She's a bit strange but she shares my interest in the occult. We dabble in it together. She's regressed me back in time. She's really good at it. We've been at it for at least a year now."

"There is no linear regression," I told him. "There is only movement through time and space, a severing of dimensions to reveal what we know of as time."

"Why do you say that?"

"I do not know," I told him sadly.

"She says that."

"Who says that?" I asked him.

"Elizabeth. My friend, the psychic."

"Elizabeth?" I said. Suddenly, I felt confused.

"Yes. She says that, too. She speaks just like you do also."

"Elizabeth?" I said again. I felt that I should know something, but as I struggled to capture that knowledge I found myself with nothing more than a vague memory of someone with the name Elizabeth. But, I could recall not a thing beyond that.

"Oh Michele," I wept. "I do not belong here. I do not belong here."

I cried in his arms and he held me tightly. He smelled like rain. I realized that after seeing my true image in the glass that my sense of sight and smell grew stronger. Michele's scent was good. It was fresh and the scent of him obliterated the foul smells that now came from beyond the door.

"Annie, I'm confused," he said as he held me.

"You smell like rain," I said. "I like it."

"I love someone else. I can't see her but I have held her in my arms. I have been with her so intimately and I ... I love her."

I noticed that his face appeared so sad, so sad that I wanted to cry again.

"Why does that confuse you?" I asked sweetly.

"Because I feel she would look like you. If I could see her she would have your face, the face in the glass."

Suddenly, I wanted to find myself in his arms again. I wanted to feel safe. The yearning was so strong I almost begged him to hold me.

"So, is it your face that completes the vision of my Annabel, or are you and Elizabeth playing some cruel trick on me?" he whispered.

"That is familiar," I said quickly.

"What?"

"The name *Annabel*," I told him.

He went very quiet and his face was set in a pained look, as though something was hurting him very deeply.

"Am I Annabel?" I asked. The name had sounded good to me.

"She is in danger. Elizabeth and I are trying to save her. She has regressed me to Salem and the witch trials," he muttered.

"I cannot follow you," I cried. "I cannot follow what you are saying but I feel that I should."

"Yes, perhaps you are my Annabel. If I could give her flesh and blood, perhaps, she would look like your image in the glass," he told me gently.

"Something fits but I do not know what it is."

Suddenly, Michele jumped up and grabbed my arm.

"I've been watching Ann's dog while she's been in the hospital."

"I have a dog?" I smiled. That seemed nice but I had no memory of it. "What kind of dog?"

"A beautiful white shepherd," he told me. "Come, she's just across the hall.

Michele took my hand and led me to his room. It was as small as Ann Peckham's but comfortable. The dog came right to him when he entered and reached her paws up to Michele's waist. Her happy barking made me laugh.

"Look who's here, Beauty," he said.

"Beauty? Is that her name?"

"No. She has a strange name. I never remember it."

The dog looked up at me and began to turn in circles before leaping into my arms and nearly knocking me to the ground.

"She's ecstatic to see you. She knows you," Michele said excitedly.

"But I am afraid I do not remember her. How did I come by her?"

"Well, actually a stranger gave her to you, I mean, gave her to Ann."

"A stranger?"

"Yes. He was very distraught and he apologized for taking the dog. Before Ann could tell him he was mistaken, that the dog was not hers, he disappeared."

"And she kept the dog?"

Michele nodded and leaned his body against the wall.

"Who are you?" he asked me as he walked up close to me and stared at my features. He was so tall that it strained my neck to find his eyes. "What's happened to Ann Peckham?"

"I do not know who I am. I am lost," I told him sadly. "And Ann Peckham is most likely dead. I am sorry, but it must have been God that called her. I did not harm her."

"How can there be death if all is now?" he asked accusingly.

Without really knowing what I was saying the words fell from my lips again.

"Death is a moment when all time meets. She is there, your Ann Peckham. It is where we all begin and end."

"Annabel?" he whispered. "Have I found you, really found you?"

He took me in his arms and kissed me. I responded to his kiss, so warm and mysteriously familiar. His lips were soft and seemed to erase all fear. The anxiety left me and I had no other feeling but the touch of his longing on my heart. I knew that if all souls are fated to mate, than mine, had found home. But this tenderness was not to last. Urbain was near. His breath was right beyond the door. His foul hand was around my neck. Evil was waiting for Annabel Horton. And evil thrives on waiting.

# Chapter 2

Ah, Elizabeth, if I had only recognized you when I walked through your door that pretty spring morning, but I did not. And if I were Annabel Horton, with all my faculties intact, would I have known the girl I left on the hill in Salem? I cannot say. Your flesh had been so altered by the chronological linear illusion of human life that I might not have known you as the wife of my son and the victim of my first offense.

No matter. You knew me entirely, and perhaps, I owe you my eternal soul because of it.

"Now remember, she's a bit weird but don't let her frighten you," Michele was saying as he led me up a block in Manhattan in the West Eighties. The woman that Michele called Elizabeth Horton Guyon, lived on the ground floor of a pretty gray building.

"Guyon? Is she your sister?" I asked. Guyon was certainly not a common name. That I knew was so.

Michele laughed and told me that Elizabeth had some crazy notion that he had fathered her husband.

"She told me she had enrolled in my class, not only to learn history, but because she noticed my last name in the newspaper."

"How could you have fathered her husband?" I asked. "You are too

210

young."

"Precisely," Michele said as he held my hand and knocked twice on the door. I heard several locks released before the door opened. I suddenly found myself staring at a woman who was gapping back at me. She appeared to resemble the image I had seen in the glass, but she was older by at least thirty years. Her mouth was open in an odd shape and her hand went immediately to her breast.

"Good God!" she cried.

I could not speak. I stared and searched her face. I knew that I knew her but I did not know from where.

Then, before I could blink again, I found the woman in my arms. She was hugging me so tightly that I felt she would knock the breath from me.

"Oh, Annie," she cried. "Oh, Annie, Annie, Annie. Where have you been?" she asked through her tears.

I could not answer her for I had no idea what she was talking about. She grabbed my hands and led me inside. Michele followed in a bit of a stupor. I could tell he was confused, terribly confused.

"It is Annabel Horton," she said at last.

"Annabel?" Michele whispered. "The girl from Salem?"

Elizabeth nodded.

"Then why do you call her Annie?"

"It is a long story." She smiled at me.

"But she's alive. How can that be?" he said.

"She walks through time as I have done. It was she that taught me."

"No. This is crazy." Michele laughed as if a very funny joke had just been told to him. "I want to believe it but it's too bizarre, even for me to believe."

"I tell you it is true," Elizabeth said fiercely and led me to the glass. "Look at her. She is in borrowed flesh. But look in the glass, Michele. Who do you see?"

He walked to my reflection and touched the image of my cheek.

"This is amazing," he said. "How do you see her?"

"It is difficult to explain but I see her as Annabel Horton, and at the same time, I see her borrowed image."

"And others? How would they see her?" he asked.

"They would see only her temporary flesh, I am afraid."

"Are you saying that the world sees her as Ann Peckham, and that would not change, even if they saw her in a mirror?"

"That is precisely what I am saying," she answered.

"Then what gives me the power to see the real Annabel in the glass?"

"You are Matthew's father. You are a witch, Michele, or a warlock, if you prefer that term, though it matters not. You have not begun to know your own power. It is the dimension you are in. It shields you from your spirituality."

She returned to my side. I had been listening intently to their conversation.

I knew she spoke the truth but I still remained vague, and without conscious memory.

"Do you know me, Annie?" she asked as she held my hand.

I could only shake my head and stare at her. I felt I should know her but I remembered nothing.

"When I left you on the hill in Salem I had no idea where to go. My soul seemed to linger forever, right above your own, but you never noticed my presence. The night the cat took you, I wept so fiercely because I could not offer you assistance. I was devastated and called out to you, but you never answered me."

"A cat took me?" I wondered what she meant.

"Oh, Annie, I waited forever in darkness. I waited for centuries trying to transport myself to Brooklyn. Eventually, I found myself there. It was like waking up after a long sleep, and yet, I knew there had been no real passage of time. It was you who taught me that, Annie. Oh, do you not remember?"

Sadly, I shook my head and she continued.

"I had crossed a dimension. I looked the same and my dress was the same, but the century had changed quite drastically. When I realized I was in the twentieth century and not in the year 1851, as I had wanted to be, I panicked and tried frantically to alter my circumstances, but I could not cross the barriers again. Despondent, I journeyed over the river into Manhattan looking for some kind of shelter in which I felt safe, for the streets of Brooklyn were not comforting. I eventually found a group of people in a beautiful church. They walked a labyrinth, just as we had done in Salem. I joined them every evening. They fed me and even began to pay me for my 'channeling' as they called it. I was able to charge enormous amounts of money to regress people in time and conjure up dead relatives."

She laughed loudly and all the bracelets on her wrists made jingling sounds. She ran her fingers back through her hair and continued with her tale.

"I found this pretty little apartment thirty years ago and I have been here ever since. I have been making my way as a gifted psychic, as they have come to call me. I stopped trying to explain that there is no past from which to discover poor lost ghosts and just decided to enjoy my notoriety. Last year, I noticed in the paper that a historian and professor named Michele Guyon was teaching a course on the Civil War. I was overjoyed to see the name 'Guyon' for I had looked for it without success. I knew I must enroll in Michele's course. I recognized immediately that he was Matthew's father for the resemblance was extraordinary. Do you remember, Annie? When we were in Salem you spoke to me of a beautiful dark man who saved you from the tree?"

She could tell by my expression that I hadn't a clue as to what she was talking about. She sighed very deeply before she spoke again.

"Much to my dismay, Michele had no earthly idea of his power, or who he really was. I have been trying to teach him. I do not think he fully believed me though until he laid eyes on you," she said and winked at him.

Her reminisces fascinated me and I followed every word carefully, though nothing of what she said rattled my memory. I could see that she was an attractive, older woman and I sensed that we were connected in some way, though I was not sure how. As I recall the tale to you, it makes me smile to tell it, for Elizabeth looked so much like a gypsy. She had a piece of bright material that went around her head, and that would have been so unlike the Elizabeth I had known. When my memory finally returned to me, I often thought of the image and it made me laugh out loud to think of it. I learned that the word for the material was a *scarf,* and it flowed like her hair, all the way down to her shoulders. Aside from all the bracelets on her wrists, there were silver rings on all her fingers and large circular rings in her ears. Her blouse was a burst of pink and orange and her skirt hit her ankles in some colorful pattern of yellow and purple triangles that was so bright I could even see it clearly through my imperspicuous vision.

"Where is Matthew, Annie?" she finally asked me. "Do you know? I have waited so long. My loneliness has brought me such despair."

"I do not know any Matthew," I said quietly and much to my dismay she began to cry.

"Matthew is the one you call my son?" Michele said.

"Yes," she told him sadly.

"I have waited an eternity for you, Annie. I have waited for you and Matthew and Philippe. I have spent thirty-one chronological years here waiting."

"Philippe?" I said.

"Yes, Philippe." She took my other hand and looked deeply into my eyes. "Do you know what became of Meredith Mae?" she asked me.

"I have no memory of a Meredith Mae. I sense that I know you but I do not recall in what way. I do not recall anything."

"You are Annabel Horton from Salem, Massachusetts. You were born to flesh in the seventeenth century. I have regressed Michele back to just before those horrid witch trials. I told him to ask you where Matthew was but you misunderstood and thought he was speaking his name to you. He could not see your face clearly then. Perhaps, now that you are here, he will be able to materialize more completely in that century. I know that you will be named a witch and sentenced to hang for it. Michele must save you."

"And if he can not?" I asked.

"Our almighty souls return to ash. You are murdered at the tree. I die at the age of twenty nine in 1724 and Matthew does not exist at all. None of it will matter to anyone, least of all, us."

"And what is wrong with that?" I asked.

"We are written out of eternity and the devil remains in. We lose one another and he loses nothing."

I looked at Michele, but he was staring so intently at Elizabeth that he did not know I needed his reassurance.

"I do not understand," I told her.

"The devil has many disciples. Urbain Grandier is one. He has many faces. He was crushed to death in the sixteenth century but he put a curse on those that killed him, and I am afraid, the curse still lives. It was Philippe who told me that in Salem while we worked the farm."

"The curse?" I asked.

"Incest, rape," she whispered. "And murder. His passions manifest in those that see him. The Ursuline Nun who turned him in to Cardinal Richelieu was spared the wrath, they say. Somehow, you are connected to her, but I do not know how."

I laughed nervously. Whatever trance Elizabeth had over Michele was broken and he came to my side.

"I must send you back, Michele," she told him as he seated himself beside me. "I think you will be able to shatter the barriers now that she is here. There is divine magic in her presence. You will soon see it."

"What do you want me to do?" he asked softly.

"You will leave her handwritten letters. Perhaps they will rattle her memory."

Michele seemed shocked. "Letters that I write in this century? I am to leave them in the seventeenth century? How can I do that?"

"Trust that all time is now and that it is only a barrier to cross within."

He held my hand more tightly. "What should I say to her?" he asked.

"Tell her that you will protect her from dying. Let her know you are not of her dimension but here now, in May of 1980. Perhaps, if she knows that you are here she will remember all that comes before and after."

"Before and after?" He laughed. "How can that be if there is no order to time?"

"The moment is alive and therefore alterable," she said simply. "And order was imposed. Perhaps, our logic required it."

"But why, Elizabeth?" he asked her. "She is here now, and safe. Why must I go back to a time that wants her blood?"

"If we do not save her, Ann Arlin Peckham will regain her flesh and the soul of Annabel Horton will find God."

"What's wrong with that?" he asked despondently.

"Your children will not be born and I will never look upon the face of my beloved Matthew. My soul will carry nothing but misery to God's threshold."

"I cannot mourn the children I do not know," he said pensively.

"I am told that the bloodline on her mother's side has willed her the power to destroy the evil seed. You are the mate of Annabel Horton, and though you are a limited witch, you will learn to master your craft, as I have. I need you to do that. I must find Matthew and Urbain Grandier must find hell. "

"For God sake, what do you want me to do?"

"Sit here and write to your beloved. Do not say too much for I do not want her father to become suspicious of the letters and question them. There is such great paranoia in her village, even within families. Simply say that you will not let any harm come to her."

Michele suddenly put his arms around me.

"Can I call her my wife?" he asked. "After all, we have children together, right?"

"Yes, call her your wife," Elizabeth told him and smiled.

As for me, I blushed so deeply that I searched for a fan in my dress pocket. Elizabeth knew instinctively what I searched for and made me one of paper. What an unusual world. I might not have remembered my

ANNABEL HORTON

name but I knew with an exasperated certainty when I needed my fan.

# Chapter 3

After the letters were written, Elizabeth took us into a small room behind her kitchen. It was dark except for candles, many candles that burned and flickered against the wall. Music came from somewhere, though for the life of me I could not figure out where. On the floor was an asymmetrical pattern, a maze that seemed to go no-where.

"Take off your shoes, Annie," she said.

I sat on the floor and unlaced the soft shoes on my feet. I was dressed in a skirt that fell to my ankles, like Elizabeth's, but it was not as bright. My short white blouse had puffy sleeves. I did not like the clothes I wore but much to my chagrin, I found them comfortable.

"Now, I want you to clear your mind and walk the maze. Think of nothing," Elizabeth told me.

"All right," I whispered.

Michele was to follow behind me. He had one of the letters in his back pocket. The letter was short and signed only with the letter *M*. There were four other letters placed in the center of the maze. Elizabeth thought it best not to confuse the girl Annabel with a name she did not know so a simple *M* as signature was agreed upon by all of us.

I followed the thick white line until I lost track of all time. I could not say how long I chanted along to the music and followed the maze. I was mesmerized by the buzz of my own voice. Elizabeth finally led me out of the room with the labyrinth and put me on the floor, inside of a circle. Michele lay on the floor beside me. His hands were at his side and in the palm of his right hand, which was turned up, Elizabeth had placed the first letter. I listened to Elizabeth's voice as she chanted and spoke in low, whispery tones. I could barely make out the words she spoke. Perhaps, they were not words, but merely sounds that resembled a language I could not discern.

"Where are you now, Michele?" I finally heard her ask.

"I am in a room. I can see it clearly," he whispered.

"Is anyone in the room?" she whispered back.

"No," he said softly, and though I could not see him I knew that he shook his head. *How strange*, I thought, *that I know that.*

"Can you touch anything in the room?" I heard Elizabeth ask Michele.

It was a long time before he answered.

"Yes. I can touch the table," he told her.

"Can you put the letter on the table?" she then asked him quickly.

"I don't know," he answered.

"Try," she commanded softly.

It was at that very moment that I was able to see the room, as well. I could see that it was sparse but comfortable. The light was dim and shone only from the moon. Suddenly, I noticed a man. He was at the table. I could not see him clearly but I knew he was terribly tall.

"Matthew," I found myself whisper.

"Put the letter on the table," Elizabeth said.

"I cannot," he uttered.

"Matthew," I whispered again.

"Put the letter down on the table," Elizabeth commanded forcefully.

Suddenly, I felt the letter in my hand but before I could enfold it I felt it disappear.

Just as quickly as I had felt it there, it was gone!

"Good," Elizabeth said to Michele, "You have done it."

"I can see her reading it," he said excitedly.

"She is in the room?" Elizabeth asked.

"Yes. It appears to be the following morning and the girl Annabel is in the room."

"Can she see you?"

"No."

"To my wife," I read aloud, "I will protect you."

I could actually see and read the letter though I knew that I was still lying on the floor in Elizabeth's living room.

"She is standing in the sunlight by the window and has put the letter in her apron pocket. Her eyes are very green and her hair has such golden hues. She looks like an angel," he said softly.

"Papa," I called suddenly.

"A man has entered," Michele spoke quickly. "He is older and wears heavy breeches."

"Who has left this letter?" I found myself speaking to the man, inquiring aloud.

"What does the man look like?" Elizabeth asked Michele.

Michele laughed. "A big, kindly man."

"It is Joshua," Elizabeth said softly.

"He is saying, 'No, daughter. I know nothing of any letters. Perhaps it is Daniel, from across the road come calling?"

I answered in a loud voice. "Oh, no Papa, certainly it is not Daniel."

I could not help anything I was saying, or doing and still remained on my back in a deep trance on the floor.

"The man has walked out," Michele said. "The girl is staring out the window and holding the letter to her heart."

"Matthew," I said again.

I heard Elizabeth sigh. "She thinks the letters are from Matthew."

"I tried to touch her hair but she cannot see me," Michele said.

"Place the other four letters about the house," Elizabeth told him as she placed the other letters in his hand. I could see what Elizabeth was doing though my eyes were closed.

"Where shall I put them?" he asked her.

"Where are you standing now?" she whispered.

"I'm in the kitchen. It is very warm and there is a large kettle on the fire."

"Can you walk through the house; perhaps back to the room you were just in?" Elizabeth said to him.

I knew again that he had nodded though my eyes remained closed. I could see myself standing in the sun. I could see the sea in the distance and a very green field. It was an odd sensation, I was there and yet I was not. I could clearly see that I was wearing a plain dress and something tight on my head.

"I have placed another letter under the candle holder and another on top of a shelf. The other two have been left on a small table by the stairs," he said.

"Come back Michele," Elizabeth told him. "We will try again in a few days to speak to her directly."

"Can I say good-by to her? She is standing in the sunlight and seems to be daydreaming," Michele asked.

"Quickly."

I felt his lips so briefly and blushed.

"I love you," I heard him whisper as his lips touched my ear.

After just a moment, I knew that Michele had sat up straight and looked over at where I was lying. I could feel the tingle of his breath though he was no-where near me. I knew he looked at me, though my eyes were still closed.

"Should we send Annabel into the seventeenth century now, Elizabeth? Can we help her?"

"I do not know, but it is time to find out," she answered and held out her hand to me as I opened my eyes.

I felt terribly dizzy as I felt her flesh on my palm. I drifted into a place in space, simply drifted from one dimension into another. I could see color and feel the pressure of Elizabeth's hand fade away in my own.

After only a moment, I found myself in a wagon beside a young man who seemed familiar. I was not physically there, and yet, it felt as if I were, for everything was so clear. The man and I were in a carriage singing a song about yellow birds, very quietly, for we are not allowed to sing. It is very enjoyable to me and I start to laugh. Soon, I recognize the man as my brother, James.

"It is hot," I hear myself saying this to Elizabeth from somewhere outside of my trance. "The sun burns brightly on my arm. I can feel the heat. I can smell the horses, see the brown backside of Lucas, yes, Lucas. That is what we call the horse."

I was excited now for I knew the people around me.

"What else?" I heard Elizabeth ask as if from very far away.

I looked around. I could see myself behind the lids of my eyes.

"She seems to have her memory back," Elizabeth whispered excitedly to Michele.

Suddenly, I felt Michele take my other hand.

"There is a girl staring at me from behind a hat," I told them. "There is a malicious smile on her face. She is familiar to me. Yes! I know her as Ann Putnam."

"This must be right before her accusation against you!" I heard Elizabeth whisper. Her voice sounded muffled and seemed to come to me through a long tunnel.

"How close is Ann Putnam to you?" she asked.

"She is on the ground beside our carriage," I told her.

"Does she speak to you?"

"No, not to me but to my brother, James."

"What does she say?"

"Brother Horton, your sister has such bright eyes. They are like emeralds."

"Do not go there, Annie." I felt Elizabeth's hand in my own once again. "Just tell me what you see but do not let your soul go there too completely."

"My brother James is laughing," I said, as I felt the wind on me and heard the birds. "He has jumped from the cart and he is holding out his hand to me."

"Careful, Annie. Do not speak to her," Elizabeth told me but I could not stop my words.

"Good morning, Sister Putnam," I uttered as I watched myself step to the ground.

"Annie, avoid her, look away!" Elizabeth called to me.

"Young Peter Hemming is running over to us," I said aloud, forcing myself to narrate and not fall too deeply into this space. "He has been standing on the other side of the road. He has a broad smile and his hair falls to his eyes. My brother turns to me and whispers, 'see how he likes you,' and he grins broadly at me."

"What then, Annie? You look frightened."

Elizabeth clasps my hand more tightly as I watch my brother lift grain into the carriage. I can feel my face turn pink. I know Peter is the only boy with the courage to flirt with me.

"'The prettiest girl in the county has now graced our town,' Peter Hemming has said."

I suddenly went very quiet and I could hear, as if from a great distance, Elizabeth ask, "What then, Annie?"

"The girl, Ann Putnam, throws back her head and laughs loudly. 'Why thank you, Brother Hemming' she smiles, but it is to me he turns. 'May I walk your sister to the shade, Brother James?' I am smiling at him as my brother nods. 'If you will help me with the grain first, Peter, I would appreciate it,' he says."

"What happens then, Annie?"

Elizabeth's voice seems to have broken up and I know that if I do not struggle I might lose her altogether.

"We watch as he helps my brother with the grain. The girl glares at me as she speaks. When we have nearly loaded the carriage, and my brother has gone to pay our bill, Peter offers me his arm and we walk to the tree near the carriage station. The girl, Ann Putnam, walks with us and takes Peter's other hand, though it is only I that he wishes to be with. I know this, for he has whispered it in my ear and it makes me uncomfortable. He sits me down on an old stone bench. A large tree shades the bench. There is only room for two. 'Your father is calling you, Ann' he says to her as he sits beside me. The girl leans her head in toward his and whispers 'She has the devil's eyes. I would not sit too close.' I feel him squeeze my hand as she runs off. 'Be careful,' he says as he turns to me. 'For she is under her father's spell and surely the only witch that I know of'.

"What then Annie?" Elizabeth whispered and I felt her hand on mine but I started to weep so much that I could not stop. I was not only weeping but soon I began to scream.

"It is all changing now. I see the tree. We are on Gallows Hill, oh, Lord, help me!"

"Annie," she cried out sharply. "Come back! Annie, please return now. You are too terribly frightened."

"They have accused me! They have accused me!" I cried.

"No!" I hear Michele's call but I have fallen into darkness.

"Annie!" Elizabeth's voice was stern and commanding. "Come back!"

But I could not return. I seemed to have no power to return. From far away I heard her call again.

"Michele, oh Michele, where are you? Oh, dear. Oh, dear. Michele? Michele? Please, come back. I think it is too soon for you to go to her."

Her cries were suddenly muffled and I struggled to leave, to vanish from this place and return to her. But I could not move. I was lost in this vision. I was being led to the tree. I was so scared that I could feel myself soil my dress. There were people all around me. I knew my eyes were very large and my breath came out of my chest in rapid thrusts. Suddenly, there was a man before me. He placed a blindfold over my eyes and whispered close in my ear. Curls graced his face and his skin was the color of a cocoa bean. His presence calmed me, somewhat, and his vision was seared into my brain before blackness covered me.

"Count to three, then turn your head sharp, to the right! Do it girl and be spared!" he commanded in a fierce whisper.

I took heed and fell quickly into darkness just as the rope was slipped about my neck. I remembered nothing about my soul's release. I awoke in Elizabeth's arms.

"It is all right, Annie. You are safe now," she whispered as she stroked my face with her fingers.

My hands immediately went to my neck but my memory had already faded.

"Where is Michele?" I asked her as I searched the room for him.

"He went to save you," she told me as she took the hair from my eyes. "It seems that his power was found in his weakest moment, when he thought he might lose you."

"Bring him back!" I commanded.

"I cannot."

"You must," I cried.

"If only I knew how to bring him back. Then Matthew would be here, and Philippe, and Meredith Mae and Emie. I would bring everyone back so that we could all be together, but alas, I cannot."

"You used him to secure the existence of your beloved Matthew," I screamed. "I would send you to hell if I could."

"If hell is having a human heart then I am already there, Annie," she whispered softly.

Elizabeth took me back to Charles Street that evening, though I did not want to leave her apartment until Michele returned.

"Ann Peckham's parents will worry, Annie. You must go home," she insisted. "They will no doubt be there by now to look in on you."

"But Michele?" I cried. "We must find him. What if he is in danger?"

"He is not," she told me confidently. "He fathers Matthew, Philippe, and Emie. Obviously, he finds a way back."

"Are you sure, Elizabeth?"

"You had memory in the trance," she said. "You have none now?"

Sadly, I shook my head. "The last thing I remember is falling asleep on the floor," I told her, "and waking up to find that Michele had disappeared."

She came to me and put her hand in mine.

"Michele will return. I am certain of that, Annie. Let us not incur suspicion. We must get you back downtown."

Reluctantly, I agreed to let her take me back to the small apartment. As Elizabeth had suspected, Ann Peckham's family had driven down from Boston to be with their daughter, after her near fatal accident in the Hudson River, and they were worried sick that she was not there. Still, I was shocked to find them sitting in apartment 2C with the pretty white shepherd.

Ann Peckham's mother was quite hysterical and ran into my arms the moment I entered.

"Good God, Ann, where have you been?" she said through her tears as she hugged me and just missed singing my hair with a foul smelling cigarette that she held between her fingers.

I started to speak but Ann's father came to my side and I found myself lost between the two bodies, as they nearly squeezed the breath from me.

"Who are you?" Mr. Peckham asked as he released his bear hug and stared at Elizabeth.

"I have just come to take care of Ann's dog but I see you have retrieved her. I ran into Ann as I was coming up the stairs," Elizabeth said and began to back out the door but I grabbed her arm.

"No, come in," I called as I released myself from Mrs. Peckham's grip. "This is Elizabeth Guyon, Michele's friend. You remember Michele? He lives across the hall. He had my dog while I was in the hospital," I told them as I brought Elizabeth into the room. "How did you get her?"

Mr. Peckham ran to the phone. "I must call the authorities and tell them you're safe. We reported you missing when we didn't find you here."

"Darling, where did you go?" Mrs. Peckham asked as she took my hand and led me to the sofa. "We were so worried."

"Well, I needed to get out. I needed air," I told them. "How did you get the shepherd?"

"Why didn't you wait for us at the hospital? They said you had some amnesia and couldn't remember your name. Is that so?"

Mrs. Peckham took some smoke from her cigarette and stared at me.

"No, no. I am fine now," I said and put my hand over hers. I noticed that Elizabeth sat in a chair and looked uncomfortably back at me.

"How did the shepherd get here?" I asked again.

"She was here when we arrived, dear." Mrs. Peckham said.

"Perhaps, your neighbor brought her home, Michele, is it?"

Mr. Peckham returned from the kitchen and sat at my other side. His weight brought the couch into an ocular slump. I nervously sat between them and stared at Elizabeth.

"We're taking you to the beach house for a rest, sweetie. I want you to pack your things," Mr. Peckham told me softly and took my other hand. Mrs. Peckham's smoke drifted before my eyes and further distorted the little sight I had.

"I am not going anywhere," I insisted.

I heard Mr. Peckham sigh as he gripped my hand more tightly.

"We're not asking you to move home, dear," he said. "It's just for awhile, to rest."

"Darling," Mrs. Peckham insisted as she stood and grounded out her cigarette, "it is for your own good. You need attention and care. You've had a nasty accident."

"Who will take care of my dog?"

"We will take your dog with us. We're driving back tonight." Mrs. Peckham stood before me and put her hands on her hips. "There is nothing more to say," she added.

"I really must go," Elizabeth announced and rose to her feet. "You know where to find me, Annie."

"*Annie,* how cute. No-one's called you that since you were a child," Mrs. Peckham said as she began to pace the room. "No-one except that damn Jacques. I told you not to go boating with him, I told you not to."

"Young Todd Sheehan has been asking about you," Mr. Peckham smiled and winked at me. "Don't upset the girl, Gloria," he said and looked at his wife.

"That's nice," I responded spontaneously and politely. I tried to get up from the couch but it was so low to the ground that I could not rise to my feet.

"Goodnight, Annie," I heard Elizabeth say.

"No, wait!" I called.

"Let the poor woman go," Mrs. Peckham told me and turned to Elizabeth. "Say hello to that nice young man. What's his name, the Black boy?"

"Michele," Elizabeth said softly.

"Black?" I said. "He is a Black man? Michele is a Black man?" I wondered why I had not seen that.

Mrs. Peckham laughed and went for another of her foul little cigarettes.

"Good God, Ann. What has that accident done to you? Although he does look a bit like a Spaniard, wouldn't you say, a dashing Spaniard?"

I looked meekly up at Elizabeth and she nodded.

"Oh," I said. I looked at Elizabeth. "Are you sure?"

Mrs. Peckham eyed me with her brow raised. "Dear?"

I ignored her and turned back to Elizabeth.

"Michele Guyon's father was from France and his mother was from one of those little islands in the Caribbean, Haiti, I believe, or is it Jamaica? Anyway, those things no longer matter in this century, Annie," Elizabeth whispered to me.

"What things?" Mr. Peckham inquired.

"Black and French European? Well, that accounts for his striking good looks, wouldn't you say?" Mrs. Peckham blew the smoke back over her shoulder.

Elizabeth extended her hand. "Nice to meet you both," she said.

"Yes, same here," the Peckhams said spontaneously.

"Elizabeth, do not go!" I cried.

"Ann! What's wrong?" Mrs. Peckham came quickly to my side.

"Michele. Michele is missing," I told her.

Both Mr. and Mrs. Peckham looked at each other as Elizabeth ran to me.

"Do not worry, Annie," she told me. "Everything will be alright. I promise."

"Is this true?" Mr. Peckham looked at Elizabeth. "Is the young man missing?"

Suddenly I became very cold and began to shake.

"Lock the door," I screamed. "Quickly! Lock the door."

But no one moved. They sat and looked at me as if I had suddenly gone mad. I began to cry louder. I made my hands into fists and began to pound them at my sides. Soon I was sobbing uncontrollably. I saw Elizabeth rise. I heard the scream fall from her lips.

The Peckham's stared at us in disbelief for they did not understand our horror. There at the door, stood Urbain Grandier. I could smell the rancid air around him though his face was clean and chiseled.

"Annie," he uttered as he came to me like lightning; his large, imposing figure swept before me like some gallant prince. He took me forcefully into his arms. "I've been beside myself in grief, so worried, my darling, so worried."

I felt his face in my neck and his long, nearly white hair before my eyes.

The shepherd began to raise her lips and growl. Urbain pushed the dog aside.

"Begone!" I hissed and threw up my hands while the Peckham's watched in disbelief.

Urbain fell back on his knees and laughed.

"Such fire in your soul, little Annie." He grinned.

"It is so nice of you to visit but she needs her rest, Jacques," Mr. Peckham said as he watched Urbain rise. The demon was dressed in black, what you would call contemporary clothes. His shirt was small and showed his massive build, his pants so tight I could see the muscles move on his thigh.

I noticed that Elizabeth stood glaring at him from a corner of the room.

"Where is Michele?" I asked him.

"We're taking our daughter back home to Massachusetts," I heard Mr. Peckham tell Urbain. "You know, we have a beach house there on the Cape."

"Is that so?" the devil said.

"Go to hell!" I suddenly called out.

Everyone in the room turned to stare at me. I heard Urbain's laughter.

"She is going nowhere with you," he said and turned back toward Mr. Peckham.

"I beg your pardon?" Mr. Peckham said in disbelief.

"You heard me," Urbain said fiercely. "I am sending her on a trip."

"What?" Mr. Peckham demanded. "We are her parents. We say where she goes, not you, young man."

"You bastard." Gloria Peckham rose and stood defiantly before Urbain. "Our daughter almost dies in your care and you dare to tell us what to do with her?"

"Your daughter almost died when the engagement ring I gave her slipped from her finger and into the Hudson River. She fell from the boat trying to retrieve it. The idiot woman got me all wet, I wound up under the boat."

"Now listen here Jacques..." Mr. Peckham began but was cut off by his wife.

"How dare you, you overblown son of a bitch. Leave this apartment before I call the police." Mrs. Peckham shook her finger in his face.

"You are threatening me?" He smiled as he said it. "I wouldn't do that."

I found myself rising. "Begone Beast!" I commanded and held my hands before me.

Suddenly he spun around. "Her anger charms me so," he said as he fell to his knees and rubbed his head. He appeared dizzy.

"Where is Michele?" I screamed out.

"The devil's curse is on you all." He spat three times on the floor and spun around again, his massive body continued to turn as we all stared in horror. "Simplistic, naïve ninnies. You deserve your God. You deserve your fate," he called out.

The shepherd chased behind him and yelped loudly as she tried to nip at his heels.

"He's insane," Mrs. Peckham called. "Call the police, Mark," she screamed.

"Get the hell out of here," Mr. Peckham demanded but did not try to stop his spinning.

"I am chewing up your souls," Urbain shouted. "And I will spit you out like soiled food."

I watched as Elizabeth came towards him with the dog's leash and began to thrash him on the back. "Return to fire, you demon!" she hissed.

"Ha ha!" he laughed. "Poor little Elizabeth." Suddenly, he grabbed her and spun her around with him. "You are old now," he told her. "At least sixty-four. What will your precious Matthew want with you now?"

"I command you to release her," I screamed.

"Didn't I tell you, Ann? Didn't I say he was a madman?" Mrs. Peckham screamed frantically.

Then, suddenly, the room became pitch black. I could see nothing through the darkness but Urbain's long white hair and the blue of his eyes dazzling the imposing nigrescent sheath like stars above the earth. I felt a loud thud, as if I had been thrown against a wall, but I felt no pain. I knew that Elizabeth had been thrown as well, for I heard another thud near me, though I could see nothing. The Peckham's voices began to dissolve and fade out. I began to cry softly. I felt Elizabeth as she held me close to her. When the darkness finally lifted, the Peckham's were nowhere to be found and Elizabeth and I, and the pretty, white shepherd, were standing on a dirt road in the middle of no-where.

# Chapter 4

We looked at our surroundings for a long time before we spoke. The dog seemed as confused as we were but after a while she began to act like a dog and sniff the ground. Soon she was running and playing in the grass on the other side of the street as if nothing unusual had happened to her.

"Good, God. Where are we?" Elizabeth asked bewilderingly.

Way off in the distance there appeared to be houses.

"This is somewhat familiar," I said at last. "We have left the twentieth century behind for sure."

"You have some memory?"

"Are you all right, Elizabeth?" I asked her.

"Oh, yes," she told me. "But where are we? Where has the demon sent us?"

"Let us go there where the houses are." I pointed ahead.

The dog followed behind us as we walked and nipped at our ankles. What a strange couple we must have made in our twentieth century clothes; Elizabeth in her brightly colored skirts and both of us in such curious shoes.

We followed the dirt road, which soon became Clover Hill and eventually led us, miraculously, to the house on Montague Street.

"My God!" I said as I dropped to my knees before it.

"What is it, Annie?" Elizabeth asked as she huddled close to me.

"I know this house as my own!"

"Your memory has returned then?"

I rubbed my head. "Yes. Everything is still a bit foggy, but yes, I seem to be remembering everything. Oh, my. My memory has returned intact, I think."

"Oh, Annie," she wept.

"Oh Elizabeth, I have missed you so terribly much," I said. "I have so much to tell you now that I know who on earth I am."

"And I, as well."

"My thoughts are coming at me so quickly that I can not sort them."

"What dimension of time do you think we are in?"

"I know not."

The shepherd barked loudly at us and began to run in circles around us.

"It appears to be early morning," I said to Elizabeth as I looked at the rising sun.

"We mustn't bring attention to ourselves," Elizabeth whispered and tried to quiet the dog, but she continued to bark and run out ahead of us.

"She's going to wake up the neighborhood," I said nervously.

"I think we are in the nineteenth century, Annie. Look at the buildings, and there are no skyscrapers."

"It is Brooklyn. We are near the river and this is the home we always spoke to you about when we were in Salem together. Everything might be perfect, if only Michele were here."

"Look, there is a man. He wears such a handsome suit. Is it a nineteenth century suit?"

"Quick! We must hide. We can not be seen dressed like this."

We tried to stand behind a tree, hoping it would shield us from the passer-by, but the dog only barked louder and circled the tree. The man eyed us strangely.

"Good morning, Ladies." He grinned broadly at me and tipped his hat. As he passed, he stopped to turn back and smile at me. He must have assumed I was with a traveling circus.

I meekly returned his smile and watched him continue down the road, swinging his cane and whistling.

"Oh my God! What form do I have?" I suddenly realized I had flesh.

"Why, I see you as Annabel Horton but I think you look the same. You are still Ann Peckham."

"How unnerving that I can walk through time and not have to kill off a body. It has never been like that before."

"Urbain willed you here, perhaps that is why," she whispered as if he lurked in the shadows.

"Urbain has no will over me." I laughed. "If Urbain willed that so easily then I have no power to thwart the Devil, and I know that is not so. I must have wanted to be here. I must have allowed it. I must have the power to cross the barriers without doing away with anyone. It is a shame I do not know how to use this power."

"Perhaps, you do," she said.

"My only weakness is not remembering my own magic," I told her.

"That must be," she said and squeezed my hand.

"Should we knock on the door?" I asked quietly. "Matthew might be there." I grinned.

"Urbain might be there, as well."

I laughed. "Yes, the devil thinks this is *his* house."

"I think it is a chance we must take," she told me, "before our pretty dog wakes up the entire city and we are left to explain why we look like misplaced actors."

"Come, Beauty!" I called to the dog and took Elizabeth's hand. With some trepidation and rapid heartbeats, we walked to the front door.

"If it is Urbain that answers, what should we do?" Elizabeth asked.

"Nothing. I will not bargain with the devil," I told her confidently.

"He feeds on pain, Annie. Are you strong enough for that?"

"Strength is a force of faith," I whispered as I pulled on the familiar chime. "And my faith is greater than the devil's game."

We waited only a moment before the door opened. Two people stood there and neither of them was Urbain, a third stood just beyond them.

"Mother!" Matthew cried as he reached for me. "My God, at last!"

"Matthew!" I wept as I embraced him.

"Grandmamma!" my beloved Meredith Mae said as she took me in her arms.

I recognized them at once as my son and granddaughter. I was so overjoyed I might have burst at the seams. Together we cried and laughed, large tears rolled down our faces. Then, quickly, my granddaughter broke away from my embrace and ran to Elizabeth.

"Oh, darling, darling Elizabeth. Is it really you?" she exclaimed.

"Meredith Mae, how beautiful you look," Elizabeth sang out as she embraced her.

Matthew did not let go of my hand and looked on quietly as the two women held each other. I wanted desperately to recapture every memory I had lost, but I was so distracted by the presence of Matthew and Meredith Mae that my thoughts were a jumble. I looked beyond Matthew to the teenaged girl that stood at the stairway and stared at me with a quiet smile. The dog had run to her and practically knocked her over.

"Rachel?" I whispered. "Look, Elizabeth," I said quickly. "That girl has Ann Peckham's face; that is why Ann was so familiar to me. See how alike they look. Why, even the dog thinks it is her mistress. She and Ann Peckham could be sisters."

I ran to the young woman and took her in my arms.

"Rachel," I cried. "Oh, how good it is to see you. Look Elizabeth, look at the similarity between Ann and Rachel."

But Elizabeth did not answer me. She was staring at my son. He remained silent and did not move. It suddenly dawned on me that poor Elizabeth was at least ten to fifteen chronological years older than Matthew.

"Matthew," she said through her tears, but my son only stared in disbelief.

"Matthew," she repeated. "Oh, Matthew, I have waited so long to hold you in my arms."

He went to her and stood before her and held her face to the light.

"Matthew," she wept. "Oh, God! Matthew."

He kissed her lightly on the lips and smiled sadly.

"You have become old," he said, as if trying to make a joke of it. I could feel Elizabeth's pain as if my own heart had been as brutally punctured.

The year was 1857 and I was home in my beloved Brooklyn with my son and my own dear Meredith Mae. The girl, Rachel, was now sixteen. Though we could not prove it at the time, we knew that Ann Arlin Peckham was a direct descendent of Rachel and the man she would marry the following year, Troy Spencer. They would have three boys and two girls. The older girl, Elizabeth Sue, would disappear mysteriously at the age of five. The disappearance would go on record as an unsolved kidnapping and the child would not be seen again for many years. Olivia, the younger girl, would marry a biologist named Ian Sanford and they would move to Boston in1880. Olivia's daughter, Jane, would marry a portrait painter just as the century turned, and they would have twin girls. One twin would succumb to tuberculosis at an early age and die, the other, little Melinda, would marry Thomas Conklin in 1914 and they would have six children. Only one of the children would be a girl. Their daughter, Cordelia Conklin, would marry late in life and only because the money from her trust was poorly invested. She would meet Terrance Arlin when she was nearly forty. They would only have one child, a daughter, Gloria Evangeline Arlin. Gloria would marry early, seventeen, to be precise. She and Mark Peckham would have three children. Unfortunately, one son would die early from a weak heart. Their other son, Bill, would become a medical student at a teaching hospital in New York City and their daughter, Ann, an art historian student at New York University. Ann would be found murdered in her own home just weeks before her forty-fifth birthday. Yes, well, you will learn of that soon enough. I would learn all this much later, as well, but I tell you now because it fascinates me so that I would wind up in poor Ann's body, a descendent of my dear little Rachel. I was so happy to see her looking so well after all she had been through with that nasty Ebenizer and Malcolm. She had matured into a fine young woman.

Matthew continued to ignore Elizabeth while we sat in the parlor after breakfast trying to fill in the events that had separated us. Matthew was eager to tell me all about the Civil War, a war that would not begin, from a chronological standpoint, for four more years. He relayed his experiences in Virginia with Philippe and Emie, and I could tell that much of it was painful for him. He told me that after the battle of Appomattox and the Union victory, Philippe and Emie had returned to their own dimension of space so that they would not encounter suspicion there, and Matthew had immediately returned to Brooklyn to search for his Elizabeth.

"I thought I would find you all here," he told me as he sat at my feet and held my hand. I noticed that Elizabeth sat on the other side of the room and kept her eyes to the floor.

"Imagine my shock to return to an empty house," he said.

"How did you wind up in such a terrible war?"

"We were pulled toward it. We thought Elizabeth was there in Virginia in 1863."

"The Civil War?" Elizabeth asked quietly.

"Yes," Matthew said and turned to her.

"I have been listening to your stories and I think I understand. You speak of many things that I have studied. Your father taught a course on the Civil War. He is a teacher of history. I took the course in 1979," she said and looked at Matthew with an expression I could not read. "Perhaps you were pulled by my own absorption in it."

"My father?" he asked and went to her. "You know my father?"

Elizabeth nodded. "Annie and I have found him in the twentieth century."

"Mother?"

I smiled at him. "Yes. Michele teaches history in New York City in the dimension of 1980, and I have met him. He sees me as Annabel when he looks in the glass, but as far as I know, he does not know of his power as a witch."

"God, Mother. I so want to meet my father." He got on his knees before me again and took both my hands in his. "Can we move in time?"

"I am afraid Michele has vanished and I do not know where he is."

My son sat back and sighed loudly. I noticed that my homecoming was not as happy as I would have imagined. Elizabeth seemed quite despondent and Meredith Mae remained sitting across the room from me as if she were trying to disappear behind her fan. Rachel eyed me curiously.

"Your mother, child, Beth Ann, how is she?" I asked her.

The girl looked at me, a bit sadly, I might add.

"I have not seen her since I was a child, but I hear she lives alone and rarely goes out."

I breathed in deeply and put my hands over my chest. It would seem that poor Beth Ann had honored Malcolm's ultimatum and never bothered with the child again.

"What of Ebenizer?" I inquired.

Rachel smiled very broadly. "He's been dead for years."

"And your grandmother, Maebelle, is she well?" I asked.

"She has not changed. She appears happy, though she doesn't know who any of us are when we visit her. They tell me she sings to herself and keeps her room tidy. We try to see her as often as we can but Long Island is so terribly far."

I recalled my encounter with poor Maebelle, and as I did, so many other memories began to flood back into my consciousness. It seems my human body was slowly acquiescing to the transition of having shattered space. All of a sudden, I was hit with a terrible recollection. Of course.

Oh, my God, my beloved Meredith Mae had been hoodwinked by an insidious imposter and had been in great danger right before my death in Malcolm's flesh.

"Good God!" I cried and rose to my feet.

They all looked up and their shoulders stiffened.

"What is it, Mother?" Matthew cried.

"Annie?" I heard Elizabeth say.

"Ann?" Rachel came quickly to my side.

Only Meredith Mae remained quiet and did not move. I turned my eyes to her and watched as she shook her head and stared at her father.

"Meredith Mae?" I whispered.

"Grandmamma?" she answered softly, her eyes wide and frightened.

"What has happened to Ursula?" I asked.

Now, I remembered that foul woman and the evil trick she had played to seduce my granddaughter and steal her estate.

"As far as I know, Ursula has never returned from Europe," Meredith Mae said quickly.

I raised my brow and continued to stare at her.

"We adopted Rachel, Louie and I. We have raised her all these years." She came to my side and put her lips to my ear. "Papa does not know," she whispered quickly.

I looked into her eyes. I was just about to ask her to explain how Louie and Ursula could be in two different places at once when they are the same person, but then all of a sudden the very scoundrel we spoke of stood at the top of the stairs in a red velvet robe and looked askance at me, as she, *or he*, as she was now referring to herself, descended the stairs.

"What have we here?" he said as he slowly walked down like visiting royalty and stood before me. My mouth fell open as I stared at him or *her*, I should say.

"Good morning, Louie," I heard Matthew utter amicably. I stared at my son, my mouth so open my tonsils must have appeared apparent.

"What is it, Mother?" My son asked.

Meredith Mae stepped behind me and I heard her whisper, "Don't Grandmamma, please, don't reveal him."

"Good morning, Papa," Rachel said.

"Papa?" My eyes narrowed as I said it.

The villain smiled and stared at me.

"Do I know you?" he asked suddenly.

"What is the bastard doing among us?" I asked.

"Mother!" Matthew cried in disbelief and ran to my side. "Louie is part of the family. He is my son-in-law. Louie, this is, ahh. This is...."

"Ann Peckham," I said as I glared at him. "I am an old family friend."

"Ah." Louie said as he shook my hand. "I could have sworn I heard Matthew refer to you as his 'mother' but how can someone so appealingly young be anyone's mother?" He kissed the tips of my fingers.

"And this is Elizabeth," I said. "Matthew's wife."

"Elizabeth?" The scoundrel seemed surprised as he turned to her. "I have heard nothing but your name for so long now. It is a pleasure."

Elizabeth seemed taken by his charm and bowed gracefully.

I searched for Meredith Mae's eyes but she held them to the floor and avoided me.

"Meredith Mae, I wish to speak with you alone," I commanded.

Matthew was surprised but looked to Rachel.

"Come, sweetheart," he said. "Come, Louie. Let us give them the time they need."

Elizabeth said nothing, but I knew she understood my dismay and gave me a curious look. I watched as *Louie* turned his back on me and proceeded toward the kitchen. The bastard still wore his hair to his shoulders. It was height that made the woman appear to resemble a young man, but with such delicate features any idiot could see *he* was actually *she*.

"Take your time, darling," he said over his shoulder to Meredith Mae. "I'll make us all some coffee."

My son put his arm around Louie's shoulder and together they left the room. Poor Elizabeth went ignored and followed quietly behind. I was furious with my son for so clearly rejecting Elizabeth, with no thought at all to her feelings, but I could do nothing about it at the moment. There was something else to attend to, something dangerous and scandalous, and so terribly decadent that I could barely collect my thoughts to communicate.

LOST WITCH OF SALEM

# Chapter 5

My darling Meredith Mae sat across the room from me and stared at the hands she held in her lap.

"Child..." I began.

"Grandmamma?" She looked up.

"Surely, you must recognize the truth now."

"Yes," she said quickly. "I do."

"What?" I was aghast. "You seem so nonchalant."

"Grandmamma, Louie and I are in love."

She closed her fan and placed it on the table.

"Louie?" I said. There is no Louie."

She turned her eyes from me and studied her fingers.

"Are you saying you are in love with this, this...?"

I could not even finish my thought.

"Yes," she said simply. "That is exactly what I am saying."

"You knew all along of Ursula's deception?"

I was so agitated I felt myself biting my lip.

"Not at first, but soon enough I did. It was a game. I played it," she said defensively. "We played it together. I don't expect you to understand."

"She is out to trick you," I said and walked to her. "To take your estate."

"Then why has she not taken it? It has been over five years that we are together."

She sat back and stared up at me. I could tell by the way she was holding herself that I would never convince her of any wrongdoing on Ursula's part.

"I am surprised that *Louie* returned to Brooklyn. Catherine accused him of masterminding the plot to kill poor William," I said as I turned and leaned against the mantle.

"We knew we were taking a chance on returning but I was so worried about Rachel. Once I learned of Malcolm's death I knew I had to come back for her. Fortunately, no-one took the accusations against Louie very seriously, though Silas did try to conjure up a case against him."

"What happened?" I asked.

"Nothing," she told me. "He failed to produce enough evidence."

"I see." I sighed. "Why did *he* not just return as Ursula? Ursula is not wanted for murder."

She blushed and turned away from me. I could see my question was not going to be answered truthfully.

"I had no idea what had happened to you," she said. She leaned forward in her chair and looked at me. "It is easier to travel with a man, Grandmama. It could be dangerous for two women alone. Luckily, Papa was here when we returned. I was happy for that but what could I say to him, with Ursula dressed as Louie? I introduced her as my husband."

"What did he say?" I asked.

I was shocked that Matthew could not see beyond this charade.

"He told me that Emie and Philippe had gone into the twentieth century. I asked about you. We were so worried. We've waited an eternity for you."

"I also found myself in the twentieth century but Emie and Philippe are not yet born."

"I see," she said.

"I found Elizabeth there, and also Michele, but I had no memory of either."

A long uncomfortable silence followed between us. Finally, I spoke.

"Matthew accepts this abomination between you and Ursula?"

I knew I had hurt her but I could not help myself.

"It is easier for Louie and I to live as husband and wife. Who would accept us otherwise? The charade had already begun. I thought it would be easier for Father to accept, and the child, Rachel, as well."

"Your father is innocent but you do not fool the child."

She returned my gaze with a raised eyebrow.

"Rachel knows the truth?" she asked, as if she did not know.

"She clearly loves you both and will not burst your bubble."

"And what about you, Grandmamma? Will you burst it?"

"If memory serves me, I followed the scoundrel to a church and found your Ursula in a devil's mass. She was about to sacrifice Rachel to the devil. Her lover, Jeanne Elemont, was about to put a stake through the girl's heart before I stopped it." I went to Meredith Mae and took her wrist and pulled her face to mine. "Don't be a fool, girl. What the Devil desires he does not love."

She pulled her arm from me and sat back.

"Ursula is a complex being but she is no friend of the Devil." She glared at me.

"What then would you call the murder of a child?" I spat at her.

"She plays at being a man and she plays at being a witch. She is neither," she said and I could see that her eyes were filled with tears. "And the child still lives, does she not?"

"She saw me as Annabel when I walked in Malcolm's flesh," I said. "She rode me like a bull knowing who I was."

"I will not listen to this." Meredith Mae rose and stood by the window. She turned her back on me.

"Perhaps her lover, Jeanne Elemont, revealed my identity," I said.

"I know of no one by that name."

"She resembles your Father Jacques, this Jeanne. Perhaps it was his seed that made her."

Meredith Mae spun around and glared at me.

"Father Jacques is the kindest man alive." She almost screamed the words.

I laughed. "You do not know when you are being deceived, do you?" I said, quite frustrated with her.

"I am not being deceived!"

"Does he still come to this house as though it were his?" I laughed.

"Yes. He uses the Library. He has my permission to do so."

"Has your father ever seen this Father Jacques?"

She shook her head.

"And why not?" I asked. "I will tell you why not. Because your father would recognize him as the man on the Ferry who sent him to Salem and who killed Seth, his step-father, and the Devil would no longer be able to trick you into believing that he is some benevolent priest."

"No, Grandmamma. It is because he reads what the church does not permit him to read. He reads philosophy on agnosticism and atheism. He reads books on the Occult. He even reads novels. The Catholic Church would frown upon that. I keep his secrets and he keeps mine."

"You are being fooled Meredith Mae though I know not for what purpose."

"You won't tell Father about Louie, will you, Grandmamma?" she asked. "I beg you."

I promised, despite my better judgment. The news of it would have sent poor Matthew into a deep depression from which he might not have emerged. I would tolerate the truth for the time being, until I learned of Ursula's motive, and I knew she had one. Ursula/ Louie Boussidan was acting on Urbain's behalf, and of this I was quite certain. But, the Devil does not share his secrets until his web has sufficiently enticed his prey of choice. Then the hand of the Devil closes tight and chokes the one within.

When we returned to the dining room my son Matthew was reading the paper. Rachel and Louie had left, probably to the rear yard, for it was a pleasant morning. Matthew was doing all he could to avoid contact with his beloved Elizabeth. I looked at her as she sat in a chair staring out the window. She was beautiful. Any fool could see that. If my son were the older of the two there would be no cause for grief. But poor Elizabeth had aged differently, in a different dimension of time and space, and the illusion of life had given her flesh the process of age. It was because of this illusion of age that this needless grief was taking place. But know this; the soul is a timeless entity. It experiences life in the body as a process of dying but the soul is not physical flesh, it only experiences physical flesh. The body is acknowledged as changing, but it is actually the soul metamorphosing and shedding the process of being in human form. Poor Matthew could not see the soul of his beloved because he could not get beyond the vanity of being human. Do you think there is such a thing as vanity when the flesh is shed? The Devil can be held accountable for that foible. The soul is timeless. Unfortunately, that knowledge is not accessible when we are experiencing ourselves as living beings in the unenlightened dimensions of life. However, despite the ignorance of Matthew's soul to recognize itself as such, I decided to intervene.

"Elizabeth." I said. "May I see you alone in the drawing room?"

"Of course," she said and followed me behind the closed door.

I took her hand and squeezed the pretty fingers.

"Men are fools," I said. "Do not be hurt by them."

"I know I am beautiful. Why does he not see it anymore?"

"My son has aged at least fifteen chronological years since I last saw him. There is a swell to his belly and more flesh under his chin than he needs." I laughed.

"Have you noticed, too, that his teeth are no longer like pearls and there is so much gray in his beard that he looks like a pigeon?"

She laughed with me until we were both a bit uncontrollable.

"And those dear curls of his are getting quite thin on top." I giggled. "So much so that I can see the dear sweet pink of his skull."

"Oh, Annie. It does me good to laugh at him. I am sorry, but it does."

"Do not apologize, my dear," I said. "He does deserve it."

"To think I have waited over thirty years to find him so disinterested."

"The Devil is a man," I winked. "Human judgment blurs the vision."

She looked at me and smiled. "That is so."

"You must use your power over his ideologies *and* mythologies."

"I do not follow you," she whispered as she came closer to me on the couch.

"Once upon a time, he loved a beautiful young girl who could not live without him. How easy and simple that is when a man is still a boy. But, he has come to fear you now."

"Fear me?" she said.

I nodded.

She looked beyond me, most likely trying to figure out what I meant.

"Men think that it is only women who believe in fairy tales. Men start out falling in love with the first of their illusions, and when they realize this, they shift their obsessions in order to allay their fear of dying, and aging, and confronting a woman's power. You must get beyond this nonsense."

"How?" she asked me.

"Seduce him," I said simply.

She laughed sarcastically. "He thinks I am old."

"What he thinks is completely meaningless. Men are lost in illusions.

Shatter them. Touch his soul. Bring him to his heart, Elizabeth."

"How?" she asked again.

"Are you not a woman?" I smiled seductively.

She puckered up her lips and stared at me for a long time. Finally, I saw that she understood me completely.

"Am I to resort to sex to win his heart?" She grinned.

"Is the magic in the act or in the actress?" I winked again.

"You are wicked," she told me softly.

"Is it only men that have the power to take what they want?"

Elizabeth stood up from the couch and I marveled at her beauty. I looked into her eyes and smiled, as I opened the door to the dining room. I watched as my son slowly looked up from his paper. Elizabeth had unbuttoned her blouse until the swell of her bosom could be seen, like two well-formed mountains rising to the sun. Her flesh had a soft pink tinge. She put her hands on her hips and ran her tongue over her lips. She then undid her hair until it fell from her shoulders. Streaks of gray ran through the brown waves as she shook it free and laughed. My son seemed mesmerized.

"I am thirsty," she said at last. Her voice was low and reminded me of velvet.

I watched the color rise to my son's face. I noticed his eyes had remained on her unbuttoned blouse and his lips fell into a quiet part.

"Matthew?" she said, her eyes smiling as she said it.

He looked up, a bit flustered.

"Bring water to my room?" she asked in her velvety voice as she walked toward him.

"Yes, yes. Of course," he said as he began to rise.

She stood before him. Playfully, her hands went around his waist and then fell carelessly past the buttons on his fly.

"I am taking to my bed," she whispered. "Do not make me wait too long for it."

"Yes, Elizabeth," he stammered, his flesh a deep red as she turned and left the room.

"If you'll excuse me, Mother. Elizabeth is thirsty," he said quickly and followed close behind her.

"Yes, of course," I called after him. "Do not worry about me. I have much to keep me busy."

But I am quite sure he heard not a word of what I said.

It was not until the following morning that I saw my son again. He was in the drawing room with his paper. He looked up when he saw me.

"Good morning, Mother."

"Good morning, Matthew. Did you sleep well?" I asked as I made myself a place beside him on the sofa.

He nodded and took my hand.

"So, you have your precious Elizabeth back at last," I said.

He nodded but looked away.

"You are still in love with her?" I asked cautiously.

"Do you know that it was I that saved you in the river?"

"You are changing the subject," I told him.

"I heard you calling me and I let myself follow your call. It led me out on the Promenade. I stood gazing out over the water, and before I knew it, I was in a boat and people were screaming and pointing to a woman who seemed to be drowning. I knew I had crossed a barrier but I had no time to sort anything out. I simply jumped into the Hudson, without even thinking about it, and I swam to the woman in distress. It wasn't until I breathed the life back into her body that I saw you take possession of her flesh."

"Why did you not stay with me then?" I asked.

"I could not."

"Why?" I turned him to look at me.

"I tried to remain, but my body came back, and I could not cross again," he told me. "I kept trying, but something held me here. I wasn't even sure of the century I had just been in. I had followed a call but I couldn't return to it."

"Elizabeth was there in that century. You might have found her."

"I love Elizabeth," he said quietly, "but she has changed."

"No, not changed. She has simply aged," I told him. "And she loves you entirely."

"Many years have passed for me here, Mother," he said quietly. "I have not been without a woman."

"More years have passed for Elizabeth. She has never stopped wanting you. Perhaps you need to discover each other anew."

"I don't think you've heard me, Mother. There are others, one in particular."

I turned him to face me and looked into his eyes. He appeared sad and yet he returned my gaze.

"Elizabeth is your wife, Matthew," I said slowly.

"I will honor that," he said.

"You must give up this other woman."

"It has been going on for quite some time, four years to be exact. I could not marry her as long as I thought Elizabeth might return to me. But I promised that I would not wait more than five years for Elizabeth. This woman has been very patient with me, and now I must tell her that I can't marry her." He looked terribly upset, "that my wife has, in fact, returned."

"Well, Elizabeth has returned just in time then," I said.

He looked away.

"I am not a young man anymore, Mother."

"What are you saying?" I asked him.

"Elizabeth is not a young woman."

"You are married!" I cried.

"I said I would honor that, but a man is entitled to a mistress," he said simply.

I stood and glared into his eyes. "Why?" I asked.

"It is a male privilege, like cigar smoking."

I laughed and sat back down.

"And hunting and pilfering and pillaging the earth? Are they also male privileges, Matthew, or male insensitivity?"

"Men enjoy what they enjoy."

He turned and scowled at me as Elizabeth walked into the room and looked at him coyly.

"And what do men enjoy, darling?" She laughed as she sat on a couch that faced us.

"Being men," he said and got up to sit beside her.

"God does not judge us by our genitals, Matthew, only by our soul," I told him sternly. "May that be your redemption."

"Oh, Mother." He smiled and put his arm around Elizabeth's shoulder, "what has the twentieth century done to you both?"

I did not answer him. I got up and left the room. Just as I closed the doors behind me I heard him call her his mature "turtledove," and I listened as she laughed and referred to him as her "handsome cock."

# Chapter 6

I needed time alone. My son's indiscretions had upset me and I had so much to think about. I went into the front room where it appeared I could find some solitude. I nestled myself on a large, overstuffed settee. Rachel unexpectedly came down the stairs. She ran to kiss me on the cheek.

"I am going to Prospect Park to watch Troy play Rugby," she said.

Since I needed to collect my thoughts I welcomed her exit.

"Troy?" I said and smiled distractedly.

She blushed and nodded.

"Is it serious with the young man?" I asked as I watched her place a shawl over her shoulders.

The girl laughed and kissed me again. I could not help but think how the once pathetic child had metamorphosed so beautifully.

"And has Louie been good to you?" I asked.

"You and I both know I have two mothers." She grinned.

I avoided her eyes.

"Ann," she whispered.

"It does not bother you?" I asked sternly.

She shook her head from side to side and smiled without showing me her teeth.

"When you were a child, she took you into Manhattan. Do you

remember?"

I held out my hand to her and motioned for her to join me on the couch.

She came and sat next to me.

"I remember my childhood very well. Unfortunately, I remember my grandfather and my great-grandfather, that horrible Ebenezer. I also remember how wonderful it finally felt to be adopted."

"You do know about me, don't you? You do know who I am, or should I say, whose flesh I was in?"

"Yes, I know everything now. Thank you for saving me."

"There was a church, Rachel."

"Yes, I recall."

"A devils Mass," I said carefully.

She laughed again.

"There is nothing funny about the devil," I said quickly.

"Oh, Ann. Papa plays at magic but has none."

"I see," I whispered. "Papa? You still call her that?"

"Why not, if it makes *her* happy?"

"Because it is indecent."

"They gave me a warm and loving home, both of them. I am grateful for that."

"He is deceiving you. *She* is deceiving you," I said.

"I'm late meeting Troy. You will excuse me?" she asked, avoiding any further discussion.

"Of course," I answered as I kissed her.

"Do you have any powers?" I asked before she could get too far from me.

"I am clairvoyant," she proudly proclaimed.

"How much do you see?"

She turned to me at the door.

"A long trip." She winked.

"Whose?"

"Yours," she said seriously, "But you will return."

"Enjoy your Troy Spencer, dear." I waved her on.

"You can't take Louie, very seriously." She stood at the open door and looked back at me.

I smiled slowly. "Oh, but I do," I told her as she let in the quiet sun. It fell on my arms and provided me with comforting warmth.

She stared directly into my eyes. "And I am serious about what I see for you."

"I hope you are wrong, dear. I do not wish to go anywhere. I have just arrived."

"Papa has kept me very safe."

"Urbain and his whores are making fools of you all," I muttered under my breath as I sat back comfortably into the seat and looked at the blue sky beyond her.

"What was that you said?" she asked.

"Nothing dear. Nothing you will not hear again."

She blew me a kiss and then skipped down the steps and disappeared into the unforgiving white shadow of the noonday glare.

I racked my brain to think of it. Why had Ursula not killed off my Meredith Mae and absconded with her estate as she had planned to do with Catherine and Malcolm? Why would she continue the marriage for five years, and what had ever happened to Jeanne Elemont? Why did she not sacrifice the child to the devil, if that was her intent, after Malcolm's death? And why was she luxuriating here in my beloved house and making a complete idiot out of my son, and my granddaughter, with this ridiculous charade as a man? The answers did not come to me right away, but when they finally came to light, and they would, even I would be startled by the truth.

I must have fallen asleep soon after Rachel's departure. When I awoke, a lovely late afternoon sun was gently filling the parlor with a brilliance of light. The house was quiet and I wondered how long I had been asleep. It felt like forever. I listened for sounds of life and from far off in the distance, I could hear laughter. I felt happy for a moment, until I remembered that several dimensions separated Michele and I, and that that wretched Ursula had infiltrated my family. I wished that Elizabeth would tire of my son and join me in the parlor. I wanted to tell her all about Ursula, and that horrid plot to steal my granddaughter's estate, but it seems I would have to wait until Elizabeth and Matthew had a temporary lapse in their lovemaking. I had not gotten the chance to speak with either of them about my sojourn in Malcolm's flesh. I put my head back on the chair and stared at the beveled ceiling. I tried to think things through, but my mind seemed dull and tired and I could not collect my thoughts. I kept sensing that I was not alone in the room, yet I saw no one else. I felt the blessed sun on my flesh as a gentle breeze played with the curtains and they danced in playful nonchalance. Suddenly, the dog began to bark. I looked up and watched as she ran from the room, as if someone she knew had called to her. I listened to her nails on the wooden floor until I could no longer hear them. It was then that I realized that both my vision and my hearing were a bit clearer than usual, if only for the moment. I felt an unsettling vertigo as the door chime began to sound. I thought, at first, it was a neighbor's bell, but then, I realized it came from my own front door. I waited to see if anyone would answer the call but no one came. Quite suddenly, I realized that I was dressed in different clothes than I had been earlier. They appeared to be from Ann Peckham's casual and rather shocking century, but I could swear I had changed into more appropriate attire. *How on earth did I get into these clothes again?* I thought. My mind felt so groggy. I tried to clear my head but the chimes did not stop and continued to distract me.

I remained on the couch, still trying to remember when I changed my clothes. I hoped whoever it was at the door would realize that no one was going to answer the wretched bell, and would desist from pulling on the chime and go away. Then, all of a sudden, I heard a key turn in the lock.

"Good God!" I called out as I sat up straight. "My God."

There he stood! The impious, malevolent, dastardly bastard!

"Annabel?" he asked slowly.

I rose from my chair and held out my hands, but the demon held a cross in front of him.

"Peace," he said.

"Go to hell."

"Amen." He smiled and walked into the room.

He wore the clothes of a Catholic Priest. His yellow white hair was tied back. His eyes were like those of an eagle but appeared as a vivid shade of blue in the light of the sun. He took up so much space in the room that I stood back from him.

"You are in my house," he said simply.

"This is my house," I told him.

He laughed and came toward me but I stepped back again.

"Where is Michele?" I asked.

"Here," he said and touched his heart.

"Where is he?" I repeated.

"Here," he said again and again touched his heart.

"Leave me!" I commanded.

He sat and crossed his legs.

"So how is our Elizabeth?" he asked.

"In bed with her Matthew."

He laughed. "Have you met the glorious Jeanne Elemont yet?" He grinned.

"I think not."

"Matthew has."

"You will not taint my son with your whores."

He laughed again and stared at me.

"What year is this, I wonder. Do you know, sweet Annabel?"

"It is 1857," I answered and the bastard laughed loudly.

"No, I think not. I think it is later than that."

"What are you talking about, Beast?"

"I am talking about time, Annabel."

"It is 1857," I said again.

"Tsk. Tsk," he said malevolently. "I believe it is 1858. You are quite lost, I think."

"No," I said. "I know exactly where I am."

"What do you plan to do, little Annabel?" he asked. "Now that I have severed you from life?"

"You have severed me from nothing."

"Ah yes, but I have. You and your precious Elizabeth do not exist. Ha! Ha!"

"I do not exist? Look, look at my flesh, demon. Look in my eyes, bastard, and tell me again I have no footsteps."

"I tell you that you have no footsteps," he said. "I have footsteps." He stood up and walked from one end of the room to the other. "There! Now let me see your footsteps, little Annabel."

"Go to hell. I will prove nothing to you."

"Look then," he said. "Glass." He went to the mirror over the mantle and cracked it with his hand. He took a piece of it and brought it to me. "See for yourself," he whispered.

"No," I said and turned my face away.

"Ah, how handsome I am," he said as he gazed at his image. "What a soul is this."

"You are slime on the water's edge," I spat.

"Dribble, dribble, dribble, just like the dung from the tongue of your precious, Jesus."

"You hypocrite. You dare to wear the robes of God?"

"God? You speak of God? I alone know God. You know nothing but dribble, dribble, dribble." He danced then. He moved about the room and waved his arms.

"Little Jesus born in a manger, three wise men and a virgin birth, son of God? Ha! What Son of God would perform miracles for the masses and not for himself? Turn wine into water for a measly little wedding and not for the whole of Israel? I turn flesh into spirit. Let Jesus top that."

"Jesus was resurrected," I said, despite the fact that I did not want to argue with him.

"Ha! Am I not resurrected, little Annabel?"

"Jesus revealed the truth to us. You reveal nothing but hell."

"Jesus wanted you all to know the kingdom of God is now. I want you all to know that God has no kingdom."

"Even you are in God's kingdom, Urbain."

"Your mind is dulled by the dung of foul authors. You think Noah had an ark? You think Adam had an Eve? You think Moses had commandments and Jesus came from God's loins? Ha! Dribble, dribble, dribble."

"Begone beast!" I shouted.

"You are a fool, like Jesus," he shouted back and pointed his finger. "Follow me."

"Never!" I hollered as I walked right up and stared into his eyes.

He turned me to the mirror above the mantle. I screamed out in horror. The bastard was right! I had no image in the glass.

The beast fell to his knees. "Hisssssssssssssssssssss."

"Where am I, you bastard?" I screamed. "Where the hell am I?"

He made the sign of the cross.

"Heaven," he said simply.

"No!"

"Yes," he answered. "Most assuredly. You are in heaven."

It was then that Matthew entered the room.

"Matthew," I cried and ran to him.

"Jeanne," he called.

"Jeanne?" I said. "No, Matthew. It is I, your mother."

"Jeanne," he called again."

I noticed the beast was on his knees. He appeared to be praying.

Then I saw her. The same Jeanne Elemont that I had seen in the church with Ursula.

"Matthew," she said as she came swiftly toward him and took the cape from her head.

I watched in horror as he took her in his arms and kissed her.

"Are we alone?" she asked.

"Matthew!" I screamed. "Matthew, where is Elizabeth? Matthew, please, why can't you see me?"

Just then the bastard lifted his head.

"You are in heaven, little Annabel. Sweet, sweet heaven, with that bitch of an aunt of yours and that idiot, Elizabeth," he spat.

"We have at least two hours before they return," Matthew said quietly as he continued to kiss her.

"Oh, this is getting good." Urbain laughed as he stood.

I watched in horror as my son began to tear the clothes from that wretched woman.

"Come, Annabel. Relieve me," Urbain called as he fell to his knees and ripped the collar from his neck. "Your son has aroused my passion."

I ran to Matthew and tried to force him from the woman he now embraced but he could not see me or feel my presence.

"Oh Annabel," the beast cried. "It is time to make another baby."

I turned back to look at him and to my horror the beast had removed all his clothes. I put my hand quickly over my eyes and ran from the room but he followed me up the stairs. I found myself weeping profusely as I ran into the library and hid behind the drapes.

"Annabel," I heard him say as he tore the drapes from their hooks. "Look, Annabel. Look what ascends for you."

He reached for me with one hand and threw me to the floor. I saw the beast for only a moment, his foul wretched body now naked, the rigid phallus crudely commanding. Then he covered my flesh with his own and the world went to darkness. I felt him moving over me. I felt his wretched organ force its way inside me. I heard the bastard moan. I screamed, but no one ran to my aid.

"Shut up," he said harshly.

"No!" I called out. "You are weak."

Suddenly, he stopped moving and stared at me.

"What?"

"You are afraid to love me, bastard," I screamed.

"Don't flatter yourself, dear Annabel. Love is God's weapon, not mine."

"Get off me, coward," I called.

"Look, Annabel." He grinned and held a long silver blade before my eyes. I felt myself spin, as if I would never stop. I heard the beast cry out

251

to Satan as he brought the knife to my cheek. Something warm and dark ran down my face. There was a foul smell. I felt myself falling into something I could not control. "Here is proof of my love, proof of my power."

I cried as I felt the blade cut me.

"Go back to your pansy," I heard him say. "His seed has filled your belly with a little Black bastard. Go in darkness, bitch!"

I felt the devil's phallus leave me and I tasted blood. I screamed out. So quickly my soul seemed to snap in two. I tried to open my eyes. I struggled to open them. I could not tell where I was but I felt the comfort of a man's arms around me. I struggled to free myself, yet the enclosure no longer offended me. Finally, I realized that the darkness had begun to lift and the man above me, making love to me, was not Urbain. His hair was dark, not blond, his touch tender, not rough, his voice sweet and reassuring. I could not control the scream that fell from my lips.

"Annabel," he said at last. "I love you."

"Michele?" I cried when my passion ceased.

He left the bed and went for the light.

"And who did you think it was?"

I struggled for a moment to remember how I had wound up in his bed.

"The doctor said there would be lapses." He looked at me intensely. "Are you having one now?"

"What doctor?" I asked.

"Good God!" he cried out.

"What is it?" I screamed.

"Your face, your cheek is bleeding!"

He ran for a tissue and came quickly to my side. When he wiped the blood away I noticed that his hand was shaking.

"Did I do that to you?" he asked. "Look, I don't have any nails."

I touched my face and tried to recall how I got such a nasty scratch.

"How long have I been here?" I looked at him helplessly.

"Been where?" he whispered.

"Here with you."

"You don't remember?"

"The last thing I remember was Elizabeth and I returning to Ann Peckham's apartment and finding the dog with Ann's parents. Is the dog here now? Is she all right? Beauty!" I called out.

Suddenly, the shepherd jumped on the bed and licked my face.

"Annabel," he said carefully. "Elizabeth vanished. We haven't seen her for over a year. You don't remember that?"

"Vanished?" I cried. "Vanished where?"

"The doctor said you'd go in and out of memory. I'm so sorry." He put his arms around me and held me close.

"Where have I been?" I asked softly. "What has happened?"

"You don't remember?" he asked again. "We were married last month. Oh boy, we shouldn't have made love. Perhaps it was too intense this time. I'm so sorry."

"Married?" I gasped.

"Look at the ring you gave me last year. You told me it was in honor of our engagement. Remember?"

I stared at the gold band, the beautiful square emerald. I shook my head.

"It is beautiful." I said. "But I do not remember giving it to you."

"What do you recall?" he asked. "Do you recall anything of the last year?"

"Just coming here from Elizabeth's apartment. You were missing. I was so worried."

"You and Elizabeth disappeared for an entire week-end. That Sunday evening, after Elizabeth had regressed us back to Salem, you showed up at my door and asked me where on earth I'd disappeared to, and Elizabeth was never heard from again."

"What happened?" I asked.

"She disappeared," he said. "Really disappeared. It was very sudden and unexpected. I went back to her apartment thinking that if you had returned from wherever you had been, then surely she would follow. But she never did, and it was as if she had never existed. No one had even heard of her. It was very bizarre."

"Did she ever regress us in time?" I asked him. "I seem to remember some success."

Michele laughed.

"Well, now I'm not so sure how real any of it was but you and I both went into a trance, of some sort, and when I awoke from it I found myself back here at the apartment. I must have walked out. It was almost like being drunk. I couldn't remember how I got here. I watched from the window as the Peckham's drove up. I didn't want to run into them so I brought the dog back over to Ann's apartment. Then, I returned to Elizabeth's place to find you, but you were both gone when I got there."

"You mean you never disappeared?"

"No, I don't think so, but perhaps … I'm not sure."

"And then what?" I asked carefully.

"You don't remember anything?" he said.

"The last thing I remember is being here with Elizabeth and the Peckham's, and that horrible Jacques, just as I told you."

"The Peckham's were killed in a car crash that evening," he told me sadly. "Their son, Bill, has been in touch with me. He keeps telling me that you are nothing like the sister he knew, that the boating accident has affected you terribly."

"Good God!" I cried.

"What is it, sweetheart? What's wrong?" he asked as he put his arms back around me.

"He put a curse on us all. Yes, I remember now. He cursed us all to hell. That is what killed the Peckham's." I wept.

"There will be no more talk of devils and curses. I will never refer to anything metaphysical or paranormal again and I'm going to insist that you refrain from it, as well. We've been happy for the last year, but you've been in a delicate state. This relapse of yours is the result of our continued interest in witchcraft and other such nonsense. I am sure of it."

"But what happened to Elizabeth?" I asked. "Shouldn't we look into that?"

"No!" he said emphatically. "I will not jeopardize your health, especially now. The doctor has advised against it. I should have listened to him. We've been careless. Your memory loss is a result of too much obsession on things that don't matter."

"And Jacques? What of him?" I asked.

"Who knows and who cares?" he said. "I've never seen him again."

"But what about us? Are we going to be all right?" I nestled my face on his shoulder and held onto him tightly.

"I certainly hope so, Mrs. Guyon. You're carrying my child." He smiled.

"Your child?" I whispered with more joy than I have ever remembered feeling.

"Yes," he said. "My child. Our child."

# Chapter 7

I lived a normal existence for quite some time after that evening. How fond I am of those years. Michele was deliciously romantic. He loved old music boxes and I would find them under my pillow, or I would hear the faint echo of a Bavarian waltz, only to discover a beautifully carved box playing from my dresser. He haunted antique malls and would return time and again with the most delightful old dolls and fine porcelain dogs. He was particularly fond of little Scottish terriers and German shepherds. We would spend hours upstate, collecting old silver, obscure prints, and satin wood tables. He loved traveling to wineries and holding my hand in public. He gave me a birthday to celebrate and made up excuses that appeased my soul's ambiguity. He eased my anxiety with a sense of balance and stability. I loved him deeply, irrefutably, and eternally.

We did not speak of the past and did not dwell on my own dichotomous image. I did not remember anything substantial about Annabel Horton and came to accept myself simply as Ann Arlin Peckham Guyon. I had no memory of Meredith Mae, or my sweet Matthew, and I certainly remembered nothing of Ursula Boussidan. I had only a vague recollection of Elizabeth, but Michele avoided any reference to her so my memory faded rapidly. Since my near drowning in the Hudson River, Doctor Jameson Welty had become my trusted physician and insisted that Michele continue to keep me as far away as possible from anything metaphysical. Doctor Jim, as we came to call him, believed that an unnatural interest in the occult too often leads to mental illness, breakdowns and even memory confusion. So, Michele insisted that we never refer to things of a paranormal nature again. My husband even gave up his own passionate interest in the occult to protect my well-being. Though it was known that I remembered nothing prior to my boating accident, Doctor Jim thought even hypnosis would be a mistake, and insisted that we let sleeping dogs lie, so to speak.

"She is very sensitive," he told Michele. "Her memory will either return or it will not. It is for the best that she does not remember her parents, for a while, at least. It takes the grief out of their tragic death until she's ready to bear it."

My brief encounter with the nineteenth century vanished from consciousness, and life essentially began for me the moment I awoke in a hospital bed in 1980 and met my beloved, Michele. My son, Philippe, was born on a cold white evening in January, in the year 1982. Two years later, on a lovely July morning, I gave birth to my daughter, Emily Elizabeth Guyon. Since her first year we have called her Emie, after Michele's grandmother. I was enormously happy, aside from disturbing yearnings to return somewhere that I could not name, much less, visualize. I explained away the yearnings as gaps in my memory that I could not fill. I accepted Ann Arlin Peckham's history as my own, but I knew I had no connection to any twentieth century childhood, or any parents named Gloria and Mark Peckham. Nonetheless, I claimed Ann's identity as best I could.

Michele called me "Annabel" and told me it was a pet name. I accepted this. Michele insisted that I not be photographed and I never questioned his request. I saw myself in the glass as Annabel Horton and I forgot that the world saw me as Ann Arlin Peckham Guyon, not the girl from Salem. I drifted even further away from whatever little memory I had when I first found myself in the twentieth century. Perhaps, it was because I was happy and I accepted my life with Michele and the children as being as near to perfect as life could get.

I did have disturbing dreams, mostly about a tall blond man with an evil smile. Sometimes, in my dreams, I encountered my son, Matthew, but mistook him for Michele and did not understand why I would find myself so undeniably sad when I awoke. I complained constantly about my foggy sight because I did not remember my state of darkness. Of course, no doctor could help me. They would prescribe prescription glasses for me, and naturally, I found them useless. I kept complaining that my hearing was poor though all my hearing tests would show perfect results. I assumed that my sense of taste was missing because of some genetic abnormality. I only ate food to keep my borrowed body alive, yet longed for the missing pleasure of taste that seemed to have the effect of a drug on others. The children often made fun of my cooking, my tin ear, and referred to me often as "Mrs. Magoo." But mostly, I appeared as solid a form of flesh and blood as anyone else.

Michele and I raised our children Catholic for that was the religion of my husband's family. We were active participants at Saint Paul The Apostle, a small Catholic Church not far from our new apartment on Morton Street, in Greenwich Village. I was not a religious woman but I believed unflinchingly in God. I accepted the concept of heaven and hell and knew without question that Jesus had profound vision, and was born from the virgin birth. I turned my back completely on the nemesis, Lucifer. There was only sin and redemption. Evil was an action, not a disciple of the Devil that walked the earth and tormented witches with the magic to confront him. I believed that I was serving God but I could not put words to this knowledge. If Urbain Grandier returned to me during these years, I did not recognize him.

My son, Philippe, was dark skinned, and Michele said he took after his grandmother, but he had my cleft in his chin and his cheekbones were high. He excelled in school. His passion was history, like his father. When he was a child, he often spoke to me of having a brother, a brother he had visited in his dreams. I laughed and told Michele how cute our son was to harbor such imagination. Once, when Philippe was only twelve years old, he came to my side and stood by the mirror.

"Do you know you are a witch, mother?" he said to the image in the glass.

I laughed so loudly the tears fell from my eyes.

"And what makes you think this, Philippe?"

"Your soul is incarnate," he said simply. "You are without your own body."

I looked into his eyes, but said nothing. He put his arms around me and hugged me tightly.

"I will protect you," he said before running from the room. "Always."

A shiver went through me but I let it pass. When I mentioned to Michele what the boy had said he sat on the edge of our bed and looked away.

"The boy has quite an imagination," he told me. "I'll speak to him about it."

"No, Michele. Imagination leads us to God."

"No! I will not have you bothered with nonsense of that sort. You are too sensitive for it. It is because of my obsession with past life regressions that you lost an entire year of our life together," he said sadly.

It was true that I never remembered my marriage to Michele, or the events leading up to that night I found myself in his bed with a cut on my cheek. This hole in my memory caused him much distress. The time between my seeing Jacques in Ann Peckham's apartment, and finding myself as Mrs. Michele Philippe Guyon, was a very vague and dark slate on which, unfortunately, nothing was written.

My daughter, Emie, was like her brother in many ways. They were both serious and sensitive children, except Emie's passion was for parapsychology and religious philosophy. She was a very studious girl and she was always reading. She and Philippe would often talk about things I did not quite understand. She was a pretty girl and very light skinned like her father, with vivid green eyes. However, my daughter was nearsighted and I had to get her glasses at a very early age. She looked adorable in them. From the time she was a child she preferred little wire glasses, with just a tinge of red to the frames.

Emie and her brother were very close and often spent a great deal of time together, even after we moved to the new house in Brooklyn, and they were both young adults and had entered college. That is when our lives started to change again. Oh, we knew our new house was filled with time chambers, holes in space in which other dimensions can be seen and entered, but both Michele and the children avoided talking about such things with me. They were afraid I would fall into another memory lapse and decided it was not worth it to threaten my mental health, so even though I knew the time chambers existed; I did not speak of them.

But, it was not my destiny to live out my final years in this century, happily ensconced in our house with my beloved husband. No, my days as Ann Arlin Peckham Guyon, in the late twentieth century, were sadly limited. I would eventually return to this dimension to record my tale and to live out my life in a form other than Ann's. But first, let me tell you how poor Ann's death came about.

It was after Michele and I bought the house on Montague Street from the church that owned it in 2001 that Annabel Horton's magic would be called upon once more. But, you must know by now that *after* is a term I use to appease your anxiety. It has definition in your language, but it does not really exist, not anymore than a word such as *before.* These words do not describe anything at all useful beyond the stasis of vocabulary. Remember this, that which was — is, and that which will be — has been.

# Chapter 8

After several successful publications and years of tenure at New York University, Michele was offered an excellent position as Dean of American and European History at a small Catholic college in Brooklyn Heights. The college offered to subsidize most of the cost of a beautiful old house on Montague Street, not far from Saint Francis College. We learned that the house was built in the early 1800's, and poorly modernized in the early 1900's, and then, restored to its original form around 1910. The last owner died in the house and left it in a will to Our Lady of Fatima Church. The church rented out the house for a number of years until the cost of repairs became too burdensome. So, it went up for sale in the year 2000. It remained on the market for one year, until Michele and Philippe saw it and fell desperately in love with it.

"There's something about the house," Michele told me. "It beckons me as you do, dear woman. It has cast its spell upon me, just as you have," he said as he kissed me.

I laughed, because I knew that if Michele and Philippe loved it, then Emie and I would have a terribly hard time convincing them otherwise.

"I hope we fall pray to its magic, as well," I told her.

And I shall never forget the morning I saw the house on Montague Street; it was in the dimension of time and space known to you as the chronological year, 2001. Of course, I had no memory of ever seeing it before, nor did I have memory of ever being in the borough of Brooklyn, but while driving over the Bridge that separated the two boroughs, I experienced an overwhelming sensation of fear.

"I do not wish to live here," I said suddenly. "Something is frightening me."

Michele gave me a concerned glance. It was late spring and my children were now between semesters, and were spending the hiatus with us in the city. Philippe put his arms on my shoulders from the rear seat of our car.

"Wait till you see this house, Mother. Am I right, Father, won't she change her mind then?"

Michele reached for my hand.

"It's a beautiful house, Annabel, and the streets are lined with nothing but trees and lovely old nineteenth century brownstones, but they are young compared to this one."

I looked out the window. The closer we came to Montague Street the more my anxiety gathered. Finally, Michele stopped the car in front of the tired, old house. I turned and stared in disbelief. It seemed to contain my history, familiar and mesmerizing in its knowledge of my soul. Someone had painted the glory of its columns yellow, and it looked a bit rundown, but it was certainly whispering its secrets to me like the shadow of prophets at my lips.

"What do you think?" Michele asked as I stepped out of the car.

"Take me inside," I whispered. "It speaks to me."

"It is out of proportion with the others," Emie cried. "It looks haunted."

"That is because it is indeed very old, my little wizard, and needs our loving touch," Michele told her as we all ran to the door.

Houses have whispers. You can hear them from the corners of rooms as you walk too swiftly by, and notice, too casually, that it is not your laughter that lingers in the echo of some indiscernible word. Houses have spirits you can feel in the night, movement passed off as creaks in the floorboards. Houses are built, as churches are built, sacred and coveted. People always say it. Houses are haunted. Yes, that it so, but it is not by ghosts from any past who linger there. Houses are haunted by time, and time is but a chamber that echoes the soul's eternal presence.

# ANNABEL HORTON

I loved the house the moment I stepped foot inside of it. The initial fear I had felt crossing the Brooklyn Bridge vanished and I knew that I was home. I knew that I belonged in the unusually large, appointed rooms, and I was comforted by something melancholic in the old grandeur. My children giggled, the way they used to when they were toddlers, and they playfully ran through the open doors and up and down the stairs. My husband walked slowly around, touching the walls as if he might claim them forever, caressing the wood and the banister, and the sills of the windows in the same way he has put his hands upon my face and stroked me before a kiss.

We gave the church our offer that afternoon and we moved in within a few months. Despite the fact that the evenings were warm, I noticed a mild chill throughout the house, but then, rather quickly, the chill would pass. I attributed this dampness to years of vacancy. But I could not find excuses for the chambers, areas in space that are vulnerable to other dimensions. Many houses contain them, and this one certainly did. I often saw shadows when I glanced through. I found my children staring into them, even coming out of them, and disappearing back in. I avoided comment, simply because Michele wished to pretend that they did not exist.

However, we were both aware that the library, which was particularly beautiful, seemed to be the most haunted of all the rooms. I always avoided it. Michele insisted on working there even though he often retired from the room in a foul and nasty mood. Still, we never spoke of the house's magic, and if my children were inspired by the ominous possibility of the chambers, and were practicing their craft in that house, I was unaware of it.

Philippe was staying with us that summer before returning to Connecticut College in the fall, and Emie was enrolled at Columbia University and lived at home. It was a wonderful summer. We were all having a grand time plastering the walls and tearing down old wallpaper. We had a big backyard, and I spent a great deal of time there planting flowers and sitting under a glorious old oak tree that provided such ample shade from the sun. I did not understand, at the time, why Emie and Philippe spent so many hours inside the house, when the weather was so delightful in the yard, but then again, there was so much to do inside, so much renovation to keep them busy; and my children had always been unusual. I never knew what to expect from them.

Emie and Philippe had always preferred each other's company and had very few friends outside the family, so I thought it very unusual when I heard a strange voice coming from Philippe's room one day, that I did not recognize. I stood at my son's door and listened intently to see if I could make out whom he was speaking with. The voice that I heard did not seem familiar to me. I knocked on the door and waited for him to let me in. I felt that if he had brought a friend to his room then I should have at least been introduced. I was shocked to find him alone.

"Philippe," I said. "Whom on earth were you speaking to?"

"Mother, you must return."

"Return where?" I asked and noticed the seriousness of his expression.

"Father says I shouldn't speak to you about this. He says it's nonsense but I know differently. Father is not confronting the truth."

I stared at him, confused that my grown son had been talking to himself. I could tell he was tremendously upset about something because he kept wringing his hands.

"Philippe, I am going to insist that you tell me exactly what is going on." I went and took his hands in mine. "Whom were you speaking to just now?"

"Matthew," he told me. "When I walk through the chamber I can speak with him."

"Matthew?" I said. "Who is Matthew?"

"That's not important at the moment, Mother. It's what he tells me that's important."

"What does he tell you?" I asked.

"That you are a witch with great power, that we are all witches," Philippe blurted out and held my hands tightly. "He wanted to come through to you, but I told him you might be harmed by it, that your memory was damaged and Father would be furious."

"What poppycock." I laughed.

"Urbain Grandier is your nemesis, Mother. Do you know the name?" he asked.

I looked at him in astonishment. Then I put my arms around him and held him close to me.

"Where did you get this nonsense?"

"I told you, from Matthew," he said.

I tried to soothe him but he broke from my embrace.

"He put a curse on you for being related to Madeleine de Brou. It was she who turned him in to Cardinal Richelieu in 1634. Urbain was a priest who turned on God and raped the nuns of the Huguenot St. Pierre du March Church. "

"Philippe, what on earth are you talking about?"

"This house has another time, Mother. I have traveled through to another dimension. Come, you can see through time as well."

With that he stood up and took my hand and began to lead me through the chamber.

"No!" I screamed. "No, Philippe I will not go there."

He studied my expression before he spoke. "Emie and I..." he broke off, yet held my eyes. "We have a gift, mother. We have always known it, but something about this house is making us stronger. I can't explain it."

I said nothing. Finally, he took my hand again and began to lead me out of his room.

"Philippe, where are you taking me?"

"Come, Mother. Please," he said and pulled me down the hall. "Emie has been trying to connect to Elizabeth. She always has great success in the library. If you will not walk through the chamber, listen then to your own daughter."

"Elizabeth?" I said. "We have never mentioned Elizabeth to you. How do you know about her?"

"She came to us in Emie's trance," he said.

The door of the library was closed when we got there. I did not wish to enter but Philippe was insistent. Whenever I researched for Michele I avoided the room, despite its beauty, and worked instead from my own sitting room, a small sunny place beyond our bedroom.

"I do not like that room, Philippe, must I go there?"

I stopped before it and put my hands over my heart.

"Emie is there, Mother. Please come, I think she is in a successful trance," he told me and opened the door.

"What?" I cried as I rushed in and ran to my daughter's side. My little girl was lying on the rug, on her back, humming like a hungry bird.

"Good, God, Emie. What are you doing?" I demanded as I sat beside her.

Philippe grabbed my arm. "No, Mother. Don't startle her. Just listen."

"Annie? Annie?"

The voice coming from my daughter's throat was clearly not her own and sounded very small, like a child's.

"My God," I said as I stared at her.

"Elizabeth is here," the voice droned like some dead spirit.

"Elizabeth?" I cried out.

"Danger."

"Elizabeth?" I said again and rubbed my temples. "I remember you. Where are you?" I asked. "Please do not hurt my daughter."

Philippe sat beside me and held my hand. "It's all right, Mother," he gently insisted.

"1857. Remember?" the voice asked, while Emie appeared perfectly safe, and in a very deep sleep.

"No." I said. "I only remember that you vanished. I wound up back with Michele but you were gone," I said quickly, fearing now that the voice would somehow disappear, and though I was frightened for my daughter, I did not want to lose it.

"Murder."

I sat back. I was aghast and horrified. "Murder? What do you say?" I asked.

"Enemies," the voice said quietly.

"Enemies?" I whispered and held onto my son tightly.

"Yes," she said.

"What enemies?"

The voice sighed. "Have you memory?"

I shook my head as if she could see me.

"No," I said finally.

"Two years have passed here," the voice uttered in a barely audible whisper.

"Elizabeth, where are you?" I asked.

"In small form."

"What do you mean?"

"Come," she said. "I need you."

"Where must I come? I do not understand." I began crying.

"1859."

"1859?"

"Yes."

"I cannot travel in time."

"Annabel Horton, lost witch," the voice uttered.

"NO!" I screamed.

"I will help you," Philippe cried.

"I cannot!" I screamed again.

"Please, Mother. My brother, Matthew, is in danger," Philippe said as he hugged me close.

"Try," the voice was very low, as if it were losing power.

"My son is a witch?" I said. "Answer me, Elizabeth. Answer me!"

But before I realized it, Emie sat up and looked at me.

"Good God, Emie. What is going on?" I asked, still horrified.

"Mother," she said. "You must return. Matthew will be murdered. Elizabeth is trying to save him. He will listen to no one but you."

Oddly enough, I laughed. "Have her tell this Matthew to save himself," I said as I looked at Philippe. "Send Elizabeth to him."

"I can't, Mother," he said sadly. "Elizabeth cannot help him now. You are the only one who can save him."

"This is preposterous."

"Mother, please. You must trust us," Emie whispered as she took my hand and pulled me toward the chamber, for the library contained the most actively visible pull of gravity in the house.

"Matthew has told me that you cannot pass through the dimensions of space without giving up the body you are in, because you are incarnate, not real flesh and blood. So, we must walk through the chamber, Mother," Philippe said to me as he took my hand. "It may work for you as it does for us."

"No!" I screamed.

"But you cannot pass through time without dying. Matthew has told me that." Philippe said.

"I will not walk through the chamber," I told him.

"All right then, let's try a trance. Perhaps it will work." He looked at me and sought my eyes, pleading with me to trust him.

"Philippe, I cannot move without memory," I whispered, praying that Michele would not return early and find his family tempting the occult.

"I will help," A voice suddenly said from the shadows.

"Good God," I whispered. "Who is that?"

My son stared at the stranger.

"Urbain," Philippe uttered quietly.

The demon laughed.

"Why, I thought I had just blinked since I saw you last," he said to me.

"We don't need you," Philippe stood and glared at the shadow he cast on the floor.

"Oh, but I think you do," the bastard sneered.

"Begone Beast!" Emie suddenly stood up. "Return to hell and taunt the noxious souls that worship you there."

The demon laughed loudly. Then, he came and stood before us. His yellow white hair fell into his eyes and his shadow moved across the floor and held us in its somber grasp.

"Like mother, like daughter, I see."

Philippe touched my forehead and asked me not to look the devil in the eyes. Emie stood by my side.

"He is not really here," they whispered. "He cannot be."

"You cannot move her body," Urbain grinned. "You cannot move the corpse she covets. Would you send her without flesh to kill again?"

I could see that he wore a priest's robe, though he still remained in shadow. A foul smell came from where he stood.

"Don't look at him, Mother," Philippe whispered.

"He has a knife," Emie said quickly.

I heard his laughter. It was so shrill it hurt my ears.

"I am Lord," he said.

"Ha! Lord of what?" Emie screamed.

"No!" Philippe said sharply. "Do not speak to him."

"You are pathetic." He laughed. "Bone and ash. Smoke and fire. Who said it? Shakespeare? Your soul tells an idiot's tale of sound and fury, signifying, in the final analysis, nothing but your mindless passion. God is nothing. That's the cruel joke of it, isn't it? Your God is an empty word, a white canvass, a burp on the universe."

"Go to hell," Philippe hissed.

"Maggot." Urbain's shadow moved about the room, his foul odor filling the air and causing me to choke. The blade gleamed in his hand.

"You need my help, little ninnies that you are. Only death moves the soul. Only life can move the flesh. She is without flesh. She is...how shall I say it? A phantom, an apparition, a doppelganger."

"You moved her flesh once. Matthew told me that you did." Philippe confronted him.

The demon stepped out of the shadows and put his foul face right up to Philippe's. I could see the lines about his eyes.

"Listen to me, you idiot. I moved that which does not exist, not that which does."

My son stood tall and stared back at him.

"What do you mean?" he asked.

"I turned the hourglass over. I moved the clock ahead. I fumbled with the brilliant notion that time is precise and reality is that which you know, not that which you are too stupid to comprehend."

With that he knelt and pulled me down to him. He grabbed my hair and held the blade before me.

"You want motion, bitch?" He grinned. "Unfinished business."

"Jesus, protect her," my son cried out just as the bastard shoved him aside and brought the blade slowly to my chest and pressed it toward my borrowed heart. I heard my children screaming. It was the last thing I heard before the breath blew out of me and I felt a mighty lunge, as if I'd been shot from a canyon. The bastard's laughter followed me. I felt a sharp pain. In my mouth there was blood. I could taste it on my lips. Somewhere, I felt pain again, terrible pain. I tried to move, but I was too much like stone. I felt despair so deep I thought I might drown in the pull of it, but then, it passed and lightness returned.

When I could finally see through the haze, I was startled to see him again, his pallid chiseled jaw, his hawk like stare. He still wore the priest's collar and my own sweet Meredith Mae was serving him tea. I knew her instantly.

The devil looked at me over his cup; his eyes rolled back in his head and his smile revealed two small fangs on either side of his mouth. With his tongue he licked blood from his lips. Meredith Mae did not seem to detect the foul odor he carried.

I felt dizzy and noticed, to my dismay, that Meredith Mae could not see me.

The bastard held his hand out to me.

"Do you believe in ghosts?" He grinned.

Meredith Mae laughed.

"No," she said.

"Vampires, bloodsuckers?" He smiled.

"Good lord, no," she answered.

"Jesus?"

"Yes, of course." She bowed her head.

"Good girl," the bastard said. "Jesus, the holy ghost, Mary the Virgin? Interesting dribble." He smiled. "I prefer other works of fiction."

"Father Jacques, you have a strange sense of humor."

"Just testing your faith, child. It is as sweet as a kiss from the holy ghost himself."

I sat in a chair and glared at him. Meredith Mae continued to drink her tea.

"I see you are still sad, my child."

"Yes, Father, I am terribly sad."

"Have faith and pray."

"Yes, Father." She managed a faint smile. "What will you be

preaching to us on Sunday?"

"Fidelity," he whispered.

I realized that I was ghostly, and I could obviously not be seen. I found it difficult to remember what had happened to me. For a moment, I could not decipher one dimension from the next, too many memories flooded my consciousness.

Father Jacques turned to me and pointed his brows. "God did not mean to confuse you. You're lost, bitch."

"Begone the Devil's toad!" I hissed but the words had no voice with which to be heard.

Obviously the bastard could see me but I was nothing but space to Meredith Mae.

"Did you say something Father Jacques?" she asked.

"Ghosts should be seen and not heard, like women." He laughed and slashed out at the air that my ghostly vision occupied.

I moved back. I realized that Ann Peckham must have been murdered. I had some movement that I could control but I would not be able to speak unless I took a body. But whose body, pray tell, whose?

Suddenly, the door burst opened and in walked Rachel with a man I presumed to be her new husband, Troy Spencer. With them they had a young girl of about two that I assumed was their first daughter. The child squealed loudly when she entered the room.

Father Jacques grimaced and stood quickly, as if the presence of the new arrivals disturbed him, particularly the child's. I noticed the grimace remained on his face.

"Children should be seen and not heard, as well," he said. "I have overstayed my welcome," he whispered to Meredith Mae and bowed slightly from the waist.

"Your presence is always welcomed," she said as she walked with him to the door.

"You know my daughter, Rachel, and her husband, Troy?"

"Yes, yes," he said and extended his hand to Troy.

"And their daughter, Elizabeth Sue?"

"Sweet," he muttered, and quickly left the room, giving a hateful sneer in my direction before closing the door behind him.

"Mother, how are you holding up?" Rachel asked Meredith Mae.

The child suddenly broke away from her father and began to jump up and down and peer into the corners of the room.

"I know you're here, oh, I do. I do," she whispered, very quietly, so her parents could not hear her words.

"Whom on earth are you jabbering with, dear?" Rachel laughed.

"The child is pretending to speak, how cute. It almost sounds as if she has a vocabulary," Meredith Mae said.

"Annie, where are you?" The child whispered from behind her little hand.

"I could almost swear she said, 'where are you?'" Rachel laughed and looked around.

"Mommy. Mommy," the child responded.

"Good, God!" I whispered from my vacuum. I was both appalled and shocked. So much so, that I did not even wonder what had made my dear Meredith Mae so upset, for I knew that she was distressed over something. I could feel it and see the sadness in her expression.

"You are here! You have done it, but you need a body. I cannot see you but I feel your presence," the child whispered into a corner I just happened to be occupying.

"How could you?" I cried from my opacity.

"Elizabeth Sue, come sit on Mommy's lap," Rachel called.

I stared through my darkness in disbelief. Why she had taken a child's flesh. My sweet Elizabeth had robbed a child of life! Why, surely it must be she that speaks from this small form.

"Is Grandfather still angry?" Rachel asked as she sat near Meredith Mae and took her hand.

"Yes, he is furious with me," Meredith Mae answered.

I moved closer to Meredith Mae so that I might understand what problem existed, but the child ran through the space I tried to capture.

"I know what you must be thinking, but oh, Annie, I had no choice," the child whispered into the air, "it is not what you think."

"Elizabeth Sue, Daddy's sweet. Do sit down will you?" Troy smiled.

"Dada," the child answered and sat quickly.

I was so shocked and so dismayed.

"Oh, Elizabeth, Elizabeth! How could you? You have robbed the body of a child? Oh good Lord above us. Oh, dear, oh dear," were the thoughts I formed.

# Chapter 9

I lingered, and listened to their chatter, until they finally ended their visit and took the little girl home. I was so upset, and found it difficult to concentrate on what I was hearing. I floated through the rooms in a vegetative state, waiting impatiently to be alone with the child.

Finally, they bid a very long and fond goodnight to Meredith Mae. I followed behind when they left. They did not live far and were able to walk. They took the girl to bed as soon as they arrived home, and spent some time kissing her goodnight. After what seemed like forever, they wished her a sound night's sleep and left the room.

I crept into the darkness and tried to speak to Elizabeth but she could not hear my words. I needed a body. My memory was quite clear, once again, and I recalled my last moment in this century. I had run up the stairs trying to escape Urbain. I looked back at the little girl in the bed and did all I could to wake her, but I could not touch anything material and I had no breath to blow on her cheek. I decided to wait. I knew she would eventually awaken, and I hoped she would feel my presence once again. To my great relief, the child opened her eyes just a few hours before dawn.

"Annie, Annie, are you here?" she whispered.

271

How could I answer her? I screamed, but it did no good.

"I sense you, Annie. If you are here, give me a sign of some sort. Make some movement, any kind of movement."

I tried to figure out what to do. Suddenly, I remembered how angry I had been at Malcolm and how the energy from that emotion had caused a faint red glare. I worked myself up into a rage and spun around the room. After a while, I heard the child giggle.

"Oh, Annie I see you. I see you," she cried and put her fingers to her lips. "I must speak low. I do not want to wake Rachel. She sits for hours and tells me stories whenever I do," she said.

I watched as she sat up and fluffed her pillow.

"I know what you are thinking and it could not be further from the truth. I did not kill the child," she insisted. "I did not kill little Elizabeth Sue."

I let out what would have been a sigh of relief, had I breath, and listened.

"The poor baby was choking in her crib when I came to her. She was dying. It was her time to go. She would not have lived had I not of given her the strength of my soul. Miraculously, I was able to keep her flesh alive once I took it over. I needed a body, and at that very moment there was no one else's to take. I did not think it would work, for I was quite sure her little heart had stopped, but then I felt it, and I knew that God had granted me a place in time, and that this little soul of Elizabeth Sue's was now in God's hands, and that I was forgiven, that fate had intervened. You cannot fault me for allowing fate to guide me. Oh, I will tell you the whole wretched story, Annie, but please do not be angry with me."

She pulled herself up higher on her pillows and rubbed her nose. You could say that I sat on the edge of the bed, though it was not really sitting, it was more like lingering.

"Matthew had an affair with some woman claiming to be a friend of Ursula Boussidan, Louie's so called sister. I imagine it had been going on for years," she began and let out a long, small breath at the end of the sentence.

I was shocked to hear that she had discovered this treachery. I remembered how I had seen my son in Jeanne Elemont's arms, and his confessions of infidelity.

"Perhaps, I really was too old for him, I do not know. But the intimacy was quite wonderful between us. It was richer and more satisfying than it had ever been in Salem when I was a young girl. But

Jeanne Elemont changed that. She was very beautiful and appeared to be several years younger than Matthew. She was constantly invited to the house because Louie insisted on having her. She unabashedly flirted with Matthew in front of all of us, including me. I began to suspect that they had been intimate."

She sighed again and I watched as her little body slid down from the pillows.

I was saddened by this news and angry with my son. I wanted to tell her that men often succumb to such deceit, and to not be too terribly hurt by it, but my words fell into nothing.

"I ignored their affair, at first, and I took myself out," she continued. "I did whatever I could to take my mind off it. I went to concerts and plays. I joined clubs. I did everything possible to avoid facing this betrayal. And then, one afternoon, quite by chance, I ventured over the bridge to New York City and decided I would indulge myself in a history lesson. I would see how different Greenwich Village looked in the dimension of 1859, compared to what I knew of it in the late twentieth century. To my amazement, I saw Louie and Jeanne Elemont shopping together on Waverly Place. They were holding hands like new young lovers. In a state of shock, I followed them to an apartment not far from where you had once lived as Ann Peckham in 1980. Louie stayed there for hours. When he returned to Brooklyn, later that evening, he told Meredith Mae that he had been bored with a client and forced into a long tedious dinner. He out and out lied to her, Annie."

I watched as the child stopped speaking. She listened intently for a moment to hear if her quiet talk had awoken Rachel and Troy. After a moment or so, when she was assured that no one had heard her, she continued.

"After that afternoon, I decided to keep a close watch on Louie Boussidan. To my horror, I discovered that he met Jeanne Elemont every Wednesday afternoon and Jeanne Elemont met my own dear Matthew on Tuesdays, when I was away with my book club. I thought this was the worst offense I had ever been privy to. I thought that things could not possibly get any darker than this when, to my horror, I discovered that this Louie Boussidan had ventured into Jeanne's Elemont's apartment one afternoon, and had emerged only a few hours later, as a woman! Do you believe that, Annie? He emerged as a woman? I knew it was the same person immediately, for Louie had a bad bruise on his cheek from a recent fall, and this woman had the very same bruise on the very same cheek. It was large enough to be seen from my hiding place across the street. How bizarre and decadent it was, and how on earth would I ever tell Matthew?"

I was overjoyed that Elizabeth now knew the truth about Louie's charade and wanted so badly to discuss this horrid state of affairs, but my voice came out like huffs of wind and Elizabeth ignored it as nothing more than the evening breeze. She continued with her tale.

"Well, I confronted Matthew immediately. First, I told him of Louie's infidelity with Jeanne Elemont and watched as his face turned several shades of red. After he was sufficiently shocked, I told him that Louie was an even greater imposter than he could ever imagine. He listened to me with his mouth agape and nearly fell over from the news of it. He was absolutely horrified, and immediately confronted Louie, who at first denied it and laughed loudly. But then, when Matthew insisted that he disrobe, he unabashedly opened his shirt and revealed two small but perfectly rounded breasts under all this wrapping tape that he had used to conceal them. As Matthew gapped in horror, Ursula spit at him. Matthew gasped and ordered Ursula from our home, right then and there. I thought it best not to bring up his own affair with Jeanne Elemont, for I knew he would never see the woman again, now that he knew of her unnatural perverse nature. To my great relief, this was correct, and Matthew returned to my bed with renewed fervor."

Elizabeth sat up and fluffed the pillows. I was relieved for my Meredith Mae but I wondered what transpired when Ursula was driven away. I wanted so badly to ask. I watched impatiently while Elizabeth took her time with the pillows. Finally, she continued.

"You can imagine what Matthew thought of his daughter at this point. Poor Meredith Mae remained silent when we confronted her, and we believed for a while that she had been duped by this charade. We foolishly considered Meredith Mae so naïve that she would not know the sex of the person who made love to her. How stupid of us, really. However, she finally admitted that she had known the truth all along. Matthew was appalled. He insisted that she marry a young bachelor he knew from his men's club, young Callen Hall. Meredith Mae was beside herself, and absolutely refused to do so. Matthew put his foot down and threatened never to speak to her again if she did not. He offered Callen a large dowry. Callen, of course, was thrilled, for he had always been very gallant around Meredith Mae. Matthew took further control of the situation and went to Silas. He told him of Louie's infidelity. Silas, still believing that Louie had something to do with his father's death, and his own incarceration, was happy to write up a new will, one that completely eliminated Louie Boussidan as an heir. Meredith Mae unhappily acquiesced and agreed to sign the new will.

The child suddenly stopped talking and turned to the windows.

"Are you still here, Annie?" she asked. "I do feel as though I am speaking to myself."

I began to spin around the room again and I could see from my opacity that Elizabeth's eyes followed me, much as they used to when she was a child in Salem.

"Ha!" she said. "I see you."

I stopped my spinning and rested before her. She leaned in toward me now and spoke in a whisper.

"Matthew did not tell Silas of Louie's real identity as a woman. He knew it would bring too much shame to Meredith Mae and the rest of the family. The truth provided some safety for Ursula, who disappeared from the house and took up residence with Jeanne Elemont, in Manhattan. I knew this because I went there and spied on them."

Again, she stopped speaking and looked around the room. I wanted to ask her about Meredith Mae, and hoped she would resume her tale. As if she had read my thoughts, she continued.

"Meredith Mae begged Matthew to allow her to see Ursula, but he absolutely refused. Meredith Mae finally agreed to honor her father's wishes and marry Callen. She really had no other choice. To my knowledge, she and Ursula were not in contact after Matthew threw Ursula out."

It was then we heard a creak on the floorboards and the child quickly held her breath. A cat the size of a raccoon jumped in her bed and nestled beside her.

"This is Sadie," she told me.

'Oh, Elizabeth, Elizabeth, please do go on;" I tried to call out, but my words broke up and fell apart.

"Isn't she pretty?" She smiled.

I began to spin again and the child followed me around the room with her eyes while the cat purred loudly in her arms.

"Matthew took Meredith Mae to Long Island to visit Maebelle," she finally continued.

I sighed some relief, though I could not be heard.

"Her wedding to Callen was planned when they returned. I was alone in the house preparing for the wedding. I had no reason to fear Ursula Boussidan for I believed that I had seen the last of her. That could not have been further from the truth. While I slept in my bed, the vicious woman stole into my room with her accomplice, Jeanne Elemont, and put a pillow over my head. I must have struggled a great deal because they could not suffocate me. So one of them broke my neck instead, just snapped it in two."

I let out a long low cry that broke up and fell into space. If Ursula had been before me I would have choked her to death. She had murdered my Elizabeth, who was now trapped inside the body of a child, doomed as I was, to an eternity of pursuit, to a murderous yearning to clothe the soul in flesh and blood. I wanted so much to speak to Elizabeth, to comfort her as best I could, but my words were contained in the prison of my fate.

"Oh no, Rachel is coming," the child suddenly said.

Rachel entered the room quickly, and Elizabeth Sue slid under the sheets and pretended to snore.

"Whom are you speaking with?" Rachel laughed.

"Da da," the child whispered back.

"Da da?"

"Mama."

"I think I'll tell you a ghost story. That will put you back to sleep, just for another hour or so, darling. It's too early to be up and about. How about the Annabel Horton ghost story?"

The child giggled.

I proceeded to listen to Rachel tell the baby some wild tale about a ghost named Annabel Horton. I grimaced to myself as I listened. I suppose it does give some amount of peace to distort truth, does it not?

I had to find a body quickly. I had to keep any harm from happening to Meredith Mae and Matthew. I knew that Ursula and Jeanne had killed Elizabeth to get her out of the way. Their original plan must have been to bring Jeanne into the family by marrying her off to Matthew after the five year wait was over, making both Ursula and Jeanne heirs to the estate. They most likely wanted to insure themselves a claim to the estate should Ursula's charade ever be found out. But their plans were badly fouled by Elizabeth when she returned to Matthew's dimension. The chances of their getting their hands on the estate now, was unlikely, unless Jeanne found a way back into Matthew's bed and Meredith Mae's will was altered again to include Ursula, as Louie, her estranged husband. Then of course, Meredith Mae would have to be mysteriously done away with. I was quite sure they had the audacity to succeed in reclaiming my wealth and I surmised that I had to act fast. I knew they were planning on murdering the members of my family one by one if I did not.

My son, Matthew, was now a widower, and therefore vulnerable, even to Jeanne Elemont. My granddaughter, Meredith Mae, would be married off and young Callen Hall would now be entitled to a portion of our estate, putting him in as much danger as everyone else. There was more than enough probability that those two insidious women would, one way or another, worm their way back into my family. I knew they would not let a fortune slip through their hands, not one sizable enough to keep Jeanne Elemont waiting in the wings for over five years. I was certain that Matthew had been quite generous with her, but of course she would be worth far more as his wife than his mistress. I also believed that Meredith Mae was still vulnerable to Ursula, and could be used unmercifully to amend any foul attempts at treachery that had failed to bring them success. This was a temporary setback for Ursula and Jeanne, for they would not let go of their wicked little plan until every dime and sawbuck of our money was in their hands. No mater, I would bring an end to Ursula Boussidan, or so I thought.

I remembered exactly where the wretched Jeanne Elemont lived in Manhattan. The image of that horrid black Mass was still fresh in my mind. I found the church that she had desecrated with her worship of the evil Satan. Her apartment house still stood in the same spot, next to the old Catholic Church that had now been cleaned up and looked rather beautiful from behind the mist of my deficient vision.

Jeanne Elemont and Ursula Boussidan seemed to be enjoying themselves that early evening, of September 14th, 1859, in the plush little room on Charles Street. I could see the shadows they cast behind the shade as I peered through the mist that shielded me. I simply floated up to their apartment and lingered on a wall near them. I prayed they would not notice the vague small shadow I cast, for the room was still in semidarkness, and a soft light from the fading moon fell near me. Jeanne's thick blond hair kissed her naked shoulders in round, wiry curls. From my caliginous gloom I could see tiny electric hairs around her head, probably not visible to the human eye, glowing as if she were lit from within. Her eyes were like Urban's, eagle shaped and the color of the sea from Salem's port. The other one's long partially clad body lay on the bed. Her straight hair was pulled back, as if wet, and her large, seductive eyes stared lasciviously at Jeanne Elemont's strong, white legs.

"You should have killed her years ago, in France." Jeanne smiled and pulled a silver brush through her hair. "Now, whatever legal claim you had is completely meaningless."

"I could never trust my legal claim, dear. It is much too dangerous to have believed I could have passed myself off as a man forever."

"She could not have gotten rid of you had you of killed her." Jeanne peered at Ursula.

"Ah, I see. We marry in America, and then, poof, she disappears in France? She is gone and I am in possession of her fortune? Surly, you realize that her father would have fought me to the death and cut me off without a dime?"

Ursula put her head back on her hands and smiled sweetly at Jeanne. "She told me her father was missing; he could have shown up at any time. Unfortunately, there he was, miraculously found when we returned from abroad. How could I know that he would be there? I would have done away with her back here in America if not for his presence. I swear it."

"I think you like her in bed. You've had years in which to get rid of her."

"Ha!" Ursula continued to stare at her friend. "I will not compromise myself because you are jealous of her. I kill her, and then I am sharing the estate with the father, and so I kill him, and then the little heir Rachel? How suspicious is that? I am no fool."

"Your costume too often confuses you and I think you are as foolish as any man, and just as weak." Jeanne put the brush down on the dresser behind her. "You are a rogue, darling, not a murderer. It was I that had to snap the bitch's neck. You barely had the strength to hold the pillow down." Jeanne laughed loudly.

Ursula looked up at the ceiling. "I do not kill foolishly," she said. "As you would have me do."

"Pussy cat, pussy cat." Jeanne purred. "You are such a sissy."

"I must gain access to the will, find out exactly how it has been altered. Once her father returned, he was entitled to fifty percent of the estate not held in trust. When I rewrote the will, for the second time, Malcolm Northrup insisted that Matthew Guyon be named an heir. How very strange it was to me then."

Jeanne laughed loudly and pulled her legs up casually to her breast, revealing a tight brown brush of hair between.

"I told you that his mother clothed her soul in that idiot, Malcolm's flesh. You do not believe me?" she asked.

"Ah, yes, Annabel Horton. I believe you." Ursula sighed.

"I'm not sure that you do, which would be terribly foolish," Jeanne said quietly.

Ursula ignored the remark and began to file her nails. "That will I wrote has since been rewritten, and now, he has altered it again. I would love to see it."

Ursula turned her body so that she was at the foot of the bed. She stared crudely up the other ones legs and smiled, so that even through my darkness I could see her teeth.

Jeanne spun around in her chair and looked back at Ursula through the mirror.

"I don't need Silas to tell me how the will is written. Matthew owns the estate and your little wife owns the trust, which is worth a great deal more. If something were to happen to Matthew Guyon his money would go to Rachel, and her family, but if Matthew has a wife, poor Rachel and her heirs would be reduced to twenty percent. Save your winsome charm for Meredith Mae, darling. Silas has to be thrown in a ditch and a new will written. You can do that. You've done it before. The new will should reflect no other heirs than Matthew's wife. Twenty percent is still too much."

Jeanne then spun her chair back around to Ursula and parted her legs again. I could tell it was a deliberate act to excite the woman.

"And what about me, darling?" Ursula asked, with a lewd grin.

"You must write yourself back into the bitch's will, as well. I'm sure she will fall prey to your charm, at least one more time," Jeanne said. "I think she should leave you at least thirty percent for your troubles. Leave her father to me. I will race you to the altar once again. Men are easier to ensnare than women."

Ursula slid off the bed to her knees and dragged the witch to her lips. Her face now rested on the brown tight hair between the witch's legs. I heard a small sigh emerge, though I could not tell from whose throat it came.

"What of your husband, Count Elemont?"

"Ha!" Jeanne laughed. "The poor man is old. He will not last the year."

"What of Matthew?" Ursula whispered as she closed the heavy lidded eyes under the soft white flesh of Jeanne Elemont's body. "How can I sneak to your bed if you are sharing it with him?"

"I will insist on my own bedroom." Jeanne Elemont laughed wickedly. "And we will have that all to ourselves. I will unlatch the window for you every night and you will fly like a vampire bat to my bed." She giggled.

Ursula joined in on the laughter as she continued to kiss the horrid creature in places I dare not name. I had to act quickly, even though I knew that Meredith Mae might never forgive me for what I was about to do.

I watched in horror as the two women rolled all over the floor together. I could hear their breath and the sucking sounds they made as they devoured each other's tongues. I knew that Ursula was at her weakest moment, as she moaned aloud and began to mount the body of the other. I knew I needed her weakness in order to emerge victorious, for if Ursula were to have had her full faculties about her, I might not have been able to claim her flesh as my next cavern of choice.

I pushed myself close. "God," I whispered, "forgive me for my participation in this dreadful debauchery, but I must do it to save my blessed soul."

I crept up the wall until my shadow lingered on the ceiling over them. Jeanne Elemont was writhing and moaning like one possessed, while the scoundrel, Ursula, covered her body with her own long legs and they moved as if under some bizarre hypnosis, smiling and dancing to some erotic legato thrusts that seemed to bring them both to plains of pleasure the innocent should not have knowledge of.

I lowered myself as best as I could to Ursula's naked back. She was too enthralled to notice that I was absorbing her flesh. Jeanne Elemont was too deeply lost in sin to tell that I had entered Ursula's blood stream, had crept there like a demon in the night. Suddenly, I felt the jolt as I was pulled through Ursula's veins and I could feel myself reeling through the warm blood that flowed there.

"Kiss me in my spot!" Jeanne Elemont suddenly cried out.

Ursula screamed in her own voice as she felt my hand on her heart.

"Kiss her there, bitch!" I hissed.

"Darling, oh darling." The other one writhed under me. "You must kiss me there quickly, please." She clung to me and began pushing my body into her flesh.

I laughed, as I felt my hands move and my body stretch out in this new configuration of form, but Ursula fought me like a tiger and I rolled off the writhing Jeanne.

I felt myself thrown against the wall. I tried to walk but I fell to my knees. I could feel the gasp from Ursula's soul.

"Jeanneeeeeeeeeeeeeeene!" she called out.

I heard the other one scream.

"Begone Bitch!" I cried and called upon my magic.

Before I knew it, Jeanne had leapt across the room and clutched my throat.

"Idiot!" she yelled, "What have you done with her? Ursula? Darling, where are you?"

"Return to the mud you came from," I hissed, though I could barely get the words out. She seemed to be crushing my bones.

"Whore." She spat in my eyes. "You sit on your finger and call my father's name."

"Your father is God's despair," I cried. I felt the air in my throat diminish and gasped for breath as her hands tightened around me.

"You will not have her," she hissed. "Do not be foolish enough to think you will."

"Begone!" I said through Ursula's teeth.

"I will devour your soul, you amateur!" she screamed. "Ha!"

It was just at that moment that I blacked out completely. When I regained consciousness my neck was so sore that I could not turn my head. I could hear Jeanne laughing somewhere from outside of the space that I now inhabited. I searched frantically for her, but she must have returned to the slime of her father's arms for though I heard her laughter, I did not see her.

Convinced that I was alone, I collapsed onto Ursula's bed and fell back into a deep sleep. When I finally awoke and opened my eyes the sky outside the window was covered in a sweet pale blue and I languished for several euphoric moments in the long, androgynous form of that beastly woman, Ursula Boussidan.

# Chapter 10

I looked in the closet for clothes. The woman had an irregular body. Her legs were so long that they simply ran into her hips, which were certainly not much broader than her shoulders. I found a purple bonnet and lay it on the bed. I had to admit that it was very lovely. I noticed a full and pretty lavender dress with white lace around the sleeve and the waist. "This will do," I said and sat down to put Ursula's hair up in a popular French braid.

I looked at her features in the glass, the aquiline nose, and the small, full bow mouth. The thick dark hair fell nicely behind her ears and the lashes over the round-lidded eyes were so much thicker and longer than I had remembered them. I stared into the glass, admiring Ursula's good looks, when, suddenly, I screamed out in horror. It took but a moment for me to realize that only the cyanotic gaze from Ursula's blue eyes stared back at me. I could no longer see the opaque comfort of my own image. Annabel Horton was nowhere to be found.

"Good God!" I cried. "She has eaten my soul!"

I wept until I could weep no more. I was gone. I existed in the body of this beastly woman and I could not find myself in the glass. It took hours for me to pull myself together. Finally, I washed Ursula's face and found some color to apply to her cheeks. I left the apartment and ran quickly through the streets. I found it difficult to locate Rachel's house for I had only seen it through my darkness, but I knew I had to find Elizabeth. It took hours but I finally retraced my steps until I spotted a pretty white porch with a red pot of begonias on either side of the stairs. It looked somewhat familiar. I went to the rear yard, praying the child would be there, but she was not. Yet I was quite sure that this was, indeed, Rachel's home. I found what I thought might be the window to Elizabeth's room. I threw pebbles at the glass until the child finally looked through. To my great dismay, she put her hands up to her ears the moment she spied me, and let out the most bloodcurdling scream I have ever heard.

"No, Elizabeth!" I cried. "It is I, Annabel Horton. Oh, please Elizabeth. Please believe me," I called up to her. *Dear God, she thinks I'm Ursula*, I thought.

But the child refused to hear a word I said and just kept screaming. In order to avoid attention, I had to flea quickly but I did not know where to go. I could not return to my own home as Ursula, for Matthew would not recognize me as his mother, and I certainly could not return to an apartment that belonged to Jeanne Elemont. For a moment, I did nothing but run in circles. I can now say, in all certainty, that I believed I was in hell, cursed to this wretched body for all eternity, without shelter or hope. I fell to my knees and begged for God to release me from my torment.

When I finally stopped my crying and opened my eyes, I found myself in a church. I had no idea how I had gotten there but I threw myself on the mercy of God and his angels. I called to Jesus and the Blessed Mother. I held my hands to the sky.

"I can take no more surprises," I wept. "I was there and now, I am suddenly here? What cruel joke is this?"

I listened for a long time but no one answered me.

"Where am I?" I cried from the depths of my darkest despair. "Lord, God almighty. Where am I?"

Just then, the doors began to rattle and the lights from the candles began to dance on the ceiling. A presence came and stood behind me. Suddenly, the air became sweet and warm, as if a thousand ripe melons had just been opened and a garden of wisteria had been placed at my feet.

"Do not look at me," the voice said. "Not yet."

I felt enveloped by his presence though he did not touch me.

"Do not be afraid," the voice whispered in my hair. "Are you Madeleine?"

"Madeleine? No. Who are you?" I asked.

"Oh, I thought for a moment you might be her," he answered.

"Why?"

"I've been searching for her," he replied.

"You know her then?" I whispered.

"Oh, yes."

"Who are you to Madeleine?"

"I am lost to Madeleine," he said.

"Are we dead?"

"I didn't say that," he told me. "You did."

"Am I where God is? Am I finally there?"

"God is everywhere," he answered. His voice was sweet, and he spoke slowly.

"Where?" I whispered. "Where is God and where am I?"

"Here," he told me, his voice so soft.

"Have you any answers?" I asked him. "Or are you just trying to confuse me?"

He laughed and touched my hair.

"Do you know any magic?" I asked. "I have lost my soul."

He took my arms from behind me and held them out.

"Give me your fingers," he said.

He put his hands under mine and pressed all ten of my fingers with his own.

"Magic," he whispered, "shall be yours, as it was hers."

"It is eerie here," I whispered back. "And you are a strange man."

He laughed. "Eerie? Look." He laughed again and pointed to a small bird that suddenly appeared out of nowhere and landed before the feet of an icon of Christ.

"Witchcraft?" I asked.

The bird was beautiful. It stared at me from the most mesmerizing fragility and flapped its wings and flew to the ceiling.

"If you like," he told me.

"What should I do?" I asked the man. "Where should I go without a soul?"

"Here," he said and touched his heart. "And there," he said and pointed to the bird.

"Do you know where Madeleine is?" I whispered.

I felt him kiss the top of my head.

"No."

I smiled to myself and held out my hands.

"Are you in love with Madeleine?"

"I do recall feeling that," he said.

I felt exasperated, but not afraid. I knew I was in a clean, safe place. The man lifted his arms.

"Proof!" He laughed and turned around three times. "Proof!" He said again and turned some more. It was the first time I was able to see him, but he moved so quickly that his face was a blur to me. I did notice that he wore a priest's gown and his hair was very dark. When he finally stopped spinning, the church had disappeared entirely and he had vanished before my very eyes, but the sweet, delicious scent of the melons remained in the faint night air, and the beautiful little bird flew just above my head. I watched as it disappeared into the glorious quiet of night with a swish of its wings against the black sky.

# Chapter 11

I had no time to analyze what had just happened to me, or to question it. The church had vanished as if it had never been there. I was standing under a gas lamp on Smith Street. I felt my face and realized I still had Ursula's form. I ran back to Rachel's house and told myself I would think about the strange man in the church later.

I could see through the windows that the family was eating dinner. I stole in through the unlocked front door and crept up the stairs to the child's room. I was almost seen by the family maid but managed to duck behind the door in time and hide myself behind a drape. I waited for what seemed like forever for little Elizabeth Sue to be put to bed, but then, I had to sit through a barrage of prayers. Finally, Rachel and Troy kissed the child's cheek, turned down the oil in the side table lamp and closed the door behind them.

I knew I had to wait for the little girl to fall off to sleep, for if I were to show myself as Ursula Boussidan, I am sure her blood curdling screams would begin all over again and the entire neighborhood would be at Rachel's door. So, I waited until I heard tiny little snores coming from her lips. I then crept to her bedside and held my hand down on her mouth. She opened her eyes quickly and struggled under my grasp.

"Elizabeth! Elizabeth! Shish! Please, please listen to me. It is I, Annabel Horton. I stole the woman's flesh and it has cost me my soul.

Listen. Let me prove it to you; Ursula would not know of my life in Salem. Hear me out! Listen to me: My father was Joshua Horton. My brothers were James and Jeremiah. Jeremiah was your father. I took you away from him. He sinned against you. Do you believe me now? Oh please, Elizabeth. We need each other. Jeanne Elemont will not give up, and men are weak. Matthew may succumb to her charms and marry the woman. Please Elizabeth, if I take my hand away, please; promise that you will not scream?"

I looked into her eyes. They were filled with tears. She nodded her head up and down and I knew she believed me and that I could now trust her.

"Annie, "she wept as I removed my hands. "I cannot see you in Ursula's features. What does that mean?"

"I do not know."

"Ursula must be a witch," she whispered.

"If she is, she is the devil's witch," I told her. "As I suspected."

Elizabeth let out a long sigh.

"You are like me, now," I said sadly. "Your original body is gone."

"When Jeanne Elemont put her hands to my throat I remembered what you told me about Michele, about what he said to you right before they put the noose to your neck."

"Turn your head, sharp, to the right. Do it girl and be spared," I said.

"Precisely." She smiled. "It worked. I lost my body but my soul is intact."

"Oh, if only Michele were with me."

She reached to hug me.

"He is safe. I am sure of it."

"What about Matthew, does he see you?" I asked.

"No. No one looks that carefully at children, unless of course, they are your own," she whispered. "And I do not want him to see me. First I return to him old, and now young, too young."

"I am sorry." I took her hand.

"Do not be sorry," she said. "I do have life at least."

"Urbain? What evil hand does he play in this game?"

"I do not know. I do know that Ursula and Jeanne want the house and the entire estate. Evil wants all."

"That is too simple for the Devil," I said. "His wants are more complex."

"I think they want to kill Meredith Mae before she marries Callen."

"Yes, they have enough heirs to deal with. But then, there is Matthew's share of the estate. That has nothing to do with what Meredith Mae owns."

"Jeanne will have to try and regain Matthew's heart," she said sadly. "If she succeeds in doing so, she becomes heir to his wretched fortune."

"No, Jeanne Elemont will never have Matthew's heart. She never did. She has a moment of his vulnerability and that is all."

Elizabeth looked away and I continued.

"Meredith Mae will have to sneak behind her father's back in order to see Ursula. I do not know if she will do that. But Ursula and Jeanne will find some way to trick her. They will plan her murder once Ursula has written herself back into my granddaughter's will."

"Ursula and Jeanne have to kill Rachel *and* Matthew *and* Meredith Mae in order to insure the estate. Wouldn't that look a bit suspicious?" she asked.

"Yes," I agreed. "So, maybe they will be more methodical in their planning, or perhaps, they simply do not care," I said sarcastically. "There's always a house fire when everyone is inside. Perhaps that's their plan."

"I think that Jeanne Elemont will probably get rid of Ursula. She will have no need for her once she snares my husband," Elizabeth said.

"I do not understand why Ursula did not kill Meredith Mae in Europe right after they eloped."

I sat back and reached for a glass of water that sat on the nightstand by Elizabeth Sue's bed and sipped it.

Elizabeth blushed. "Sex, I imagine."

"Oh, I see."

I turned away myself.

"The witch desired her; she still does. Meredith Mae is quite beautiful."

"Then how did she keep Jeanne Elemont from killing her in a jealous rage?" I asked.

"I have a theory."

"I'd like to hear it."

"Well, I think that our Jeanne Elemont is using Ursula to her own advantage, but every time Ursula botches the plan she becomes more and more disposable. Personally, I do not think she cares one way or another who Ursula takes to her bed."

"But what of Ursula?" I questioned. "How does she insure her fortune if Jeanne convinces my son to marry her?"

"Didn't you mention that Ursula will write herself back into Meredith Mae's will?" Elizabeth asked.

"Yes." I nodded.

"Well, Meredith Mae's trust is worth more than Matthew's estate. It is Jeanne who needs Ursula, I would say. She stands to inherit more money if their wicked little plans work."

"I suppose so." I shuddered.

"Do you think they are immortal?" she asked.

"I do not know," I said. "But if Urbain was crushed under the stones of Loudun in 1634, his daughter must be quite a hag by now."

Elizabeth giggled.

"We could use her beauty secret one day."

"Yes," I said simply. I brushed the hair from her forehead, as if she were really a small child. "I wonder why they did not kill Rachel after the devil's Mass? They must have wanted her dead. It was clearly a sacrifice."

I closed my eyes. I could see the vivid image behind the darkness of Ursula's lids, poor little Rachel at the altar and the stake at her heart. Oddly enough, I suddenly felt tremendous fear. I did not know if it was my own emotion or Ursula's.

"They call it the devil's reprieve," Elizabeth said. "They believe that Satan saved Rachel, not Annabel Horton. So they let her live."

"Perhaps." I smiled. "Or perhaps they are not really evil."

"They are evil to me."

"What shall we do?" I whispered.

"Maybe we should try and convince Matthew and Meredith Mae that they are being deceived. Perhaps they will believe us and flee the century. Have you ever seen Jeanne and Ursula in another dimension? Perhaps they can not follow us."

"I will not forfeit my fortune," I said.

"What? You will allow harm to come to them?" Elizabeth shot up in bed and glared at me.

"What of Rachel and Troy?" I questioned. "You would leave them in the hands of the devil?"

"They are not witches. They cannot cross time."

"Rachel?"

"She is only clairvoyant. She can see through the dimensions but she cannot cross."

"But you live in her child's body. Will you take that from her?"

Elizabeth sighed. "She will have another child," she said softly. "Her child lived longer than she would have because of me. I have spared her some grief."

"Whatever we do, let us make sure we do not let fear cost us our security."

We sat in silence for a long time and stared at the reflection of the moon. It was as if neither of us wanted anything more than the simplicity of a night's rest, for both of us began to nod off.

"Well, what are we to do?" Elizabeth's head came up sharply and she shook it. "I can think of nothing."

I turned and took her hand again.

"I have no thoughts yet, either," I told her. "How is Matthew? I want so much to comfort him."

"He is despondent and distraught over my murder. He blames himself for leaving me alone."

"Is Jeanne Elemont succeeding in turning his head around?" I asked.

"Yes, she has been going to the house and asking to see Matthew. He has refused to see her, but I can tell he is weakening, even Rachel mentioned it."

"Why do you not go to him and tell him to stay away from her?"

"I cannot go to my husband as a child. What can I offer him now?" she wept. "That is why I needed you. It is too painful to have him look upon me as a baby, even when I have the truth to give him."

I put my arm around her small body and held her in the arch of my shoulder.

"And Meredith Mae?" I asked. "Now I know why she was so sad. What can I do for her? I know she must be suffering so much."

"She hates Callen Hall but she must marry him. Do you know that she refuses to believe that Jeanne Elemont was Ursula's lover and is trying to convince her father that I made the whole thing up, out of jealousy, because I knew of his affair with Jeanne? I think Matthew is beginning to believe it." She sighed.

"Then we must act quickly," I said. "If Jeanne Elemont convinces Matthew to marry her then my son and my granddaughter are in terrible danger."

"What about Meredith Mae? She'll see that you've murdered Ursula." Elizabeth said quickly.

"She won't see. Annabel Horton is lost in Ursula's features. I will have to keep up the charade. I will not have her hate me for Ursula's murder, if in fact, I have actually succeeded in doing away with her."

"Oh, what should we do?"

"I think that we must go to Matthew and convince him to convert our money into gold."

"For what purpose?"

"We will all flee the century with our fortune intact. We can transport material objects. I am sure of it. My clothes travel with me; why not my gold?"

"But what if Jeanne Elemont can follow us? She will just continue to seduce my husband and I have a child's body. I cannot compete with her."

"We will find a way to age you, somehow, but the gold will be converted to cash in the twenty-first century and deposited into several different investments, all under the name of Ann Arlin Peckham Guyon." I smiled. "I am afraid Jeanne Elemont cannot seduce me."

I noticed that Elizabeth squinted up her eyes and looked as if she had just swallowed bad food.

"What is it, Elizabeth?" I asked.

"Oh Annie. I am so terribly sorry."

"Sorry? Sorry about what?"

"You were murdered, Annie. Ann Arlin Peckham Guyon was found stabbed in the library of her home. I have been in a trance with Emie. Your children were present. Urbain came there and he...."

I sat back and gasped. I had forgotten, for an instant, what the beast had done to me, but now it settled in my brain, and I cried out so fiercely that the child quickly sat up and put her hand over my mouth.

"Michele and the children are grieving terribly," she told me.

"Oh, my God!" I cried. "You must tell them that I am all right."

"But you are not all right, Annie. You cannot be seen in Ursula's features. That frightens me."

"You must tell Michele that I am fine, Elizabeth. You must relieve his pain. You must tell my children that I live and breathe," I whispered fiercely.

"Michele has gone into the time chamber, Annie. He went in search of you. Philippe stood just outside the chamber and watched as Urbain followed Michele. Philippe told Emie to wait on the outside of the chamber — that he would send for her, and then he ran to follow his father."

"No!" I cried.

"Michele quickly told Philippe to act as a manservant and stay at his side.

"'I will follow you, Father. I will never leave you,'" Philippe said. "Michele told him to protect you, that Urbain was gaining hold of him."

"'When we find your mother, remain with her. Do not give her too much information at once. Protect her, Philippe,'" Michele said.

"My God, what will happen to them?" I wept.

"Emie communicated to me that they vanished, all of them, Michele, Philippe and the bastard, Urbain."

"Where have they gone?" I asked.

Suddenly, Elizabeth shot up in bed and stared at me.

"You had better leave now."

"What?" I cried.

"They must have gone into the dimension you spoke of so often. Oh, my God. They have gone to Matthew's birth. Of course!"

"What are you saying?"

"They have gone to seduce Patience Stokes and give birth to Matthew Joshua Horton Guyon."

"Good God!" I cried.

"Michele said Urbain was gaining hold of him. They must be there in that dimension now. Philippe kept his promise and stayed with you, right before you came back to Salem. Destiny is being written and we must allow its course, for it has happened."

She stood from the bed. "You must go. Ursula will return to her flesh and surely murder me once again. I do not think I can stand anymore violence."

"I have no-where to go."

"You did not murder Ursula. Perhaps, Jeanne Elemont was able to protect her from your grasp. So, now they are having fun with you. Ursula is momentarily hindered by you, but not gone or dead. When she regains consciousness you may disappear and won't be able to help me."

Suddenly, I felt cold; a sharp jab went through the left side of my head. I looked at the child as she stared at me strangely. My vision went dark, so dark that I quickly lost sight of everything.

"Oh, my God. You are right," I called out. "Run, Elizabeth! She is regaining her strength. She will force me out."

But, just as Elizabeth ran to the door, I was thrown to the wind, thrown from inside Ursula's form. I regained a shadowy vision, and as if watching through white smoke, I saw Ursula reach out her hand and put it over Elizabeth's mouth. I tried to stop her but I was no longer inside her body. I had become nothing but thought and I could not control Ursula any longer. I watched helplessly as Ursula went to the open window and jumped to the ground below with the child in her arms.

I had been forced out of the body of Ursula Boussidan as if blown by the wind of a hurricane and I landed back in the darkness from which I had arrived. I fell into an abyss from which I would not awake until startled by the playful call of the man from the church. Oh, so many dimensions of time and space would alter and shift before the stasis my soul now lingered in would lift.

# PART III

# DOMINUS

# Chapter 1

I went to that place where all time meets, and in that eternal second I heard the melody of a song, the squeak of a box, the sound of wind. Ah, yes, I felt the coolness of porcelain and the warmth of wool. I tasted wine on my lips and giggled. I saw blood on my hands and wept. I felt the delirium of love, oh how deeply I obsessed in it — the obliteration of grief, oh, how fine was that. I ached for language and was given ink. I was moved by innocence, haunted by the stroke of an artist's brush. I was drowned in guilt, consumed in the weight of it. Oh, so briefly, I picked up the scent of a rose, the taste of fruit. I knew desire and wallowed. I felt defeat and withdrew. I wiped away tears that were not my own and sadness choked me. I did not turn away and compassion freed me. A white tailed doe made me stop to smile. The soar of an eagle made me stop to dance. I called to my mother and her arms enfolded me. I wept for my father and his smile returned to me. I prayed for my children and an angel heard me. Friendship blessed me. Loneliness left me. I cursed this taunting hum of a universe that made me cold enough to shiver, and then, so hot I burned. I lingered over the fall of a leaf, the sight of rain, the rage of thunder. I knew myself so profoundly that I gave up all fear. I lost my self so completely that I ached an infinity. I saw nothing but darkness, then nothing but stars. The earth closed around me, and then opened anew and I cherished it. Oceans slapped against the shore and the moon slid into my hands like magic. Hatred passed before my eyes and left me empty. Humility consumed me and left me full. Snow fell. Grass grew. Sweet, sweet air left its kiss on my lips and my breath made ripples in the universe. I worshipped the Lord with all my heart and he clothed me in silk. Where am I? I am at the point where all time meets. I am in the eyes of God and the sight of God's presence is on my soul. Therein, I see you.

"Annabel?" he called.

I had ears to hear.

"Annabel?" he called again.

I looked all around me. It was the church I saw, familiar and aglow with candles. The Virgin guarded the lights that flickered, and Jesus looked so sweet. I went to the statue and touched his feet.

"Oh, Annabel?" he called again.

So now I had eyes to see.

"Who goes there?" I asked.

"An angel," he whispered.

I now had a nose to smell, wood and incense, flowers too. His cloak left a scent of musk in the air, a scent of rain.

"Michele?"

"I'm afraid not," he said again.

I sighed louder and held out my hands. Nothing.

"Where am I?" I asked.

"Here," he answered.

I went to him. His face was shielded in shadow but I noticed a beard, dark and full. His hair curled. His form was large. He appeared young one moment and old the next.

"I want answers," I demanded.

"I have none," he said.

"I am without form," I told him.

"Of course," he said. "Have you found your soul?"

"My children? My husband?" Where are they?" I pleaded.

Now it was his turn to sigh.

"Time holds them," he answered.

"How do they fare there?"

"They fare there."

"I must go."

"Wait!" he called.

I turned and watched as his shadow moved across the floor.

"But I must take form."

298

"Find her!"

"Find who?" I asked and stared at his face. His features were sharp and well pronounced. I could see the line of his nose, the glow from his eyes.

"Madeleine de Brou," he whispered. "It is your destiny."

"Who is Madeleine de Brou?"

"Find her," he whispered.

"Where shall I look?"

"In the devil's heart."

"You know Urbain?" I gasped.

He smiled and walked away.

"Wait!" I called. "I do not know where to go."

He snapped his fingers and I heard the sound of nails on the wood. In an instant, she stood before me, her sad brown eyes smiled up at me, her tongue hung out so pink against the white mouth, and her saliva made a puddle on the floor.

"Beauty," I laughed. "How did you get my dog?"

"She is her dog," he said. "Her name is Annascha, not Beauty."

"Annascha? What does that mean?"

"Anything."

"She disappeared one day. We never found her; how the children wept. How did you get her?" I asked again.

"I took her back. I made a mistake. I thought I had found Madeleine. She was so similar, so like Madeleine, but you see when I return I become confused."

"You were the one that gave the dog to Ann Peckham?"

"She is looking for her mistress," he said. "Perhaps she will guide you to her. Once you have found Madeleine, Annascha will be happy. But then, I will be alone."

I looked at Annascha and put my arms around her. The dog licked the air I consumed and I laughed.

"She will take me to Madeleine?"

"I think so."

"She is a magician?" I laughed.

"No," he smiled. "She is a dog."

I reached out my hand to stroke her but I had no form to follow through with.

"I must take a body," I whispered.

"Do not kill."

"I kill only evil."

299

He glared at me and I could see his hand reach out for the space I claimed. I feared for a moment that he was going to banish me.

"I kill only evil," I said again.

But the man did not respond. His hand disappeared, and though I called his name he did not answer. I searched the church but could not find him. Only the dog followed behind me.

"Hey!" I called out. "Come back to me."

I ran up and down the pews looking for him. The dog ran behind me and barked.

"Hey!" I screamed.

Out of the quiet and serenity of the church I heard a door slam. I stood very still. Footsteps followed. A form appeared. Annasha did not recognize the scent and began to growl.

I felt a heart beating in my chest.

"Oh, my God," I whispered.

I held my hand before my eyes and saw flesh.

"Oh, my God," I said again. "He has given me form."

I looked quickly to the dog and then to the altar. A priest stood there staring at me.

"Can I help you?" he asked as he walked towards me. "Is that a dog? There are no dogs allowed inside the church."

I stood silent. I could not speak. *How on earth did I get form?* I wondered.

"Father?" he whispered.

"Good God!" I proclaimed.

"Father? Are you all right?" The priest reached out tentatively and touched my shoulder. Annascha continued to growl and he jumped back.

"It is all right, Annascha," I said.

"You look weak," The priest whispered as if speaking louder might cause me to fall.

I held my hand before my eyes. I touched my beard. I picked up the scent of musk from my cloak.

"Oh my God," I uttered aloud.

"What is it?" The priest asked.

He had given me *his* form. I wore *his* cloak. I carried *his* scent. The beard I now stroked had been the very beard I had seen on his face. He had given me his form and I had only known him as an angel. Of course, it could not be. He could not have really been an angel.

"What is your name?" The priest asked. "Who are you?"

300

I stared into his eyes.

"Aaah. Julian, Father." I told him. "Julian Rouvrey." The name slipped off my tongue easily.

"Ah, French," he uttered as he took my arm and sat me down. "You are a curate? You wear a robe."

"Yes. I am a curate," I told him. I noticed that I spoke with a French dialect.

"Where?" he asked.

"At the Huguenot St. Pierre-du-March Church," I said.

"Ah," he said. "Huguenot St. Pierre-du-March?"

"Yes, Father." I nodded as I put my head in my hands and rubbed my temple. I was saying whatever popped into my head. "I am a Priest from Loudun but I do not recall how I wound up here. I must have fallen and bumped my head. I cannot seem to remember anything. Can you tell me where I am?"

"Brooklyn."

I looked up quickly.

"Brooklyn?"

"Why, yes."

"What year is it, Father?"

"It is Christmas Day. We have just finished our Mass."

"What year, Father?"

"1896."

"My God." I sighed and fell back.

"What is it, my good man? What is wrong?"

"1896?" I cried. "Oh God, I am too late; they could all be dead. Yes, surely thirty-seven years have appeared. They must all be dead."

"What's that you say, Father? What is it? Who must all be dead?"

But I could not answer him, sobs tore through my chest and I could not speak.

# Chapter 2

Father Terrence Donovan gave me a room at the rectory and had Annascha taken to the basement. For three days he held my head in his hands and fed me. When I awoke from my despair, I saw him sitting there in prayer. When I screamed out in pain, he rocked me in his arms and told me that I was a child of God. I wanted to die and the old priest knew it. I wanted all the illusions of heaven to be real and to sweep me up in the sweetness of angels with harps. I wanted death to be peaceful and the murky white light to reveal the eternal spirit of my son. I cursed the truth and whispered the lies in my sleep. The heart in my chest ached, and my soul carried the tedium of despair like a bird carries a torn wing. It was not until I had the dream that I relented and squeezed the priest's hand. Oh, how I welcomed the dream. In it, my son Matthew spoke to me in my sleep. He waved his hand and whispered that he lived in a seashell. He told me to search the ocean's floor for the echo of his voice, and like a jewel on a battlefield discovered in the aftermath of war, I grasped this tender dream and did not let go. It was my omen. It was my hope.

"Well, you seem to be feeling better."

The priest smiled, his kind blue eyes appeared like fine light silk. As I looked about me, I was surprised to see that this was the very same church that had stood over forty years ago, and had harbored my

302

granddaughter. After I sat up in bed, and had eaten some cereal that a nun must have brought to my room, I could not help but ask Father Donovan if he knew of a Father Jacques. For some reason, it was the first clear thought I had. The old Priest scratched his chin and thought for a moment.

"There was a Father Jacques here at St. Joseph's right before I came, but he returned to France, I think. I never met him. I heard he died there. Either that or he left the priesthood," he told me.

"Really?"

"Did you know him?" he asked.

"I knew of him."

"Well, you must get some peaceful rest now that you seem to have your strength back. You tossed around so much in your sleep that I tired watching you. If you like, I will check the books and see exactly when your Father Jacques left our Church."

"I would appreciate that, Father," I said. I wondered if the bastard Urbain could have really died. If something so mundane as death could have snuffed out his soul.

"I will bring you some clean clothes now. Then you will have something to wear when you awake. Your robe seems a bit archaic," he whispered as he closed the door to my room. "I am just on the other side of the hall if you need anything."

As soon as he shut the door, I went immediately to the mirror over the small dresser and searched for my image, my real image, but nothing stared back at me but the concerned gaze of the mysterious Julian Rouvrey. I sat on the edge of the cot and looked at the foreign grasp of fingers that no longer contained the reflection of my soul.

I must have sat there for only a few minutes before the good Father returned with a pair of shoes, a white priest's collar and black pants and a shirt.

"Take these," he said. "The pants will be small, and the shoes big, but I think they will work for the time being.

"Thank you, Father," I said as I took the clothes from him and laid them on the cot. From my window, I could see a large imposing bridge that seemed to reach across the Hudson River into Manhattan. Of course, I knew it immediately as the Brooklyn Bridge. It must have been recently built, though. I went to the window and stared at it. Father Donovan came and stood by my side.

"Beautiful structure, isn't it?" He smiled.

"Yes. It certainly is."

Father Donovan laughed very suddenly and I turned to look at him.

"Have you seen the Spider Lady?" he asked with a gleam in his eye.

"No, Father. Who is the Spider Lady?"

"Not *who* but *what*." He laughed again. "Well, I will take you downtown and show you the elevated tracks we have running from Court Street all the way out to Coney Island."

"And you call these tracks the Spider Lady?" I asked. I had never heard that, nor did I remember any elevated tracks in Brooklyn from my days in twentieth century New York.

"Oh, yes." He laughed more heartily now and seemed quite proud. "I wonder if your fair city of Paris has anything like it."

I laughed with him. "I cannot remember," I told him.

He looked at me seriously. His eyes had a certain sparkle, even though his mouth was set firm.

"But you remember being in Brooklyn?" he asked me.

I nodded.

"What do you remember about Brooklyn?" he inquired cautiously. "When were you here?"

I looked at his face. Nothing but kindness and concern looked back at me.

"A long time ago, I think." I sighed and did not speak for several moments. "Do you know a family named Guyon?" I asked, as if I had suddenly remembered something.

"Guyon? Guyon?" He scratched his chin again and came to sit on the edge of the bed.

"Oh, yes! Yes, I knew them," he said after giving it some quiet thought. "My God, I haven't seen them for a while, but yes, yes I do seem to remember them. It was when I first came to this parish in 1859."

I went quickly to his side and sat down. He turned his face to mine.

"Matthew Guyon. Yes, I remember. He converted to Catholicism right before he married. I counseled him. That's why I remember. Oh, I was a much younger man then, but I do remember him. He died shortly after his wedding, poor man."

"Matthew Guyon? Dead? Are you sure?"

The old priest nodded, "Yes, I am sure."

I swallowed hard and remembered my dream.

"When was that?" I whispered.

"Oh, quite some time ago. I don't even think his children were born yet."

I stood up and went back to the window so he could not see my face.

"His daughter makes it here every now and then, the older one from a prior marriage. They always sit in the very last pew. She comes with her companion. Yes, what is her name now?"

The priest looked up and scratched his chin so judiciously I thought he would rub away his skin.

"Meredith Mae?" I asked softly.

"Your memory is returning." He stood and stared at me.

"Somewhat," I told him meekly. "Who is this companion of Meredith Mae's?" I asked and dreaded the answer.

"They have one of those Boston marriages, you know." He sat back down again and whispered. "Spinsters."

"She never married Callen?" I asked before I could stop myself. I was so surprised that I began to pace the room. It was then I realized for the first time that the good priest had clothed me at some point in an old dressing gown and I began to feel a bit foolish walking around in it.

"Callen? You mean old Callen Hall?" The priest laughed.

I stopped and turned to look at him.

"Old? Why yes, I guess he is by now. What happened to Callen Hall?"

"How do you know these people?" the old priest asked.

"I have a cousin who knew them," I told him quickly. "Please Father. It is helping me to remember. What happened to Callen Hall?"

"Well, it was quite a scandal at the time. He was engaged to be married and he ran off with another woman. The woman worked with Ellen Terry, I hear. Ah, yes! He was engaged to Meredith Mae Guyon, I'm quite sure of it. He ditched her for an actress," he leaned in and whispered to me.

"Did he marry the actress?" I asked.

The old priest nodded. "As far as I know they are still married. He is not a Catholic but she is. Callen had some kind of falling out with the older Guyon, probably over his jilting the daughter."

"The older Guyon? You mean Matthew?"

I kept seeing my son's face in the dream. He was young and he kept waving at me to follow him.

"Yes," Father Donovan said. "His wife baptized the children after his death. That surprised me."

"Callen's wife?"

"Oh, no, no, Guyon, his widow baptized their children.

"Children?" I asked.

"Twins," he said.

"Twins?" I gasped and sat at his side again. "Matthew Guyon had twins? Who did he marry?" I asked and held the sleeve of the Priest's shirt.

"I don't know her name. I just saw her once or twice."

"Was it Jeanne Elemont?" I asked sadly.

The priest went to scratch his chin again and thought better of it. Instead he pulled on his ears.

"What does she look like?"

I took in a deep breath. "She is cold," I told him. "Beautiful, blond and cold as snow."

The priest laughed. "Yes, that's her. Jeanne Elemont. Must be her. She still looks good. I haven't spoken to her since his death. She was never much of a parishioner, probably why the children never show up here, but her name and her picture is always in the paper. She gives money to charity, well, why not, saves on taxes, huh?"

"You mentioned twins?" I asked quickly.

"She told me she baptized her children because she likes the ritual. Ha! I remember that. I tried to council her but she disappeared. Is that all religion was to her, ritual?"

"Father, there were twins?" I asked, trying to bring him back to the matter at hand.

"Yep, boy and a girl. Strong resemblance between them. I see them around but never in church."

"Father," I said. "I hope you will forgive me, but you are right about that peaceful sleep. I could use a nap about now."

"Yes, of course. I hope I've been of some help to you?"

I put my arms around him and held him to me.

"Yes, Father. Bless you," I whispered. "I am going to sleep for awhile and when I awake I will change into these nice clean clothes, you so kindly provided me, and take my dog for a walk. I have so much to think about. A walk will help."

"I will go with you," The old Priest said. I took his arm.

"No, Father. I must go alone. I will think better."

He looked at me carefully. His pale blue eyes still sparkled. After a moment, he nodded.

"You will be careful?"

"Yes, Father. I will take the address of the church with me and if I lose my way I will find some kind soul to lead me back."

"We will pray when you return," he said.

"Of course." I smiled and took his hand.

My head was spinning as I thought about my son, now dead, and my granddaughter, now old and possibly broke. I was tired and knew I needed sleep.

I took the dressing gown off and stood before the mirror naked. I had nothing on but a gold cross around my neck. Father Julian Rouvrey was an unusual contradiction. He was a big man with delicate hands. His nose was long and his eyes were large, yet his mouth was almost pretty, as his upper lip showed pink beneath the hair that covered it and his lower lip swelled slightly in a soft, moist swell. The hair on his body was black as night and covered him in curly dark strands that stopped miraculously at his shoulder and did not run down his back. His skin was dark, and yet, his eyes were blue. The hair on his head curled and fell to his shoulders. His beard was heavy and needed trimming. He appeared small boned yet his phallus was thick.

The cross he wore appeared to be rusted. When I held it in my hand, I could see that it had weight and was the size of my finger. The chain was carefully linked in the same dull gold. I took the chain off my neck and studied it. I saw nothing unusual, except for some dents on the side of the cross, as though someone had tried to scratch something in the rust. There was a compelling beauty to the cross. I went back to the mirror to return it to my neck and stared in utter amazement as my own dear face looked back at me.

"Good God, my image has returned!" I cried out as I gazed into the eyes of Annabel Horton. There I was, smiling miraculously back at myself from behind Julian's features. But, when I placed the cross back around my neck my vision disappeared entirely. I stood before the mirror and did this several times and each time I removed the cross, I regained myself, and when I returned the cross to its rightful owner, Annabel Horton vanished back into the obscurity that claimed her.

# Chapter 3

I slept only an hour or so. When I awoke, I dressed quickly and stole quietly down to the basement to retrieve Annascha, who was sitting up and staring at the door as if she knew I would come for her.

"There's a good girl," I said as the dog jumped to my waist and let out loud, happy barks.

"Shiiissssh!" I commanded.

I could not find a leash for the dog so I took the belt from around my waist and tied it quickly around her neck. I led her up the stairs as quietly as I could, for I did not wish to be detained by idle chatter. I took her out through the small kitchen and we left by the

back door. On my way through, I passed a kindly nun who told me she had given the dog some meat. Annascha barked happily at the sight of the nun and tried to run to her, but I pulled her back.

"I love dogs," The nun told me. "And she is so pretty. I knew a dog like that once. What is her name?"

"Annascha. Thank-you, Sister," I uttered as I pulled the dog out the door. The nun stood staring after me as I ran to the street, pulling the dog behind me. The nun seemed familiar, but I had no time to stop and study her features. I was eager to find my old Brooklyn home and discover who had stolen it out from under me.

The good Priest had been correct about the clothes. They were tight and my short slacks pulled at my crotch. The shoes he had given me were a size too large and I found it difficult to keep them on my feet. I must have looked an odd sight with my shoulder length locks and large flapping shoes, and my beautiful white dog pulling me down the street. I tripped several times trying to keep up with Annascha, who led me right to the door of the house on Montague Street with out even stopping to sniff at a tree.

I would not have known the house if Annascha had not stopped before it. I stared in disbelief and held my breath for several seconds. Some idiot had painted my beautiful home an obnoxious shade of blue and had trimmed it in red. It was a ghastly sight! A huge white gazebo took up most of the space in the front yard and almost dwarfed the house it was so large. The gazebo was grotesquely adorned with wooden lovebirds and large bells. An addition to the house had been added on the right side which looked like a Cathedral. The front door had been completely altered. Instead of the beautiful old original wooden door, I found myself staring at a red, thickly embodied fortress covered in snarls and terrifying gargoyles. Two huge lion statues guarded the sides of the house with open stone teeth.

I was just about to ring the chime when a woman came through the front door and glared at me.

"Can I help you?" she asked.

I was shocked. There stood Jeanne Elemont, the devil's blood disciple. I could not move my tongue to answer her. She had barely aged since I saw her last. There were lines near her eyes and around her lips but she did not look any older than forty-one or two.

I stammered something about being there to see the master of the house. She told me to ring the door again and Calvin, his servant, would help me.

I watched as she passed and continued down the walk. She was magnificently dressed and wore a large green feather in her hat. She had looked through me, as if I hardly existed. I knew then that my image was hidden in Julian's features and could only be seen by another witch if I removed the cross. Of course, I wanted to kill Jeanne for what I knew she had done to my son, but I simply stared at her until she was out of sight.

I anxiously rang the door chime. It played back some ridiculous tune that I could hear reverberating on the other side of the monstrous door, which finally opened on a servant who peered at me from behind his starched white shirt and his kind Black smile.

"May I help you, Father?" he asked.

"Yes," I told him. "I'd like to see the man of the house."

"Who should I say is calling?" He looked apprehensively at the dog as he inquired.

"My dog is gentle."

The man reached out and stroked the top of Annascha's head. The dog wagged her tail.

"I am Father Julian, from St. Joseph's," I began to explain, when I noticed that another man had appeared at his side.

"And you have a message from God?" the other man bellowed as best he could, for his voice was quite squeaky.

The servant quickly backed away. I stared at the man that I now surmised was Matthew's son.

"Wait, Calvin!" he quipped as he snapped his fingers. "Take this creature to the back and tie him to the old apple tree." He looked me up and down and smiled at my appearance. "I do not like German shepherds," he said as he squeezed the skin on his nose up and narrowed his eyes.

"Yes, of course." I handed the leash to Calvin who had a strained expression on his face. He appeared frightened.

"I will take good care of him, sir," he said apprehensively.

"*He's* a girl." I smiled.

"Come, sweet girl." He took the leash from me and petted her again. "What's her name?"

"Annascha," I told him as he continued petting her. I noticed that the young man raised his eyes to the ceiling and sighed loudly, as if his patience had been stretched to the limit.

"Let's move along now, Calvin," he finally said and peered in my direction.

"Yes, sir." Calvin frowned. "Come on, Annascha. You come with me."

The man stood back after Calvin took the dog. He extended his hand and motioned for me to enter.

"Please come in, Father," he said. "I can give you a small donation and even less of my time. Come, I'll get my checkbook."

I walked past him into what had once been my old parlor. Thick red drapes hid the sun from the room and large paintings of naked children adorned the walls.

I stared around me in disbelief, and almost walked into a wall, as I sadly surveyed the renovations. I gaped incredulously at the monstrosity this idiot had turned my home into.

"I am Luther Guyon. Ah, but you must know that. Please, be brief. I'm a busy man," he said as he stood by an ornate marble fireplace and motioned for me to sit. "What little charity have you come in earnest for?"

I stared at this pompous fool. He appeared to be the same age as his mother. His moustache fell below his jaw line and his lank brown hair came to his shoulders. His eyes were black, so black that they looked like small dark holes. His lips were very thin and his skin was unusually pale. On the bridge of his nose were several freckles. I noticed he was short, for a man, but he appeared to stoop over. His front teeth fell over his lip and made him look rather foolish. If indeed, he had a twin, the poor girl was surely cursed by the devil if she bore resemblance. Certainly, he bore no resemblance at all to our side of the family.

"Actually, Luther, I am here because I knew your father." I carefully watched his reaction. His face remained passive and he appeared bored.

"Really?" he said. "Mother tells me he was quite useless."

I dug my fingers into the offensive fabric that covered some claw-footed chair in fat naked cherubs and forced a smile.

"On the contrary," I said, "he was quite remarkable."

"In what way?" he asked, suddenly averting his eyes. I watched as he let out a brief cry and ran to the window in a state of panic. I realized that Annascha was barking and assumed that Calvin was playing with her in the rear yard.

"Calvin!" Luther screamed and turned back to me. "What stupid people these coloreds are. I absolutely don't know what they are good for. But alas, they work more cheaply than those horrid Irish."

I could not help myself and laughed. He eyed me sharply. Apparently he did not know he carried twenty-five percent Caribbean blood in his veins, if indeed, he were Matthew's child.

"Do I offend you, Father?" He smiled.

Calvin entered the room and stood just at the door with his hands in front of him.

"Yes?" Mr. Luther?" he said.

"I told you to tie the beast up, not let him run fancy free in our yard," Luther screamed as he walked to poor Calvin and stood only a foot from his face.

"Yes, sir. Sorry, sir. I'll attend to it right away, sir."

Luther snapped his finger in the air and waved him off.

"Useless colored." he said.

"God would not think so," I answered.

"Well, dear Father, I am afraid that I am not in agreement with God. Now, what is your purpose with me? As I said, I'm a busy man."

Suddenly, I noticed it. I almost fell out of my chair and on to the floor. I stared over this idiot's head in amazement and held my breath. There, on the wall behind Luther, was a painting of the sea. The waves were high and one lone bird flew in the sky. The frame looked as if it had been made out of seashells.

"What is it, Father? I must get on with my day." He scowled, apparently not noticing my fascination with the painting that took up just a small portion of his wall.

I turned back to him. "Is your sister about? The message from your father is to both of you," I said.

Luther looked at his watch. "Gillian is probably even less inclined to care what message you carry from a man we never knew."

"Your mother?" I asked. "Was it she that just left?"

"Oh, now the dead man has a message for mother? Really, Father. I don't mean to be rude, but I have an appointment with my attorney and he is due any minute."

"Your half sister, Meredith Mae, where does she live now?" I asked quickly. "She used to live here."

"That old witch? Don't tell me the poor dead bastard has a message for her as well? I never see her. She is a recluse. My sister visits her from time to time." He grinned. "For money, no doubt."

I glared at him and watched as he brushed his mustache.

"Actually, I would like to visit with her myself. I have not seen her for several years," I said.

Luther walked to a large desk with huge swans carved at the sides and opened a drawer. He scribbled something on a piece of paper and handed it to me.

"Here," he said. "She lives there."

"Thank you," I replied. "Now, may I meet with your sister and yourself, later this evening? I did promise your father. Oh, and I would appreciate your mother being here, as well."

"Really? My father has been dead for many years. Why do you come now?" he asked with an astonished look on his face, as if he'd swallowed a goldfish.

"He gave me the day and time to come to you," I said. "I think it is imperative you hear your father's message. It will be to your advantage," I assured him.

"Really? Well, all right then. I am a curious enough man to hear you out. Come back at five. I will have Gillian here, I'm sure this will amuse her."

"And your mother?"

"I will try, but mother has a mind of her own and may not be in the least interested to receive a message from one of her dead husbands."

"Try, Luther." I smiled. "Tell her my message from the dead might bring gold to the living."

He squealed like some strange animal caught in a trap.

"That will do it!" he said finally.

"Thank you, Luther," I said as I stared into those black holes of his. "By the way, whose house is it now?" I asked. "I am told that it used to be Meredith Mae's."

The evil one took my hand and shook it. His flesh was cold to the touch.

"I don't know if it's any of your business, Father, but unfortunately, this house belongs to Union Pacific Bank and everything in it belongs to me. To my knowledge, it never belonged to my 'half sister' as you call her."

"Your mother remarried then?"

"Four times widowed since my father's death, four times willed a fortune. Some people have all the luck, wouldn't you say? The poor dear is momentarily unattached, lucky for male society."

"Yes, I suppose so." I studied his features; nothing of him resembled either Jeanne or Matthew. "Well, I will see you at five, Luther," I said as I stood up and faced him. I realized he barely hit my shoulder. "May I have my dog, now?" I asked him and took one more look at the painting with the seashell frame.

"Go to the back of the house, Father. You will find her tied to the apple tree. If she is not there, please let me know. I will enjoy giving that Black fool my strap."

The door behind me closed sharply and I shuddered to myself as I walked down the front steps. *This monster cannot be of our blood*, I thought. *My poor dead son could not have proliferated this.*

I started toward the back of the house when I noticed Calvin standing by the road, as if he had been waiting for me. He waved to me frantically and I walked to him as briskly as I could in my flapping oxfords. Annascha sat by his side, panting patiently in my direction.

"Some people come from the devil," he told me as he handed me the belt that I had tied around the dog's neck. "The good Lord don't have nothing to do with people that sit with the devil. That's just the way it is. Some of us going to heaven and some of us going to hell."

"Thank you for watching my dog, Calvin." I noticed his sadness.

"Don't bring her back here, Father. He'll put a stake through her heart, sure as I'm standing here. Please, Father. She's such a nice dog."

I studied Calvin's expression as he looked back at the house. He appeared to be trembling.

"I will not bring her back, Calvin," I said softly.

"Come back over here where he can't see us," he whispered as he walked in front of some large high bushes and bent down.

"What is it Calvin?" I asked. Deep lines ran from his eyes down to his lips, yet he was still a handsome man.

"I seen him kill dogs just for some ritual he does in that cathedral he built."

I sucked in my breath sharply and stared at him. I saw before me a deeply troubled man. I reached out and put my hand on his back. Somehow, the simple gesture made him break down.

"What is it, Calvin? Let me help you."

"Priests come here all the time asking Mr. Calvin for money, but none of them ever brought a dog."

"No, I suppose not." I gently rubbed a place on his back, hoping it would comfort him.

"I could never get close enough to talk to any of them."

"What is it, Calvin? What is it you want to tell me?"

"You'll hear my confession? He don't let me step foot in no church, else I would have told the Lord"

"Of course, Calvin." I knelt before him and closed my eyes. "Kneel with me."

"I ain't a Catholic, sir, but I got to get this off my chest," he said as he got to his knees and faced me.

"Go on," I said quietly.

"It ain't just dogs, Father."

I saw the grief in his eyes and found tears in my own. I feared what he would tell me.

"Little children, sir. He brings them into that Cathedral. He does bad things to those children, little sweet children no more than eight or nine years old. Sometimes, even younger."

"Go on," I urged him gently.

"I think he's been murdering those children. It gives him some kind of pleasure to do bad things."

"What?" I grabbed his arm and held on to him tightly. "Do you know what you are saying?"

"I sure do, and I can't say nothing about it. I can't do nothing about it. He'll hunt me down. He'll kill me if I ever open my mouth."

"Do you have any money? Can you get away from him?"

"No, sir. He's threatened me something bad."

"How do you know he kills children?" I asked.

"He has me burying bodies. He says they're the dogs. He kills those strays up on the altar and puts them in bags and gives them to me to get rid of. Some of those bodies don't feel like dogs. They feel like people, like little innocent people. Good God, almighty. He knows I know and I can't say nothing." Calvin cried and fell on the ground before me. "Forgive me."

I knelt before him and held on to his arms.

"Why?" I asked. "Good God, Calvin, why does he kill them?" Even as I asked the question, I knew the answer. Evil kills because it is bred by Satan to do so.

Calvin was crying so badly that I could barely understand what he said to me.

"He says some hocus pocus words and all these people swaying and chanting some prayer I never heard. Oh my God, Father. He promises them the world to get them into that cathedral and then he takes the world from them. He promises them money. He steals the children from poor women, he buys them, takes them off the street, steals them from the orphanages, gives them hope; then kills them like he kills those stray dogs, like their lives mean nothing."

I held the man in my arms for what must have been a half an hour while he cried and asked me if God would ever forgive him for burying those poor innocent little bodies.

"I promise you, Calvin. I will stop this bastard. I swear I will avenge these senseless deaths," I finally said. "You must go back inside before he wonders where you are."

"You can't say nothing to anyone or you'll get me killed. Priests can't say nothing 'bout what's been told to them, ain't that right, Father?"

"I will not betray you, Calvin, and I will not betray the children he has harmed. One more thing, Calvin," I called to him as he ran toward the house.

"Yes, Sir?"

"Does he have a pistol?"

He stared at me for quite sometime before he nodded.

"Yes sir, and I know where he keeps it, too."

"Is it loaded?"

"Yes, sir."

"I want you to steal it and meet me here at precisely 4:45 this afternoon. Do not let him catch you."

"I'll be right behind that bush at 4:45, Father. He won't catch me."

"Bastards be damned," I said as I turned to go, "Damned to the forfeiture of God forever!"

# Chapter 4

I did not really know why I told Calvin I needed the pistol. I was formulating a plan in my mind that I could not fully attend to, but felt some power to initiate. I was so grieved by the malice against children and animals that I begged God not to reveal this monster as my grandchild. I prayed that his blood was not of my kin. I was too consumed with grief to find an immediate solution to his murderous and scandalous acts, but swore that I would avenge them.

I looked at the address the demon had scribbled for me. I knew that I must seek Meredith Mae's help. If we did, indeed, have magic, I needed that revelation now to rid the earth of this slime.

The address for Meredith Mae was not far from Montague Street and I knew I could walk there in under ten minutes. This time, it was I who pulled Annascha forward as I nearly ran toward Lafayette Street, stumbling once again over my own feet.

I was pleased to find a beautiful home on the corner of Lafayette and Carroll, shielded by lovely maple trees that gracefully swayed before the tall, white columns that adorned the porch. I was relieved that my precious granddaughter had not been living in abject poverty all these years and wondered briefly how she had avoided Ursula's evil hand.

I paused a moment before the door to catch my breath before ringing the chime. Annascha sat at my side with her ears pointed up and her head cocked to one side as if she wasn't quite sure what to expect.

I also anticipated what I would find and I paced anxiously as I waited. Finally, a rather pleasant looking woman of about fifty answered the door and stood nervously looking beyond me. When she was sure that I was alone she looked into my eyes and smiled in friendly fashion.

"Yes?" she said and stared curiously at my rather ill fitting clothes.

"Oh," I was immediately disappointed. "I was looking for Meredith Mae Guyon."

"She's inside resting, Father. Can I help you? I am Miss Eugenie Anderson."

Annascha suddenly broke from my grasp and jumped up on the woman.

"Annascha!" I called. "Oh, I am so sorry but she appears to like you."

"Annascha? That is an interesting name. Well, I love dogs, Father. It is perfectly fine," she said, as she petted the top of Annasha's head. "Now, what can I help you with?"

"Well, actually it is rather important that I speak with Meredith Mae."

She looked at me for a long moment before she spoke.

"All right, please, come inside, Father, and I will tell her you are here. Who should I say is calling?"

I thought for a moment. I knew that Meredith Mae would not be able to see me behind Julian's features, but I would remove the cross and reveal myself the moment we were alone, for I could not trust exactly who this Eugenie Anderson was.

"Tell her I am Father Julian Rouvrey. I have a message from her grandmother."

Eugenie Anderson stopped dead in her tracks and turned to me.

"Her grandmother? Are you quite certain?"

"Well yes, I am quite certain."

The woman eyed me oddly. She studied my face. After looking into my eyes for several seconds she threw back her head and laughed.

"Really, Father? How very strange. You see, I know Meredith Mae so well and you certainly do not appear old enough to have known her grandmother."

"Well, the message has been passed down," I blurted out quickly as she led me into a very simple but pleasant parlor.

"We have lived together for many years and I have never even heard her speak of her grandmother. How very unusual," she said as she moved some books and made a place for me on the couch.

Annascha jumped up before I could sit and made herself comfortable by kicking all the cushions to the floor and curling up in a little ball.

"Oh, I am terribly sorry," I said quickly and clapped my hands at Annascha. Eugenie Anderson laughed again.

"I don't mind, Father," she said. "But Meredith Mae will have herself a fit if she sees the poor sweet dog on her couch."

"Off!" I commanded as the dog continued to sit.

"You know, I knew a shepherd once with the same beautiful white fur."

"You don't say?" I answered over my shoulder as I removed Annascha and had her sit on the floor near my feet. I was thinking how out of character it was for Meredith Mae to have a fit over a dog on her couch.

"How strange," I uttered. "Meredith Mae always loved dogs."

"You knew Meredith Mae?"

"Well, no, but her grandmother told me."

"People change." She smiled.

"How many years have you lived here?" I asked.

"Several," she answered, and then very abruptly added. "Which parish did you say you were from, Father?"

"St. Joseph's." I smiled broadly. "How long do you know Meredith Mae?"

"I met Meredith Mae over twenty years ago. You are French?" she asked me curiously.

I nodded.

"Meredith Mae wanted to return to France but we so love this house."

"Really?"

She smiled again and crossed her arms over her chest.

"You look surprised, Father?" she said.

"Well, I am surprised that Meredith Mae would want to go to France when she is an American."

"Ah, yes that may be so, but she was born in France and it is such a beautiful country."

"Yes, indeed."

"You will see that her dialect is still rather thick," she said nonchalantly over her shoulder as she left the room.

I sat there with a disturbing sensation in the pit of my stomach. My

Meredith Mae was not French. I wondered why she felt it necessary to tell this woman that she was, and how in God's name could she have a dialect?

I stood up and walked to the window. As I looked out over the pretty street I began to feel that something was terribly wrong.

I did not have to wait long for Miss Eugenie Anderson to return to the drawing room with Meredith Mae. At first, I could not see her face. She was over seventy years old and walked with a bit of a stoop. But when she stood before me and raised her eyes to mine, I fell back and tripped over those colossal, large shoes, and wound up on poor Julian's *derriere*. From the floor of her parlor I stared up in horror. There stood the evil familiarity of an aged Ursula Boussidan.

"Father?" she uttered.

"My God!" I cried out.

I was appalled to see that she must be passing herself off as my granddaughter and had obviously been doing so for years. My mind raced quickly. She must have successfully murdered my darling Meredith Mae, just as Jeanne Elemont had successfully gotten rid of my son.

"Are you all right, Father?" The bitch asked.

I could do nothing but gasp.

"I will get some water," Eugenie said alarmingly and ran from the room. Annascha came to me and pulled at my sleeve with her teeth.

"Nice dog," she said suspiciously. "I have seen her before, no?"

"Perhaps so, Miss Guyon. She attached herself to me while I was walking by Prospect Park, just recently. Perhaps you saw her on the street?" I said as I got to my feet.

"Umm. Yes, perhaps. Pretty dog." She called to the dog but Annascha did not go to her.

Eugenie quickly came to my side and handed me the water. I found my way to a chair.

"Are you feeling better now?" Eugenie asked.

"Yes, thank you, Miss Anderson."

"Now, what brings you to my home, Father? Eugenie mentioned you have a message from my grandmother, but as you can see, I am quite old and my poor Granny is long dead."

"I am from Loudun," I said.

*Oh, la campagne est si belle en ce moment. Venez vous souvent?* she asked.

*J'essaie,* I found myself responding. *D'ou etes vous?*

I watched as she moved her lips in an unusual way, as though settling her teeth. Finally, she responded.

"Bordeaux," she said. *Je n'y suis pas retourne depuis longtemps mais je m'en souviens comme d'un tres joli village.*

*Oui, oui c'est tres joli.* I smiled.

We went on to speak French for some time. I was amazed at how easily it fell off my tongue. I was amused that Ursula had no idea that Annabel Horton sat in her parlor and conversed with her in French about the wonders of Paris and the glory of the countryside. Finally, I turned to Eugenie and asked if I could speak with Meredith Mae alone.

"Of course, Father," she said. "I haven't been able to follow your conversation, anyway. My French is very rudimentary. However, it is time for refreshments. I am sure you would like a cup of tea?"

I nodded, and she left the room, promising to return with tea and biscuits. I stared at Ursula. She had aged well, but she was definitely not immortal. I assumed she had finally carried out Jeanne Elemont's wishes and had gone through with Meredith Mae's murder. She must have taken her share of the money and bought this house. I could tell she was living well.

"You are staring at me, Father," she said. "Is there something wrong?"

I shook my head. I was not quite sure what I was going to say but a plan was taking shape in my thoughts as I spoke.

"Forgive me for staring." I ran my hand through my beard. "You are a very attractive woman."

"For my age? Is that what you are implying, Father?" She laughed.

"Does it matter? Good looks are not altogether fleeting."

"I've sold my soul to the devil but I am not as blessed as Dorian Grey." She laughed and looked into my eyes. "Do you like Oscar Wilde?"

"Would you really give your soul for youth?" I asked. "If it meant the devil would walk in your shoes?"

She looked at me seriously and leaned forward.

"Are you making me an offer, Father?" She laughed gleefully.

"Perhaps," I said solemnly.

"What an unusual question for a priest. I thought you were a man of God, not a dream weaver." And she laughed even more loudly this time.

"Tell me, Miss Guyon; for I am quite serious, would you really sell your soul to me if I were the devil, and in return for your precious soul, you could skip down the lane like a young girl and throw your legs

321

around your lady friend once again?"

She gasped and threw her head back. She looked at my face for a long time. Then she took a small cigarette from her purse and lit it.

"Who are you?" she asked slowly.

"I am a magician," I whispered.

She blew the smoke out from the left side of her mouth and continued to stare at me.

"And what can you do for me?" She grinned and I noticed then that her teeth were rather yellow.

"I can share secrets with you that will transport your soul," I told her casually.

"And why would you do that?" she asked.

I stood up and sat by her side. I took her hair in my hands and pulled her face toward mine. I slapped her hard across the cheek and held on to her flesh until it turned a blotchy crimson.

"I need you," I told her.

She reached out her hands to push me from her but she was too weak to fight me.

"Father Donovan tells me you show up in church with your lady friend. Why do you go to church, Ursula?" I hissed. "Why do you defile the house of God?"

She opened her mouth to scream and I put my hands around her throat and began to squeeze until I saw her eyes bulge. "Listen, bitch. I know who you are and I know you are evil, but you are not favored by the devil. You have a conscience. Your old age has frightened you back to the church of your youth. But now, you must redeem yourself. I will help you. I am going to teach your soul to fly and your flesh to swallow the blood of your enemies. You are going to have eternal life, should you want it. You are going to walk in Jeanne Elemont's skin. Do you remember her? Well, you are going to take your prayers to Jeanne Elemont's lips. You will taste the salvia that runs down her chin once again."

"Please," she gasped. "She is a witch."

"That will be your problem, dear Ursula. You will steal her flesh and you will bear the consequences. You will give me Jeanne Elemont's money, all of it; including the fortune she has since stolen from all four of her husbands. I will allow you to keep twenty percent of this great legacy. That is more than most people can count."

"What if I won't do it?" she gasped.

I leaned in close, my lips so near to hers I could smell her horrid breath.

"I will kill you anyway," I whispered. "But your soul will not metamorphose in flesh. Your soul will wither on God's doorstep. You are quite insignificant. Evil has no weight with God."

"No," she whispered, "the devil will avenge it."

"The devil be damned," I said, and threw her back in her chair as I rose and stood over her. "Do not fret, Ursula. I am making you rich and beautiful. The devil's daughter does not age. I have seen her. She still looks thirty-five and she must be several centuries."

"What will you have me do?" She sighed.

"Send Miss Eugenie Anderson on a trip. Get rid of her. Get her out of the house. Wait for me to return for you. I will send someone this evening, or I will come for you myself. If you run, I will find you. Death will only be a transition for you, dear, Ursula. You will finally learn to master your vicious soul. It will be an easy journey."

Eugenie walked into the room at that moment with a tray of biscuits and hot tea. She screamed out when she saw Ursula's condition, for the wretched woman's hair was askew, her face a red and blotchy mess, and she gaped at me as if I held a guillotine over her head.

"Oh, my darling, my precious, are you all right?"

Eugenie ran past me and sat beside the old woman.

"Father, what have you done to her?" she asked me with the most horrified expression on her face.

Eugenie held the old hag in her arms and began to straighten her hair.

"Who are you?" Ursula whispered and stared in my face with the most confused expression.

I bowed at the waist but said nothing. And as I turned to take my leave Ursula looked up at me in absolute horror, as if I had given her a death sentence and not the promise of eternity.

# Chapter 5

I ran back to the church as fast as I could in those ridiculous shoes and threw open the doors of the sanctuary. I felt completely lost. I had no real plan and I was finding it difficult to think clearly. Sobs tore through my chest as I fell to my knees before the altar. My beloved son had fallen victim to evil. My granddaughter had innocently loved the devil's own disciple and had paid for it with her life. Children were being murdered by a madman while the world turned around and around, oblivious to the nightmare.

"Do you sanction this, Jesus?" I screamed. "You that have given me magic, give me the Lord's good grace to apply it. Please guide me." I screamed. "Guide me!"

The most miraculous thing happened. I swear that I saw it, and even now when I think of it, I shudder. A bird flew into the church and circled the icon of Jesus, a bird just like the one I had earlier seen in the painting with the seashell frame. The wooden eyes of the icon looked at me for a brief moment before closing. I held my breath and walked up close to the statue. His face seemed deeply sad. I touched his cheek and felt the tear he'd left there. I stared in disbelief as he opened his eyes again. He did not look directly at me but he shared my pain. He seemed to take it from my body and hold it in his own. I fell before him. My tears ceased. The bird flew over my head, its long white wings barely

324

flapping as it flew up toward the crown on the head of Jesus and sat in precious dominion over its Lord.

I heard a whisper from behind and I turned sharply only to find the nun that I had seen in the kitchen earlier that morning, softly praying in the third pew.

"Did you see that?" I asked as I stood to my feet. "Did you see it?"

The nun looked up. I could see that she was pretty, not terribly young but certainly not old.

"See what?" she asked.

"His eyes."

"What about them?"

"Come here," I said to her.

She got up slowly and walked toward me.

"What is it, Father?"

"His eyes moved."

The nun laughed.

"Father Donovan will not be pleased to find your dog in the sanctuary." She chuckled.

"You look familiar," I said as I stared at her. "Have we met?"

"Yes." She smiled.

"When?"

"This morning you passed me with your dog."

"Oh," I said. "Yes."

"I told you that I had given her some meat."

"Yes, but I meant beyond that."

"Are you all right, Father? I heard you crying so deeply that I stopped to pray for you."

"Thank you sister," I said. "I will take my dog down to the basement. I am fine now. Really, I am."

"What were you saying about his eyes? Did you mean Jesus?" she asked.

Now that the moment of shock had worn off, and my breath had returned to normal, I assumed she would think I was mad if I told her what I had seen, so I decided not to say another word about the blinking eyes of Christ. By then, I was pretty sure I had hallucinated anyway. I was so overcome with grief that I might have thought I saw anything.

"No, it was nothing, really. Well, I must take Annascha to the basement." I smiled graciously. "Good day, Sister."

But before I could reach the side door with Annascha, Father Donovan entered in a great hurry and I almost ran into him as I myself

325

hurried out.

"Father Julian, I was beginning to worry! You made it back all right?" he asked as he put his hands up and prevented me from toppling him over.

"Yes, Father. Annascha and I had a nice walk."

"Good afternoon, Sister Elizabeth." He turned to her and bowed his head.

"Elizabeth?" I said quickly.

She looked at me in the kindest way and searched my face as I stared at her's.

Father Donovan turned back to me and put his hand on my shoulder.

"I have located that Father Jacques you asked about."

"You don't say?"

I continued to stare at the nun. The familiarity slowly began to make sense. Could it really be, I wondered?

"And what are you doing here, missy?" Father Donovan asked as he bent down and spoke to the dog.

I reached behind my collar and quickly took the chain in my hand. I slipped the chain from around my neck and looked back at Sister Elizabeth, while Annascha's tail made swishing sounds in the air.

The nun gasped out loud and fell back into the pew.

"Annie!" I heard her exclaim.

"Your Father Jacques was a priest in this parish from 1840 to 1859. He returned to France and died shortly thereafter," Father Donovan told me as he took the belt I had tied around Annascha's neck and handed it to me. "There's a portrait of him in the third floor sitting room. Would you like to see it?" he asked.

"Yes," I said quickly.

"Take this beauty to the basement and meet me up there." He grinned and patted the dog again.

"Yes, Father. I will be there shortly," I told him and watched as he left the sanctuary.

I turned to look at the nun. Great tears ran down her face.

"Elizabeth?" I said softly. I noticed that while I held the cross in my hand that I could see Elizabeth as I remembered her from Salem, and I could also see her as I remembered her from Manhattan. But with the cross around my neck, I could not recognize the true soul. I saw only the borrowed face of the nun.

"Where on earth have you been?" she asked me as she ran to take me in her arms.

"I cannot say, but it certainly was not earth," I told her sadly. "It felt as if I were in a transitional universe waiting to be born."

"Do you know that Matthew has been dead for many years?"

"Murdered?"

"I cannot prove it."

I studied her face as she went on to tell me that she had not returned to Brooklyn until the dimension of 1879. I noticed that her speech had become resigned and her eyes were sadder than I had ever seen them.

"What has happened to you, Elizabeth?"

"That wretched Ursula dropped me when she jumped from the window. I hit my head, but I was only stunned from it. Fortunately, she ran away and left me. Rachel came outside looking for me and calling my name, but I was too afraid to answer her. I ran off in another direction. I ran as far from Ursula as I could get."

"And then you returned to Rachel?" I asked.

"No, I did not see Rachel again. I was too afraid that Ursula would find me if I went back home. I ran downtown. I must have looked frightful and a bit pathetic. I hid in the doorway of a fancy store until morning, and before I knew it a nice young couple stopped to speak to me. They bought me ice cream and a whole new set of clothes. I told them I had to get away from an abusive father and begged for them to take me."

"And they did?" I asked her incredulously.

"Yes. They took me to their home in Pittsburgh, Pennsylvania, and raised me as their own. They believed they saved me from violence, which they did."

"So you are Rachel's little Elizabeth Sue all grown up?"

"No. The body of Elizabeth Sue passed away naturally. It was just before I planned to return to Brooklyn. Then I, too, drifted in what you refer to as a transitional universe."

"How did you become a nun?" I asked.

"When I finally regained some semblance of consciousness, I found myself here at the church. I must have been willing myself to find Matthew and my soul led me here. I was aware that there was an evil woman at the convent. From my opaque distance I could see her beat the children. I had to have someone's flesh, so I forced her to flee her body. Oh, I think I have mastered it, Annie. I used her body to regain life and the evil in her soul fled with her. I thought I would find

Matthew here in Brooklyn, just as I had left him. I knew he would be old when I found out the year, but I thought that I could care for him in his aged skin. I even fantasized that he would find a young evil body to take and I would leave the convent so that we could be together. But, then, I found out that Matthew had been dead for nearly twenty years. I was devastated and saw no reason to leave the convent after that. There is no other for me but Matthew, why not then, serve God?"

"How did Jeanne kill him and get away with it?" I asked sadly.

"They say he died of natural causes in his sleep," she told me. "But I know she poisoned him. She must have. She has married four times since and each of them has died in their sleep. Oh, except for one who accidentally fell in front of a train."

"Have you met his twins?"

"No, I only know of them and I hear that they are horrid. They are both quite notorious. I do not believe that Matthew is their father. I simply do not."

"Why do you say that?" I asked quickly.

"Well, for one, they were born only seven months after his marriage to Jeanne."

I took her hand in mine. "Unfortunately, they may still be his children," I said. "We cannot prove otherwise by that."

"You have taken on very fine flesh this time, Annie." She winked at me.

"Thank you, Sister." I grinned.

"Behind this habit, Sister Elizabeth is quite pretty. Her real name was Angelina Navarro and she was born right across the street from this church some forty years ago. I do not know how she became so mean, but now, she is kind, and I am not sorry for it. Will God forgive me for robbing her life, I wonder?"

"God does not rationalize our actions," I said.

"Perhaps not."

"What about Meredith Mae?" I asked. "How did Ursula get away with her murder?"

"I do not think Ursula murdered Meredith Mae."

"What?" I said in the most shocked manner. I could not believe I had heard her correctly.

"I spoke to Ursula many years after she took over Meredith Mae's identity. It was right after I took Angelina's flesh in 1879."

"I don't understand. My God, why didn't you do something?"

"I couldn't."

"Why not, Elizabeth?"

"Matthew had been murdered so many years by then. Silas was dead by that time, so there was no one to claim that Ursula was not really the real Meredith Mae. How would a twenty-three year old Sister prove the identity of a fifty-year old woman? Besides, I felt it was not wise to reveal the truth."

"Not wise?"

"Look, perhaps I should have gone right to the authorities and told them to investigate Ursula, yet somehow, I felt that would have been a mistake and it was best that I tell no one what I knew."

"You were still afraid of Ursula?"

"No. It was not because I was afraid, but because I had the feeling I might harm Meredith Mae if I exposed Ursula as an imposter. So even though I knew she was passing herself off as my dead husband's daughter, I kept my mouth shut. Ursula may have taken her name and her money, but she did not kill her. I was certain of that. I still am."

"Are you suggesting then that it might have been some plot between them?"

"I think it is quite possible."

I thought that it was completely preposterous to imagine that Ursula underwent an epiphany of some sort and had avoided killing off my granddaughter when so much money was involved, but I listened to Elizabeth politely, assuming, of course, that a life serving God had blinded her to the evils of others.

"I think Ursula Boussidan protected Meredith Mae. I think she kept her from Jeanne Elemont's evil reach," she said innocently.

"You think, then, that Meredith Mae is alive somewhere, perhaps in another dimension?"

"I do."

"Oh, please." I laughed aloud. "You expect me to believe that Ursula has been protecting Meredith Mae all these years?"

I found myself unable to control my disdain for this theory for even though I wanted my granddaughter to be alive, I could not conceive it, not with the evil Ursula as her only chance of survival.

"Listen to me Annie, Ursula came to the church and spoke to me. Of course, she saw me as Sister Angelina. It was not so long ago. I recognized her immediately, and of course, my first impulse was to run away because she had frightened me so much when I was a child. But she stopped me with the sadness of her call, and I listened to my heart. I apprehensively sat with her and I heard her anguish. She spoke to me for many hours. She clutched my hand and wept many a tear. I never saw her again. Though I hear she comes to the church and sits in the farthest pew. I know she has a companion but I have never seen her either. I barely leave the convent and always sit in the first row for services."

"A confession? Why not speak to a priest," I asked and crossed my arms over my chest.

"It was not a confession. It was more like a desperate woman purging herself, begging for redemption, trying to find God again."

"Yes, Father Donovan also told me she comes to church. What did she say when she spoke to you?"

"She told me she was a sinner but she wondered if she had redeemed herself by saving someone she loves."

"Really?" I turned to look at Elizabeth. I still found her theory a bit far fetched but she seemed to earnestly believe it.

"I think Ursula was supposed to set herself back up in Meredith Mae's will before she could marry Callen Hall and then murder her right after the will was rewritten. But I do not believe she was able to go through with it."

"Then what happened to my granddaughter? Where is she?"

"I do not know."

I thought about the Jeanne Elemont I had known and wondered, if Elizabeth's theory was correct, why the evil Jeanne had not killed Ursula for betraying her. But before I could ask the question, Elizabeth gave me the answer.

"I am sure Jeanne Elemont really believes that Meredith Mae is quite dead. I think Ursula tricked her. I do not know where Meredith Mae is, but I do not believe she was murdered."

"I hope you are right." I put my arms around Elizabeth. "But I do not believe it is possible. How could Ursula have gotten away with fooling Jeanne Elemont? Urbain is ubiquitous. He would know the truth."

"I am not sure." She sighed.

"Unless of course the great Urbain is not conscious."

"What do you mean?"

"I am not entirely clear. It is just a feeling I have."

"What are we going to do to reunite our family?" she asked. "It must be possible somehow."

"Well, first, we are going to look at the portrait of the notorious 'Father Jacques,' and then we are going to perform a little witchcraft."

Elizabeth stood up and stared at me.

"What is it, Elizabeth?" I asked.

"I have been a Catholic nun for over seventeen years. I cannot perform witchcraft!" she uttered in a hoarse whisper.

I walked to the altar and stood before her.

"Look about you, Elizabeth. Look well at this church. Look at Jesus on his cross and the Virgin Mary at his side. Ask yourself why millions of souls are led here, led for centuries to worship the Virgin and her son. How do they know to do that? Why do they do that? How can a man and a woman who lived nearly two thousand years ago still perform miracles and heal the afflicted? Why is it that the name of Jesus is still on the lips of the dying and in the praise of the living? Let me ask you this, how do the lost get found in his name and why is it that his compassion is revealed in an act of mercy to this day? Why are the dying still led to his arms? Why do our souls end in his promise and begin with his blessing? Elizabeth, we celebrate him still. We speak to him daily. His death still makes us weep and his birth has brought us joy. What is this, Elizabeth, if not what we as witches know? My God, Jesus has no distance in a universe that has no time but his. Jesus is here, as we are here, and he lives behind each of us, and he lives before all of us. Is this magic, Elizabeth? Magic? Or is this Almighty God? Isn't this God the eternal blessing, the despair and the hope, the magic, and the miracle of being a substance born to thought and to heart and to language, and to the confounding soul of its own moment? Where is this line between witchcraft and God, Elizabeth, between magic and miracles?"

She held her rosary in her hands and stared at the Virgin Mary.

*Hail Mary full of grace, the Lord is with thee. Blessed art thou amongst women and blessed is the fruit of thy womb, Jesus,* she prayed.

I waited patiently and watched her.

Finally, she sighed deeply.

"I am with you," she said. "I am always with you, Annie. What ceremony do you speak of?"

"An exorcism," I said carefully. "This form of Julian Rouvrey," I told her as I slipped the cross back around my neck, "gives me knowledge that I did not previously have. Just pray I have the power, as well, to exercise it."

# Chapter 6

Elizabeth and I stood transfixed before the portrait of Father Jacques. He wore brown bangs and his skin was pockmarked. His eyes drooped like a spaniels and he registered nothing but kindness.

"Do you remember him?" Father Donovan asked me.

"No. This is not the Father Jacques I remember."

"Uhmmm. That's curious," he said. "Perhaps you have confused a name with a face?"

"Perhaps."

"Well, I have some lessons to attend to. Do you teach? We could always use a good teacher at the boys' school?"

"Oh, there is a school here?" I asked.

The Father smiled proudly.

"Yes, St. Joseph's School for Boys. We have mostly private students but we also take in several children from Holy Name Orphanage," he told me.

"Father, have any of the boys disappeared from the school recently?" I asked.

"No, not from St. Joseph's but the orphanage has had some problems. Several boys ran away. They haven't been found yet."

I looked at Elizabeth, who eyed me curiously.

"Why do you ask? Have you spied them somewhere?"

"No, no Father," I told him quickly. "I heard something about that on my walk and wanted to be sure to keep my eyes open."

"Yes, yes. We should all do that. Well, tomorrow I would like to talk to you about leading Sunday's mass. What do you say?"

I smiled and nodded.

"Good. I shall look forward to that. Well, good afternoon, my children."

"I will see you at dinner, Father," Elizabeth said.

"Yes, Sister. Hash tonight, isn't it?"

"Yes, Father," Elizabeth said.

"Well, perhaps I will skip dinner. I have a lot of work. God bless you."

He patted my shoulder as he retreated down the stairs.

I quickly turned to Elizabeth.

"We don't have a lot of time and so we must make haste. Come to my room," I told her and took her arm.

"Father, that is most unusual," she said as she followed me swiftly down the stairs.

I shut the door behind us as Elizabeth sat on the edge of my bed.

"That was not Father Jacques," I said. "He looked more like the priest that Meredith Mae always said he was than the bastard I knew him to be."

"He must have stolen the poor man's flesh," she whispered.

"Do you think it's possible that Meredith Mae did not see the same Father Jacques as I did?"

"How could that be? She has the vision."

"That is so, but look what happens when I take this cross from my neck."

Elizabeth watched as I removed it and smiled.

"Is it possible he had such a cross?" I asked.

"But you both saw him at the same time, did you not?"

I thought for a moment and realized that every time Meredith Mae and I were in the presence of Father Jacques, I was in spirit form and not in flesh.

"I think it is possible. When I am in spirit form I do not see flesh as I see it now. I could have easily been tricked. Meredith Mae might have only seen the real Father Jacques while the demon hid behind the puppy dog eyes of that poor man. Perhaps he has a cross like Julian's, or perhaps, he simply has the power to will himself to be seen however he chooses to be seen."

"Why did you ask if any of the boys were missing?"

I took the chair from across the room and sat facing her.

"I have had some disturbing news from Luther's houseman, Calvin."

"Luther? Jeanne Elemont's son?"

I nodded.

"What news?"

I gripped the sides of the chair and looked away.

"He has stolen children from the street. He has stolen them from orphanages, from wherever he can get them."

"What? Why?" She leaned over and tried to find my eyes.

"Calvin believes that he offers them to the devil in some horrid Mass that he performs at our old house. He has built a Cathedral there, or so he calls it such."

"Offers them to the devil? What do you mean?"

She glared at me but I said nothing. I could not find the words to tell her more.

"What do you mean?" she repeated. Then she put her hands to her heart. "Mother of God, he harms them so horribly?"

"Yes," I said quietly.

"Good God." She sighed.

"We will avenge the bastard."

"How?"

"I am not sure yet. We have a lot to do and no time to do it in. What is the hour?"

"Well, it must be nearly three. Father Donovan always retreats to his office at three."

"What do you know about the girl twin, Gillian, is it?"

"She has quite a reputation." She smirked.

"How so?"

"Well, she and the boy squander their money. They had to mortgage their house to the bank. I hear the mother does not bail them out either and they will both most likely be broke before they're forty. The girl has a thing for the theatre, it seems. She fancies herself an actress. She also fancies pretty men and buys as many of them that will have her. She prefers very young men and there are always several of them at one time, never anyone in particular. She grooms them and endows them with enormous gifts, clothes, and fancy rooms. She makes gentlemen of them, but she tires of them easily. After setting many of them up in a glorious lifestyle, she then cuts them off quite drastically without a dime. It is cruel, really, and many of these poor boys wind up at our doorstep begging for a place to sleep. The worst of it is that she blacklists these poor actors with producers by refusing to put her money into a show they might be cast in, and she succeeds in ruining many fine careers. She does it simply to be cruel, I think. She has probably manipulated the fate of every show on Broadway with her threats. I have heard several people have tried to have her killed for using her own money to control and destroy so many people. Fortunately, she herself has stopped performing because of so many dreadful reviews."

"How do you know all this?" I uttered.

"Nuns do gossip," she said. "Many of the women here would prefer to be elsewhere and gossip more than they pray."

"Then why are they here?" I asked.

"Perhaps they are avoiding marriage. Following God instead of a husband seems like the lesser of two evils, for many women, not that Catholicism is evil. Oh, Annie, I did not mean to say that. I just meant that giving up ones independence one way is a lesser evil to some, than giving it up another way. Many nuns do have the true calling, perhaps most, but so many women have so few choices, it is either God or marriage. One's heart is all one can really follow, hopefully it is followed wisely."

"I heard the girl is ugly." I smiled.

"I have never laid eyes on her but I hear she looks like a well fed rat."

"Do you know where Ursula lives with her friend?" I asked.

She looked at me and shook her head.

"It is right off the corner of Lafayette and Carroll. It is very lovely, with tall white columns and a pretty porch," I told her.

"I am sure I can find it."

"I want you to go there at four thirty and bring Ursula to the Cathedral, the one that idiot has built on our property. Have her there by ten of five. Tell her I sent you to retrieve her, and it is for her own well being that she accompanies you. Tell her nothing else."

"And what about you, where will you be?"

"I will be there," I told her. "We must act quickly. I am expected to be at Luther's door by five this evening. But I must intercept Jeanne Elemont before that hour."

"What is going to happen, Annie?" she asked as I opened the door and checked to make sure there was no one in the hall.

I turned back to her and smiled.
"Just a little revenge," I whispered.

# Chapter 7

Actually, I still had not formulated a concrete plan in my head. I was following some instinctual notion that dictated my actions. I knew I had greater physical strength than I had ever had before, and I heard prayers on my lips that I had never before uttered, prayers that I felt certain would guide me.

I found Father Donovan in his study behind a pile of papers. The room was dark and comfortable. A lamp glowed on his desk and gave off a gentle but indiscriminate hue. I remembered the very first time I had seen electricity as Ann Arlin Peckham, how I had turned the switches off and on because it had so fascinated me. Now I stared at the simplicity of the electric lamp he used. I thought of his excitement over the elevated tracks he referred to as *spider lady* and how he admired the great dramatic sweep of the Brooklyn Bridge. I felt a tear in the corner of my eye as I recalled how he had held my head in his arms and fed me. The tears increased and ran down my cheeks, tears I did not attempt to hide. In that moment, I loved this man. I loved his innocence, his moment upon the earth, the physical presence that was his alone. I stood there crying like a fool in his doorway until he raised his head in my direction.

"Father Julian! My good man, what is it?" He peered at me over his glasses. He stared at my weeping face.

"God bless you Father," I whispered. "God bless your sweetness, the goodness you attempt to instill, the God you worship and the souls you save. God bless your time in

this one brief moment of eternity in which you are held to God's lips, with your faith and your compassion."

"Father?" he whispered.

"I love you," I said. "Your despair and your joy will not die with your flesh. Your beauty will not fade. You are magnificent, sir. You are quite divine."

"Father?"

"I have come to say goodbye."

"Goodbye?" he uttered.

"I do not have much time."

"Time? Time for what?"

"I am a witch," I said quickly.

"What?"

He stood up tall and stared at me.

And so I told him everything, as I knew it. I spoke quickly and did not look at him as I revealed my soul. I doubt if he believed in my magic, but he listened.

When my tale was told, I looked into his eyes. I am not sure what I was looking for, forgiveness, perhaps. I wiped away the tears and stood up to leave.

"Julian?" he called.

"It is Annabel, sir."

"It is not rational. All that you have told me, it is not rational."

"No, I whispered. "It is not rational."

"God is not only an act of faith. We can reason the existence of God but not...this hocus pocus you speak of."

"If I can affirm that I am here then I can also affirm that I am not," I said. "Perhaps there is logic in that, perhaps not, but it is so."

"I've always believed in the afterlife," he told me.

"Father," I said. "There is no afterlife. We are all....gone. We are all...here."

"That is not rational either," he said again.

"We will not find God through reason, never through reason."

"What's that?"

"Passion, Father, the stroke of a brush on canvas — the sweep of a violin — a dancer's graceful leap —a soldier's grief — autumn unfolding in the crisp yellow gold of death, there's God. But reason is too long a road to take to find that connection to the Almighty. It is passion that will lead us to God, not detachment."

"Lead? To lead is to follow forward toward a future you say we do not have."

"In reality, it is only the spirit that moves, but the spirit moves not back and not forward," I said softly. I felt weary. "How can the spirit move forward or backward without step or motion? The spirit can only move through God."

"*In the name of the Father, the son and the holy ghost*" he recited, and it sounded like a song from his lips.

It was then I took his hand in mine and kissed his fingers before taking the white collar from around my neck and leaving it there on his desk, under the glow of his electric lamp. I could hear him blessing me as I walked out the door.

It was so unlike September. Early evening had a chill and night was falling with a hint of frost. Leaves were abundant and snapped beneath my feet as the wind kicked up and blew my jacket collar up to the tips of my ears. The knuckles on my fist were whitening from the grasp of my hands over my closed lapels. My breath was tight and kissed the air in smoky rings. The sky was cast in a charcoal light that draped across the fading sun.

Calvin called to me as I approached the absurdity of my old dear home, its distasteful bright colors sadly contradicting the somber nebulosity of the darkening sky.

The pistol he placed in my hand was small and cold against my flesh. I took the weapon quickly and sent him back to the house. I told him I would call on him shortly and not to wait in his room but to keep his eye on Luther. He did not question my intension and so I told him nothing more.

Jeanne's carriage was precisely on time. I surreptitiously watched behind a parade of bushes as she emerged. Her cape, swept lightly by the wind like strokes of affection, was lavender and full and fell to her ankles. Her heels made taps on the concrete street and I could almost hear her breathe as her brisk steps came toward me. She had the air of wealth, so scrubbed that her ivory skin peeked out from her fur-lined hood and beguiled the darkness.

I felt in my pocket for the rags and cord that I had taken from the church kitchen. I slipped my finger near the trigger of the pistol's wooden handle and pointed it toward her approaching form. I felt quite masterful. I let Jeanne Elemont pass me on the walk and then I slipped through the bushes and followed her step. When I felt for certain that she was far enough away from the street, and yet not too close to Luther's door, I jumped her from behind and held the pistol to her temple. She gasped loudly but did not scream out. I forced her to the ground on her stomach and pushed the pistol into her back.

"I am not above murder if you resist me," I told her harshly.

I quickly grabbed all the rags and cord and stuffed her mouth. I tied a rag around her mouth so she could not scream. I pulled her hands behind her back and tied them as well. Next I bound her feet so she could not kick me when I turned her over. As I did so, she searched my face and stared into my eyes. I searched hers and smiled. She was frightened and confused. I reached up and I lifted the chain from my neck and removed the cross. I watched, as she took in the image of Annabel Horton, and it was like watching someone die without the ability to manipulate the unfolding second. And as the shadow of my features left its darkness across her white skin I embraced the fear I found in her eyes. She went limp in my arms and I thought for a moment that she might have fainted.

I picked her up and carried her inside the cathedral. She was lighter than I expected and felt like nothing more substantial than a pile of clothes in my arms. I placed her on

the altar. I had passed the five- pointed star and the stone and wooden statues of Gods that I did not know. The witch was mumbling. It sounded like a prayer or a call; I could not tell. I watched the silent statues, their stone eyes, and the long, curled tails. I thought I picked up the scent of something rotting but it faded fast.

The back door opened with a start and a clamor and I looked up, the pistol poised in my hand. Elizabeth entered with Ursula Boussidan, but stopped abruptly when she saw my weapon. Ursula, however, was not afraid and walked slowly to the altar where Jeanne Elemont lay bound. She said something that I could not hear, and then spit in the witch's face. I could tell, despite the rag that covered Jeanne Elemont's mouth, that she was calling on her demons to defend her. The statues were slowly turning and their eyes appeared to quiver, but I could not be sure. I could not dwell on the possibility that they might have power.

Ursula, now old and slow to movement, walked back to where I was and stood before me. She looked long and hard at my face. She closed her eyes and began to mumble the Lord's Prayer. She reached for the cross around my neck and kissed it, called out the name of Jesus once again, and fell to her knees.

"I am ready to die," she whispered.

Elizabeth watched from the shadows as I pulled the old woman to her feet. I removed the chain and cross from around my neck and stared at her. She looked at me quizzically for quite some time.

"There is no recognition?" I finally whispered and showed my surprise to Elizabeth.

The old woman shook her head. "What recognition?"

I grabbed her and took her to the bound body of Jeanne Elemont.

"Tell her who I am, daughter of the devil," I commanded as I removed the rag from her mouth.

"It is the lost witch from Salem," she spat.

"Annabel Horton?" Ursula gasped and turned to stare at me.

"And you do not see it?" I said bewilderedly.

"No," she said softly. "I do not."

I stuffed the witch's mouth again and then put the cross back around my neck. I sat Ursula in a chair.

"So she is not a witch," I said to Elizabeth. "How is it you came to be Jeanne Elemont's lover?" I asked Ursula as I turned back to her.

"Jed."

"Jed?"

"Yes, Jed, Catherine's brother. We became friends. He told me all about his family when I was there, in Loudun, passing myself off as a boy to avoid the convent. I worked as a tutor and I taught him French. He told me his half sister was very rich and his father was furious that he could not gain control of her estate."

"Ah yes, Jed," I said. "He also knew Father Jacques?"

"Yes. That is how I met Jeanne. It was Father Jacques that told Jed to look up the daughter of an old friend while he was studying for the priesthood at Loudun. The daughter he referred to was Jeanne Elemont."

"And it was Jed that introduced you?"

"Yes. Jeanne and I became fast friends, as you know."

"Go on," I said.

"Well, the story about Jed's half sister filled much of our evening conversations and we devised a plan while we drank red wine and cooked our meals. It began first as a fantasy, something we joked about. But then, before I knew it, we stopped our joking over it."

"And you came here to follow through with murder?"

"We came to America with the plan in place, but I really did not take it seriously, at first, even though we had gone over and over it."

"Jed knew of it?"

"No. Jed had nothing to do with it. It was Jeanne that came up with it once she learned how good my charade as a man was, and how much money was at stake."

"What was the plan?"

"You know of it."

"Tell it to me," I commanded.

"As Ursula, I was to seduce Malcolm into trusting me. I was to become his mistress and make him part of the plan. Then I was to seduce Catherine, in the guise of Louie.

Malcolm, of course, knew of my intention to manipulate his daughter. He didn't care. He wanted only the money. Once I had control of Catherine, I would get her to kill off the lawyer, William; I believe his name was. With William out of the way I could write up a new will."

"And then?" I asked as she paused.

"As Catherine's husband, I would inherit Catherine's share of the estate and Jeanne and I would then abscond back to Europe with the money and live happily ever after, or so I thought."

"And Malcolm?"

"The new will, if you remember, would have been sizable. He would not have cared, even if he knew of my relationship with Jeanne. He was to become too rich to care. Besides, he was not in love with me, he loved no one."

"How perfect. Did you not know Jeanne was a witch?"

Ursula laughed. "I knew she *said* she was a witch. It frightened me to hear her say that but I tried not to believe her. I didn't believe her, not really."

"They planned to murder Rachel, to sacrifice her to Satan. You knew it. You were there. And you murdered my granddaughter, as well. What is that if not evil magic?"

"I did not murder anyone," she said adamantly. "I was relieved when you came to the church and saved Rachel. I even tried to stop William Davenport's murder. I began to get cold feet, but Catherine was obsessed with the idea and followed through, despite my protest. It was then I began to realize the hole I was digging for myself. I was scared to death of Jeanne Elemont once I realized she was capable of anything.

That is why I had to continue being her lover when I had come to hate her. I was petrified. At first, it was only a game. I told you, I never really believed we were ever serious about murdering anyone. But as we got deeper and deeper into the plan I realized she was fiercely capable of all things evil."

"I don't believe you," I hissed.

I lifted my hands in the air and felt magic so powerful that it swept me off my feet. I knew in that moment that I could easily swallow the soul of one woman and move it into the body of the other through nothing more than will and an ancient prayer on my lips, a prayer that emerged from my consciousness like primal memories coming to light.

"No matter," I said. "What does it matter, now?"

I knew that as powerful as Jeanne Elemont was, she was no match for Annabel Horton. I smiled at Elizabeth who watched me curiously.

I turned to the old woman and told her that she would soon be clothed in hair like woven gold, skin as fine and flawless as a porcelain doll and lashes so long and thick that they would flirtatiously shade her sea blue eyes from the admiring glances of young and handsome women.

"And why would you do that for me?" she asked.

"It is not for you, dear Ursula. I have selfish reasons. Without you, I cannot get my hands on my own money. When you become Jeanne Elemont, you will return the house to me and my family, the entire estate, as well. As I said, I will allow you a percentage for your troubles."

"I pray then that you are every bit the witch they say you are," Ursula said as she clutched my arm.

I did not hear the rear door open but I suddenly felt that I was being watched. I looked abruptly behind me. I noticed a shadow that stood near a badly disfigured stone figure. Elizabeth followed my gaze and stood quickly to glance behind her. I put the chain back around my neck and held my arms in front of me. I feared it might be Urbain that stood ready to pounce on my flesh.

"Release her at once!" I heard a woman call out.

I let out a sigh of relief. My fear subsided and I lowered my hands for I had no reason to fear a woman. She stepped out of the shadows and walked toward me like a soldier prepared to meet the enemy. As she got closer I gasped.

"Good God," I cried. "It is Eugenie Anderson!"

She moved her hand like a whip, and as she did, my body was thrown to the floor with a terrific force. Poor Elizabeth had been thrown near me and seemed to bump her head rather badly on the wall. I could hear Ursula laughing.

I looked up to see Eugenie standing over me. She turned to look at the body of Jeanne Elemont, which was tied to the altar. She appeared confused and stared back at me.

"What is this?" I heard her ask, with her hands outstretched like weapons. "Who are you and what are you doing?"

"Oh my God," I heard Elizabeth utter and I watched as Eugenie turned to the nun. To my amazement, she cried out and ran into Elizabeth's arms. The two women began sobbing and clutching each other like long lost schoolgirls while Ursula and I stood by and gaped.

Finally, Elizabeth looked up and laughed.

"Oh, if only I had left the convent and ventured to your door. If only I had known."

"I thought I'd never see you again, dear Elizabeth," Eugenie said.

"Remove your cross again, Annie," Elizabeth smiled at me.

"Annie?" I heard Eugenie utter.

I slowly took the chain from my neck and lifted it. The minute I pulled it over my head I saw my own dear Meredith Mae behind the sweet, tender features of the woman I had recently encountered as Eugenie Anderson.

"Good God." I smiled through tears.

"Oh, Grandmamma, if only you had taken off that magical cross when you came looking for me. You would have seen me right away. I thought you brought harm. I came to protect Ursula. We planned it after you left. We thought you were some servant of Jeanne Elemont's that came to destroy us."

I ran to Meredith Mae and took her in my arms. As I held her, I whispered that I was going to attempt to move Ursula's soul into Jeanne Elemont's flesh.

"No!" she cried. "She cannot move her soul. She is not one of us."

"You must trust me, Meredith Mae. Elizabeth will guide her spirit and you will send Jeanne Elemont's soul to hell. Jeanne Elemont does not have enough power to fight the three of us. I am so glad that you are here."

"How do you know Jeanne will die?" she asked.

"This cross. If I press it to her chest while I am taking her, I am sure she will never again walk the earth."

"But you will doom Ursula to the devil's wrath," she pleaded.

"Urbain Grandier cannot harm us. Together we are all too powerful.

But if he does return, we will protect her."

"How?"

"Julian Rouvrey is more powerful than Urbain Grandier. I do not know how I know that but I do."

"I cannot let you risk Ursula's life to gain back Father's money." Meredith Mae was adamant but I knew I had to convince her.

"She is over seventy years old. Would you not prefer her young and beautiful?" I asked, as Ursula stood and walked to us.

"*I* agree to it," Ursula said sternly. "I will sell my soul to look like that again, and she is not even that young, but she is still every bit the rose in the garden, isn't she?"

Meredith Mae sighed and went to the old woman. We knew we did not have much time for the statues had begun to close in on us, and the five-pointed star had begun to turn.

Meredith Mae took Ursula's hand and looked into my eyes.

"This is not revenge, is it Grandmamma?" she asked.

I shook my head slowly. "No, not anymore."

"You do not know the whole truth," she said.

"No, I do not," I said. "Why don't you tell me?"

Meredith Mae then proceeded to explain how she and Ursula had staged her death and how Ursula handed over all but twenty percent of the entire estate to Jeanne Elemont.

"Ursula risked her life to protect Jeanne from killing me," she said.

"Why?"

"It was the only way to get rid of her, Grandmamma. I knew I could avoid Jeanne Elemont behind the flesh of Eugenie Anderson. Jeanne had to believe I was dead. Ursula took my identity immediately after my death in order to get the money for Jeanne. We just wanted to get rid of her."

"No one recognized the truth? What about those awful twins?"

Jeanne Elemont's children never saw me until they were much older. Gillian came to visit us many times when she needed money, and we always gave it gladly, but by that time I was already in Eugenie's flesh. It was through Gillian that we knew what Jeanne was up to. We could always stay one step ahead of Jeanne. It was Gillian that told us that her mother hated Brooklyn and only visited in order to berate Luther for spending his inheritance. We knew that Jeanne was usually far too busy traveling the world with her husbands and lovers to care whether or not she ever saw Ursula again. However, she did think rather highly of Ursula for being so crafty, and that is just the way we wanted it, absent admiration. It is a pity to shatter her illusion, but I shall do just that, I'm afraid."

"So it was you who came to church with Ursula and sat in the back?" Elizabeth asked.

"Yes, Elizabeth," Meredith Mae nodded.

"If only I had paid attention, I might have seen you."

I watched as Meredith Mae left the old woman's side and went to where Jeanne Elemont lay bound. She leaned over her and kissed her cheek.

"I will soon have my way with your ageless form," I heard her whisper.

"How did you do it?" I asked as Jeanne Elemont struggled desperately to free herself.

"I went to a hospital ward to search for a body. I came upon Eugenie Anderson. She was a nineteen year old girl dying from Encephalitis."

"Why didn't you just go back to France or hide somewhere?" Elizabeth asked.

"We knew that my body would have to be identified as my own in order for Jeanne to believe that I was really dead. I could not just disappear and get away with it. Jeanne is too crafty for that. She knew Ursula loved me. As long as she thought me alive, I was a threat to the estate, and to her, I suppose."

"Besides," Ursula interjected, "Jeanne insisted on seeing Meredith Mae's corpse for herself. She would not have taken my word alone."

"I see." Elizabeth made the sign of the cross.

"I did not know if it would work, my taking on a dying body, but I had to try. I knew that if we did not stage this death quickly, that surely Jeanne Elemont would lose patience and murder me herself so that she could inherit my trust. I had no other heirs then, and even if my will decreed my money to charity she would have fought it. She kept pressuring Ursula to do it, so we had to act fast. I did not know if I had your gift, Grandmamma, but I took the risk that I could indeed, transport myself into a dying body."

"You might have gone to God and not to this poor girl," I said. "There is no guarantee."

"I know."

"It was like the time I took Elizabeth Sue, Annie," Elizabeth said as she came to my side. "The baby was dying, but when I entered her flesh the disease died with her. It was her time. It was that simple. Fate, so many people call it."

"Oh, Elizabeth, we were so angry at each other then that I never knew you took the child. I never looked that seriously at little Elizabeth Sue's face, I was so distraught," Meredith Mae said sadly.

Elizabeth reached out and took her hand. I noticed that the chanting increased in volume and Jeanne Elemont was murmuring softly.

"We went to the girl's room and told her we were going to end her suffering. I had two vials of cyanide in my hand. The girl begged me to relieve her. I swallowed the vials and died in a fair amount of time, but I did not regain consciousness in the girl's flesh for several hours. I believed that the dying girl would find peace when I took her but she fought me despite her tragic fate. Fortunately, for me, she eventually accepted death and her soul eventually left quite blissfully. It was when I took over her new flesh that I gratefully realized that the disease was no longer present. It was Ursula and Jeanne that put my old body in a trunk and sunk it to the bottom of the Hudson River, even before I fully became Eugenie Anderson, the medical miracle. For years I was written up in all the newspapers, how I had defeated death through prayer. Thank-God Jeanne Elemont never suspected. Ursula became Meredith Mae Guyon without much effort, Papa was already dead and there was no one to doubt Ursula's identity."

"What about Rachel?" I said.

"Rachel has always loved us and trusted our decisions."

"How much money did the bitch receive?" I asked.

"We kept only twenty percent of my estate in order to get rid of Jeanne Elemont forever, and it worked. She is worth a fortune. She had no further use for Ursula after I vacated my flesh. She had all the money she could take from us. It was not Ursula who had harmed me. Ursula saved me, Grandmamma. Ursula has always loved me."

I put my arms around my grandchild and held her. I told her we had to begin our ritual before Jeanne successfully called the devil to aid her, but I did not apologize for doubting her devious friend.

Meredith Mae went to her lover and whispered something to her that I did not hear. I called to Elizabeth and we made a circle around Ursula and Meredith Mae. I called out my incantations and clutched my cross. I whispered prayers that I cannot reveal to you. They are very powerful prayers and I knew as I uttered them that I had only scratched the surface of the magic they held. Elizabeth called on Jesus and clasped her rosary. Meredith Mae took the pistol and held it to the back of Ursula's head as she prayed on her knees in her native French to the abandoned Virgin of her childhood.

After I had chanted for a good twenty minutes, I left the circle and lay myself over the body of Jeanne Elemont. I picked up the rotting smell I had detected earlier and I heard the chants of the evil Gods emitting from the stone statues as pieces of the stones began to fall around me. I ignored their intimidation. They came from a dimension that Jeanne had successfully brought to the surface, but I was not afraid to defy them. I removed the rag once again from Jeanne's mouth and covered her with my lips so that she could not scream. I felt her tongue forcing itself down my throat, nearly choking me. I held the cross to her chest as I pushed my flesh into hers. I felt her struggle. I did not wish for my soul to enter her body. I only wanted to make the space in order for Elizabeth to direct Ursula's soul into the flesh of the dying Jeanne. I kept my mind focused. I feared that the powerful Jeanne would not allow her soul to exit. I remembered my failure with Ursula's body, caused no doubt, by Jeanne's interjection.

Suddenly, I felt a snap in my veins and blood seemed to gush from my skull. I sensed the opening I needed. I had forced Jeanne out by the weight of my magic and I knew I had succeeded by the sense of nothingness I felt around me. The demon fought hard but I was too strong. I lifted myself out and away from her organs and blood vessels just as I knew that the consciousness known as Jeanne Elemont was beginning to dissolve. It was the most incredible emptiness I had ever felt. I yelled out to Meredith Mae.

"Shoot her now!" I called.

I heard the shot ring out and felt Ursula's soul fly past me. I felt the immediate impact of the body being taken. I jumped off Jeanne quickly.

"It has happened. Her soul crumpled into nothing," I whispered.

Meredith Mae and Elizabeth came to the altar and watched as I untied the wrists and the feet of Jeanne Elemont. She seemed to be in a deep sleep and her eyes remained closed. I looked cautiously around me as the chants from the evil wooden statues grew louder and I caught the fleeting reflection of a large blond man in the ominous glow of a dying candle. His eyes seared into my back, and I could hear a low growl, like that of an angry cat reverberating off the stones like fading echoes.

# Chapter 8

The growl and the chanting stopped abruptly the moment Ursula opened her eyes in Jeanne's flesh, sat up and stared at us. Meredith Mae held her breath. The body of the old Ursula lay in a heap, the blood from her wound still ran from her head and the silver gray hair was matted and wet. Ursula, now in the body of Jeanne Elemont, sat upright and touched her face with her fingers. She kissed the palms of her hand and then began to sniff the fur on her cape. Meredith Mae went to her, and Ursula, in all the glory of her new body, showed off her perfectly aligned teeth with a coy smile.

"It worked, my precious," she uttered and threw her arms in the air.

"We must make haste," I commanded and took the pistol from Meredith Mae.

"What are we to do, Annie?" Elizabeth ran to my side and grabbed my arm.

"Do you know where Matthew is buried?" I asked them.

"Evergreen," the two said in unison.

Luther was quite startled when we entered the house. He must have assumed we had taken his mother hostage, for Ursula, clothed in Jeanne's presence, entered with us.

"What the hell?" he said as we stood before him. What an odd parade of characters we must have seemed.

Gillian immediately broke into tears when she saw Ursula's old body in Calvin's arms.

"Sit down!" I ordered and revealed my pistol.

"Good God!" they gasped and quickly did as they were told.

"Take Ursula's body to one of Luther's carriages," I said to Calvin. He did what I asked and left the room.

"Take the old Clarence," Luther called after him. "I will not have blood on my new Runabout. And don't touch the new Timken, either."

After Calvin left, I noticed that Gillian had fainted. I asked Elizabeth to attend to her. Luther, on the other hand, had become accustomed to us by now and was quite furious.

"Just what wretched charade are you playing, passing yourself off as a priest? Who the hell are you to threaten my family?" he commanded. "What was that nonsense about a message from my father? What do you want of us?"

I placed my hand around his throat and forced him into a chair. His fleshy legs hung over the side and he looked ridiculous, but he sat there and glared at me.

"Be still!" I bellowed.

"Mother?" he said and looked to Ursula, who now appeared to be his mother, of course.

Ursula ignored him and sat herself in a comfortable chair.

Gillian finally regained a semblance of composure by the time Calvin returned. But when I began to point the pistol, and order them all outside and into the carriage, she started to cry again and beg for her life. I calmly assured her that we meant her no harm.

"Then why have you murdered my half sister? You are degenerates. That was Meredith Mae's body Calvin carried in his arms."

"Ahha!" Ursula suddenly exclaimed. "I forbade you to see that woman."

To my surprise, Ursula's French dialect was tempered by her transformation and she spoke more like Jeanne, whose origin of birth seemed indiscriminate.

The girl made an ugly scowl. "You do not understand my intoxication for the theatre, Mother. You are too pedantic. Meredith Mae understood. She always acted a role when I went to see her and I had to guess who she was. She could do a marvelous French accent, as well. She used it all the time to please me. I loved it so."

"Ha! Intoxication for the theatre? Why yes, one would have to be intoxicated to bastardize Ibsen, turn Shaw's comedies into high drama, and Strindberg into farce. Weren't those your very reviews? Yes, yes. That makes sense. Ha!"

Gillian threw her face into a pillow and began to wail once again. Ursula raised her eyebrows and winked at Meredith Mae.

"Of course, I knew that you managed to talk your poor half sister into throwing money into your flops, after you went through your own funds. Ah, you are absolutely wretched," Ursula said, in Jeanne's voice.

Ursula was treating the twins with so much disdain that they did not detect the truth. Still, I ordered Ursula quiet, and told them all to get into the carriage.

Calvin had covered the body with a blanket and had put it on the floor of the back seat. I told Ursula and Meredith Mae to drive up front with Calvin while I sat behind them with the twins, and Elizabeth. Unfortunately, we had to put our feet on the body and sit quite close together. Gillian was practically in my lap, and Luther and Elizabeth sat to my right. It was a very tight squeeze and we had to keep the horses at a slower trot for fear poor Elizabeth would fall out the door.

We drove to the Evergreen cemetery and it took us nearly an hour to arrive. The rain was falling quite heavily and the night sky was covered in a black cloud. The moon shone through, from a listless indifference, as the clip clop clip of the horse's hooves splattered the carriage in a spray of mud.

It did not take long to find my son's grave. Both Elizabeth and Meredith Mae went right to it. Calvin, Luther, and I, began to dig up the dirt. Luther worked slowly, and after a good hour or so he began to quiver. He looked to his mother for help before he finally collapsed and began to whine.

"Why is mother allowed to sit where it is dry?"

"Keep digging, Luther," I ordered.

"No, I cannot do this anymore. I won't. Shoot me if you will," he cried and threw his shovel down.

"It is all right Luther. We are almost there," I told him as I felt my shovel hit something that felt too big to be a rock. I could see the wood of the coffin and reached down to shake off the dirt with my hands.

Gillian was sobbing loudly and sat on an old cement slab in the ground, with the hood from her cape up over her face. The rain had let up considerably by this time, but the chill was causing an ache in Julian's poor bones.

"You are all crazy," Gillian suddenly cried out. "What will you do with us? Throw us in the ground with my dead father? Bury us alive?"

I ignored her outburst and had Calvin help me lift the coffin up. Elizabeth had remained back in the carriage with Ursula and Meredith Mae, but when she saw the coffin being raised from the ground she ran to me.

"Wait!" she called.

I removed as much of the dirt as I could from the wood and watched as she stopped near the hole in the earth and fell to her knees. Meredith Mae followed closely behind and stopped just behind Elizabeth. Ursula remained in the carriage and watched us carefully.

"What do you hope to find, Annie?" Elizabeth cried out.

"I am not sure," I said as I handed the pistol to Calvin and told him to watch the twins.

The coffin was easier to open than I had thought and took only a few thrusts from the shovel. The top creaked as I lifted it. I could see that even Gillian had ceased her wailing and stared at me with owl like eyes.

"What is it, Annie?" Elizabeth whispered and clasped her heart. "Dear God, what do you see?"

I let out a horrifying sound as the bones of my dead son stared back at me.

They all stood and watched as I sobbed. Finally, Meredith Mae came to my side and held me. I pulled myself together enough to tell Calvin to bring the old woman's body and put it in the hole in the ground, and we would put the coffin back over it and re bury it.

Elizabeth was sobbing, as well. "What did you hope to find, Annie?" she wept.

"The dream was so real; he beckoned me to him ... I thought he might have escaped death, somehow, as he did in Salem," I cried.

I stood up on my feet and threw the shovel down. Luther seemed speechless, and Gillian simply stared out into the night sky, quietly whimpering. I looked over at Ursula. She appeared dumbfounded and kept preening her head to see what we were doing, but remained warm and dry in the carriage.

"Matthew!" I called and fell to my knees. I watched as Elizabeth's concerned face stared back at me. I felt exhausted but I knew what I had to do. I remembered my dream so vividly, the boy motioning for me to follow, the painting I had seen at Luther's, so like the dream. I stepped back and looked at the moon.

"Call him!" I commanded to Elizabeth and Meredith Mae. "Call on his soul and demand that he hear you. Are we not witches?"

"What are you saying, Grandmamma?" Meredith Mae asked me.

"He came to me in a dream. If Ursula can take the body of Jeanne Elemont, my son can take the body of..."

They looked at me as I glanced over to where Calvin held the pistol on Luther and Gillian.

I took in a deep breath and began to chant.

"OMEREO, LISTERN, OEREUS. COLISTRUM, DOMINUS, HERUM, DOMINUS, COLISTRUM, DOMINUS!"

Meredith Mae fell to her knees and held her hands to the sky. She closed her eyes and swayed under the moon. The children looked on in horror. Calvin began to cry out loud but kept the pistol steady.

"OMEREO, LISTERN, OEREUS. COISTRUM, DOMINUS, HERUM, DOMINUS, COLISTRUM, DOMINUS," I repeated over and over again. I do not know from where the words came. But, if I had to guess, I would say that my despair found the ancient prayer in the deepest recesses of my soul. You may use the ancient words if you wish. If you close your eyes and trust what comes to you, the severing of dimensions will occur. If you have power, you will cross the dead.

Ursula stood from the carriage and watched tentatively. The moon moved behind a cloud and the sky became black. The twins were sobbing loudly now. Calvin continued to sniffle, but he kept the pistol aimed and ready.

Elizabeth called to Jesus.

*Our Father, who art in heaven, hallowed be thy name, thy kingdom come, thy will be done on earth as it is in heaven.*

OMEREO, LISTERN, OEREUS, COLISTRUM, DOMINUS, HERUM, DOMINUS, COLISTRUM, DOMINUS.

Suddenly, the cloud that shadowed the moon faded. We heard Luther scream. When I turned toward him, I saw that his body lay flat on the earth and his eyes seemed to stare at nothing, as though he were looking inward.

"Help me!" he cried out.

We all stood quickly and went to him. We watched as he went into spasms. I believe we were too shocked to know what to do, so we did not react at all.

"Do something, you horrid people." Gillian screamed into the night wind.

Suddenly, Luther grabbed his heart and his eyes came to life and flickered.

"Help him!" Gillian wailed.

"Heart attack!" Luther whispered. "Help me."

"Do something!" Gillian called out frantically.

I watched as the breath was sucked from Luther's body by the hand of death.

"It is too late," I said.

"You did this. You murdered him." Gillian ran to me and pounded her fists on my chest. "You scared him to death."

"Look!" Meredith Mae ran to Luther's body and held his head up.

My son's face was appearing slowly in Luther's features, as Luther's soul vacated the flesh and went to Satan's door. I heard Elizabeth gasp. You might have called this transformation a phantom, a ghost from the shadowy graves of the earth possessing the recently deceased, but I knew immediately that the man appearing in Luther's dead flesh was my son, Matthew, and he had taken the body and blood of Luther Guyon and given life to the still form.

Finally, after fifteen minutes or so, my son looked up at me from the ground. Julian's face was the first he saw.

"Father," he said, "Where am I?"

"Matthew!" Elizabeth cried out.

He turned sharply.

"Good God!" he cried.

"Matthew, my darling," Elizabeth ran to him and grabbed his hand.

"Elizabeth," he reached up for her lips and began to stroke her hair, but when he noticed the habit she wore, he sat back.

"Forgive me," he said. "Forgive me, Sister."

"No, Matthew, darling." She reached out for him once more, but he leaned away from her and looked around him. Then he stood up tall and took in his surroundings.

"Where am I?" he asked.

I went to him and took him in my arms. I removed the cross from around my neck, and smiled so broadly as he recognized me.

"Mother. Oh, my God. Mother." He stared at me in disbelief.

He looked to his daughter as she stood there weeping.

"Papa?" she said and held out her hands.

"Meredith Mae?" He threw back his head and laughed. He took her in his arms and lifted her up.

I could see him clearly now in Luther's form; his dark hair was wet and fell on his brow. Here again was my handsome son, my boy, my

Matthew, appearing like a vapory mist behind the startled eyes of Luther Guyon.

Gillian stared at her brother curiously. Calvin had not moved or uttered a sound. Matthew squinted his eyes toward the carriage and stared at the bemused Ursula.

"Good Lord, is that...?" he began.

"No, it is not Jeanne. It is Ursula," I said quickly. "I will explain. She saved Meredith Mae and we transported her soul into Jeanne Elemont's."

"What?" he gasped. "Jeanne's dead?"

"Yes. I will tell you everything, but we must leave quickly before we are spotted here."

Matthew looked at Calvin and grinned. "And who are you?" he asked.

Calvin smiled back.

"Calvin Nathaniel Johnson, sir. You don't know me?"

"Should I?"

Calvin looked in my direction.

"What's happened to Mr. Luther?" he asked.

I told him he had had a transformation and would never be the same.

Calvin slapped his leg and let out a laugh. "It will only take me a moment to finish filling this hole, Father."

"Good. Work quickly, Calvin," I said.

"You have taken the form of Luther Guyon. Did you know? Did you murder him purposely to take flesh?" I asked.

"No. I heard my soul being called and I followed it. It was like that time I found you in the river, Mother. I discovered myself in this young man's flesh. He was dying. His heart, I think, but he was young. I am young, aren't I?"

"He is around thirty-five. They say he is your son and he is named Luther Guyon. The girl over there is his twin."

My son walked over to where Gillian sat on the ground. She stared at the man she still saw as her brother.

"Luther?" she whimpered.

My son studied her features.

"When were you born?" he asked.

"Are you insane? You know our birth date." She turned to me frantically. "What have you done to him?"

Meredith Mae went to her father and answered him quickly.

355

"Their birth date was August 23$^{rd}$, 1860."

Matthew looked back at Elizabeth. "I did not touch her after your death," he said. "I should never have touched her at all. I only did so because I thought I would never see you again, and she was very persuasive. Forgive me. I was a very foolish man."

Elizabeth had tears in her eyes."I, too, was foolish," she said. "Jeanne Elemont broke my neck and I took a child's body, Elizabeth Sue's. I did not know what else to do, and the child lay dying in her crib. I should have gone to you, and told you, but I could not. I was vain and could not go to you as a baby after I had lost you as an old woman. That, too, was foolish."

Matthew smiled sadly, "I thought I could be happy after I married Jeanne, but my distrust only increased, and I began to suspect she had harmed you for the estate. I might have even gone to the authorities had she not fed me the poison so soon. I do not know who these children are, but they are not mine. I would not go near her for quite some time, and she did not seem to care."

"Thank God," I uttered.

"Emie and Philippe? Where are they?" Meredith Mae asked.

Matthew sighed. "I do not know where I have been. Perhaps, death is a place too vast to recall. What chronology is this?"

"1898," I told him.

"I will be curious to see how the world has changed."

"Where is Michele?"

"I do not know, Mother. My last memory of Philippe was right after I learned of Ann Peckham's death. He and Emie think we are all dead, I am sure of that. There has been no telepathy between us and I do not know how much chronology has passed where they are. But Philippe always said he had lost only moments when he walked through the chamber and returned," my son told me.

"We must find our family. This form of Julian Rouvrey that I now wear is very powerful, and the magic I hold can reunite us, but I have made a promise that I must fulfill first."

"All in due time, Mother," Matthew said. "First though, I think, you're right, we must find our family. Meredith Mae, try and communicate to Emie. Perhaps, if you go into a trance you can bring Philippe and Emie to our dimension."

"Yes, with you and Elizabeth here, and Grandmamma, we will have the power to reach her. I am sure of it," Meredith Mae exclaimed happily.

"Everything will be fine now, Mother. I promise. Everything will be fine," my son told me.

# Chapter 9

But everything was not fine. We noticed the police carriages outside Luther's house when we were halfway up the block. I told Calvin to halt the horses and pull off the road.

"Elizabeth and I will walk past the house. We will meet you on Lafayette Street soon after. Go to Meredith Mae's home at once. Elizabeth and I will walk there from here."

Gillian began to scream and Matthew quickly put a hand over her mouth. Elizabeth and I got out of the carriage and watched as Calvin safely turned the horses and rode off. I knew, even before we approached the gate, that the bodies of the children had been discovered on the property, and there would be a warrant out for Luther's arrest. My son now wore this murderer's flesh and would surely be arrested on sight. I realized that this century would never be one we could claim as our own. I had dreamed of that, finding my beloved Michele, and sharing my home and my wealth. I knew that my romantic Michele would surely appreciate the early nineteenth century, for despite his birth in your chronology; he is a man of manners. But unfortunately, now we must flee this dimension and save Matthew from the gallows once again.

"Good evening, Father."

I smiled at a young policeman, and watched as he kept looking behind him, for there was a great commotion and many men in blue suits.

"Seems to be some excitement here," I said.

"Oh, yes. There sure is, Father."

"Well, what seems to be going on, officer?" Elizabeth asked.

"Oh, I'm not an officer, Sister."

Elizabeth smiled politely and inquired again. I noticed that the young man was embarrassed to tell us the gruesome business that had been discovered.

"Anyone murdered here?" I asked. "There seems to be so many police on the property."

The young man blushed. "Yes, sir. Children, sir."

He blushed again. I could see the faint red tinge to his cheeks under the light of the streetlamp.

"Children?"

"Yes, Father."

"Are we needed?" Elizabeth asked.

The young policeman shook his head.

"The perpetrator is at large, Sister. But we'll get him. Don't worry. We know who he is."

"May I ask how you know?" I inquired.

"Anonymous tip, sir."

Of course, I knew the anonymous tip had come from Urbain. It was his only weapon of defense against us now. I was too powerful in Julian's form to fear him, and too, with so many other witches against him he had little recourse but to try and destroy, at the very least, my son's new life.

"Don't worry, Father. We'll find this monster," the young policeman said and put a hand on my shoulder.

We bid him a fond good night and walked swiftly back to Lafayette and Carroll.

I could hear Annascha barking as we breathlessly approached the porch.

"How did the dog get here?" Elizabeth asked.

"I do not know, but it will save us a trip back to the church basement," I told her as I hurried inside.

They were all in the parlor when we walked through the door.

"How did the dog get here?" I asked Meredith Mae.

"There was a priest outside when we arrived. He brought her," she said as the dog leaped up on me and barked.

"A priest? What did he look like?"

"His face was covered by a cloak. I could see nothing, not even his eyes."

"She is supposed to lead me to Madeleine," I said.

"I think she would prefer to be led to the kitchen for some food." Calvin smiled.

"You offer food to the dog and not to me?" Gillian suddenly yelled out. "Something criminal is going on at my brother's house and he sits here like a different man and seems not to care. You people will pay for this. You have altered him somehow."

"Take this creature to the kitchen and give her something to eat, Calvin," I said.

I heard Ursula snicker.

"Yes, sir," Calvin took Gillian by the arm. The pistol was still visible in his hand. Annascha followed behind.

"What are we to do, Annie?" Elizabeth asked as Matthew sat at her side and looked at her sheepishly. I noticed that he would not take her hand, though I knew he wanted to.

Meredith Mae sat on a small sofa with Ursula and waited for me to speak. I did not have a definitive plan. The discovery of the bodies on Luther's property changed everything.

"There has been an anonymous tip," I began, and went on to explain that the wretched Luther had used helpless children in his devil worship, and then buried their remains on his property.

"And the anonymous tip?" My son asked.

"Urbain," I said softly.

"Did you know of Luther's activities?" I asked Ursula.

"Of course not," she said quickly.

"The police will come here to ask Luther's half sister what she knows of the murders. They will also question his mother," I said to Ursula. "We do not have much time."

"What are we going to do, Mother? Obviously, we must cross a barrier," my son said.

"Yes, I know," I answered.

"I have always wanted to share Philippe's time. Perhaps, that is where we should go. The twenty-first century, how frightening it sounds, but how exciting," Matthew said.

I wished I could accommodate him but knew in my heart that I could not.

The very next morning the daily papers were filled with headlines about the murders. We read the articles aloud to each other until we had devoured them all. The anonymous tip was mentioned briefly. The reporter said a letter had arrived by courier revealing the whereabouts of the bodies and naming Luther Guyon as the killer. Gillian denied the charges against her brother to all of us and accused Calvin.

I immediately sent the transformed Ursula to the bank. Of course, every-one believed she was the actual Jeanne Elemont and she continued to play her part well. I accompanied her to insure that everything was done exactly as I requested. I insisted that she transfer her cash and sign over her bonds to Eugenie Anderson. I had her pay off the mortgage the bank was holding on our house and transfer the deed to Luther Guyon's trusted houseman, Calvin Nathaniel Johnson, and his family. I had her set aside an adequate trust that would enable Calvin to live independently for the rest of his life.

Matthew wrote a suicide note and confession and signed it in Luther Guyon's hand. It was mailed to the police chief post haste. His suicide note made the afternoon edition the following day, and the police went on a manhunt to recover Luther's body, which fortunately, would never be found.

I bid Calvin a fond farewell and he thanked me for the home I had given him.

"Take care of it, Calvin for I do not know when I shall ever see it again."

He embraced me with all his might and promised to destroy the Cathedral, and the gazebo, immediately following the close of the investigation.

"And please paint the house white again, will you?" I smiled.

"I love you, Father," he whispered. "I seen firsthand. You're a messenger of the Lord."

"Perhaps," I said softly. "Perhaps."

That evening, Annascha was quite agitated and began to run in circles all over the house. We decided to tie Gillian to a chair in the upstairs bedroom and gag her mouth with a rag to prevent her screams.

We began our trance downstairs in the parlor. We lay on the floor with the dog very near us. Matthew was to my immediate right and held my hand as we listened to the steady breath of the white shepherd. To Matthew's right, I could hear Elizabeth saying the Lords' Prayer. On my left, lay Meredith Mae. I could feel the strength of her hand in mine. Ursula held her other hand and prayed in her native French. I had drawn a circle around us for protection.

I did not lead the prayers, but only listened to the dog's steady breathing, and trusted Julian's words, that somehow she would guide me to Madeleine Le Brue. I thought of Philippe and Emie, and my beloved husband, but I had made a promise to Julian and knew that he was calling upon me now, to honor it.

Hours passed. The moon crossed the room and faded, and the sun burst in the sky in a pattern of fire. No one spoke, nor slept. Our prayers never ceased.

Perhaps a day passed, perhaps two. I cannot say.

Quite gradually, Loudun appeared before me, a village covered in stone, unmercifully loud and yet, mysteriously lovely. Bells clamored in song as I stood. I called out. No one answered. I clasped the rusted cross to my breast only to see that the rust was gone and the gold shone. I called out again.

"Matthew?"

There was nothing.

"Elizabeth?"

Silence.

"I cannot fight the devil alone!" I screamed. "Meredith Mae!"

But alas, no one but the pretty white shepherd, heard.

# PART IV

# LOUDUN

God, how I would come to hate Loudun, the majesty of its stone walls, the twists and turns of its endless spiraling roads; every inch of it would disgust me, the smell from its hibiscus, the far away call of its surrounding hills. Not even the magic of its purple and yellow meadows could seduce me. Madmen roamed the streets and followed me through the village, calling upon my prayers and begging for my mercy. They pulled upon my robe and fought to kiss my feet. The bells were everywhere, loud and overbearing, so much so that the city's sky held not one bird's wing. The madmen rocked their heads to the sound and screamed like gulls at sea against the barren sky, while merchants smiled into my eyes and children fought playfully, children covered from head to foot in the dirt kicked up from the well-traveled roads of Loudun.

The church stood high on a hill, way above the village, its walls barely visible from the road below and the climb was fierce. The dog ran before me. My heart beat loudly in my chest as I walked, and when I finally reached the Cathedral door my mouth was parched and dry from the summer sun.

I entered through a long dark hall. The nuns peered at me from behind their habits, their faces strangely contorted, and like the imbeciles below; they sought my ring, my hand, and the hem of my gown as I passed them. I stood inside the church and stared. The shepherd sat at my side and followed my gaze.

It was an enormous Cathedral, lit by fire lanterns and a multitude of candles. I was startled by the smells, intense and overwhelming. The wine from the altar had the scent of vinegar, the wood smelled like rain, and the glass, like fire.

"Father Julian! Welcome back," someone called to me as I stood in the cold stone church amidst the flames of torches. I could not see his face well in the shadows, but I knew he wore a priest's gown and his step was quick. I stood very still and waited for his approach.

"Father Julian," he called again and I could see that he had raised his arm to me.

I smiled as if I knew him. I could hear his feet on the floor as he finally reached me. There in the semi darkness, with shadows of firelight shielding his face, I sought his eyes.

"Father Julian," he said, more quietly this time, but with an excited intensity.

Oh, my God. I could not believe what I beheld! I sighed so deeply that I might have stumbled. Yes, as I remember, I did stumble. His smile was so affable. His eyes were so blue I might have wept. His cheeks had a slight energetic blush from his breathless desire to get to my side. It could not be, and yet, it was.

"Urbain?" I whispered.

He fell to his knees and kissed the hem of my robe as the nuns had done. Then, so suddenly, my hand felt the lips, so soft and full of sweetness against Julian Rouvrey's flesh.

"I have so wanted to speak with you. You have been gone so long. Where have you been, Father?"

"I am sorry. I had to prolong my journey," I told him, but he seemed not to hear and continued.

"My situation grows worse."

He remained on his knees.

"I need your blessing, Father."

He seemed to be weeping. He appeared so young, so very young, and there was earnestness to him such that I had not seen. Surely, this boy cannot be the devil's apostle.

"Please, Father. I am so distraught."

I made the sign of the cross on his brow. It was a natural instinct that I seemed unable to control, like the French I spoke.

*In Nomine Patris, et Filii, et Spiritus Sancti. Amen.*

"Thank you," he whispered.

"Where can we talk?"

"Here, follow me," he said as he led me up a stairway and into a small, back room, dank with the odor of urine. The dog stayed at my side as I entered. I felt ill from the smell and I found myself opening the window that looked out over a small graveyard, overgrown with hungry weeds that crept around the tired stones, like spider legs.

"They do not believe me," he told me as he knelt at my feet once again.

"Is it true then?" I asked him, knowing of course, to what he referred. "Have you ever violated them?"

"No. It is they who try to violate me. I pray for their souls every night. It is not I. It is someone else ... something else that offends them."

"What do they say you do?" I asked as I stared at the confusion in his eyes.

"They say that I harm them. They say that I rape them. I cannot do that. I love them and would not, could not, Father. I swear," he said, so excited now by his fear that his voice rose to a shout and his face was pinched by grief.

I clutched the cross around my neck and stared at him. I gasped out loud and fell to my knees, as well.

"What is it, Father?"

"You are not the devil," I whispered fiercely.

He moved close to me and held my head.

"They say that I am. The nuns have proclaimed it. But I am not the devil, Father. If you know that, you are the only one that does."

"Madeleine Le Brue. Bring me to her quickly," I commanded. "We will leave the dog here, in this room for now."

"It was Madeleine's father that turned me in."

There was so much sorrow in his voice that I reached for him in a gesture of comfort.

"Why?" I questioned and he continued in the same high pitch.

"I do not know why the nuns blame me. It is they that call to me at night and clutch my robe. It is they that tear at my skin. They press against my lips. Good God," he cried.

"Take me to Madeleine!" I demanded.

She was beautiful. Her hair was hidden by the habit she wore but I could see the dark strands. She looked so much like Ann Peckham and Rachel that I knew immediately that we were of the same blood. Her eyes were so clear, and the color so deeply brown, as Rachel's had been. As I entered, she ran to the boy and called his name. Urbain held her in his arms. I could see his tears from where I stood.

I was frightened and terribly confused. I noticed the tenderness between them. I stared at the cold stone floor for a long time before she finally left his side and approached me. I was repulsed by the odor she emitted, though the beauty of her face kept calling my eyes to hers.

"Julian," she hissed. "I forbid you!"

She began to strike me. She hit me all over my body. I tried to shield myself and grabbed her arms. It took both Urbain and myself to force her hands down.

"Why am I being led to you?" I cried out in desperation.

"I do not want your love," she screamed at me.

I put my hands to my forehead and called out to God.

"What do you want me to do, Father?"

I looked at the innocent priest and this poor nun. I could smell her unwashed body and watched, in horror, as she reached out to strike me again.

"Madeleine" Urbain called. "Get back, for God's sake."

"Please," she begged. "Please, leave him for me."

"Get me out of here," I commanded.

"Coward!" she spat at me.

"What trick is this? You have nothing to tell me, do you? You have no answers."

"Oh, but I do," she said as she leaned into me and her lips touched my ear. I tried not to breathe in the odor she carried, like some dark muddy puddle of cow's dung.

"Be quick then," I said and held her back from me at arms length.

She spoke very low, and clearly did not want the boy to hear. She spoke to me in English and that surprised me.

"Help Urbain, Julian. Only you can save him. Satan calls him now," she cried. "Do not let the evil one swallow his soul. I will give you anything if you save him. I will give you anything I can. He is commanded to violate the others by the devil you called forth. But he has come to love me, and I have come to love him. It was never rape, as it was with you. Do not rob me of this love."

"Rape? Ah!" The thought repulsed me. "What can I do?"

"Work your magic, Julian. Please. Do not sacrifice him."

I stuttered and could not find a thing to say. She became restless and grabbed my arm.

"Listen," she continued in English. "It was I who turned him in to Cardinal Richelieu."

"I know."

"I did it to save his soul. I thought they would surely call the priests for an exorcism but that is too simple for these idiots. Now they will crush him to death. God forgive me. Please, Julian. Help him. He is not one of us."

"I will do everything I can," I whispered.

"May God bless you then," she said softly as she put her head to my shoulder. "If you mean it, I will love you for it. Annascha, Julian."

"What?" I asked, dumbfounded that she would refer to the dog I had left behind in the tiny room.

She stared at me and took my face in her hands. She studied every inch of my features. She knew that I did not understand.

"My God." She sighed so deeply she appeared almost to faint.

Urbain ran to her side.

"I see borrowed flesh. I should have looked more closely. He has sent another to alter Urbain's destiny? That is not good. Fate must be against me now."

I looked away. She took my hands and turned me back to her.

"Who are you?"

"I am sent by Julian," I whispered while Urbain eyed us curiously.

"He is too much of a coward to face me then?"

"Why has Julian sent me to you?"

"To save his soul, I suppose."

"What do you mean?"

"Julian loved me. It was he that stole into my room and raped me. It is his child I carry, not Urbain's."

"What?" I exclaimed as my eyes went to her stomach. I could faintly see the swell.

"It was Julian that brought the devil here by his sin against God. The devil went mad and obsessed on Urbain. He possesses the most innocent one. Julian is damned."

"And do you know the fate of this poor boy?" I asked harshly.

"No."

"So, Julian is given a chance to save his soul and Urbain's?"

"I do not know," she cried.

"I feel so lost." I looked at Urbain as I said it. His face was turned away from mine and his hands clutched the cross he wore.

"Annascha is a term of farewell among witches," Madeleine whispered quickly. "God's light is pure white, and we begin and end with it. 'Annascha' was what God called to us when we were let out of this light to live in the divine moment. And so, it is used to say farewell. Find God in your heart and spare my beloved. There has been nothing to need, or love, but Urbain. Julian dishonored me. He has not. I chose Urbain. I wanted him. It is his face I see in my dreams. I must love something. I must love someone. Whoever you are, do not break my heart."

"Urbain abandoned you."

"My father forced him to."

"Why not love Julian then?" I found myself saying.

She spat at me. "There is nothing I can do? Your love for me will kill him, you bastard."

I kissed her out of some overwhelming desire to force her will.

"No!" She screamed as she pushed me off her.

"Madeleine," I said softly. "I am sorry."

I knew at that moment that she hated me, and yet, I could not prevent it. I did not understand what she expected of me and stood helplessly before her. Her eyes bore into my soul, and for a moment; I thought she had caused me to faint. I opened my mouth to reassure her again, and not a sound came out. She turned away and put her head to the wall.

"Take me away!" I said to Urbain in French.

As he led me out of the room he took my hand in his and held it as if I were his father. I could feel his terror as he clutched it.

"They are going to kill the nuns, as well, you know. They will kill us all — me included if you do not stop them."

"I? What can I do?" I asked.

"Tell Cardinal Richelieu it is a mistake. I have done nothing but serve God. I do love Madeleine. For God sake, I am a man, Julian. It happened between us, something I could not control, something I could not help, nor want to help. Is this my punishment? Help me if you can. My trial is tomorrow. You have power here, Julian. They will listen to you. Madeleine and I will leave this place forever. England will be good. We'll go to England."

"How did this all come about?"

"The nuns are pregnant. One child has already been born."

"What?"

"The mother is deformed and awful but she had a beautiful baby."

"Where is the child?"

"She was taken to Paris and given away. The mother was exorcised."

"And there are others still pregnant?"

"Several others, all nuns. They will all be killed to prevent any seed of Lucifer to prevail. He rapes them and tells them to damn me with his sin."

"Who rapes them?"

"Lucifer."

I sat back and stared at him.

"Then take me to Lucifer," I said quickly.

"Well, I'm not sure that I can."

"You must take me, Urbain, for the benefit of your soul and mine."

"And if I do. Please. Tell no-one?"

"I swear, Urbain. I swear, I will tell no-one."

We found the demon in the darkest dungeon of the Huguenot St. Pierre-du-March Church. He wore a cloak of black so cumbersome that I could not see his face. His eyes were fierce and the color so indiscriminate, but they glared out at me like stars of amber light. His height was impressive, and yet, he seemed not to fill the very cloak he wore. I saw books everywhere I looked, some with old and torn covers, and some with no covers at all. Flame torches lit the dark and threw shadows on the stone, shadows that I could not justify.

The boy shook as we entered. I held his hand tightly. Julian's cross burned against my chest and I cried out in pain. The demon turned from his altar when he heard me and

laughed so loudly that I clutched my ears. Urbain knelt before the bastard and wept profusely.

"Get up, you idiot." The demon said as he walked over the boy and came to me. "What the hell do you want, Julian?"

"Leave the boy alone," I said softly.

"Leave the boy alone?" He bellowed. "He is not a boy. Why, he is forty-four years old and still such a fine specimen. I can find none greater. How then can I leave him alone? He has such a fine organ with which to satisfy those whores."

His voice had a reverberating echo. As I sought the demon's face, I realized that he had not flesh nor blood. He was spirit only, and behind the cloak only eyes existed. I quickly surmised that he possessed Urbain and in his flesh he raped the women.

"You're a freak, a parasite. Go back to your darkness in the name of God," I said as I held the cross before me.

He leapt from the darkness with such speed that I was thrown back against a stone pillar.

"In the name of God? What? Are you insane? Do you think God cares if I am in darkness or in light?"

The demon stood over me. I felt his presence, though he had no shadow, not even from his cloak. I scrambled back away from him as quickly as I could.

"The great Julian is afraid of me? Well, why not? I carry nothing in my soul but envy and envy should be feared."

"What? What do you envy, demon?"

"You don't know?" he said as he walked to his books. "Look here, every crime against humanity is recorded here. Every crime of passion, insanity and debauchery is recorded here. And there, on the other side of this identical wall, every act of courage, every act of love committed in the name of God is recorded there," he said, as he seemed to fly to the other side of the room like a stroke of lightning. "I envy that which I am not. If I am here, I envy not being there."

"You envy God?" I asked, confused at his response.

"Envy God? Of course I don't envy God. I belong to his creation just as you do. I am his consequence."

"Nonsense, you bastard," I yelled as I ran to him and stood before his towering figure while Urbain continued to weep in a corner. "That is such utter nonsense."

"Nonsense? You call God's universe nonsense? Your God conceived a universe of opposites. That's all there is, good, bad, dark, light, man, woman. Opposites! I must exist in your world, Julian, because I am your counterpart. Where you are good, my sweet one, I am not. Your oh so perfect God could not create life without death, or joy without pain or me with out you. Opposites, a universe of opposites includes my ugly soul as well! It includes the ugliness in you, Julian. It was you who brought me here. Do not forget that. Your passion for the whore has damned you."

"God is all good!" Urbain suddenly cried out.

"God, as you call him, includes the dichotomy of evil. God accepts it as such, my oh, so handsome man. God has deemed that the emptiness of nothing includes the magnitude of everything. I am nothing, and you, my salvation, are everything. Both of us together and apart equal God."

"Have you no heart? He is innocent. You mark him with the stain of your evil and he is forever bound to perpetrate your damnation. Go to the streets of Loudun and find a madman there for your wickedness," I shouted. "Leave the boy alone."

"Ah," he sighed. "I see you do not understand. Then I will show you my face, Julian. I will show you my face."

"No!" I shouted. "I do not wish to see it."

"Oh, but you must, my pretty one."

He came to my side and knelt before me. I felt myself weak from the odor he carried. I felt a hand on my shoulder, and as his cloak dropped from his face, I knew he had hold of my chin. I clutched my cross, and in my fear I felt it rip from my neck. I looked down to see the chain in my hand. When I looked up, I saw the face behind the cloak and screamed uncontrollably, "No!"

My screams frightened Urbain and he suddenly became very quiet. I screamed out again and I kicked my legs toward the demon's cloak.

"No! Please! No!"

I hit my head upon the floor. Urbain crawled to me, despite his fear, and tried to hold my hand.

The face behind the cloak was mine — Annabel: beautiful, suffering and joyfully present!

"Julian, are you all right?" the boy called.

I held on to my grief, my pain, and the joy in finding myself, even in the creation of a demon's reflection, alive enough to grieve.

"Please," I begged the demon, "do not take my soul."

The demon laughed.

"Please."

I groveled at his feet as I held Julian's cross to my lips.

"I'll bargain with you, lost witch."

"Anything," I whispered.

"The woman in the chamber upstairs? The mad philosophic witch I take when I am too tired to bother with the stupid ones, your whore, Julian? Your whore and the keeper of his heart." He pointed to Urbain. "She can live. She will give birth to Annabel Horton's soul the way you have fathered her soul, and she will be born the beautiful Annabel Horton in the new land, to English parents, and a fate that is only hers to will."

"Yes. Yes, that is the way it turned out. My mother, Caylus, was beautiful."

"Madeleine, aunt of Caylus, great aunt of Annabel Horton. From one witch to another your blood passes like the piss of that dog of hers."

"I begin with Madeleine. He told me that. Madeleine's avenging angel he called me," I said and pointed to Urbain.

"Yes. So he did. But he sees you as Julian for the moment, you fool." The demon grinned. "Come here, Urbain."

Urbain reluctantly left my side and stood up as straight as he could before the hideous Lucifer, that still bore my own dear face behind his cloak. He took Urbain in his arms and looked at me.

"Well, is it you, or the magnificent Urbain Grandier that I cloak in my greatness?"

"What?"

"Simple, bitch. Follow what I'm saying. I will take his flesh, or yours. Madeleine lives if you let me have *him*. If not, well, your soul is mine and he will live to sprinkle holy water on the whore's dead ass."

I heard the boy gasp.

"No!" I called.

"No? All right."

He put the boy down and came towards me. He stood over me and lifted me in his arms. He was moving me toward the big, dark hole behind his cloak. I was shaking with fear, and then, all of a sudden, the beast dropped me. I fell to the floor. Urbain, had kicked this thing that held me, and now he kissed the cross I clutched as he lay on the floor beside me.

"In the name of Almighty God," he whispered. "Almighty God," he said again. "I love you, Julian. I love my Madeleine. I love my faith, my despondent Jesus. Forgive that which I command my soul to do. Bless me, Julian. Bless me always."

I reached out for him. I wanted him to know that I returned his love, when suddenly, he let out a wild scream and ran furiously again toward the cursed Lucifer. The thing grasped him in some dark hold, while Urbain shook the cloak that covered him until it fell to the ground. Then, this thing, this dark empty hole, swallowed Urbain entirely. The light Madeleine had spoken of, the sweet white light glowed quickly in the fury of this consumption, and I heard the demon's howl, so much despair was in that cry that I could hardly stand it, and I held my hands up over my ears.

When I raised my eyes, after several minutes, I saw nothing but a large imposing shadow. As I stared at this dark and menacing form, the shadow took on flesh and blood. Finally; he stood before me, Urbain Grandier, as I had always known him: evil, heinous, and calculating. The demon smiled into my eyes, as the empty cloak lay crumbled in my arms, and Julian's cross turned to rust in my hand.

I knew that a simple act of love had saved my soul from the demon's grasp. A simple trick of fate had written my journey outside of the devil's hold. They came for Urbain Grandier before he could raise his hand against me. It took ten or twenty men to hold him down.

"No!" I called as they led him away. "Wait!"

"What is it Father Julian?" One of the priests asked as I tried to prevent their exit.

"Where are you taking him?"

"He is sentenced to die."

"What? Shouldn't there be a trial?"

"We have had it."

"Shouldn't we have an exorcism?" I pleaded.

"Father, none will come to lay hands on this evil."

As they led him away I could hear his laughter.

"Urbain!" I called.

"Eternity can have you now, Annabel," the demon shouted out.

"No!" I screamed but they did not listen and took him away.

"Julian. Julian, please help me. Julian," I called, but I called in vain.

I lay there and cried for a long time. I knew they were placing Urbain Grandier beneath the stones. I knew I had to witness it. I thought, perhaps, I could do something to prevent it, to call upon the devil's mercy. But alas, the devil has not mercy.

I walked to the hill behind the church. The graves were nearby. It was under the bright white sky that they placed one stone upon the other, covering his body. He bore the weight of so many stones before his eyes showed tears. He sought my face amongst the many and cursed me, calling me now, Annabel. He cursed all of us who stood there, watching him die, and he cursed the descendents that would follow us. I gazed at Madeleine as she wept. I stood on the sidelines and watched Urbain in his suffering. I prayed to God for intervention.

Urbain refused to die quickly and the priests panicked. They called him a demon, a son of Lucifer and held a brief meeting in which they decided he should burn. They ran out calling for ropes. They tied him up to a large cross in the cemetery behind the Huguenot St. Pierre-du-March church, and they set him afire. He was weak but alive as the flames leapt up and consumed him. They laughed as his screams rang out over the bells, and the imbeciles ran in the streets below and stuck their hands in each other's mouths, mimicking what the handsome priest had done to the nuns.

I fell to my knees and whispered his name. I watched as the body burned and saw as the soul fled, the great heart of humanity that had once been Urbain Grandier, beating in the devil's hand.

I went back to the dungeon that had housed the demon and stayed there in prayer, on my knees, for what seemed like forever.

I saw daylight again when I heard the shouts. The nuns were to die. They were murdered, all of them, one by one, burned behind the church like leaves, except for Madeleine, spared for turning Urbain over to Cardinal Richelieu. They believed they were saving Loudun from the devil's children, and perhaps, they were.

Annascha had escaped her room and had found Madeleine's side. She would not leave her, though I tried to take her away.

375

"She stays with me," Madeleine commanded. "I must have something to love."

"All right," I said.

"Xorgnot, Julian. Xorgnot!" she said sadly and looked toward the sky.

I knew she was damming me.

"What will you do now?" I asked her.

"Some man will have me. Certainly, I cannot stay at the convent."

I knelt before her.

"I can help you get to England," I said.

She turned toward me and laughed.

"You do not know, do you?" She laughed again. "I am afraid you can help me with nothing."

I longed to save her from any more grief, but of course, I could not. My heart was filled with sorrow.

"You failed to save Urbain," she said it softly, and did not look at me, but up toward the hill where the body lay. "Now, love is dead, as the devil would have it be."

"I tried," I said. "Urbain saved us both by sacrificing his soul to the devil. You would have died if he chose to let the demon take Julian's flesh. He must have loved you. We were given an ultimatum."

"So be it."

"You must forgive Julian."

"What becomes of his soul?" she asked me.

"You do not know? You never see him again?"

"No. Julian has died by his own hand. His body lies there, by Urbain's."

"What?"

I stood up quickly and ran to the hill. Madeleine followed me. The bodies lay together, unburied in a shallow grave. Urbain was barely recognizable. Julian's body was covered in blood. I wept softly. I felt Madeleine's hand on my shoulder.

"Return." She whispered. "Return to whatever dimension claims you."

"And you, Madeleine? I promised Julian I would find you."

"You have found me. Annascha, witch."

I sought to see her face but it appeared to be fading from my sight. I brought my hand up to my eyes to see if it was the sun that blinded me, but I saw nothing. I stood and looked for my robe, but nothing clothed me.

"Return, great witch," she said, and with that, she, and the beautiful white shepherd, vanished.

I looked everywhere for her. I roamed the streets calling her name but it was as if she had never existed. Soon, I could not see the road before me and I began to fade back into the opacity of my destiny. I allowed it. I had had enough of Loudun.

I awoke, as if from a deep sleep. Julian was at my side. The church surrounded us and the beautiful white bird was perched on the shoulder of Christ.

"Thank you," he said softly.

He led me to the altar. The colors of the glass in the windows was so bright it would have caused me to squint had I eyes to do so. The reds were abundant and the green glass robes of the apostles so brilliant I wondered if they were etched in emeralds.

"You used me," I uttered.

"No. The moment was yours, not mine."

"You used me," I repeated.

"He chose his own destiny, Annabel."

"What became of Madeleine?"

"She followed him."

"Where?"

"I don't know. I thought the dog would take us, but both are gone now."

"You raped her. It was you who brought Lucifer to Loudun."

"It was my right to take her."

"Your right?"

"I am a man."

"You are a coward," I said and spit on the ground near his feet. I felt his pain.

"My loss is punishment enough. I loved her."

"I am sorry for you."

"Suffering is endless, isn't it?"

"I must return. Can I?"

"To what?"

"To my husband, my children."

"You would leave me as well?"

"I am sorry."

"I have sinned. History will blame the arrogant Urbain but it was I.

It was always I."

"I need form, Julian. I am lost again, without a body."

"So be it."

He kissed the air I filled, and I immediately took on flesh. It was so sudden, and a tingling sensation filled my entire being.

"My God!" I exclaimed. "I can feel blood in my veins."

"She had a child, you know."

"What?"

"A girl."

I looked at him with a strange expression, now that I had a face to do so.

"What are you saying?"

With that he stood up and brought me a mirror. I took the glass from him and brought it to my face.

I was amazed at how much I resembled them both. Her dark clear eyes and his rich thick hair. Why, I was almost as beautiful as my original form.

"But what happened to the girl?"

"Nothing."

"How can that be? If I wear her flesh she must then be dead."

"No."

"Explain that to me, Julian. I do not understand."

"Madeleine is a witch. A witch can choose to prevent the entry of a human soul to be born in her body."

"So this child was born without a soul?"

"I am afraid so."

"You give this body to me now?"

He nodded and took my hand.

"This body will not die as the others have. You can move through the dimensions in this form and never kill again. Please, no more killing."

"How did she grow with-out a soul?"

"I willed her to age. I wanted it so."

I cried in his arms for a long time while he stroked my hair.

"She would not have my child," he said sadly. "But I kept the child's body with me."

"Will I ever see you again, Julian?" I asked.

"In the eye of God," he answered. "We will all be found."

And with that, he disappeared entirely, and I was left standing in the old church alone. I called out his name but he did not answer me. The white bird flew toward the ceiling, which opened its high peaked roof to reveal soft puffs of clouds in a light blue sky, so light it seemed translucent. As I stared above me, I began to lose my balance, and before I knew it, the sky faded from sight and I returned to an enveloping darkness. I drifted inside this darkness. For a long time, I heard nothing, and then, a voice appeared out of no-where. Soon I recognized it as my own.

I finally began to see light; I looked toward it, and there, beyond its shadows, Philippe's face peered into my eyes. And there was my daughter, Emie, holding my hand so very tightly in her own.

"Welcome home, Mother," they said in unison.

"Philippe, Emie!" I exclaimed as I reached out my arms to enfold them. "Where am I?"

Philippe smiled. "Brooklyn, Mother."

"What chronology?" I asked as I looked around the familiar room.

Emie nestled her head in the crook of my shoulder.

"2010," she told me.

It seems I had simply walked through the chamber and had appeared in the library, as if out of nowhere. I now wore the face of Julian and Madeleine's child, and it startled my children a bit. My, my, but I had so much to tell them. It took several days to catch them up and they questioned me incessantly, as you can imagine.

You might wonder why I chose your century to call home when I have cursed it so often. Well, I have my precious memories with Michele and the hope that he will one day return to his family. I have always loved this house, and my children, Philippe, and Emie, prefer these modern times into which they were born. I think they are most comfortable with it. Besides, it matters little, for we cross the dimensions so often. Time and space are irrelevant to us. There are chronologies that you would refer to as "future" that are somewhat more appealing than the twenty-first century, but my house is lost to me by 2100, demolished for a five city block shopping development, and the city of Brooklyn becomes so thick with people that I find it overbearing.

So, 2010 will do. Yes, I remain in your dimension for the most part, though much about it annoys me: your crowds, your crimes, your bang, bang music. I avoid those horrible underground things you travel through in your harried chronology, those dirty and thoroughly inhuman tunnels, "Subways" I believe you call them. I have a driver take me from one point to another, even though I detest the speed of your automobiles. I miss the horse and buggy, but so be it, I must make some sacrifice. Modern life, as you would claim it to be, is not altogether distasteful. There are benefits. I enjoy wearing slacks, smoking an occasional cigar, a left over addiction, I would assume, from my time in Malcolm's body.

I know that you wonder if I am ever to find Michele again. Well, I am searching through every inch of space imaginable looking for my husband, but I am unable to call upon his soul, to keep him in one place long enough to wait for my presence. I am sure that being the history buff that he is, he is thrilled to search the dimensions and find all those significant historical eruptions, as he referred to them. But I do not give up; no, certainly, I never shall. How I miss him! I often receive music boxes when I awake from sleep. I must have thousands of them by now, and they play music from every period of what you call "time." They make me so sad though. Are they Michele's gifts to me, I often wonder, or was my husband nothing more than a trick of perception, an illusion living so very briefly in an imagination ripped from my soul, by the evil Lucifer? One can put nothing past the devil.

Still, Philippe and I search the chambers for Michele, but we seem just to arrive somewhere after he has left, which assures me that he still exists. We are so often told that a tall, dark man fitting his description has mysteriously vanished. There is fear, of course, that the evil Urbain is holding him captive just to torment us both. But I will find the answer soon enough. I must find the answer.

"Father has gone to look for you," Philippe exclaimed after I returned from Loudun in the body of Madeleine and Julian's daughter. "We split up in Rome in 5BC. I willed myself to return here in search of you, but Father stayed. He told me he just wanted to await the birth of Jesus and he would join us."

But he has not joined us, and even Emie's attempts to contact him telepathically are not fruitful. But we continue to search and to call out to him. Philippe and I went immediately to trace his last encounter, believing him to be in existence during the first century of Christ, but when we entered that chronology he was not there. So we stayed, and followed Jesus until his crucifixion, but Michele did not appear in that dimension again.

Ah, how proud I am of my son Philippe. He has altered so many lives with his magic in centuries past, as you call them, and he continues to pursue with a passion, what you refer to as, the future.

For the most part, my daughter, Emie, also remains in the twenty-first century and we always find her as we leave her, deep in study. She travels as a witch quite frequently now and moves from one dimension to the next, looking, I suppose, for as much knowledge as her soul can hold. She tells me often that everything she learns is necessary for the discovery of the new transition.

Matthew never left Elizabeth's side again. The family split our vast fortune and Matthew and Elizabeth took theirs to early twentieth century Rome. They have a beautiful home not far from *Via Giulia*, and there they remain, safe from the warrant against Luther Guyon. Elizabeth often joins me in my quests into other dimensions and has truly mastered the joy of being a witch. I am so proud of her. She moves her soul with such speed that it rivals my own. But my son, Matthew, refuses to join us in your year of chronology, the century I now call home. He refers to it as a terrible disappointment, a loud, vile hell in which too many poorly clothed unenlightened people run amuck. He says it depresses him.

I still find my dear, sweet Meredith Mae, with that horrid woman, Ursula, though they are constantly on the run. I learn from Emie's psychic communications with my granddaughter that they must stay one step ahead of Urbain. They fear he will retaliate against Ursula for taking Jeanne's flesh. I can only hope neither one of them will age, for poor Ursula cannot cross time, and my Meredith Mae will not leave her side.

In one of my nostalgic trips through the chamber, I learned that Gillian Guyon was institutionalized after the wild and outrageous tales she told about people who disappeared before her eyes. I also walked past the old house in the chronological year 1937, and learned that Calvin lived out a quiet and productive life on Montague Street. It seems he used his money to adopt African American orphans and he provided shelter for abandoned German shepherds. He died in 1936 somewhat of a local hero.

I am grateful to Julian for giving me this body that will most likely sustain me for some time, and though I still suffer from insufficient hearing and taste, my sight appears to have improved. The body is agile and very much like Jeanne Elemont's, in that I believe it will age slowly.

Oh, I have enjoyed sharing my secrets with you, but I must admit that we have only scratched the surface of my experiences. You see, great witches, like myself, have touched the hand of Jesus and looked past the aftermath of destruction. Oh, there are tales worth hearing in that.

And through it all, I am still Annabel, I am still just a girl on a hill playing with my brother's dog and seeking solace in my father's love. I am still Annabel, a young woman longing for the summer wind off the sea as it catches my hair and causes it to fall on my brow. God! Salem! It will always haunt me, the sound of the water running in Frost Fish Brook, delighting my ears, and the call of the birds over the meadow by Northfields, teasing my senses and beckoning me to follow their song all the way back to my heart's first joys. How I loved the white winter sun, as it caught the sea like a sheet of glass over the heart of Salem, before the town went mad. Yes, the years before the witch trials, the blessed prayers on the lips of those who graced the church, and chased the pigs behind the barn, and lied on the earth and stole kisses on Gallows hill, yes, that is what I miss.

I will cross that dimension again, even just for the split of a second. It seems I long for nothing more than that, a time of innocence, perhaps. And I will go home and look, as if looking back, but it is only when I look within that I catch sight of something lost forever. Yes, I will cross to that chronology, I will return and I will lie in the shade of my father's favorite tree and dream that I am safe forever. I will dream that I do not know the devil's smile......

You must excuse me for I have to put my pen down for a moment because my daughter Emie has knocked at my door.

"Mother?"

"Yes, my dear?" I ask.

She holds out her hand to me. In it is a small music box.

I find her eyes. "What is this?"

"There's a man downstairs. He wears a cloak that covers his face. He has brought the box to you."

"A stranger?" I asked and took the box from her hand. "Send him up."

"Are you sure, Mommy?"

"What do I have to fear anymore? I have conquered the devil."

"Fine, but I will be right downstairs."

I watched her leave and brought the box to the light. I saw that it was very old as it seemed to fall apart in my hand. The wood was badly damaged and as I lifted the lid, a foul odor filled the room. The music it played offended me, horrific loud chords from an organ that hurt my ears, as if a child had banged upon the keys. I dropped the box to the floor and it shattered into pieces.

I turned as I heard footsteps on the stairs.

"Annabel," he said as he entered.

There in the semi soft light of dusk he stood. It was Julian.

"You are being summoned," he said. "The Black Witch commands you."

"Black witch?" I uttered.

Slowly he took the cloak from his face. He appeared handsome but drawn.

"Julian?" I whispered, though I could not see him clearly. "You are Julian, aren't you?"

"Only if you wish it so," he answered, and with that he swiped his hand across the room and I heard my daughter scream.

"No, Julian," I shouted, as he choked me in the fabric of his cloak. "I don't want to go anywhere," I told him.

"But I'm doing this for you. The box was his, she ripped out his Mozart and danced upon the keys in her bare feet. She wanted you to have it."

I looked at the broken pieces on the floor. "I don't want it."

"I'm taking you to her, it's where Michele is."

"Michele? What are you saying, he is her captive?"

Julian laughed softly. "I am afraid so."

Listen, tales are endless. For me, they never stop. Julian covered my eyes and told me to dream. As I did, my darling Michele came into view. From his arms I looked up, he was shackled in chains.

"Annabel," he said. "Is it really you?"

Pain was not far off, of course, lingering in the devil's malcontent, and in the fumes from the Black Witch of Pau's cauldron my fate churned. Who is she, you might ask? Exactly who is the Black Witch of Pau? She is everywhere you might think she is not and she is patiently waiting for my return, her hands around my beloved's heart, her potions stirred with insidious strokes, her poisons made with one purpose known, to strike Annabel Horton down. But I, Annabel Horton, lost witch of Salem, will not be consumed by the witch's hand. You saw for yourself, not even the devil could defeat me. But oh, how perilously close I would come to that consumption.

Read on, I will tell you more.......

# Annabel Horton
# and the Black Witch of Pau

**Book Two**